GW00500481

A MANSION BY THE MERSEY

Lorna Mathews has grown up in a loving home, safe in the knowledge that her parents think the world of their bright, capable daughter. However, when her mother hears the name of Lorna's new employers, Lars Wyndham & Sons, she has to confess that Lorna's real father was Oliver Wyndham, who died before Lorna was born. For Lorna, her job becomes a quest to learn more about her father, and when Jonathan Wyndham falls in love with her, she wonders if she can trust him with the truth – or will she in turn be abandoned by the powerful Wyndham family?

A MANSION BY THE MERSEY

A MANSION BY THE MERSEY

by

Anne Baker

Magna Large Print Books
Long Preston, North Yorkshire,
BD23 4ND, England.

British Library Cataloguing in Publication Data.

Baker, Anne
    A mansion by the Mersey.

    A catalogue record of this book is
    available from the British Library

    ISBN   0-7505-2133-3

First published in Great Britain 2003 by Headline Book Publishing

Copyright © 2003 Anne Baker

Cover illustration © Gordon Crabb by arrangement with
Headline Book Publishing & Alison Eldred

Published in Large Print 2003 by arrangement with
Headline Book Publishing Ltd.

Magna Large Print is an imprint of Library Magna Books Ltd.

Printed and bound in Great Britain by
T.J. (International) Ltd., Cornwall, PL28 8RW

Family Tree

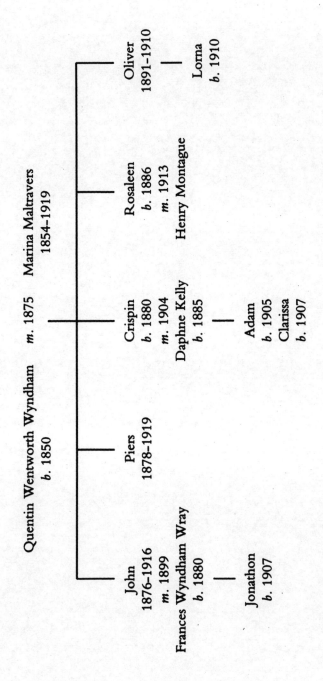

Quentin Wentworth Wyndham   m. 1875   Marina Maltravers
b. 1850   1854–1919

John   Piers   Crispin   Rosaleen   Oliver
1876–1916   1878–1919   b. 1880   b. 1886   1891–1910
m. 1899   m. 1904   m. 1913
Frances Wyndham Wray   Daphne Kelly   Henry Montague
b. 1880   b. 1885

Jonathon   Adam   Lorna
b. 1907   b. 1905   b. 1910
                                   Clarissa
                                   b. 1907

Chapter One

July 1930

It was a close and sultry evening. Lorna Mathews was bursting with triumph as she hurried home. She turned the corner of a dusty street near the docks and saw her father's stockily built figure ahead of her, taking home two planks of wood on his shoulder.

'Pa,' she called, 'wait for me.'

Samuel Mathews stopped and adjusted the weight of the planks. His shirtsleeves were rolled up to show strong bulging muscles.

'Hello, love. Your mum'll be pleased to see you. Have you got a day off tomorrow?'

'No, I was coming to tell you my news. Pa, would you believe it?' Lorna was bubbling with elation. 'Mrs Cartwright's got a buyer for her shipping agency and he wants to take me on to help run it.'

'That's marvellous,' Sam smiled. 'So you won't lose your job. It's what you hoped for, isn't it?'

'Hoped for, longed for, prayed for,' Lorna laughed. 'I love dispatching goods by sea and rail to the four corners of the world. It was bicycles this afternoon; I booked them on to the mail boat going to Freetown. I like to think of them being sold there, and being ridden round the streets.'

11

'You've done wonderfully well, learning to cope with all the documents too.'

'What's all this wood?'

'Your mum wants some shelves putting up.'

'Here, let me give you a hand.' Lorna was slimly built and a fraction taller than her father. She went behind him and took part of the weight on her own shoulder, sniffing with pleasure at the scent of newly cut wood.

'That's better,' he said. 'Aren't I lucky to have such a big strapping daughter?'

'Not so much of the big and strapping.' Lorna sensed her father was a little sensitive because she'd grown taller than he. Her brother, Jim, who was now at sea, said openly that he wished he had her inches.

'A kind daughter then, who is always smiling and happy. A beautiful daughter.'

'That's better.' Lorna laughed again. Not that she honestly thought she was beautiful. Her freckle-covered nose and sea-green eyes didn't add up to that, and she wished her teeth could be straighter.

'Shelves for the scullery? Mum doesn't give you much of a rest when you come home.' Her father was a stoker on the SS *Mary Hampton* and on brief leave from his ship.

'It makes a change. Mum'll be right pleased to hear your news.'

'I'm thrilled.' Lorna shook her hair back from her forehead. She had shoulder-length curls of rich brown that had golden highlights by the end of each summer.

They walked up the streets of small flat-fronted

12

houses, built eighty years ago to house the dock workers. Most of the doors stood open on this warm evening. Chairs had been brought out on to the pavement and the Mathewses' neighbours greeted them as they passed. Sam brought Lorna to a halt in front of their own front door in the middle of a long terrace.

'Got to manoeuvre this through to the back yard,' he said. 'Be careful, love. We'll be in trouble if we scrape the paint.'

They lowered the planks before stepping straight into their living room where Lorna's sister, Pamela, was setting the table for their evening meal.

'I'm keeping my job, Pam,' Lorna sang out.

'You lucky thing!' At fourteen, Pamela was six years younger than Lorna and would be leaving school at the end of the week. 'I went after a job at the Maypole today but I didn't get it.'

Lorna was sympathetic. 'Selling butter and bacon? Are you disappointed?'

'I'd rather be a shop assistant than a domestic servant.' Pam, dark and thickset like their father, backed herself against the wall out of the way. 'Domestic work is just about all there is at the moment.'

'Something will come up, love,' Sam comforted.

He and Lorna manhandled the planks diagonally across the table and through the door to the scullery, where her mother was cooking.

'Hello, Mum.'

'What's that? You're keeping your job?' Alice Mathews turned from the stove, her dark eyes shining with satisfaction. 'That's marvellous!'

13

'Those sausages smell nice. Will there be enough for me?'

'Yes, I'll do some eggs with them. Will you be able to live at home from now on?'

Lorna had lived in with the Cartwrights since she'd left school at fourteen and started working for them as a housemaid. In six years she'd made herself indispensable to their business.

Her father grinned at Lorna as they went out to stack the wood in the yard.

'She's worried our Pam will be leaving home to go into service and she'll be left here alone.'

Mr Cartwright had died two years ago and his wife had been grief-stricken and wanted to go to live with her sister in Cumberland. She'd never had anything to do with the agency and didn't understand it. Her solicitor had advised her to sell up.

'I'll have nothing to sell unless you can keep it running for me.' Felicity Cartwright had looked desperate when she'd said that to Lorna.

'The business has always made a profit,' Lorna had replied, knowing Mrs Cartwright needed that to support herself. 'There's no reason to think it won't go on doing that.'

The depression and Mr Cartwright's long illness had reduced the turnover, but the clients that remained had been with them for years and gave regular repeat orders. The amount of business was small but it was solid.

'I'll do my best to get the new owner to employ you,' Mrs Cartwright had promised Lorna. 'You've been good to me and Alfred, and you're very capable.' But getting a buyer had proved a

14

long-drawn-out process and Lorna hadn't dared hope.

'I'll be living in to start with, Mum,' she said, 'but not for long.' She tried to explain. 'My new boss says his family have always lived in this old house, a mansion, but it's too big now, and in a bad state of repair. He says they can't afford the upkeep and they can't get the staff to run it, so they're selling it and having an auction to get rid of all the stuff they can't take with them when they move out.'

'I thought you said you were keeping the job you've got.'

'I am, and it'll be run from their Liverpool office, but first they want me to help sort and catalogue their furniture and books and that.' Lorna beamed. 'Mr Wyndham seems very nice. He told me—'

'Who?'

'Mr Wyndham, the new owner. He's an old gentleman, very pleasant. His son's in charge now; they're in much the same line of business as the Cartwrights but it's a bigger firm. He told me all about the family—'

'Who did you say? Who's bought the Cartwright business?'

'Mr Wyndham. Lars Wyndham and Sons. Have you heard of them?'

Her mother's plump and pretty face was suddenly working with anxiety. 'You can't go there! You can't work for them!'

'Why not? They have a small office just the other side of Hamilton Square, though they say they're closing that too. Their main office is in

15

Water Street in Liverpool. I can get the ferry–'

'No, Lorna, no!' Her mother collapsed on a chair and mopped her face with her apron. 'No!'

'Mum, it's what I want. Exactly what I want. I've been on tenterhooks this last eighteen months, ever since Mrs Cartwright put the business on the market. You know I have. It's been hanging over me that I might be out of work. I'm so relieved that I'm not.'

Her mother shook her head and groaned. 'I want you to come home and look for a different job.'

'Mum!' Pam let out a little yelp and leaped at the frying pan. 'You're letting the sausages burn.' She flicked them over and turned down the gas.

Lorna was upset at the effect her news was having on her mother. She'd never known her issue an ultimatum like this before.

'Mum, with the depression, jobs aren't easy to find. I'm lucky to have this. I'm thankful that Mrs Cartwright helped and gave me a good reference.'

There was only one thought in Pam's mind as she shook the sausages in the pan. 'You've got the luck of the devil, Lorna. I know what happened was terrible for the Cartwrights but for you...'

'I was lucky that Mrs Cartwright believed she had no head for business.'

'In this life, Lorna, you make your own luck,' said their father.

'Things worked out well for me. I've had daydreams about buying the business for myself,' she said, helping by cutting some bread. 'I know I could run it and earn far more than I'd ever

16

earn in wages.'

'We could never find the money to help you do that,' Sam said sadly.

'I know, Pa, so this is the next best thing for me – being able to keep the job I enjoy.'

Mum's face was drawn. 'Lorna, I don't want you to go to work for the Wyndhams.'

Lorna was nonplussed. 'Why not? I thought you'd be pleased for me.'

As her mother's anguished eyes met hers Lorna felt her abdominal muscles tighten. Mum was frightened! 'Do you know them?' She could see she did! There was ice in Lorna's stomach; she shivered. 'What have you got against them? You've got to tell me.'

But with a gasp of dismay, Alice fled upstairs, leaving Lorna stiff with dread.

Alice slammed her bedroom door and flung herself across the double bed, which almost filled the small room. Panic was constricting her throat. Lorna was asking about things she'd kept secret for twenty years, things she couldn't possibly tell her, about a past of which she was ashamed.

For all that time, she'd tried to banish it from her mind but had never quite succeeded. It was always there, a heavy weight of worry. Lorna had brought thudding back with terrible clarity every detail of the nightmare she'd lived through.

Suddenly, when the last thing Alice was expecting was trouble, this had bubbled up. Now she was heavy with guilt because of what she was about to do to Lorna.

If she said no more and let her go to work for

17

the Wyndhams, Lorna might be hurt, even permanently scarred in the way she herself had been. And if she spoke up and told her daughter the painful truth, that Samuel Mathews wasn't her natural father...? That would change for ever the way Lorna thought of him – perhaps reduce him in her eyes. He'd accepted Lorna and treated her as his own, and she'd always shown great fondness for him.

Alice had considered herself very lucky to have met Sam Mathews. She'd never had the passion for him that she'd had for Oliver, but he'd understood that and been a good husband. Even now, she didn't dare let herself think of Oliver; it would bring back the pain. They'd both been so young and innocent; the passing years hadn't dulled the longing for him, or the dream of what her life might have been.

Alice heard the stairs creak and knew Sam was coming up. He'd offer comfort, but there was nothing he could do about this. She felt the bed springs sink as he sat on the edge of the flock mattress they'd used all their married life, felt his arm go round her shoulders.

'I can't let Lorna go to that family,' she sobbed. 'What if...'

'I didn't realise. Not at first.' His voice was anguished. 'I didn't think of it being that family.'

Alice shuddered. 'If only it wasn't.'

'I told her I was pleased.'

'She can't go. We'll have to stop her. She'll have to find something else.'

'Alice, Lorna wants to go. She's all excited and looking forward to it. You know how determined she is. You'll not persuade her out of it.'

'We've got to.'

'You'll have to tell her the reason. Lorna's grown up now, she'll understand.'

Alice couldn't suppress another shudder. 'I should have listened to you and told her sooner. I didn't want her to know – that you weren't her father.'

'Alice, love, they say truth will always out.'

His other hand was feeling for hers. It was rough; black coal dust had become impregnated in his skin, his fingernails were black and broken. Poor Sam, he was very attached to Lorna. He had a hard life, just on forty-two now and easy to see he'd spent all his adult years shovelling coal as a stoker. He had a craggy, time-weathered face but his eyes were gentle and kind.

'But like this? No inkling, until all of a sudden... It'll be such a shock for her.'

'Just tell her you once worked as the Wyndhams' nursemaid, that you know the house she'll be going to. Warn her what they'll be like.'

'She knows I used to be a nursery maid, that once I helped to look after babies.'

'There you are then. Tell her how the family treated you.'

Alice blew her nose. 'They put me out on the street without notice. They couldn't get me out fast enough when Oliver asked for permission to marry me.'

She heard Lorna calling from the foot of the stairs. 'Tea's ready, Pa. It's on the table. Are you and Mum coming?'

'Yes, all right,' Sam called. 'Come on, love.' He

19

half lifted Alice to her feet. 'Let's go down and tell them.'

'Pam too?'

'There's no way we can keep it from her.'

Alice knew it must be obvious to the girls that she'd been upset at Lorna's news. She felt shaky now as she followed Sam down to the living room.

It was small, like her bedroom. Tonight the grate was empty. The teapot was under its cosy, the girls had cut the bread and divided the sausages between four plates.

Lorna sat down at the opposite side of the table and came straight to the point as she always did.

'What's the matter, Mum? What did the Wynd-hams do to you? You don't like them, do you?'

Lorna's feeling of triumph had gone. She could hardly believe the change that had come about when she mentioned the name Wyndham. She stole a glance at her mother, who'd put a piece of sausage in her mouth but was finding it impossible to swallow.

Alice's dark straight hair had been cut into a bob months ago and was now in need of a trim. She was plump and rather dumpy in build, but her face was unlined, making her look younger than her thirty-seven years. Tonight her dark eyes looked worried and her cheeks had lost their colour.

Her father put down his knife and fork; he too looked on edge.

'It's like this, Lorna... Very hard to say these things. Should have told you years ago, but somehow we haven't.'

She was alarmed. 'Told me what?'

There was a silence, then in a reluctant, barely audible whisper he said, 'I'm not your father.'

Lorna couldn't suppress an empty laugh. 'Don't be daft, Pa!'

'I mean, not your natural father.'

'Not your blood father,' her mother added.

Lorna was paralysed. It put everything else out of her mind. It seemed an age before she could choke out, 'Then who?'

Her mother said, 'It's like this. The man you saw, Mr Wyndham – Mr Wentworth Wyndham – I know his family. I know the house he lives in.'

Pamela's dark eyes looked as though they were about to pop out of her head. 'You were their nanny?' she asked.

'Nursemaid. They had a nanny who took charge. Nursemaid to the Wyndham children. There were three of them in the nursery then. Two of them were Crispin's.'

Lorna's mouth was dry. 'And he was my–'

'No! No! Mr Wyndham had four sons and a daughter. John was the eldest, then there was Piers, Crispin and Rosaleen. It was the youngest son – his name was Oliver.'

Lorna kept her eyes on her plate, chewed end-lessly on a crust, couldn't take it in. 'But what happened?'

Sam said roughly, 'Once the women of the family knew Mum was "involved", as they put it, with Oliver, they paid her off and sent her away while he wasn't there. They gave her an hour to pack her bag and get out of the house.'

'I was seventeen,' Mum said haltingly. 'Oliver was nineteen. He said he was in love with me. I was fool enough to think I was going to have a fairy-tale sort of life. When he asked his parents for permission to marry me, they refused.'

Lorna saw her mother gulp. 'They wanted me out of the way, so Oliver could forget me. I wasn't good enough to be his wife.'

'Mum! How dreadful.'

'I had nowhere to go, my own mother had died and my father had married again and was living in Bristol. Clara, the parlourmaid, found me an address where I could rent a room and I went there. She told Oliver where to find me and he came to see me that night.' None of her family was eating, the food going cold on their plates.

'He said we'd go to Gretna Green and be married. He knew ... about you coming.' Mum dabbed at her eyes with a damp handkerchief. 'Oliver was so sure everything would be all right.'

Lorna swallowed hard. Clearly it hadn't been.

'I never saw him again. I waited and waited, expecting him to come at any moment, but he never did.'

'Mum!' Lorna felt sick. 'Why not?'

'Clara came a few days later and told me that Oliver had drowned in a boating accident but she didn't know exactly what had happened. The family were in a terrible state but were whispering together, and not letting any details be known. The accident was reported in the newspapers but I learned nothing new there. I just couldn't believe it. Oliver had no intention of going out in his boat – I don't know why he did. It was a foggy day – no one in their right mind would take a boat out. He said he was going home to pack a few things and get some money for the trip.'

'*Did* he drown?'

'Yes, no doubt about that. There was a big funeral. I went to the church, stood in the background, saw them lower his coffin into the ground. I felt terrible, bereft.'

'Did his family know about me ... being on the way?'

Alice shook her head sadly. 'I don't know whether Oliver told them. He hadn't when I last spoke to him.' Her mouth twisted in pain. 'I went to see them a few weeks later. I was desperate for money by then, I had to. I asked to speak to John's wife–'

'Who was John?'

'Didn't I tell you he was the eldest Wyndham son? I thought his wife, Frances, would be the one most likely to help, but Clara told me she wasn't at home. I didn't like Crispin's wife, Daphne. I was afraid she'd not be sympathetic but I couldn't go away without seeing somebody.'

'Yes. Go on, Mum.'

'Mrs Crispin said she'd see me and I was shown to her sitting room. Rosaleen, his sister, was with her but she was showing no sympathy either. I told them I was pregnant and Daphne called me a slut. When I named Oliver as the father, Rosaleen called me a liar and had me put out. The door was slammed in my face.'

'Mum! How awful for you.'

'They have no thought for anyone but themselves. That's why you can't possibly go to work

23

for them. I'm afraid you'll get hurt too.'

'Don't you worry about that,' Lorna said. 'I'm tougher than you, Mum. Older too; better able to fight them.'

Beside her, Sam chuckled. 'D'you know, Lorna, there's Wyndham blood running in your veins. I do believe you're like them.'

Lorna leaped up and threw her arms round him. She wanted to cry. 'I've always thought of you as my pa. I can't believe you're not.' She gulped. 'When I was small, I hated to see you going off to sea.'

'Lorna, love, you make me feel proud when you say things like that. You used to clap your hands and dance when I came home. You always gave me a real welcome.' His arms tightened round her in a hug. 'You were a pretty little thing – everybody took to you. We won't let anything change, will we? Even though you know I'm not your real father?'

Lorna felt the tears run down her cheeks. 'You are my real father. The fact that you aren't my blood father–'

'Natural father,' Pam corrected.

'It won't make any difference – not to the way I feel. How can I have any feelings for someone I never knew?'

Her anger grew at the way her mother had been treated. 'I'd like to pay the Wyndhams back for what they did to you, Mum. They won't know who I am. I could.'

'No!' Alice cried. 'No, I don't want you to go anywhere near them.'

Lorna couldn't look at her. 'I'm going. I want

to see these people. Mum, you can't stop me.'

'But that's why I've told you – so you won't go. I don't want you to get hurt.'

'Nothing you say could stop me going to Otterspool House now. I can't wait to see the place and the family.'

Alice cringed into the cushion on her chair. After a lifetime of trying to shut the Wentworth Wyndhams out of her mind, she'd broken her silence without thinking of the consequences. She should have guessed she'd awaken Lorna's curiosity. That was only natural. She'd asked endless questions, raked over everything. What Alice hadn't foreseen was the effect her disclosure would have on her own peace of mind.

She'd tried to accept that her life was here with Sam and her children, but she thought of him as second best. For her, things could have been very different. She might be a romantic fool but she'd loved and trusted Oliver Wyndham.

Since his mysterious death, though, uncertainty had burned into her mind, and doubts had left her perplexed and unable to rest. If only she could find out whether she'd been right to trust Oliver, or whether he'd been about to go back on his promise; if she could only get at the truth, perhaps it would settle her and she'd find peace.

He'd been planning to take her to Gretna Green the next day. She couldn't understand how he'd come to be on a boat. It was March, and foggy – a real peasouper that night. Nobody in his right mind would be out on the river in that.

Lorna's probing had brought back the awful

endless day when Alice had waited for him to come back, and her growing unease that something had gone terribly wrong. She'd never forget the feeling of being abandoned...

Pamela's face was flushed. 'I think it's exciting, Lorna, to find you've got a rich father. We saw a film once with a story like that. Fancy you being related to the Wyndham family.'

'They don't want to know about us,' Alice tried to insist.

'Lorna isn't ordinary working class.'

That stung Lorna to protest: 'Yes I am. This is my home and you're my family. The others won't want to have anything to do with me.'

Then she looked at Sam and said, 'This must be awful for you, Pa.'

'I've known about it all along.' Sam was taking the events of the evening in his stride as he did most things. 'It hasn't come as a shock.'

'This means we're only half-sisters,' Pam went on.

Lorna sighed. 'I've often wondered why I looked so different from the rest of you. I mean, I'm a touch taller than you, Pa – even a bit taller than our Jimmy. And look how much smaller you are, Pam, and you've got olive skin and dark straight hair, like Pa's.'

'You're a different build,' Alice added, 'curly hair and paler skin, lighter colouring.'

'You're different in other ways,' Sam smiled at her. 'You're the sort that goes after what you want in life.'

Alice sighed. 'You're encouraging her, Sam.'

Lorna was trying to smile at her mother. 'I want

26

to know all about the Wyndhams. You must tell me everything you know.'

Alice still felt reluctant to talk about them. 'Well, if I can remember...'

'You must remember!'

Alice tried because Lorna's sea-green eyes were pleading. 'They aren't like us. They're very grand. High and mighty and so proud of their position in life. They behave like gods because their forebears earned a fortune.'

'How did they do that?'

'They were ship owners. They talked of how Liverpool grew to become the second biggest port in Britain in the eighteenth century. You'd think it owed its prosperity entirely to them.'

'But they didn't found a big shipping line, did they? Not like Holts or Elder Dempsters.'

'I think they did, but in the time of sailing ships, when they were small and made of wood.' Alice felt bitter and knew she was showing it.

'Their share of the trade went down once ships became bigger,' Sam said. 'Somehow the Wyndhams lost out. Other shipping lines expanded and became more important.'

'But the Wyndhams still think they're a cut above everybody else,' Alice fumed. 'They still think they're all-powerful and entitled to have every whim granted.'

Lorna put a hand on her arm to stop her. 'Mum, I've met Mr Wyndham. He talked to me for quite a time, asked me how the Cartwright business was run. He didn't strike me like that. He was very old. He'd be Oliver's father?'

'Ye-es. He must be nearly eighty by now.'

27

'I thought he seemed a sad person. He told me he'd retired and his son was running the business.'

'That could be Piers or Crispin.' Alice was back in the past. 'John was killed in the Great War. I saw his name in the paper. I looked after his son, Jonathon, as well as Crispin's two children, Adam and Clarissa.'

'And they all lived together, even though they were married and had children of their own?'

'Yes, in Otterspool House. They all had their separate apartments but ate dinner together most nights. There was only one nursery.'

Alice was lost in thought. 'They were lovely children. Nanny Smithers was very strict about their manners. They had to say please and thank you to us.'

'How old were they?'

'Jonathon was the youngest – he was three when I left. Adam was five, and Clarissa was also three. They were taken to see their mamas at tea time every afternoon. Jonathon's mother came to the nursery to see him quite often, but not Adam and Clarissa's. They got a bit jealous about that.'

She sighed. 'I don't know, Lorna. All this was twenty years ago. You said the house was going to be sold?'

'That's what Mr Wyndham told me. That's why he wants me there to help with sorting and cataloguing the furniture. It's the land that's of value. The house is in such bad repair it's going to be demolished, he said.'

Alice shook her head. 'I can't believe he'd sell such a beautiful place to be knocked down.'

28

'Did you like him?'

'I didn't really know him, he was always out at work. He had nothing to do with the running of the house or the care of the children. It was the women of the family I came in contact with: John's wife, Frances, and Crispin's wife, Daphne, mostly. There was Mr Wyndham's wife and his daughter, Rosaleen, too, of course.'

'Did you like Rosaleen?'

'No.' The staff had been scared of Rosaleen's temper. 'She was arrogant, always complaining about something or somebody. I was glad I didn't have much to do with her. Lorna, I'm afraid they'll treat you as a menial, that you'll get hurt.'

'I'll take good care I don't.'

Alice hesitated. 'Will you tell them who you are?'

Lorna shook her head. 'I don't know. Now I've learned some of what happened I want to find out more about them, particularly about Oliver and why he died like that.'

Alice mopped at another tear as it rolled down her cheek. 'I'd love to know what really happened. Rosaleen didn't believe Oliver could do any wrong. She accused me of making it up that Oliver and I were in love, to get money from them.'

'That was horrible.'

Alice shuddered, feeling she could stand no more supposition about the Wyndhams.

'Why don't you have an early night?' Sam suggested.

To Alice, that seemed to offer escape.

Pam said, 'You go up, Mum. I'll make you a cup of cocoa and bring it to you.'

29

Chapter Two

Lorna settled back in her chair, shocked and confused. Sam Mathews not her natural father? That brought a feeling of insecurity. She wasn't who she'd supposed she was.

She sighed. What had she supposed? That she was an ordinary working-class girl who meant to better herself by hard work. A little shiver of fear ran down her spine. Sam was beside her, staring silently into the empty fireplace. Pamela and her mother had gone up to bed.

She said, 'That's why my name's Olivia? After my father?'

His eyes, full of hurt, met hers. 'Olivia Lorna Mary. Quite a label. Your mother,' his voice shook, 'wanted you to be known as Olivia. I thought it would be a permanent reminder, you know. I persuaded her to call you Lorna.'

'Was there another Lorna?'

'No, love, your mum just liked the name. Mary was after both her mother and mine.'

'Three names like that, I've always thought it sounded, well...'

'Posh?'

Definitely not working class. She'd been proud of her names. She knew her mother had worked for a rich family and thought she'd taken on some middle-class ideas. Lorna had been the only person in her class at school who didn't call

30

her mother Mam. Mum, she'd said, was much nicer.

When Pam had suggested it was exciting to find she had a rich father, she'd denied it. It had been Sam's face that made her do that. But she *did* feel a thrill that her natural father came from much higher up the social order, that he'd come from a rich family. Who wouldn't? It was romantic, wonderful, opening up a new window in her humdrum life. As Pam had said, rather like the heroine in one of the films they occasionally went to see at the Coliseum.

From as far back as she could remember, her mother had been telling her to 'make up your mind what you want and where you're going in life. Get on with it. Don't let things happen to you. Don't let other people alter your plans. Don't drift. You'll end up in trouble if you do. You must chart your path and stay on it. Control what happens to you and stay in charge. Then you'll have life on your terms. It'll be a much better life that way.'

Lorna could see now why Alice had held forth so many times with the same advice. Mum must have known from the start that Oliver's family would not approve of her, that it would be a forbidden love affair. But she'd drifted into it and she'd let herself become pregnant. She'd taken enormous risks and they hadn't come off. Mum had been warning her not to do the same.

At school, she'd worked hard at sums and enjoyed reading. Mum had taken her to the library, where she'd taken out a book every week. She'd learned deportment by walking round with a book on her head, and could recite a lot of poems from memory. She'd drilled and marched and played rounders in the school yard, danced round a maypole and played in a percussion band.

By her fourteenth birthday, Lorna could read and write and add up, but didn't feel she'd been taught enough to go out in the world to earn her living. But the time had come for her to start work and she had little choice about what she did. Live-in domestic work was just about all that was available to her.

Her mother picked out her place, choosing it because it was near enough for her to walk home when she had time off.

Lorna could remember very well just how scared she'd been when her mother took her to the Cartwrights' house in Hamilton Square for her interview. It seemed very different from their own – a gracious, grey stone town house in the middle of a terrace surrounding the premier square in town.

In the fanlight over the front door, Lorna read the gold letters that spelled out 'Alfred C. Cartwright, Shipping Agent, Exporter and Importer to the Empire and New World'.

'Look, there's two bells here, one for the residence and one for the office,' Mum had whispered as they waited on the step.

A uniformed maid, old and rather surly, let them in. Lorna saw several offices on the ground floor as they were led upstairs to the drawing room. Mrs Cartwright was sitting near the window with embroidery silks on her knee. She was

32

quite young and pretty, and Lorna was reassured.

'For the job as housemaid?'

Her mother produced Lorna's school leaving reference. It said she was a bright girl who had worked hard, was conscientious and well-behaved. Her friend Edith's said exactly the same thing.

Mrs Cartwright had put her embroidery aside and smiled at her. 'I pay twenty-five pounds a year to start, you'll live in and have all meals. Uniform is provided but not shoes and stockings, which need to be black.'

Lorna was wearing black shoes and stockings, new ones. Mum said she needed to look smart.

'Time off?' Mrs Cartwright had smiled again. 'Every Sunday afternoon and one full day a fortnight.' Mum had thought that acceptable; generous, she'd told Lorna later. More than she'd had when she'd started work.

Lorna had found she was to start her month's trial right away. Her heart had hammered with terror as she was handed over to the surly maid who had brought them up. Alma, Mrs Cartwright had called her. On the landing, Mum had kissed her and gone downstairs without her. Lorna had had to follow the woman up another flight to an attic bedroom.

'Good view,' Alma had puffed.

From the window, Lorna could see for miles straight over the docks to the Mersey and down towards its estuary. If she put her head against the frame and squinted sideways and down she could see Cleveland Street, but not as far as her home.

'It's the stairs that get me.'

Lorna discovered there were five floors and a basement kitchen.

'Up and down all day – I can't be doing with it at my time of life. You'll have to answer her bells. Never stops ringing, always wanting something, she is.'

Lorna discovered a whole lot more that day. Mr Cartwright had been a bachelor until he was fifty-three and Alma had been his housekeeper for the last twenty-six years.

'Single-handed I was, apart from a daily cleaning woman, and never once did he complain about anything.'

Lorna gathered she didn't see eye to eye with her new mistress.

'Thinks a lot of herself. Always buying new clothes. You should see the scent she's got on her dressing table.'

'She's pretty,' Lorna said.

'Pretty! She uses paint, you know. Paints her lips and her cheeks. Got plenty of powder too. Anyone could be pretty with her money. Only been married a year, quite the old man's darling. He didn't ask me if I needed more help, just expected me to look after two instead of one, with never a thought about the extra cooking and washing. I had to tell him I couldn't do everything.'

'Is that why I'm here? An extra pair of hands?'

'Yes, and not before time.'

Mr Cartwright was taken ill shortly after Lorna started work and he very soon became bed-ridden. Lorna had to act as messenger between him and the ground-floor office, while he did his best to carry on his business from his bed. In the emotionally charged atmosphere of sudden severe illness, Mrs Cartwright, who'd never done a day's work in her life, sat wringing her hands and despaired of being able to cope.

When she asked Alma to set up a card table in her husband's bedroom so they could eat their dinner together, the housekeeper said, 'It's extra work, as well as another flight of stairs. I've told you, I can't be doing with the stairs.'

In a rare show of strength, Mrs Cartwright insisted. That threw Alma into a bad temper for the rest of the evening, and the following morning when Mrs Cartwright came to the kitchen to order the meals for the day, she gave in her notice.

'You can get your own meals,' she told her, and left the house with her suitcase within the hour.

Mrs Cartwright had collapsed at the kitchen table in tears. 'What am I going to do?' she asked.

'I can cook a bit,' Lorna offered. 'Stews, that sort of thing.'

'Mr Cartwright has asked for an omelette for his lunch. His appetite's poor. Can you make omelettes?'

Lorna shook her head. 'No,' she'd never eaten one either, 'but I could do scrambled egg on toast.'

Felicity Cartwright smiled. 'I'll ask him if that'll do. I'll have to think about getting another cook.'

Lorna heard them talking. The country-wide depression and Mr Cartwright's incapacity had reduced the amount of work his business was able to attract. They were worried about the cost

35

of employing another cook-housekeeper.

Mrs Cartwright said she'd do the cooking herself, and a daily woman was hired to do the rough work.

Lorna felt sorry for them and did all she could to help. When she'd first come to work here, Mr Cartwright had employed two clerks, but the most senior one decided to retire. When his secretary left to get married, Lorna carried her typewriter upstairs to an unused bedroom and managed to type a few letters for him using two fingers.

Within weeks, the remaining clerk found himself another job, saying he couldn't do the work of three people. Lorna saw the worry that gave Mr Cartwright, as it was her job to listen for his bell and run up to answer it.

'I've got to keep the business going,' he agonised. 'It's our only means of support. Poor Felicity, how will she manage?'

In order to bring in a little extra income, he arranged for the ground floor of their house to be rented to a dentist, and the spare bedroom became their only office. Lorna did her best to make it look professional, because occasionally their clients called round with documents.

As Mr Cartwright's illness became more acute, more of the work fell on Lorna's shoulders, but she was learning how to handle it and he was only in the next room if she needed advice. She was taking on more and more of the office work and both the Cartwrights said they were grateful. They paid for her to go to night school to learn to type properly. The splendid Georgian houses in Hamilton Square were too big and too difficult to look after without plenty of domestic help. These days, fewer of them were being used entirely for residential purposes. The Hamilton Commercial School had been set up in a nearby house and Lorna found it very convenient.

She went home regularly when she had time off. Her mother was still offering words of wisdom based on her own experience. 'There are two sorts of people in this world,' she warned Lorna. 'The rich who expect to have everything they want in life and know how to get it. And the poor who serve them and are grateful for the crumbs that fall from their table.' Lorna was in no doubt as to which group she belonged to.

But she could see that the Cartwrights, though rich by Mathews standards, certainly didn't have an easy life. It was as much a struggle for them as anyone else. Felicity Cartwright told Lorna she couldn't manage without her help, and it was the only thing keeping her sane. Mum wasn't right about everything.

Lorna still lived in and enjoyed her job immensely, particularly the feeling of going up in the world and of being really needed. She'd been hired as a housemaid but now she was running a business and had certificates to prove she could type. But even so, she felt she'd drifted, she'd gone along with what the Cartwrights wanted and done her best for them. In return, they'd treated her well, and in that she'd been lucky.

Lorna thought Sam looked deep in thought. His usual serene expression had gone. She'd had time

37

to think about what her mother had told her.

'Pa, I want to know what happened to Mum, after Oliver was drowned. She said she had no money and was all alone.'

He reached for his packet of Gold Flake and lit up. She heard his gusting sigh.

'And how did she meet you?' There was a long silence. 'Aren't you going to tell me?'

'I don't know whether I should.'

'Pa! Why not?'

'It should be her telling you.'

'She won't want to. She hates to talk about any of it and I want to know. What's wrong with that?'

He sighed again. 'Your mother was desperate, Lorna.'

'Yes, what could be worse than being left on one's own, wondering how and why things had gone wrong?'

'She was without money, and with you on the way she was unable to work. There was the disgrace of it too.'

'What did she do?'

Another long pause. Lorna had the feeling that something terrible was coming. Something worse than anything she'd yet heard.

His face screwed with hurt. 'Your mum threw herself in the river.'

'What?' Lorna felt suddenly sick. 'You mean she tried to commit suicide?'

He nodded silently. 'She couldn't see any other way out. She was only seventeen, lodging with people she didn't know and couldn't pay. She'd gone to the Wyndhams and begged for money but had been refused. As you know, people

38

generally are very hard on girls in her condition.'

'Oh, goodness! Poor Mum, what she must have gone through! Tell me, come on.'

'I'd just been discharged from the SS *Sea King*. It was the end of the voyage and we'd tied up late in the afternoon at the Duke Street Wharf. I was going to spend a few days at home with my grandmother.'

'Your granny brought you up, didn't she?'

He nodded again. 'It was almost dark, unloading wasn't due to start until the next morning and there were only a few people about.

'I had my kitbag on my shoulder and was enjoying the feel of the wind in my face instead of being down below in sweltering heat shovelling coal. Behind me, other crew members were heading the same way, going to a pub. Ahead of me, further along the dock, I saw what looked like a bundle of rags fall into the water. I heard the splash and that told me it was too heavy to be just rags. It went under. The tide was going out and I saw the rags swirling towards me. Suddenly I glimpsed a white face clamped in a mask of absolute terror, then she went under again.'

Lorna was paralysed with horror. 'What did you do?'

'I yelled, "Man overboard!" Daft, wasn't it, when we were no longer on a ship? Then I stripped off my boots and jacket and jumped in too.'

'Pa! How brave.'

'Not really. I didn't stop to think what I was doing. She surfaced and I grabbed her. Then I thought she was going to do for me. She was in a

39

right panic and fighting like a drunken sailor, but others of the crew had seen me, and Connor Murphy, one of the deck hands, threw me a life belt – they have them along the dock. Just in time – the tide was strong and we were being swept away. I put her in it and the others heaved us in to one of those iron ladders.'

'You saved her life?'

He was frowning. 'Yes, but she wasn't pleased.'

'Oh, my life too! I'm pleased you saved me. Then?'

'We were both coughing and spluttering. The Mersey tastes horrible and leaves mud on the tongue. The dock police came and there was an awful fuss.'

'She must have been very upset.'

'Yes, we were all sorry for her and took her on board the *Sea King*. Those left of the crew gave her rum while I towelled myself off and put on dry clothes. It seemed very strange to have a woman in our crew's quarters. None of us felt we could ask her to strip off her wet clothes; we had nothing she could decently wear. The men wrapped her in a blanket and wanted to find a relative to look after her. When she said she had none and didn't want to go back to her lodgings, we didn't know what to do.

'In the end I took her to my grandmother's house. She looked a bedraggled bundle and was crying pitifully. My gran washed the Mersey mud out of her hair and gave her some of her own clothes. She looked quite different once her hair was dry and clean. It was such a change to see a pretty young face on top of my grandmother's shabby black dress. On Gran, the bodice hung slack and empty, on Alice it was ... well, you know, nicely curved.

'Even then we didn't know what to do with her. She told us a little of her story and Gran thought the best plan would be for her to go to her father's house in Bristol. We helped her compose a letter to him and a few days later she had a reply telling her to come. I bought a ticket for her and put her on the train.'

'And she was all right after that?'

Sam shook his head sadly. 'Alice said her father was welcoming, reasonably so, but her step-mother wasn't pleased to have her living with them. Once you were born, they wanted Alice to have you adopted so she could earn her own living again. She said they pressurised her, saying adoption was her only course, but she refused to part with you. She said she had to get away from them and brought you back here when you were three months old.'

'And your grandma took her in again?'

'We were both very pleased to give Alice a home by then. Soon after she went to Bristol, Gran had a bad fall and broke her leg. She'd been in hospital for weeks. With you and Alice back, she had someone to look after her.'

'And you and she got married and lived happily ever after.'

'Gran never really got over her fall. She died when you were seven months old. I'm glad she was able to spend her last months at home. I know she was happy there and Alice was very kind to her.'

'You weren't there?'

'I was away at sea most of the time. It took a weight off my mind to know your mum was there. Gran liked to nurse you.

'So you see, we did Alice a good turn and she more than repaid us. I kept asking her to marry me, but it was only after Gran died that she agreed. Now you know the full story.'

It wrenched at Lorna's heart. 'Such a sad tale. Poor Mum. I understand now why she doesn't want me to have anything to do with the Wyndhams.'

Sam smiled at her. 'Just don't fall in love with one of them, Lorna. Don't do what she did.'

'Don't worry, I'm not likely to after hearing all this.' She sighed. 'It's time I went back. Mrs Cartwright will wonder where I am.'

'I'll walk to the square with you,' her father said. 'I could do with a breath of fresh air.'

That night, when Lorna got into bed she couldn't sleep. The world as she knew it had changed. It had never occurred to her that Samuel Mathews was not her father. He'd shown no less love for her than he had for Pam and Jim, given no sign. In fact, she'd believed herself closer to him than they were; she loved him. And that was before she'd found out she owed her life to him.

The little house in Cleveland Street had seemed to be the centre of her tight-knit and supportive family. To hear suddenly how it had become hers was disorientating.

Only this morning, everything had seemed so normal when she'd answered Mr Wyndham's ring

42

on the doorbell and taken him up to her office. He'd been slow to mount the stairs behind her and she'd waited so as not to rush him. He was tall, over six feet, but stooped, and he'd used a silver-headed cane.

Mrs Cartwright had gritted her teeth and sat herself down beside him to talk about the business she was selling.

She said, 'Lorna ... Miss Mathews will explain the books to you. She's been running the business single-handed since my husband died.'

He listened attentively to what Lorna had to say. She showed him the figures for the last few years.

'Lorna was my husband's secretary and has helped us both enormously.' She thought Mrs Cartwright embarrassingly full of praise for the work she'd done.

'More than the average secretary,' he said to her, 'if you've been doing this on your own. You live in?'

'Yes, she always has.' Mrs Cartwright smiled at her and made no mention of her starting as a housemaid. 'That's been a great comfort to me, especially since my husband passed away.'

Lorna saw Mr Wyndham's pale damp eyes turn to study her. There seemed a profound sadness about him. She felt for him some of the protectiveness she herself had for Mrs Cartwright.

She asked, 'Would this business fit in with yours?'

'Yes, but with the depression these are hard times. Nothing's as lucrative as it used to be. Officially I've retired; my son Crispin deals with

43

the day-to-day work.' His smile was wan. 'I suppose no father trusts his child to run the family business as he would himself.'

'My business has increased over the time Lorna's been looking after it,' Mrs Cartwright said. 'In recent years, the depression hasn't touched us.'

'Yes, I noticed.'

Lorna said, 'Our client base isn't large, but it's sound. We get a lot of repeat business.'

'It's what I'm looking for. I'm having to sell what's left of an estate that's been in my family for two hundred years. The house has proved too expensive to upkeep and it needs an army of servants to run it. We can't get them any more and couldn't afford them if we could. We can't afford to let our income drop further.'

'Lorna can turn her hand to anything,' her employer went on. 'Everything we've asked of her she's managed to do efficiently. I can't speak too highly of her.'

Mr Wyndham turned to her then. 'May I ask what plans you have for the future?'

That made Lorna shiver. As this was the only job she'd ever had, she was afraid she'd find it difficult to get another she liked so well. She was earning two pounds ten shillings a week all found; that was more than her father earned, more than Jim. She was able to help her mother by giving her a pound each week.

Mum was delighted to receive it. 'I've never had things so easy. I'm able to have a few improvements in the house, shelves and that. I can even put away a few shillings for our old age.'

'Would you consider working for me?' Mr Wyndham asked, and to Lorna that felt as though the sun had broken through heavy clouds. He offered the same salary.

'I'd like you to live in too, just for the first months. We'll need clerical help to catalogue the countless things we'll have to sell. My family's accumulated a good deal over the years. We'll not have room for half of it in a smaller house.'

'The sale will be by auction?'

'Yes. It's going to break my heart to part with things I've lived with all my life. There's a library overflowing with books. Some of them might be valuable.'

'I know nothing about values.'

'Neither do I. I'll have to get a professional valuation. It'll be a mammoth job to sort through everything and decide what we must part with and what might still be useful.'

'I think I'd enjoy helping with work like that,' Lorna told him. 'But it wouldn't be a permanent job, would it?'

'Afterwards, I'll arrange for you to work in our Liverpool office. That would be the sort of work you're used to.'

'Thank you. Then I'd be very pleased to accept your offer.'

'That's a weight off my mind. The task seemed daunting,' he said. 'There'll be a good many private papers to sort through. We're a great family for writing letters and keeping journals. Every drawer I open seems stuffed tight with them, and it's all family history that would be lost for ever. I don't want anything like that destroyed now.

'Age is a great handicap. I'm bored when I have nothing to do, yet tire so easily if there's too much.'

Lorna said, 'When the sale's completed and you've moved to your new quarters you should write your family history.'

He smiled. 'I've thought of doing it. I could take my time over it. It would be a labour of love to read through old documents belonging to my ancestors and set out exactly how they founded our business. I'm sure there's a wealth of forgotten details to be discovered. Most of the papers have been undisturbed for decades. I asked my granddaughter, Clarissa, if she'd like to help me do that, but she said it sounded boring.'

'It wouldn't be for me,' Lorna told him. 'It sounds fascinating. I love old documents.'

'My grandson Jonathon would be interested but he's just starting work in the business. It wouldn't be right to keep him at home doing things like that.'

Lorna had seen Mr Wyndham as an interesting stranger, and had been delighted that he'd offered her a job. Now she found it impossible to equate what her senses told her with her mother's comments. Had Mum's tragedy made her bitter, made her memories turn the Wyndham family into ogres when they were nothing of the kind? She wished she knew. It seemed that if things had worked out as her mother had hoped, she might have been calling the old man grandfather.

Lorna tossed and turned, unable to get her mother's confidences out of her mind. She felt haunted by what she'd been told. It altered

46

everything – her feelings about the Wyndhams and about her new job. She was filled with curiosity about them; dying to find out more, particularly about the man Mum said had fathered her. And Mum needed to know how he'd come to die at such a crucial time for her.

Over the following days, Lorna felt they were all edgy. Even Felicity Cartwright was wound up, though her business had at last been sold. She was nervous about solicitors and the need to sign it away to the Wyndhams.

'I know nothing about business matters,' she fretted. She hated taking responsibility or doing anything on her own. Her husband had taken all the decisions and, while he was able to, done all the work. 'I never expected to have matters of this sort pushed on me. I need to be looked after. Alfred promised to do that.'

She took Lorna with her when she went to her solicitor's office to sign the documents, and left all the subsequent practical arrangements to her. In the following days, Lorna made sure the ledgers were up to date and tidied up the files. The Cartwrights had been in awe of the Wyndhams and seen them as their main business rivals. In slack moments, she'd looked across Hamilton Square at their office, but though she'd seen cars park outside, and men go in, she had no way of knowing if they were family members, employees or clients.

When Mrs Cartwright heard that the sale was complete, she asked Lorna to go across and see what the Wyndhams wanted her to do with the paperwork and files. Lorna was jittery as she set out, wondering if she'd see members of the Wyndham family.

The notice over their office read: 'Premier Shipping Agent to all Parts of the World'. The front door was open. The gold script on the glass door of the vestibule read: 'Goods dispatched by rail, sea and air. Best service guaranteed. None better in the land.'

There was a counter with a bell on it in the front office but nobody about. A notice invited her to ring for service.

A clerk came immediately. 'Good morning, miss. How can I help you?'

'Would Mr Wyndham be here?'

'I saw Mr Adam here earlier. I don't know whether he still is.'

'Oh!' She'd learned enough about the family to know Adam was one of the children her mother had looked after. That would make him a sort of cousin to her. She explained about the files that needed to be moved from the Cartwright house.

'Mr Buckler's here now. He's our accountant, the person you should talk to. I'll find out if he can see you.'

Moments later, Lorna was being ushered into his office. He was middle-aged and portly, somewhat dandified and overdressed; perspiration was glistening on his forehead. Lorna explained why she'd come.

'How much paperwork is there?'

'I was told you'd need all the files for the last seven years.'

'Yes, I'll ask Mr Adam to go over to fetch them.

He'll be working on them.'

Lorna could feel her cheeks getting hotter. 'Mr Wyndham asked me if I would come and work here for a few hours to explain how we've been doing things.'

'Mr Wyndham? Mr Crispin Wyndham asked you?'

'I'm sorry I don't know his given name. White-haired...'

'Oh!' She saw enlightenment dawn on his podgy face. 'Old Mr Wyndham. A bit confusing, so many of the family working in the firm. That's why we call them by their given names. Mr Wyndham has retired. His son Mr Crispin runs the firm now.'

His pale eyes levelled with hers. They were small and almost lost in loose folds of flesh. 'I doubt if we'll need much help. We'll run the Cartwright account in with our own business.'

Lorna didn't like his manner. 'I'm going to be Mr Wyndham's secretary. I'll be living in at Otterspool House for a few weeks, to help sort out his personal papers and catalogue his belongings for the sale. He's offered me a permanent job, but it could be in the Liverpool office.'

Mr Buckler's face told her he wasn't pleased at that. 'I can't see why old Mr Wyndham needs a secretary. As I said, he's retired now.' She thought that was a bit high-handed from an employee. 'I hope there'll be room in the Liverpool office, because we'll all be there soon. We're closing this place down. Anyway, Miss...?'

'Mathews.'

'Mr Adam isn't in at the moment. I'll get him

49

to come over for the files tomorrow.'

Lorna stood up, feeling she'd been dismissed. Her first encounter with the Wyndham firm had reduced her confidence.

Chapter Three

The following morning, Lorna was working in the office when the front doorbell rang. She ran down to answer it and found a young man in the lobby.

'Adam Wyndham,' he said in a lordly manner. 'You're expecting me, I understand.'

Since Lorna had been told he would visit she'd felt apprehensive. Now, seeing him for the first time, her knees felt weak and her heart began to hammer. She stammered out her own name and was glad to turn her back on him and lead the way back to her office.

She'd got a grip on herself by the time she sat down at her desk and could look him in the face. He was a very attractive young man, expensively dressed. He removed his Homburg to show well-groomed golden curls. He was *her cousin!* Ill at ease, she threw open the cabinets to show him the contents.

'These are the files. I had a letter this morning from one of our clients, a firm called Ellwoods, they want—'

'I haven't much time to spend on this today.' Adam's manner was languid, as though he had all the time in the world. He was at the window staring out into the square. 'I've asked one of our porters to bring a trolley over. He can make two journeys if he has to. We might have to get some more filing cabinets first.'

'You can take these.' Lorna had already cleared this with Mrs Cartwright.

'We bought the fixtures and fittings too?'

'Just the filing cabinets.'

'Oh, right.'

Lorna decided she didn't like him any better than Mr Buckler. 'Mr Wyndham asked me to spend a few days with you in your office,' she said, 'to explain how I keep the ledgers.'

'Cartwrights were shipping agents in a small way?'

Lorna nodded. 'Not all that small.'

He shrugged with indifference. 'Shouldn't give us any problems. We do this sort of work all the time.' He was showing little interest in her or the files he'd come for. 'But if Grandpa's arranged it, you'd better come. Start tomorrow then?'

The front doorbell trilled through the building. 'I expect that's your porter now,' said Lorna. 'I'll let him in.'

When she returned with him and pointed out the cabinets, he scratched his head. 'I'll need a hand to get them downstairs.'

Lorna looked at Adam Wyndham expectantly. He said disdainfully, 'Could your porter or one of your clerks help him?'

'We haven't anybody like that. I do everything.'

'Oh!' His blue eyes swung to her face for the first time. He didn't seem to like what he saw.

51

'You'd better fetch someone from our office, Jenkins. Right, I'll see you tomorrow then?'

'Nine o'clock all right?'

'Make it ten.'

The next morning, she went across at five minutes to ten and was kept waiting until twenty past for Adam to arrive. After spending sessions sitting at his desk on each of the following three days, Lorna knew her first impressions had been right, Adam had no interest in the work. He treated all she told him about the clients as being of little importance. She'd been dealing with them for years and knew some of their staff well. She was afraid they'd not be satisfied with the service they'd get from him.

Mrs Cartwright was packing, her house was sold and she was preparing to move up to Cumberland. Apart from a few favourite pieces, all her furniture was going to a sale room. Great mounds of clothing that she didn't want to take were building up too. There were clothes that had belonged to her husband, and hats, dresses and good warm winter coats that Lorna knew her mother would love to have.

Mrs Cartwright had always been generous. She said, 'If you can find a use for them, Lorna, you take them. They won't bring much in the sale. And what about the typewriter? You know how to use it and I don't.'

Lorna was thrilled. 'But ... that could certainly go in the sale.'

'If it would be of use to you, I'd like you to have it.'

'It would, thank you. My sister would love to

52

learn to type. Perhaps I could teach her. She wants to work in an office if she can. She's quite jealous that I was given the chance to learn.'

Mrs Cartwright was tearful when the time came to say goodbye. She gave Lorna twenty pounds in addition to the money she was due. Lorna, too, found their parting a wrench. It had been a job in which she'd managed to find her feet. She had to hire a boy with a handcart to help her carry home all the things she'd been given. She hoped, as she trailed behind it, that she'd be as happy in her new place as she'd been in the old. She had a few days' rest now before starting work at Otterspool House, but already she was feeling nervous about going.

She was still carrying in her things when Pam returned from a job interview.

'I didn't get it.' She looked disappointed. 'A factory job, making ice cream.' Pam was wearing her navy-blue best frock. 'They took on six girls, but there were crowds of hopefuls waiting.' She pulled the pins out of her severe little bun and shook out her dark straight hair. 'Mum said I mustn't go with my hair flying everywhere, they wouldn't want that near ice cream, but it did no good.'

'Next time, love.' Her mother was trying to smile. 'Don't give up.'

'That was my eighth attempt,' Pam grimaced. 'I've tried for a job in the Co-op since I saw you, Lorna, selling shoes. I'd have loved that, but it was no good, too many others after it. It looks as though I'll end up as a housemaid after all.'

Lorna had never seen Pam look so despondent.

Her school had broken up for the summer holidays three weeks ago and she wouldn't be returning in the autumn. It was the end of an era for her just as it was for Lorna. Only the three of them were at home; Pa and Jim were away at sea. Mum had had a card from Pa posted in Baltimore only this morning.

Over their evening meal, Lorna said to her mother, 'I've seen Adam Wyndham. I don't like him much.'

'He was such a pretty little boy.'

'He's still pretty. Got butter-blond hair and deep blue eyes, but, Mum, he's got a big opinion of himself.'

'Most of that family have. You won't find them as easy to get on with as the Cartwrights.'

'Mrs Cartwright gave me an extra twenty pounds,' Lorna smiled. 'She said it was to reward me for all the additional work I'd done for her.'

'She's been very generous,' Mum said.

'Very. When I started, that was almost a year's wages.'

Pam's mouth opened wide. 'You have no end of luck. I can't believe it. What are you going to spend it on? A gramophone? That's what I'd buy if I was you.'

Lorna smiled slowly. 'I've been giving it some thought as I walked home.'

'And?'

'How would you like to take a secretarial course in September instead of looking for a job?'

'Lorna! Would you do that for me?'

'Course I would.' Lorna felt Pam's arms go round her to whirl her round. 'If you had a skill, you wouldn't need to skivvy for anybody.'

Lorna felt rewarded when she saw her sister's face light up with elation. 'I'd be able to get an office job! That would be wonderful. I'd be able to wear nice clothes all the time. I'd be like you.'

'There's the Hamilton Commercial School where I went to night classes. They do a full course in the daytime. You could get certificates in typing, shorthand and book-keeping.'

'Lorna, I'd love that. There was a girl in my class at school going there. Polly Evans from the dairy on the corner. We were all green with envy.'

'We'll go tomorrow and see if they've got a place for you.'

'I can't believe it.' Pamela's dark eyes were shining. 'I'll pay you back as soon as I start earning.'

Alice said, 'You see, Pam, you have your luck too.'

'She'll be able to live at home with you, Mum. No need for you to worry about being left on your own.'

'I'm so glad. Very grateful you're doing this. You're saving our Pam from domestic work. Wait till your pa hears about this.'

'Lorna, I'm made up.' Pam waltzed her round the room. 'Absolutely made up. Nobody could have a better sister than you.'

Half-sister, thought Lorna, but she was glad that that had not occurred to Pam.

Alice Mathews had been living in the past ever since Lorna had told her she was going to work for the Wyndhams. She'd relived every precious moment she'd ever spent with Oliver. The

55

tremulous joy of being alone with him, of meeting him behind the stables; sometimes if it was a wet night, inside the stables. Of walking through the woods with their arms round each other's waists, knowing they couldn't be seen by his brothers and sister. The aching joy of kisses given and received on top of the sweet-smelling hay. The warmth of his body as he held her against him and the desperate need for more. She could remember so much of what he'd said to her, his gestures, his pleasure at being with her.

She could see him clearly in her mind's eye even now. This was something she hadn't allowed herself to do for years. It was an extravagant indulgence, and it brought wave after wave of guilt.

From the beginning, Alice had known Sam was falling in love with her, but she could think of nobody but Oliver. Sam had been so good to her. She owed her life to him, and her baby daughter's. She was grateful, but he'd wanted more from her than she could give. She did her very best both for him and his grandmother to repay them for their kindness, but she couldn't give him love.

She was living in his home at his expense. She kept it clean, used his money as thriftily as she could to buy food and coal and she looked after his grandmother. When she knew he was coming home, she prepared special meals to make a fuss of him.

Always when he came in at the front door, he kissed his grandmother, and very soon he was kissing her too, and it didn't stop at greetings or

56

goodbyes. Alice didn't welcome his kisses but she couldn't push him off: she owed him too much. She pretended to enjoy them more than she really did, but soon found that awakened him to greater passion. He asked her to marry him quite soon but she'd said no. She'd been a romantic fool, expecting another rich man to come and sweep her off her feet.

She was pregnant for a second time before she came to her senses. Sam had swept her into his arms when she'd told him, and they'd gone together that same afternoon to book their wedding at the register office.

'You won't regret it,' he'd promised. 'I'll do my best for you and both your children. You know I love you.'

Having such memories brought back like this was making Alice feel fluttery, and she wept when she was alone in bed at night.

For the last few days, she'd been looking forward to having Lorna home. Seeing her now across the table she was reminded that she'd always been her favourite child. Alice knew she shouldn't have favourites and she tried hard not to let it show, but Lorna reminded her so much of Oliver, in both her appearance and her quick wits.

If Pam had started work as a housemaid, she'd never have managed to become a secretary as Lorna had, even if she were given the same opportunity.

'She's not stupid, Mum,' Lorna had rebuked her when she'd said as much to her. 'She'll learn as easily as the next at Commercial School.'

57

Lorna never stopped questioning Alice about the Wyndham family, and she was finding it easier to talk about them now. After tea last night she'd taken her daughter into the bedroom she shared with Sam, pulled open the drawer in her dressing table and taken out the tooled leather box with the address of a high-class Liverpool jeweller inside.

'Oliver gave me this ring,' she'd said, snapping it open. Lorna's bright curls fell forward as she bent her head over it. 'He told me these red stones are garnets and I mustn't confuse them with rubies. He said it wasn't worth very much.'

'It's very pretty.'

'He promised to buy me a better one, one day. He hadn't started working, you see – not properly, although he spent all his holidays in the office. He was planning to go to university, to Oxford. He had a place to start that October. He was cleverer than his brothers; none of the others went to university. But because of me he'd changed his mind about going. He wanted to stay working in the business, earning a living for us.'

'You were both very young.'

That reminded Alice that Lorna was already three years older than she'd been then. She hadn't felt too young.

'I'll be in a wonderful position to find out what really happened to him.' Lorna's sea-green eyes were shining with sympathy.

'You mustn't trust any of them.'

'I won't.'

'If you give them the slightest inkling–'

'I won't. I don't want to be put out as you were,

58

don't want to lose this chance. You deserved better than you got, Mum. I'll be very careful.'

It was the next to last day of September, the appointed day for Lorna to go to Otterspool House. She felt torn in two; more than nervous, though she wouldn't admit she was.

To find she was related to the Wyndhams, closely related, was making her sweat. To hear how her mother had been treated by them, to see raw terror on her face was more than scary. But the more Lorna learned about the family, the more curious she became and the more determined that nothing would stop her going. She wanted to see her relatives; she meant to find out, if she could, exactly what had happened to prevent Oliver returning to her mother, and why they'd treated her so badly.

Lorna caught a tram at the Pier Head, and the journey through strange streets seemed to take an age. At last the conductor told her this was the stop she'd asked for. She got off and looked about her at the newly built terraces of small houses.

A woman swinging a shopping basket was coming towards her. Lorna asked, 'Please could you tell me how to get to Otterspool House?'

A road running alongside an eight-foot stone wall was pointed out to her. 'That's the estate in there,' she was told. 'It's quite a walk to the house.'

Lorna's suitcase was heavy. She was glad to see the huge ornamental gates, though one had broken off its hinges and had been propped against the wall. Both gates were rusting and the gatehouse looked near derelict.

She was halfway up the drive when she met a huge removal van travelling at walking pace to avoid jolting its contents in the ruts and potholes. She had to take to the verge to get out of its way. The grass was rampantly overgrown and reached above her knees.

The house was surrounded by trees and shrubs, but when at last the view opened out, Lorna was able to appreciate the marvellous position it had on the banks of the Mersey. She could see not only across to the Cheshire bank, but also along the river. Ships were scudding up and down, some with black smoke streaming out behind. She could see the tide was full in, waves were splashing against the small beach and a crumbling jetty.

She turned round and saw the afternoon sun glinting on the huge mullioned windows of the house. It was an enormous building; to her it seemed more the size of a hotel. Built of mellow bricks, in the shape of a letter L, it had ivy spreading lushly across the front façade in two separate places. The roof was of uneven blue slate, moss-grown in places, with chimneys that were tall and twisting and beautiful. It looked very old.

On the far wing of the house she could see another large removal van being loaded. Two men in green baize aprons were manoeuvring a mahogany table out through one of the windows.

Lorna was enthralled. From a distance this beautiful mansion suggested a life of great comfort and unlimited wealth. There was an aura of peace and tranquillity about it. She was thrilled to find she had connections to a family living in such a grand style.

As she went nearer and looked more closely she could see the stamp of disrepair and neglect on everything. Rosebay willowherb was growing two feet tall in the gutters of the house. All the trees surrounding it needed cutting back and only small areas of grass were being cut and kept as lawns. Everywhere else was a tangle of briars and nettles, the hedges and shrubberies growing wild.

A circle of shallow steps led up to an important-looking front door. Should she go round the back? It was all rather intimidating, but no, she was clerical staff not kitchen staff. She mounted the steps to a large bell with a rope hanging from it. Beside it was a notice on curling paper that read: 'Please use side door.' Only then did she notice the grass growing between the stone slabs and realised the door could not have been opened for some time.

Lorna couldn't see a side door. She headed towards the removal van and met the two men bringing out a huge mahogany bed. They pointed back the way she'd come.

'By the main door. A new one made in the window.'

She could see it now. The windows were tall and reached down to within a foot of the terrace. Part of one windowsill had been roughly cut away, and a glass door had been fitted. She pressed the electric bell beside it. A girl wearing the black dress and starched white cap and apron of a parlourmaid came to open it.

'Hello, I'm Lorna Mathews.'

'Mr Wyndham's new secretary?' The girl was Lorna's age, buxom and lively. 'We're expecting you. Come in.'

Lorna was pleased to be described as Mr Wyndham's secretary; pleased to have got inside the house, but after what her mother had told her it felt like stepping inside a lions' den. She could feel herself quaking. 'Couldn't find the way in.'

'You're not the only one.'

'Why don't you use the main door?'

'Won't open. Something the matter with the lintel or the frame – it's collapsing. Hasn't been used in years.'

Lorna was in what seemed once to have been a sitting room. She followed her guide and couldn't suppress a gasp of admiration as she stepped into a great hall. It had a ceiling that went up to the roof and was so high that the heavy black beams and trusses were lost amongst shadows.

'Is that what they call a minstrels' gallery?'

'Yes. It's very grand, isn't it?'

The main staircase swept upwards and divided in two. It was lit by windows of stained glass through which shafts of coloured light dappled the marble floor and gave the hall a warm radiance.

'You might not think so to look at it now, but it's a cold and draughty place in winter. I'm Connie.' The young woman's smile was friendly and welcoming. 'Shall I take you up to your room?' Connie made to take her suitcase.

Lorna said, 'I can manage it, thank you.' She

wanted to make a friend of Connie. She liked her open manner.

'We're supposed to use the luggage stairs, but Mr Crispin's family is moving out today and there's furniture coming down them. We'll go this way.' It was a grand staircase but obviously not the main one. To Lorna, everything seemed larger than life-sized.

Connie lowered her voice. 'Miss Rosaleen said we were to give you a room on the attic floor.'

Lorna paused for a second on a landing where there was plenty of carved oak and Turkish carpet, then her guide led her through a door and up another flight of steeper stairs, lino-covered this time. She could guess what attic rooms meant in a house like this. Miss Rosaleen classed her as a servant even if Mr Wyndham thought of her as his secretary.

'It's not as though there aren't plenty of other empty rooms that are better.'

Lorna had reached the attic floor. It looked drab. 'Not a good place?'

Connie shook her head; a lot of reddish hair escaped round her cap, standing up like a halo.

'The rain comes in, look.' She threw open a door. The ceiling had large brown stains and the place smelled musty. 'Feel this wall. It's always wet. Not a fit place for anyone to sleep, really it isn't. Even the bedclothes feel damp, and in one room along there the whole ceiling's come down.'

'Oh, gosh!'

'We decided you'd better have my room.'

'Really? Thank you, but—'

'I'm leaving. Well, I'm going with Mr Crispin's family, though I don't want to. It'll just be for a few weeks until they get their own staff.'

'Oh no! I was thinking you'd be easy to get on with, that we might be friends.' Lorna tried to smile. 'You know how it is in a strange place.'

'That's nice,' Connie giggled. 'But you'll have to make friends with Hilda or Sissie. They're the ones staying on.'

'Are they easy to get on with?'

'Hilda can be a bit sour,' she whispered. 'Sissie's sick. She's got flu; she was coughing all over us. They called the doctor to her and he sent her home for a few days. Here we are. I've packed all my things and we made up the bed clean for you.'

Lorna looked round. The room was plain and sparsely furnished, with a deal wardrobe and an iron bedstead. She went straight to the window.

'What a magnificent view. I can see right across the river.'

'Yes, but that window gets the full force of any storm. It leaks too, quite badly. You'll find pools on the windowsill from time to time.'

'I shall be happy enough here. It won't be for long, after all.'

'That's right, but it's unsettling, not knowing where we're going to end up.'

'Haven't they found another house?'

'No, nothing's good enough for them. Miss Rosaleen likes the grandeur of this place. Hilda can't see them going anywhere. The old man looks round and finds a place but when he takes her, it's always too plain, and not nearly big enough for all of them.'

'How many of them are there?'

'There's Mr Wyndham and his sister, Mrs Carey. She's a widow and has lived here since her husband was killed on the Somme. She's staying with her married daughter in London this week but she'll be back soon. Then there's his daughter, Rosaleen, and his grandson Jonathon. Rosaleen doesn't like the place Mr Crispin's found for his own family – she thinks that's too small too – but it's a really lovely house. Do you want to unpack, or will you come down to the kitchen and have a cup of tea?'

'I think I'd like the tea.' Lorna knew it wouldn't take her many minutes to put her clothes away and she wanted to learn all she could from Connie. As they were going back down again she could hear raised voices.

Connie turned to her with her hand half covering her mouth. 'Quarrelling again,' she whispered.

The voices became clearer as the girls descended the stairs.

'Is one of them French?' Lorna asked.

'Yes, that's Daphne, Crispin's wife. The other is Rosaleen.'

She had an accent like cut glass. 'Really, Daphne, you can't take that dressing table with you. It was Mama's. I'm sure Father will want it as a keepsake.'

'Nonsense, I've been using it for the last decade at least. He hasn't once mentioned it to me, or been to see it in all that time.'

'It's Chippendale–'

'Don't be silly.'

65

'It's eighteenth century and very valuable. Even if Father doesn't want it, it ought to go in the sale.'

'I'm attached to it. I'll ask him if I can have it.'

'He's gone out and you know it.'

Connie pulled Lorna into the warmth of the kitchen and closed the door so they could no longer hear. 'Always having a ding-dong, those two, and it's usually about money or possessions. Come to think about it, Rosaleen's always having a row with somebody.'

The kitchen was vast and stone-floored. A large mahogany trolley was set with sparkling china and a delicious selection of sandwiches and scones. A stout woman in a cook's striped dress and large apron was making room on the trolley for an iced cake on a silver stand. It had 'Happy Birthday' in blue icing written on it.

'This is Hilda,' Connie told Lorna, going straight to an enamel teapot keeping warm on the hearth. 'And it's the old man's birthday. He's eighty today.'

Hilda moved slowly. She was approaching retirement age. 'You still here, Connie? You'd better hurry. Mrs Crispin came down five minutes ago looking for you. She said you mustn't let the last furniture van go without you.'

'Ooh, where's my coat?' She turned to Lorna. 'I'll be back tonight. See you then.'

Hilda explained. 'Mr Crispin and his family are coming back for dinner tonight. Bit of an occasion, being the old man's birthday.'

'I'm on my way. So long.' The kitchen door

66

slammed behind Connie. Lorna was sorry to see her go.

'A bit scatterbrained, that one,' Hilda said severely, 'but I don't know how I'll manage without her.'

Savoury scents were coming from the coal-fired range. Hilda lifted out an enormous pan to inspect and baste the contents.

'Saddle of lamb with thyme and parsley stuffing for tonight.' Her white cotton cap was large and worn low across her forehead, showing only a hint of iron-grey hair.

Lorna savoured the tea, hot, strong and restorative.

'Would you like some cake?' A large tin was pushed in front of her and the lid removed.

'No thanks.' Coming to this job had banished Lorna's usual appetite and dried her mouth. She had the second cup of tea steaming in front of her on the scrubbed table and was just beginning to relax when one of the line of brass bells on the kitchen wall began to jangle.

Hilda got up to swing an enormous kettle over the hot plate. 'That's the drawing room. I expect they're ready for their tea now. Warm the pot for me, there's a good girl.' She leaned against the trolley and rolled it out into the passage. 'I'll tell them you've arrived.'

Chapter Four

Lorna looked round the kitchen as the sound of tinkling china died away. The wall clock fussily ticked the seconds away and the kettle began to sing. On the other end of the table was a massive silver tray laden with the paraphernalia used for serving tea. She inspected the slop bowls, the silver strainers and sugar tongs before warming the teapot and hot-water jug.

Hilda's footsteps were returning. 'You're to come and have tea with them,' she told Lorna, as she spooned curly black leaves into the pot.

'Gosh, I've just drunk two big cupfuls.'

'These will be daintier.' Hilda edged another china cup and saucer on to the tray and picked it up. 'They're in the white drawing room. They always have their tea there.'

'How many drawing rooms are there?' It seemed unbelievable to Lorna that any family could need this much space.

'There's the white one – they use that mostly – but there's also the red drawing room and the summer drawing room. Lots of sitting rooms too.'

Lorna trailed behind her, looking around with avid curiosity. She'd thought the Cartwrights had a fine house, but it had had nothing of the grand baronial style of this place. It was a veritable palace. Well, once it had been; now it was worn, shabby and threadbare.

'Here we are,' Hilda whispered, stopping at a door.

Just then, the cut-glass voice Lorna had heard earlier said, 'Father, you haven't had a secretary for years, not since you retired. What can you possibly want with one now? A gross extravagance.'

Hilda cleared her throat as she led the way in, Lorna following.

The woman was tall and thin to the point of being gaunt. Lorna guessed this must be Rosaleen, Oliver's sister and her aunt. She was in her forties, a faded blonde with deep lines of discontent running from her nostrils to the corners of her thin lips.

'Oh!' she said, turning to glare at Lorna. 'You must be the new secretary?' Eyes of blue ice were assessing her.

'Yes, Lorna Mathews.'

Mr Wyndham was on the other side of the room. She thought of him as an ally and moved closer. He struggled to his feet and offered his hand.

'Glad to see you. Found your way all right? I hope you'll be comfortable here with us for a few weeks.'

Rosaleen was pouring tea. 'She's come to work, Father, not to be comfortable.'

He seemed more aged than Lorna remembered. His scalp showed pink through a scant haze of white hair.

'Are you going to cut your cake, Father?' Rosaleen asked.

He said, 'You do it for me.' That made her cluck with impatience but she brandished the knife and did it with quick nervous movements. She seemed out of patience with everything.

'Many happy returns, Mr Wyndham,' Lorna said. 'I see it's your birthday.'

Before she realised what Rosaleen was doing, she'd been presented with a large slice. It was too late to refuse it.

'Had too many birthdays. I'd like to forget them.'

'It's no good forgetting birthdays,' Rosaleen said irritably. 'The years add up just the same. Why don't you relax and act your age? Forget about work and secretaries.'

'We'll need secretarial help, Rosaleen, to sort and catalogue things for the sale. You know that.'

Lorna reminded herself she must show no dislike, no fear of Rosaleen, though her heart was thumping. She'd need to be careful.

Mr Wyndham said to her, 'In a house of this size nothing is ever thrown away. When things are no longer used, they're put away in case they're needed again. So there'll be a lot for you to sort through.'

'It seems a very big house.' Lorna nibbled at the cake half-heartedly, though it was delicious.

Rosaleen said proudly, 'We have seventy-four rooms here. Many are not used, or used only occasionally for visitors. We've always had space for everything.'

'Seventy-four rooms?' Lorna was astounded. Home as she'd known it had been a two up two down, until Pa had fixed a skylight and a ladder up to the attic to make a room for Jim, and none of them was this size.

'Seven staircases and two courtyards,' Rosaleen added with even more pride. 'Plenty of room for several generations of the family to live in comfort.'

The old man sighed. 'But we're splitting between two smaller houses now. Crispin and his family have moved out today.'

'None of us wants these changes,' his daughter shuddered. 'I hate the thought of moving from here. I've looked at so many places, and you won't agree to any of them.'

'We haven't seen anything to suit us yet, Rosaleen,' her father sighed. 'We've lived here together generation after generation. I'm afraid breaking the family up will mean we won't be as close in future.'

'Have we been close in the past?' Rosaleen asked pointedly.

Lorna remembered the voices she'd overheard on the stairs. Rosaleen and Daphne hadn't been close.

The old man helped himself to another slice of cake. 'I've tried to look after my family but the struggle's become too much. All this century, the city's been growing. We're surrounded now and it threatens to overwhelm us. This old house will be pulled down and an estate of little boxes built here instead. We had forty acres of grounds once, now we're down to three and soon there'll be nothing left.'

Lorna let her eyes go round the huge room. It was very formal, with family portraits in gilded frames crowding the walls. There were two white pillars holding up the ornate ceiling; both that and the pillars were yellowed with age. There were several groups of well-worn sofas, all gilt-framed, rather spindly and not comfortable to sit on. Lorna knew little about antiques but thought the furniture could be worth a good deal. The carpet square was well worn and shredding beneath her best shoes, but Mrs Cartwright had been agreeably surprised at how much her worn carpets had made in the sale.

'I'm afraid many valuable things will be lost when we leave here.' Rosaleen's cheek kept giving a slight jerk; it took Lorna a few minutes to realise she must have a nervous tic.

'Many valuable things will be sold, Rosaleen. We have to do this.'

'There must be letters and diaries and business reports dating back over two hundred years. Nobody will pay much for them but they're our family history. Even I know very little about our past.'

'That is why Miss Mathews is here. I want her to make sure no family papers are lost.'

Lorna felt Rosaleen's cold eyes rake over her as though she didn't believe her capable of that.

'That's a portrait of Captain Lars Wyndham over the mantelpiece,' Mr Wyndham told her. 'We're very proud to have him as one of our forebears.'

Lorna admired the picture. One of my forebears too, she thought, seeking in him some family resemblance to the current generation.

'He built this house in seventeen seventy-three.'

'Not entirely, Rosaleen. The west wing was added in Victorian times.'

Lorna said, 'Leaving it after all this time must be very painful for you.'

'Yes, there are untold plans and maps relating to it,' the old man said. 'Watch out for them and keep them safe.'

'Do they matter?' Rosaleen asked impatiently. 'If the house is to go, why keep the plans? Nobody's going to build another like this today.'

'The plans will be all we have left.'

Rosaleen's manner changed, became less aggressive. 'Father, I told you about the house I saw yesterday. It might suit us. I wish you'd look at it. There are stables and two paddocks for the horses.'

'It's in Southport. That's too far out.'

'You're not working any more so distance from the office isn't important.'

'What about Jonathon? He'd have to travel in daily.'

'It's a lovely house. Why won't you look at the details?'

She took a sheaf of papers over to him. He grunted in protest but felt for his glasses. A moment later he snatched them off.

'It has twelve bedrooms, and goodness, look at the price!'

'We don't need to live in a hovel, Father. Don't pretend we do.'

'We can't afford this. There'd be little point in moving. It's too big.'

'Twelve bedrooms is not big compared with this.'

'We need only four if there's attic rooms. Six without. Mossley Hill, perhaps, or Gatacre would be good places to look.'

'Father, I've tried. I've tramped round every agent. They have nothing I want to live in. So few houses have room for staff.'

'We can't get staff, Rosaleen. You're always complaining about that.'

'There's Hilda and Sissie and...'

Lorna felt Rosaleen's eyes settle on her again. 'My mother's quite keen for me to live at home,' she said hurriedly. 'I won't be here for long.'

Rosaleen ignored her. 'There's nothing on the market.' She sounded exasperated. 'Believe me, I've looked.'

'Perhaps the other side of the river,' her father suggested. 'That's the dormitory for Liverpool, after all. It's easy to get into town from there.'

'We've got to have a house that's halfway decent.'

'Of course we have.'

'You're not going to see this one?'

'No, it would be a waste of time.' He crumpled the details into a ball and tossed it on the fire. Yellow flames spurted up to devour it.

Lorna heard Rosaleen cluck with impatience, and in order not to appear to be listening to what seemed a private squabble, she moved to one of the drawing-room windows that looked out over the river. She was soon lost in her own thoughts.

She found it difficult to imagine her mother married into this family. Would she have been able to settle in such grand surroundings and to such a different way of life? Mum was very sure

74

she'd have been happy here with Oliver, but she'd said the staff were scared of Rosaleen. Now Lorna had met her she thought Rosaleen would have made Mum's life a misery. She'd have been forever needling her.

Of course, Mum had worked here for several years before her affair with Oliver, but Lorna was sure she'd have seen little apart from the nurseries and the kitchens. Mum surely wouldn't feel at ease in this vast cold drawing room, with its two crystal chandeliers and plaster cherubs and trailing ivy on the moulded ceiling.

She saw Rosaleen was watching her and blushed, although she couldn't know what she'd been thinking.

An open MG sports car was coming along the drive. It pulled up on the forecourt and a young man got out and came to the entrance.

'Jonathon's home,' Rosaleen said.

Lorna braced herself to meet another of her cousins, who'd been three at the time of her mother's crisis. He came in a few moments later, bringing a gust of cold air with him. He was tall and slim, like all the Wyndhams. Though not unattractive, he wasn't strikingly handsome like Adam, his colouring fair though hardly blond.

Rosaleen said, 'This is Miss Mathews, Father's new secretary.'

Jonathon smiled at her, his teeth ultra-white against his bronzed skin. He shook her hand and said, 'Miss Mathews? Gee, Aunt Roz, such formality?' His blue eyes levelled with hers; his suntan made them seem as bright as sapphires. 'Don't you have a first name?'

'Lorna,' she said. 'I wish you'd all call me Lorna. I'd prefer that.'

Rosaleen added coldly, 'Jonathon's just back from America. He's spent two years there and unfortunately, he's picked up some very trans-atlantic habits.'

He pulled a face; his expression was ever-changing. It wasn't hard to guess what he thought of his aunt. He said 'Grandpa tells me you're going to help him write the family history.'

'Before you start on that there are more important things to be done.' Rosaleen's tone was severe. 'Rooms to be turned out and cases packed.'

'Is there any tea left, Aunt Roz?' He cut himself a slice of birthday cake.

'It's cold – you're later than usual. Ring for Hilda.'

'I'll fetch it.' Lorna got to her feet and took the tray to the kitchen. She needed some respite from the glacial atmosphere. Hilda was washing cabbage at the sink.

'Fresh tea needed? Why didn't they ring?'

'I can't sit back and let you do everything.' Lorna felt she had to make a friend here if she could. 'I'm not used to that.'

'I heard Mr Jonathon arrive and I put the kettle on again.' Hilda was tipping out tea leaves and slops and making more while she spoke.

Lorna took the tray back, which was heavy and needed two hands. Once in the drawing room, she slid it back on the table in front of Rosaleen, who ignored it.

Jonathon got to his feet. 'More tea, Grandpa?'

76

'Yes, please. I'm very pleased with the fountain pen you gave me this morning, Jonathon. It writes beautifully, thank you.'

'Good. How about you, Lorna? More tea?'

She could hear a faint American lilt in Jonathon's voice. 'No, thanks.'

'Aunt?'

As Rosaleen pushed her cup silently forward, Lorna noticed that her nails had been bitten down to the quick. Jonathon helped himself to a scone and winked at Lorna. He seemed to imply they'd have something in common.

His grandfather asked, 'Jonathon, has Adam spoken to you yet about the Cartwright business?'

'No, he left early. They're moving into their new house today.'

'I know, but I thought they'd leave that to Daphne. If they're as worried about the business as they say they are, I'd have thought they'd want to work. I suppose Crispin did?'

'Haven't seen him all day, Grandpa.'

'Good Lord! Daphne has Clarissa and she took Connie to help. Why would she need Crispin and Adam as well?'

Rosaleen looked up sourly. 'Moving house is hard work, Father. You've never done it. You don't realise what it entails.'

'It doesn't entail cooking. I understand they're all coming back to have dinner here tonight.'

'It's your birthday, Father. That's why. I thought you'd like to have them here.'

'They pleaded for Connie. Said without her they'd never be able to get their beds made up before they'd need to use them.'

'Father, wait till we have to move – that's if you ever find a house for us to move to.'

The old man got stiffly to his feet. 'I think I'll have a glass of whisky. It might soothe me.' His silver-headed cane tapped slowly out.

Jonathon smiled at Lorna and whispered, 'Bickering as usual. You must forgive our family.' He pulled himself to his feet, collected the jacket he'd shed, and said in his normal voice, 'See you later on at dinner.'

Lorna was returning the tea tray to the trolley and nodded her agreement.

She saw Rosaleen purse her lips. 'Dinner tonight will be a family occasion,' she said. 'Take yours in the kitchen with Hilda.'

'Yes, Miss Wyndham.' Lorna hesitated. 'Is that just for dinner tonight?'

'No, all meals except breakfast. You can come down for that at eight o'clock sharp. Then you'll be ready to start work with Father by half-past.'

'Yes, Miss Wyndham.'

Lorna pushed the trolley back to the kitchen, feeling relieved she'd not have to face the family at dinner. Hilda was rather strait-laced but she could cope more easily with her.

She found her making pastry.

'They shouldn't take Connie away like this,' she complained. 'They order a special dinner for Mr Wyndham's birthday, then leave me to see to everything on my own.'

Lorna cleared the trolley and washed up the tea things. She had to make an ally of Hilda. 'What else can I do to help?'

78

'Peel and slice those apples, if you would. I'm making an apple pie.'

Lorna did so, wondering about Hilda's life. She asked, 'Have you been working here long?'

'Going on thirty-one years now.'

Lorna suppressed a gasp. Hilda would have been here with her mother. She'd have known all about her affair with Oliver.

'Connie isn't pleased to be going?' Lorna knew she had to ask questions to get information about what went on here.

'She doesn't get on with Rosaleen, though Mrs Crispin's not easily pleased either. What Connie would really like is a job in a clothes shop, then she could rent a room for herself.'

Lorna smiled. 'Wouldn't you like to work in a shop?'

'I've always been in domestic service. It's what I'm used to.'

'A cook?'

'Or a cook-general. With Connie here I did just the cooking but it was for a family of eight plus the staff. Now I'll be back to doing everything again.'

'What about the girl who's off sick?'

'Sissie Smith? She's useless. No help at all. I'm getting too old to do all this. I'll be sixty next year.'

'You'll be thinking of retiring then?'

'Chance would be a fine thing,' she said sharply, thumping her rolling pin down hard on the pastry. 'They'll probably keep me in harness till I drop.'

Lorna said nothing. It seemed Hilda could be touchy. After a few minutes' silence, she went on:

79

'I've set the table for eight. I didn't know whether you'd be eating with the family or here with me.'

'With you.'

'Then I shall have to remove one place setting.'

Lorna put the apples she'd sliced in front of her. 'Shall I do that? I'm to have all my meals with you except breakfast so I'll need to find the dining room.'

Hilda chuckled. 'The ladies have their breakfast in bed, but there's a breakfast room where the men eat.'

'Oh! Where's that then?'

'You go through the green baize door back into the big hall. The breakfast room is the first on the right, the family dining room is next to it. You cross the hall to get to the main dining room.'

'Three dining rooms?'

Lorna wasn't sure what to make of Hilda. There were moments when she seemed to be normally good-humoured, but others when she was decidedly off-putting and her eyes had a steely glint.

'That's right,' Hilda said. 'The main one seats forty-six, but I've never had to cook for that number, thank goodness.'

'Gosh, how many does the family dining room seat?'

'Up to twelve.'

'I'll see if I can find it.'

Lorna went through the kitchens, opening each door she passed to look inside, and saw store-rooms, pantries, rooms for ironing and washing clothes. Once on the other side of the green baize door she paused. She'd been this way to the white drawing room earlier.

Lorna was fascinated by the great hall's huge fireplace with a canopy of hammered brass and a chimney breast that rose to the ceiling. The empty hearth looked large enough to roast a whole ox and was furnished with firedogs and pokers and brass buckets.

The light coming through the stained-glass windows had faded now. Lorna thought its size, age and dim light gave the hall something of the atmosphere of a church. As she crossed it, she saw Rosaleen coming down the sweeping staircase in a grey full-length dinner gown. Lorna had reached the door of what she took to be the family dining room when she heard her call out, 'Clarissa?'

Lorna knew well enough who Clarissa was, and thought it was no concern of hers. She took off one place setting and was moving up the other knives and forks to fill the space when Rosaleen came to the door.

'Clarissa?'

Lorna turned round.

'Oh, it's you!' She was staring at her. 'I thought you were Clarissa.'

Lorna gripped the edge of the table. She'd not seen Clarissa yet – could it be that she resembled her? She hadn't considered such a possibility. Now that she did, it scared her.

Lorna suppressed a shiver. 'I'm helping Hilda. Taking a place setting off. She thought I'd be eating here.' She was nervous and spoke too quickly. 'Hilda's busy because Connie isn't back yet.'

Lorna returned to the kitchen feeling quite shaky. She wanted to ask Hilda if she looked like Clarissa but dared not. Such fears must not be mentioned in this house.

The back door slammed and a man in a flat cap and the heavy boots of a gardener came in, bringing a large basket.

'This is Harold,' Hilda introduced him. 'Lives over the stables with his mam and dad.'

'Harold Jones,' he said. 'I've brought you some plums, Hilda.'

'This is no time to be bringing stuff in. Morning is when I need it.'

'There's only me, Hilda, to do all the outside work. I've got the car to drive and the horses to take care of.'

'There's your dad, he still does a bit. Got more sense than you. If you'd brought them plums sooner I could have used them tonight. Would have saved us peeling apples. Why didn't you tell me they were ripe?'

'I don't have time to stand and gossip with you.'

'Your mam does. Nothing stops her gossiping. She was here earlier – why didn't she say?'

'We can't think of everything, Hilda. Thought you'd like the plums to make chutney.'

'I haven't got time to make chutney, not these days,' she said crossly. 'I'm on my own too.'

At that moment, Connie returned, looking hot.

Harold said, 'You seem to have plenty of help here tonight, if I dare say so. But I'll take the plums away. Tip them on the compost if you don't want them.'

'No, I'll use them tomorrow.'

'Mrs Crispin brought me back to help tonight,' Connie said. 'I won't be staying.'

'Neither will I,' Harold retorted, and with a nod at Lorna, stamped out, slamming the doors.

Connie started to complain. 'They've been at me every minute: put up those curtains; unpack this linen; take this to that room and carry that somewhere else. I'm shattered, but they hate the thought of letting me rest. Can't even make a cup of tea for themselves.'

'Is there any rest for me? At least you'll have a smaller house to look after now,' Hilda reminded her.

'Still big, and they haven't even found a daily char yet. And there's no peace. It's not just the work – the family never stop sniping at each other.'

'What d'you mean, sniping at each other?' Lorna asked.

'They were at it here, weren't they, Hilda? Rows and arguments almost every meal time.'

'For months.'

'Years more like.'

'What about?' Lorna asked, trying not to look too interested.

'There's always something to upset them,' Hilda said. 'Something different all the time.'

Connie giggled. 'It's Clarissa's boyfriend at the moment. They don't approve of him. They've been at her to give him the push. She chose today to announce she's going to marry him whether they like it or not. It's put them all in a foul temper.'

'What's the matter with him?' Lorna asked.

'Not good enough to marry into the Wyndham family. He's a doctor but has no money. They kept giving dinner parties, didn't they, Hilda? Trying to find her someone better but she's determined to have her precious Dr Vincent McDonald.'

'You shouldn't be gossiping like this,' Hilda reproved. 'They'd be in an even worse temper if they heard you.'

Lorna decided that Hilda was of the old school who did her best to please her employers, whereas Connie had a tendency to chatter and didn't put herself out to do more than was essential. She'd learn more from Connie and she was more fun. The bell summoned Connie to the drawing room before she'd got her pleated cap and apron adjusted to her satisfaction.

'What can they possibly want now? Won't lift a finger,' she was saying as the kitchen door banged behind her.

Hilda was watching the kitchen clock as she lifted the saddle of lamb on to its serving dish. Lorna could feel Hilda's tension building as the time to serve dinner approached. She kept her busy with a stream of instructions and jumped on Connie the moment she returned. 'Sound the second gong to get them to the table.' At precisely five minutes to eight, it rang through the house.

'Just the gravy to make now.' Hilda was starting on that.

Connie returned to pour the soup into the serving tureen. 'What sort is it? They always ask.

84

Could you get the soup plates out of the oven for me, Lorna?'

She was back from the dining room a few moments later. 'They're sitting up, not wasting any time tonight. Where's the bread?'

'The bread! I've forgotten it.' Hilda snatched the rolls from the oven where they had been warming.

'They'll say they're too crunchy.' Connie rejected two that had turned brown, tossed the rest into a bread basket, covered them with a fancy napkin and rushed them to the table.

'Sissie's not much good but I miss her. We need another pair of hands. Mash those potatoes for me, there's a good girl,' Hilda directed Lorna, 'and get them into a dish.'

'They have mashed as well as roast?'

'Yes, croquettes as well tonight.'

Lorna had the pan of mashed potato poised over a serving dish when the electric light went out, plunging them all into pitch darkness.

'Hell, not again!' Hilda dropped a spoon. 'What a time to lose the lights!'

Lorna stood stock-still until she heard a match strike, then she gingerly pushed the pan she was holding back on top of the stove. In the feeble light she could barely see across the room. The bell jangled more loudly than ever from the dining room.

'Damnation,' Connie swore from the door. 'They'll be wanting light, but they don't give anybody time to find the dratted lamps.'

'Take some matches. There's candles there. They can dine by candlelight.'

'I've got to be able to see my way there, haven't I?'

'Be glad it's the last time. You won't have to put up with this again.'

Hilda wrenched a cupboard open and started lighting oil lamps. 'Take one for the drawing room and another for that table in the hall. Good job I trimmed the wicks before putting them away.'

The dining-room bell jangled again, louder than ever. 'Damn you, you'll have to wait a minute,' Connie shouted at the wall.

'Don't let them delay dinner,' Hilda said furiously. 'Tell them it'll spoil if they do.'

'Does this happen often?' Lorna wanted to know. An oil lamp had been lit on the dresser so she could see again.

'Things break down all the time. If it isn't the electric then it's the hot-water system. It's all so old. They had the electric put in before the turn of the century. Plenty of money in them days for all the latest gadgets.'

Connie came back. 'Mr Wyndham says hold the next course for a while. Adam and Jonathon have gone to see if they can fix the light.'

Hilda slumped on to a chair. 'You told them it was all ready? Eight o'clock she said and eight o'clock it is.'

'I told him. Rosaleen wants another bottle of sherry, they're having it with the soup.'

'Oh bother! I wish I could sit down to a glass of sherry. You'll have to get it from the butler's pantry.'

The electric light flickered twice and went off again.

86

'Shouldn't be long,' Lorna said, trying to soothe her.

'Here,' Hilda lit another lamp, 'take this to the sideboard so Mr Crispin can see to carve. Ask him if you can take the joint in.'

Lorna was taut with tension because she'd see Clarissa there and be able to judge for herself if they resembled each other. That had been on her mind since Rosaleen had made the mistake. Connie had positioned oil lamps and candles at intervals in the passageway and corridors, so they could see their way to and from the dining room. Lorna could feel her heart pounding as she went. The dining table looked very elegant, lit as it was with a candelabra of six candles at each end. She looked for Clarissa as she put the oil lamp down.

'Is there any moonlight?' Clarissa had left her seat at the table to open the curtains. She had her back to Lorna, but she was tall and slim and her hair was curly and did not look very different from her own. Lorna could feel panic rising in her throat.

'Oh, Miss Mathews.' Mr Wyndham got to his feet. 'Whatever is the matter with me? I meant you to dine with us. This will be the only chance to introduce you to some of the family. This is Daphne, my daughter-in-law.'

Daphne seemed barely interested, but Lorna felt unable to move. Would anyone notice a resemblance between herself and Clarissa? Perhaps not in this dim light.

'My son Crispin. He runs the business now.'

He was already on his feet. A haughty-looking man, he offered his hand, but spoke over her shoulder to his sister.

'When are we going to be fed, Rosaleen? We've had a hard day moving house. I need to get to bed.'

'At least have the patience to wait a few minutes. This was meant to be an occasion. Don't spoil it like this.'

'And this is my granddaughter, Clarissa.' The chandelier flashed twice, before it steadied and hardened to white light.

'Hello.' Clarissa turned round and smiled at Lorna. Everybody was blinking in the sudden brilliance, exclaiming with delight to have it restored. 'Pleased to meet you and all that.'

Waves of relief were washing over Lorna. Clarissa's face was nothing like her own. She was really pretty, with a pert upturned nose and high cheekbones. She was wearing a becoming gown in midnight-blue silk, low-necked but long-sleeved. Lorna had been worrying for nothing.

Mr Wyndham said, 'Do sit down and eat with us. It's what I intended. I forgot to ask you; please forgive me. Why isn't there a place set? Rosaleen?'

'Here, have my chair.' Jonathon had returned and was lifting away his soup plate, which was still almost full. Adam was spooning his soup down.

Lorna was overcome with embarrassment. It was the last thing she wanted. 'It's very kind, but no thank you,' she said as firmly as she could. 'This is a family occasion for you. I can't push in now.'

'Course you can. Connie, can we set another place here?'

'No,' Lorna protested. 'I mustn't.' Most of the men were in formal dinner dress with black tie, the women in ankle-length gowns. 'I haven't changed.'

'Neither have I,' Jonathon pointed out.

Lorna had chosen to wear her stone-coloured skirt today with a plain jersey of almost matching colour. She'd felt smart and up to the minute, but it felt wrong now when the other women were wearing dinner dresses.

She'd brought a dinner dress with her that had belonged to Mrs Cartwright. It was of black jersey and rather staid. It had the waist-line dropped to hip level, which had been fashionable in the twenties but was now completely outmoded. Lorna had brought a belt to wear with it to disguise that fact.

'You're lazy, Jonathon,' his Aunt Rosaleen told him. 'You should have changed. It wouldn't hurt you to make more effort.'

'Sorry, Aunt Roz. I sat down to read for a while after tea and fell asleep. The second gong woke me and I didn't have time to change then.'

'You should get to bed earlier.'

'It's not that. I've been on my own in the office today.' He pulled a face. 'I haven't stopped.'

Lorna felt she'd had a hard day too. She was tired and could no longer concentrate. She was backing towards the door.

'I'll ask Hilda to send in the joint,' she said, and turned to flee just as Connie was coming back with the saddle of lamb on a large platter and blocked the door. Lorna didn't feel safe until she'd reached the kitchen again.

89

Chapter Five

Jonathan was afraid his grandfather's birthday dinner was not going well. None of them was in a party mood; they needed cheering up. He stood up and raised his wine glass.

'I think we should all drink to Grandpa's eighty years,' he said. 'Happy birthday, and many more.'

'Hear, hear,' Clarissa smiled. 'To Grandpa.'

'Eighty years is quite an achievement.'

'It's not an achievement at all.' His grandfather was smiling. 'It's something that overtook me. It'll overtake you too in time. The alternative seems worse.'

'It's still a big occasion. My mother told me about the tremendous parties you used to have,' Jonathon went on. 'Parties of all kinds – tennis parties and picnics.'

'In the summertime. That was your grandmother's doing. She was very sociable, always wanted people here.'

'I heard you had good parties in the winter too. Fireworks to celebrate birthdays. I should have got some.'

'For the children – when they were young. Those were family parties. Marina made much of the family.'

The food was good. Jonathon tucked in; he was hungry. He'd cheered Grandpa up but, apart from Clarissa, the rest of the family still seemed in a dour mood.

'Family is important to us all,' Rosaleen said.

'Very,' Aunt Daphne agreed. 'I do wish you'd realise that, Clarissa.' She glared at her daughter.

'Don't start nagging, Mother. Not now.'

'I don't know why you can't settle for Edmund,' Daphne said irritably. 'He'd make a very suitable husband.'

'Who's Edmund?' Jonathon wanted to know. 'Edmund Wyndham Yates, your cousin.'

'Cousin? I didn't know Edmund Yates was a cousin.'

'Yes, of course he is, a distant cousin.'

'Distant? At least fifteen times removed, if not twenty. Why call him a cousin at all?'

'I hate Edmund,' Clarissa spat. 'He's a pain.'

Jonathon didn't care for him either; he went to Clarissa's assistance. 'Gee, Aunt Daphne, you want to choose Clarissa's husband?' He laughed at the very idea. 'That's crazy. It's up to her.'

'Thanks,' Clarissa said.

Crispin was at his most pompous. 'In a family like ours a good marriage is important.'

Daphne was attacking her lamb with gusto. 'Clarissa can't marry just any Tom, Dick or Harry. Besides, this doctor wants to take her away from us. Your place is here with the family, Clarissa.'

Jonathon felt restive as he listened to the reasons: The family must come first... Keep the line pure... Carrying on life in the traditional way...

Aunt Roz said, 'What about you, Jonathon? You'll need to think of marriage soon.'

Aunt Daphne's face broke into a radiant smile.

For the first time he realised she might have been good-looking when she was a girl. 'You and Clarissa? An eminently suitable match.'

Jonathon felt gall rising in his throat. Hadn't he spent his youth trying to hold his own against Clarissa and Adam? They'd both tried to squash him on every possible occasion. He didn't fancy being married to her! He was so angry he could hardly get the words out.

'That's an outrageous suggestion. Who we choose to marry has nothing to do with you, Aunt Roz. You can leave all decisions about that to us.'

'Hear, hear,' Clarissa said again, baring her teeth at her mother.

Jonathon was relieved when Crispin took his family home, glad they'd found another house to move to, glad he could escape them.

'Shall I ring for another pot of coffee?' Aunt Roz suggested.

'Not for me.' Grandpa stamped off to his study and slammed the door.

'No thanks, not for me either.' Jonathon strode upstairs to his bedroom and threw himself across his bed. What was the matter with all of them? They never stopped sparring.

Frustration had niggled at him all day. He'd tried to hide it in the office, get what information he could from the staff and tackle the jobs he felt capable of doing. Now resentment exploded within him.

It was two weeks since Grandpa had taken him to the office and shown him round, told him how worried he was about the downturn in the busi-ness. Jonathon had been steeped in the family

92

history during his childhood. He knew they'd once been ship owners, but now they were reduced to dealing in the export and import of other people's cargoes and even that business was falling off.

He'd been pleased to be given an office to himself, though it was a mere cubbyhole compared to Adam's. He'd wanted to settle in, learn what was expected of him and do his share of the work to get the business back on its feet.

Grandpa had said, 'Adam will bring you up to date on what we're doing and Crispin will explain your duties.' They'd both been there and heard him say it, but neither had made the slightest effort to do what he'd asked. Tonight at dinner, Uncle Crispin had looked a typical manager of a big company in his dinner jacket with starched shirt and gold cufflinks. His toothbrush moustache, growing paunch and aura of good living, no expense spared, reinforced that impression. But a typical business manager he certainly was not.

Jonathon was afraid that Crispin was not pleased to see him back. He hadn't been given any duties at the office though he'd asked for them twice more. Neither did Crispin want to discuss any aspect of the business with him. It seemed he wanted to keep control of it and didn't mean to give his nephew any power. He preferred to restrict that to himself and his son.

Jonathon didn't like it but he could understand it. What he found beyond his comprehension was that neither Crispin nor Adam was doing anything to improve business profitability. They'd told Grandpa they were concerned about it but they acted as though they hadn't a care in the world and spent very little time in the office, though there was work crying out to be done. He'd told Grandpa that today, dropped them in it. It was almost as though they didn't care if the business went bankrupt.

Jonathon pulled himself off the bed. He couldn't rest while his head whirled like this; he had to busy himself with something. He went to the room his parents had used in the west wing. It was still known as Frances's room and kept just as she'd left it, as though waiting for her return.

Crispin and Daphne had moved in to the apartments in this wing and had taken over Jonathon's mother's boudoir and his father's study. The wing was still and silent now they'd moved out.

His mother's room smelled musty and airless. The bed had been stripped and covered with a dustsheet. It looked small for two – the one he slept on now was the same size. Odd to think he'd been born in this bed and no doubt conceived in it too. He sat down on it and looked round. His mother had thought his roots were here and so had he.

There was a silver and cut-glass powder bowl on the dressing table. He got up to look at it, his mother's initials, F.C.W.W., were on it. Frances Charlotte Wyndham Wray. A gift from her own family before she was married? She must have packed in a hurry to have left it behind.

Jonathon had returned to Otterspool expecting to be taken back into the bosom of his family, but he felt he was on the outside looking in. The family didn't accept him. He was beginning to wish he hadn't come at all.

Yet his father had been his grandfather's heir and he could claim to be Wyndham on both sides. His mother had been a Wray, another family claiming relationship with the Wyndhams. She thought of herself as a distant cousin but like Edmund Yates, she was a cousin dozens of times removed.

This afternoon, when he'd first seen Lorna Mathews, he'd thought that, like his mother, she must be another distant Wyndham cousin. Lars Wyndham, who was said to be the father of the family, was described as having eyes of sea green; mostly they were dark like the depths of the ocean, but they could change to turquoise as though the sun was glinting through the fathoms. Lorna had eyes like that.

She also had a very ready smile that could light up her face. Even when she was serious, it seemed to hover on her lips and in her eyes like the sun waiting for a break in the clouds. When her smile came, she had a dimple in her cheek. He found himself watching for it. He'd asked why she wasn't at dinner.

'Not family,' Aunt Roz had said with disdain. 'An employee. She's eating with the staff.'

She seemed to be warning him off Lorna and he didn't like that. The Wyndham pride was beginning to stick in his gullet. How many times had he been told they were one of the greatest Liverpool families, that Liverpool owed its prosperity to them, that they'd put the city on the map as England's second port? The Wyndhams had done great things in the past and they were so sure they could do so again. They thought themselves above the common man.

According to Aunt Roz, the Wyndhams were such an important family that not even those with the most distant kinship wanted to forget the link. They were all so proud of it.

Jonathon opened a drawer. It had scarves and handkerchiefs in it and smelled of old lavender. The sachets were still here too. Another small drawer under the mirror held beads and bangles and brooches. Probably none was worth much but they were his mother's personal belongings. He picked out a pretty necklace of coral and decided he'd pack the best of them and ship them out to America to her.

He was going to look for some tissue paper and a box when his eye caught the millefiori paper-weight on the mantelpiece. It pulled him up sharply. She wouldn't want that. He picked it up, it was heavy. Had she once told him it was Victorian? The variety of the close canes was infinite and very beautiful. Colours sparkled up at him, yellow, blue and particularly red. His mother hadn't been accepted by the family here either, though she'd married the heir and lived here for years.

'Things were all right while your father was alive,' she'd told him. She'd left when Jonathon had gone to boarding school, saying the situation had become difficult between her and Aunt Roz.

It had taken her a long time to get round to telling him that after an argument about something

96

completely trite, Rosaleen had snatched up the paperweight and hurled it at her head. His mother had been on the point of turning and it had caught her a glancing blow to her shoulder instead. It had been painful for weeks all the same and she didn't doubt there'd have been dire consequences had it hit her on the head.

His mother had thought Rosaleen hated her. She'd grown used to the verbal arguments, but this was too much. She'd confessed she was afraid of Rosaleen and had decided to leave to make a new life for herself in America.

Aunt Roz had grown more sour in recent years. She was finding fault with him though he'd only recently returned. She too needed to make a life of her own, possibly marry again. But she wouldn't: she'd be too fussy, looking for a man from a family of at least equal status, and anyway, she'd be afraid of losing her share of the Wyndham inheritance if she didn't keep a close watch on Crispin. It brought a nasty taste to Jonathon's mouth. He'd been treating Aunt Roz with kid gloves, but she couldn't physically hurt him. He had twice her strength. He could cope with her if he had to.

As he emptied the drawers and wardrobe, deciding what could be thrown out and what his mother might like to have, his mind worked overtime on other things.

Adam too seemed actively to dislike him, and he couldn't get him to give any explanation of the work in hand. If anybody asked him, Jonathon would have said Buckler, the accountant, was actually running the business, but he wasn't managing it or providing leadership to the staff, and he was keeping Jonathon at a distance too.

And it wasn't just in the office. Even in the nursery he'd been the odd one out, but then he'd been the youngest. Now they were all grown up he'd expected to have more in common with them, but it wasn't like that at all.

Jonathon felt exhausted now. He could do no more tonight. There was nothing more tiring than trying to ease oneself into a new job. He got into bed and, almost immediately, he could feel sleep coming.

In the peace of his study Quentin poured himself a glass of whisky and sat down to savour it. Once his family had meant everything to him, but he'd lost those he'd loved most. Now, he felt responsible for those who were left, and guilty that he wasn't providing for them as well as he'd expected to. Not as well as they'd expected either, as they sometimes reminded him. They were quarrelsome and demanding rather than loving, and he no longer had the energy to fight them.

Quentin let his eyes travel round the room and felt sad. This had been his father's study before it was his, and his grandfather's before that, back through the generations. Nothing had been changed here for a hundred years. It was the same wherever he looked in this house, and to think of it being demolished and the familiar furnishings scattered depressed him.

To leave the house he'd lived in all his eighty years was bad enough, but his ancestors had built it in 1773 and his family had lived here ever since. A house like this was held in trust by each generation for the next, and he was the one breaking that trust. The family would count him a failure.

And it wasn't just the house. He'd also inherited a profitable business, and in his lifetime he'd seen much of that slip away too. The losses were increasing year by year, chiefly in recent years since he'd retired, but that didn't make it easier to bear because neither he nor Crispin knew how to stop the decline.

Quentin couldn't remember a time when he hadn't devoted himself to the business; his employees and his family made up his whole life. He'd worked hard and honestly, and hadn't expected such an outcome. He hadn't expected to disgrace himself.

At the outbreak of the Great War, the younger members of his staff had volunteered to fight for their country. British factories were no longer making the goods he used to ship abroad; they were turning out armaments, and the Germans were sinking British ships. Trade was decimated and his business had been brought to a virtual standstill.

On the spur of the moment, he pulled himself to his feet and went to his bureau. He very rarely opened up his leather-covered albums these days. The memories were too painful. He'd had a photograph of his employees taken on the annual outing every summer. He used to hire horse buses to bring them here, where they'd played cricket and run egg-and-spoon races and three-legged races. He'd always provided a good lunch, set up tables and benches under the trees if the weather was fine, and, if not, in the great hall.

From July 1914 two lines of young men smiled out at him: employees he'd trained and relied upon to run his business. Some were people he'd expected to go far. Instead they'd been mown down in their prime on the Somme and in the trenches.

His gaze lingered on Eric Turnbull and Arthur Digby, two of whom he'd been especially fond. He'd written glowing testimonials, recommending them for officer training. Digby had been killed as a second lieutenant within two weeks of reaching the front. Turnbull hadn't lasted much longer. He'd wept for them but things might have been different for him if his own boys had survived to run the business.

John, his eldest, had perished in the trenches of the Great War too. He at least had died a hero and they could all be proud of him. From an early age Quentin had taken him to the office and explained details of the business to him. If John had survived, things would be easier today. Quentin had no great faith in the way Crispin was managing. Even though the business seemed to be haemorrhaging profitability, Crispin resented any suggestions from him.

Of course, the Great War had ruined many a business, but even before that, theirs had not been weathering the changes too well. Their business had been at its peak in the years of the late eighteenth and early nineteenth centuries, when Lars Wyndham and Sons had owned a fleet of twenty-six sailing ships. The company hadn't prospered too well since Victorian times, when the large steam-driven iron ships, carrying more passengers and goods than the Wyndham vessels, had made their fleet less profitable. The world had changed radically since he'd been a lad and he hadn't been able to keep up with the changes.

The Wyndhams had always been driven by the need to earn and accumulate money. He only had to hear Rosaleen's shrill voice to know she'd inherited the family obsession, but, never having earned any money herself, all her efforts were directed to hanging on to every penny she could.

Unlike other great Liverpool families, they'd never interested themselves in good works for the poor and needy, or in embellishing the city in which they based their business. He couldn't boast, as the Rathbones could, of having started a district nursing service to ease the burden on those who were ill as well as poor. Nor had they built hospitals or churches or schools. They'd never been altruistic.

His family had wanted only to provide for themselves and their future generations, which made it all the more surprising that they were seeing their fortune seep away like this.

Perhaps in the present depression even the Rathbones and the Roscoes were not as rich as they'd once been, but at least they'd have the comfort of knowing they'd given some of their money to the poor. Quentin didn't know where his fortune had gone. He'd tried to restart the business to provide income to support his sister Maude, and Rosaleen, and John's fatherless lad.

'Father.' Rosaleen came bursting in in a pink satin dressing gown. 'What are you doing down here at this time of night? You should be in bed.'

He pulled himself wearily to his feet and sighed. 'Reviewing the past. Eighty! I'm old. It gives me a lot of years to think about.'

'I woke up and thought I was alone in the house. It's so quiet with Aunt Maude away.'

Quentin sighed again. Rosaleen had always lived on her nerves. 'She'll be back soon. I'll come up now.'

She smiled. 'You sit down here drinking by yourself and forget everything.'

If she'd missed him from a nearby room, he knew she must have been anxious. Rosaleen's state of mind was a big worry.

At breakfast the next morning, Quentin was eating his bacon and egg and thinking about the work that had to be done before they moved out of Otterspool. For years, he'd been unable to look through his wife's diaries, journals and letters, and still couldn't. Neither could he bear the thought of anybody else touching Marina's personal belongings. He'd keep all her papers separate and read them when he felt ready to write the family history.

He sighed. He'd have to open up his safe and empty the contents before he left. It was very old and had been bolted to the floor. He'd get himself another, smaller one. He ought to give Marina's personal jewellery to Rosaleen and Clarissa; it ought to be worn, not shut away in a safe. He wasn't too fond of Daphne, but he'd find some trinket to give her so as not to make it too obvious.

He'd keep the more expensive pieces for as long as he could. He had antique jewellery that had belonged to the ladies of his forebears. It was as good as money in the bank. He'd hang on to some of their more important portraits too for the same reason. The thought of selling any of the many pictures in the house was painful.

Jonathon had been tucking into his egg and bacon in companionable silence at the other end of the table. Now he said, 'Grandpa, I know you're going to get your new secretary to sort through everything...'

'We've got to make a start now.'

'There's a lot I'd like to do myself – turn out the room my parents used, for instance.'

'I thought you'd done that already.'

'Well, yes, but not thoroughly enough, and also Uncle Piers's room.'

'If that's what you want. Ah, here's Miss Mathews now.'

'Good morning,' Lorna said.

He watched Jonathon stand up to lift the silver covers from the dishes on the sideboard for her. He was being very attentive.

She helped herself to bacon and egg. 'We were discussing how to share out the jobs that need to be done,' Quentin told her.

Jonathon said, 'The most important thing now is to find another house, Grandpa. It's getting urgent. We must decide on that. I'll go round the agents today and pick out particulars of any I think might be suitable. Then we'll look over the details when I come home this evening and see which we should view.'

'Rosaleen wants to choose it. Begged me to let her.'

'But she isn't doing anything about it, is she?'

Quentin sighed again. 'She's got such big ideas, that's her problem. It's no good getting another mansion like this. But if you take over she'll be cross with you and hate everything you show her.'

Jonathon smiled. 'I'll try to find something you'll both like.'

He pursed his lips. 'If I can afford it, I don't expect to like it.'

'Grandpa, you're as bad as she is. You've sold this so we'll have to move out. We'll involve Aunt Roz, show her all the brochures, and take her when we go to view. Until you choose a house it's impossible to decide what you need to keep.'

'You're right, of course,' his grandfather said. 'You're the only one with any practical sense. I'm sure the house Crispin's moved to is far too big. I'm glad he's rented rather than bought, though Daphne says this is only a stopgap to give them more time. The fact is, there's plenty of room in it for the rest of us. I feel we should stay together and half expect that's where we'll end up. Eventually Crispin will see it that way too.'

'It might please you,' Jonathon said, 'but it sure as hell wouldn't please Aunt Daphne or Aunt Roz.'

That made Quentin feel the generation gap. He hardly knew what they were thinking nowadays.

When Jonathon left to go to work, he took

104

Lorna to his study.

She said, 'Isn't it equally urgent that you appoint a firm of auctioneers to handle your sale? It'll take them time to catalogue and assess the value of everything and they'll probably need to call in expert help. You have valuable antiques here.'

'You're right too, of course, I'll have to. What you and I need to plan now is how best to go about sorting through all we have.'

'Systematically,' Lorna said, 'room by room and floor by floor. Start at one end of the house and empty every drawer and cupboard and spread the contents out where they can be seen. Group similar items together. Make lists, one of furniture, one of china, that sort of thing.'

'You've done this before?'

'Yes, for Mrs Cartwright.'

Quentin liked the look of the girl. She had her brown hair clipped back this morning and looked business-like, she was keen and willing, and seemed to know what she was doing.

'Good, but I want you to keep separate all private documents, photographs, personal items, that sort of thing. I don't want to part with any of them. I'll need them anyway when I come to write the family history.'

'Perhaps if I found a trunk to put them in?'

'Yes, there are plenty of those in the attics. Bring one down to use.'

'I'll label everything I keep, or put it into envelopes so you'll know what you've got.'

Lorna had to concentrate on what Mr Wyndham

105

was saying to get a clear picture of what he expected of her. She knew it would take her some time to find her feet.

Rosaleen came into the study after they'd been going through one drawer for what seemed like hours. 'I've come to help, Father,' she announced. 'I've drawn up a plan of action for you.'

'Good, let's hear it. We're beginning to struggle.'

'I'll make myself responsible for the silver and the plate. I'll turn out the butler's pantry and list everything there, and I'll do the china cupboards too.'

Her cold eyes lingered on Lorna. 'You can start in the library. Make a list of all the books; the title, author, date of publication, condition, that sort of thing. Then I can take the list to a book dealer to find out which are the valuable ones.'

Her father ran his hand through his wispy white hair. 'But we have thousands of books.'

'All the more reason to find out their worth. Come to the library and I'll show you what I mean.' Rosaleen escorted them there and showed them a ledger she'd ruled up. 'So you can fill in the details I need,' she told Lorna.

Lorna felt daunted as she looked round. It was a big room and each wall was fitted with shelves that were crammed to capacity with books. In addition, every table, desk and bookstand held many more.

'It would take weeks of work,' she said slowly. 'Is this the most important job?'

There were books of every sort, some almost as old as the house. She lifted a huge leather-bound volume to the table. It looked as though it hadn't been disturbed in decades.

'You could dust them while you have them out.' Rosaleen appeared to be taking charge.

Lorna said, 'Wouldn't I also need to number the shelves and mark the position of each book? Otherwise we'd never find them again.'

Quentin said, 'Perhaps if I appointed the auctioneers, they could send a valuer in to sort through them here.'

Lorna was delighted to be able to say, 'Much the most practical way of going about it.'

Mr Wyndham was frowning. 'But how does one choose a firm of auctioneers?'

'There's the one Mrs Cartwright used. I could find the phone number. It was the top Liverpool firm,' Lorna assured them. 'Mrs Cartwright had only a fraction of what you've got here, but the auctioneers brought in a man to value them. A professional opinion is what you need. She had a few valuable volumes and a few more that brought a shilling or two, but the rest were said to be virtually worthless.'

'What did she do with those?' the old man asked.

'I tried to interest a dealer with a stall selling second-hand books in the market, but he wanted only popular titles. Mr Cartwright had a lot of text books that were out of date.'

'I don't even know what we've got here,' Quentin sighed.

'Perhaps if we had a quick look round now...' Lorna suggested. 'Are they in categories or any sort of order?'

'The old ones are all in this bookcase.'

'They all look old to me.' Lorna shook her head. 'You've never had them indexed?'

She could see fiction and non-fiction of all sorts jumbled together. It looked to her as though they'd been pushed haphazardly on to the shelves once they'd been read.

'I could achieve more by sorting through the guest rooms. Perhaps if I did that first?'

'Yes,' Mr Wyndham said. Lorna could see Rosaleen looked more than a little put out that her suggestion had been vetoed.

'I didn't know you'd done this sort of work before,' she said testily.

'Yes, Mrs Cartwright sold up everything she had before moving to Cumberland.'

'Mrs Cartwright couldn't speak highly enough of Lorna's work,' Quentin told his daughter. 'She looked after their import and export business too.'

Lorna felt she had to explain. 'Her house was nothing like this, though.' She remembered then that Wyndhams had an office nearby. 'You'll know her place, just opposite your own office in Hamilton Square.'

Rosaleen drew herself up to a haughty five foot eight inches and looked down her nose at Lorna.

'No, I don't. I have nothing to do with the business. I don't work for my living. Ladies don't, you know.'

Lorna winced, knowing that was intended as a snub, but she could not resist retaliating. 'Mrs Cartwright never worked either, but I think it left her at a loss. She felt unable to cope when her husband died.'

'It would be impossible for me to work, wouldn't it, Father?' Rosaleen was indignant. 'For a woman in my position, of my family, it just isn't done.'

Lorna was going to hold her own. She smiled disarmingly. 'I've always had to work and I don't think it's done me any harm. It's interesting, you know, to see new places and talk to other people. Get inside other people's houses too. I enjoy it.'

Chapter Six

Lorna started work that first morning in the wing Crispin and his family had vacated. Mr Wyndham walked round with her to show her what he wanted. She thought she'd never be able to find her way round this huge house alone.

'There are no straight corridors or passageways because it grew haphazardly,' he told her. 'Every generation added something, so it's in a con- glomeration of styles.'

'This wing looks Victorian,' Lorna said.

'Yes, they added a great deal.'

Most of the furniture and fittings had been taken from the rooms. The soft furnishings were shabby or had perished, and with the yellowed ceilings, faded wallpaper and the odd cracked windowpane, this part of the house looked as though it had been laid waste. Lorna had only to sort the rubbish to one side, take down the curtains and light fittings that remained and make a list of the few things she thought were worth keeping.

She found that comparatively easy upstairs, but in the downstairs rooms the curtains were of heavy velvet, very wide and ten feet in length. They seemed in good condition. Lorna was strong but she needed help to lift the weight off the hooks. She was crossing the great hall to ask Hilda to give her a hand, when she saw Daphne, Crispin's wife, coming towards her. Arrogant dark eyes challenged hers as they drew closer.

'Who are you?' she demanded in a heavy French accent.

Lorna was somewhat affronted by her manner, but, needing to stay on good terms with the family, she answered politely, 'I'm Lorna Mathews, Mr Wyndham's new secretary.'

'Oh!' Daphne, middle-aged and of stout matronly build, continued to stare.

It gave Lorna some satisfaction to say, 'Mr Wyndham introduced us last night. You're Mrs Crispin, I believe?'

She didn't answer.

This was the woman who had refused to help her mother, Lorna thought. She added, 'I'm to help sort out things for the sale.'

The woman expanded her huge chest to its proud maximum. 'The silver and plate in the butler's pantry needs a good clean. It's all very tarnished. It won't realise half its value unless it's polished up.'

'I'm sure you're right,' Lorna said, 'but Mr Wyndham has asked me to start in the west wing

110

and then go upstairs.'

Daphne took off across the hall without answering, her high heels clicking as she went. Lorna smiled to herself. If Daphne didn't recognise her, she hadn't made much impression on her last night. Mum hadn't liked her and Lorna could see why. She was glad Daphne had already moved out of this house.

She found Hilda was busy making scones so she left the curtains and set about the next task that Mr Wyndham had given her, turning out rooms in the main part of the house that had not been regularly used. Lorna did exactly what she'd been asked to do: emptied every drawer and cupboard, wiped the dust of decades off wardrobes and polished up antique dressing tables. She listed washstands and chamber pots, water jugs and soap dishes. Each room was a mixture of old and new.

With forty-five bedrooms for family and guests and ten bedrooms for servants, there were only three bathrooms.

'When the family was larger, the housemaid had to take hot water up to the rooms in copper jugs,' Hilda had told her. 'And empty the slops.'

Lorna was to share one bathroom with the rest of the staff, one floor down from their attic bedrooms. It was a large room with an ancient iron bath on splayed feet on one side and an enormous washhand basin on the other. Their lavatory was out in the yard beyond the kitchen, three floors down.

She spent the rest of the morning laying out the sheets, blankets and coverlets she found in the drawers, some so fragile she was afraid they'd turn to dust as she opened them. She found candlesticks by the score, rugs of every sort, some fine, some threadbare. Some rooms were equipped with horsehair mattresses on fine mahogany bedsteads. In others, there were four-posters with threadbare hangings and mattresses of goose feathers on top of the horsehair. She found mahogany steps to help the elderly and infirm climb into the high beds.

She studied the paintings hanging on the walls, because Mr Wyndham had asked her to look out for watercolours by Samuel Palmer; his mother had been keen on them. She found several, but there were many others that were faded and spotted with damp. Spotted mirrors too with frames that needed regilding, a few books, shaving mugs and contraptions to hang pocket watches on. In every room there was a thick powdering of greyish dust covering the furniture, and curtains of cobwebs looping the ceiling. She discovered multitudes of dead flies and disturbed armies of spiders. Every room smelled musty, and in many the ceilings and walls were stained with patches of mildew.

She completed four rooms, all of which had been used as guest rooms in this century, and if they'd belonged to any member of the family in the last, it was not obvious. Apart from the furniture, she didn't think she'd come across many treasures and she was not empowered to throw out the rubbish.

Her stomach told her it must be near lunch time. She'd heard bells ringing and a gong sounding through the house. Rosaleen had already made it clear that she didn't want her to eat with the family, but Mr Wyndham seemed to assume she would. Lorna wanted to settle that. She was trying to find her way back to the kitchen when she saw Rosaleen hurrying across the great hall with her head down, looking neither to left nor right.

'Miss Wyndham,' she called.

'Yes?'

'I was wondering... I'm to have my meals with Hilda?'

'Yes, I've already said so, haven't I? Better if you stay in the kitchen.'

'Your father seemed to assume–'

'So he did.' She looked distracted. 'Well, you could come to the drawing room for tea, that should be enough.'

'Yes, I'll do that then.' Lorna was not dissatisfied with the arrangement.

'Breakfast and tea with Father – more than enough.' Rosaleen was irritable.

After lunch, Lorna started on the fifth room with as much enthusiasm as she could muster. What she wanted to do was to learn more about the members of the family who had lived in this century, not those of the distant past.

She was burning with curiosity about Rosaleen's brothers, particularly Oliver. Lorna wanted to ask about him, but she knew she must not. She had to keep quiet and keep her eyes and ears open.

Daphne Wyndham looked round the drawing

113

room of Ravensdale House, feeling a glow of satisfaction. The Turkey carpet and the crimson velvet curtains complemented each other beautifully. Choosing and furnishing their new home had given her great pleasure. She sat back in her smart new armchair, savouring its comfort. All the hard furniture had come from Otterspool, of course – it would have been impossible to buy antique pieces of this age and quality – but she had chosen most of what was here.

Crispin had brought his favourite pieces too, but he went for intrinsic value rather than looks, so Daphne was more than willing to give them houseroom. The huge picture of Captain William Wyndham and his wife, Viveca, over the fireplace, in its newly gilded frame, was rather overpowering in this room, but it was impossible to part any Wyndham from reminders of their glorious past.

What gave Daphne most pleasure was that Ravensdale House was for her, Crispin and their children. She'd got away from his horde of relatives at last. Quentin had been hinting quite openly that he and the rest of them wanted to come too.

'Nine good bedrooms there, as well as accommodation for staff,' he'd said, rubbing his hands with satisfaction. 'Room for us all.'

Daphne had been determined not to have any of that. She wanted to live like a normal family for a change, and fortunately Crispin wanted to get away from his father too. The very last thing she needed was to have Rosaleen here with her.

'Connie?' Crispin's voice echoed along the hall.

114

'Connie, I'll have a tray of coffee in the drawing room.' He burst in with the morning's newspaper under his arm. His pale eyes met Daphne's. 'Oh, you're here.'

Daphne flinched: 'Why shouldn't I be?' Crispin's manner could make her hackles rise.

'I thought you were going out.'

'I've already been to Otterspool this morning. I thought you were going to the office.' She wished he'd spend more time there, like a normal husband. 'You're a bad influence on Adam. When he sees how little effort you put into the business, he thinks there's no need for him to work either.'

Crispin opened his newspaper and ignored her. It was what the Wyndhams did. They'd never truly accepted her, even after nearly thirty years of marriage. At first, she'd thought they would in time. She'd believed as the mother of two children, real blood-line Wyndhams, she could consider herself part of the family. But they never had. They'd always kept her at arm's length.

Now the children were grown up, she was worried, especially about Clarissa. She'd rushed out after breakfast saying she was going to play tennis, but she wouldn't be surprised if she didn't see her for the rest of the day. Daphne was afraid she was out with that man again.

Neither of her children had any sense. They were ready to throw away the position that Daphne had fought so hard to maintain for herself. She really didn't know what to make of Adam. He was a grave disappointment. She hadn't expected to find his abnormality in the Wyndham blood.

And as for Clarissa, she had no thought for her

social position or comfort in later life. She didn't value it. She said she was in love and wanted to throw everything away on that. What was love but a fancy that could soon pass? Crispin had been deeply in love with her but it hadn't lasted. Clarissa ought to have some thought for her own future.

Daphne stood up to wipe a few specks of dust from the mahogany bookcase with her lace handkerchief. It was a favourite piece of furniture, made in the time of George III. Connie came in with the tray of coffee and slid it on the table.

'You haven't dusted properly in here this morning,' Daphne told her.

'There's only me and I can't do everything,' Connie said quickly, with a toss of her red hair. She was a cheeky bitch and didn't give her the respect she gave the Wyndhams. Flighty too, and her work was anything but thorough. 'You said you were going to get more staff. You'll have to, if you want the place spick-and-span.'

Daphne suppressed a gasp. It would give her great pleasure to hire her own staff and send Connie back to Otterspool.

'I thought you were too,' Crispin said, crunching into a ginger nut. 'We need a gardener as well.'

In a flash of anger, she said, 'I'll go down to the domestic agency this afternoon and see what they have on their books.'

'Do you good to get off your backside and do something.' Crispin was reaching for another biscuit.

Daphne waited until the door closed behind

116

Connie before she lashed out. 'Don't speak to me like that in front of the servants.'

This was why they showed her no respect. She'd get rid of Connie as soon as she could. She'd like to get rid of Crispin too. She slammed out and went to the small sitting room she'd furnished for herself, and collapsed on the sofa. Things hadn't turned out as she'd hoped all those years ago. Daphne could feel tears prickling her eyes. She turned her face into the new cushions on the sofa, but she couldn't stop her mind roaming back over the family folklore that had been told and retold to her when she was growing up.

Her father, Bill Kelly, had been the cook on a small coastal tramp trading between Liverpool and the ports of the Mediterranean. One hot afternoon, he'd gone ashore in Marseilles while the crew were loading cargo. Two streets behind the harbour, in a district where fishermen, sailors and dock workers lived, he found a pleasant bar. He sat down at a pavement table and drank too much red wine.

It made him sleepy, and though he hadn't intended to, he dozed off. When he woke up he found the sun had gone down. Never had his feet covered the ground more quickly but when he reached the harbour, he found the ship had sailed without him.

Bill Kelly had wandered back to the bar in a state of shock. He had no clothes but those he stood up in and very little money left. Luck hadn't entirely deserted him, when he poured out his troubles to Jacques, who was tending the bar.

117

Jacques also owned the Pension Mirabelle, which was directly opposite, on the other side of a busy road. That morning, the cook at the *pension* had departed in high dudgeon following a disagreement with Mirabelle, Jacques's wife. Bill was hired to take his place and was also to help in the bar. It was meant to be a temporary arrangement, but he soon learned to cook their local dishes and his hotpots and scouse were popular with their customers.

Jacques and Mirabelle had a daughter called Esmée, and within a year she and Bill were married. Daphne had been born in the *pension* and brought up there. She was fluent in both French and English.

When she was fourteen her grandfather died following an accident. Jacques had grown so used to flitting across the road between the bar and the *pension* that he hardly noticed the big drays pulling heavy cargoes down to the docks. One day, a bicycle almost ran into him, he sidestepped to avoid it and stumbled under the hoofs of a heavy horse pulling a dray, and was trampled on.

Daphne would never forget the grief and the heart-searching her family went through at that time, or the indecision about what they should do. Mirabelle was nearing retirement age and didn't want to carry on running the *pension* and bar. Bill was homesick for England and didn't want Esmée to take it over. Eventually, the businesses were sold and her grandmother retired to live in modest comfort in a village house a couple of miles away from the hustle and bustle of the busy port.

Her father returned to Liverpool, his birth-place, and brought his family with him. To support them, he became licensee of a pub, the Lord Raglan. It was a typical Liverpool public house, but not one of the drinking dens on the dock road like the Seven Steps or the Baltic Fleet, full of flat-capped dockers and ship repairers. The Lord Raglan was higher class, in the centre of the city, and well placed to serve both the business community and the young wanting a drink when the theatres and cinemas closed.

Daphne thought their home, in the rooms above it, was no worse than their rooms in the *pension*, but her mother hadn't been able to settle. She couldn't adapt to the cold, damp weather, the river fogs and the dark winter days without sun.

Daphne had been brought up to help in the *pension*. She was used to waiting on tables and pouring glasses of wine. Now her mother wanted her to learn a trade that would take her away from being a barmaid. She was sent to a commercial school to be trained as a secretary, a job in which being bilingual might enhance her prospects.

Daphne had enjoyed working in an insurance office. It was there that she realised there was a British class system. She never advanced beyond being a general secretarial assistant, but she translated one or two letters for the firm and once even acted as an interpreter. At home, she kept the accounts for her father and helped her mother with the cleaning. It was hard work for all

119

of them.

The Lord Raglan was a man's world; not that women were barred, but they were confined to the back parlour. To start with Daphne was confined there too. Esmée didn't like her nubile daughter serving in such men-only surroundings as the public bar.

'Men will get quite the wrong impression,' she complained to Bill. 'A Liverpool pub is no place for a good-looking girl like her. It is not like the *pension.*'

When needed, Esmée worked there herself. They sold a wide range of traditional mild and bitter beers, all brewed locally and on tap from their barrels, which were set out in a long row behind the counter. Esmée missed the red wine as much as she did the sunshine.

But once Daphne was eighteen, her father pressed her to help out in the pub on busy evenings to save the expense of paying another barman. She met Crispin there. He was twenty-three at the time, a personable young man who liked a drink and a bit of fun.

Crispin couldn't take his eyes off her and Daphne was dazzled by him. Esmée was a strict Catholic mother who had pointed out that it was essential to stay well away from the men in the bar. Daphne would ruin her reputation if she was too friendly with them. She'd been very glad she'd listened to her when Crispin came on the scene and had fallen in love with her. Maman had whispered that he was rich and would be a real catch as a husband. She helped Daphne play her cards right.

'You have to play a man like a fish,' she told her.

'I want to marry him.' Daphne knew she was reaching for the moon, but she was in love too and could see a rosy future for herself miles away from the Lord Raglan.

'Don't tell him that, whatever you do. Not yet anyway. You'll frighten him off.'

'What should I do?' By then, in the early years of the century, Daphne fully understood the rigidity of the English class system.

'Play hard to get. Don't jump at his invitations. When he mentions marriage, let him think you don't believe he's serious. Don't let him sweep you off your feet. Kisses, yes, but no more. You're a good, wholesome, clean-living girl. Keep your wits about you, encourage him but always stop him in time. Never give a man what he wants,' she'd warned. 'If you do, he won't offer marriage. He'll think a girl from your background is probably one of easy virtue, and quite unsuitable to be his wife. He'll enjoy what you give, but he'll tire of you and be off after another. If he finds there's no other way he can get you to bed, you might just get him to put a ring on your finger.'

Crispin began taking her to expensive restaurants, and because Esmée was interested in food and cooked in the French style, Daphne was used to what Liverpool considered sophisticated food. More sophisticated than Crispin himself, she loved being able to show off her knowledge to him. She had been enjoying his company and lavish life style for some time when her father had a heart attack in the bar and died suddenly. That plunged her and her mother into crisis. Daphne gave up her job to help run the pub and Mirabelle arrived from France to lend a hand. They managed well enough – they were all used to such work – but Esmée wanted to return to Marseilles.

'Liverpool is a dark miserable place. I miss the sun. I can't stay, not now your dad has passed on.'

Mirabelle, Daphne's grandmother, wanted them back near Marseilles. She offered to take them all in; there was room in her house. It was the last thing Daphne had wanted. She was feeling close to Crispin by then and didn't want to leave him. When he kissed her that night, she wept on his shoulder. His arms had tightened round her in sympathy, she was sure he was on the point of proposing.

But Esmée told the brewery she wanted to leave, and the company set about finding another licensee for the pub. When he arrived as they were packing up, Daphne got her dearest wish. Over dinner that evening Crispin said he couldn't bear the thought of losing her and offered marriage.

Daphne thought of that as her moment of triumph. He was everything a woman could want, and all that she'd dared hope for. She thought her fortune was made. She knew he came from a wealthy background, but she didn't understand just how wealthy. Crispin frowned as he held her hand across the restaurant table.

'I'm a bit worried about how my family will see yours,' he said.

Even now, Daphne could still remember how

her heart missed a beat, afraid he was changing his mind, but he said, 'We'll have to change things a bit. Don't tell them you lived in the Lord Raglan, for God's sake. Or that you worked as a barmaid.' That had made her wince. 'They think all public houses are dens of iniquity.'

He concocted a very different social background for her, and she was ready to go along with anything that would allow her to marry Crispin. Quentin and Marina were told her father had been English and in the Diplomatic Service. He'd met Esmée while serving a term of duty in France. Mirabelle's husband, Daphne's grandfather, had also been a diplomat.

She was to say that her father had retired and they'd been touring England, unsure of where they would settle. They'd stayed for some time in Liverpool because they wanted Daphne to have some way of earning her own living. She'd gone to a commercial college and had polished up her knowledge of languages and hoped to find work as an interpreter. They'd lodged in the Adelphi Hotel and that's where he'd met her, but in the restaurant, not the bar. A friend had introduced them, some months before her father had had his heart attack.

With her mother and grandmother, Daphne was invited to Otterspool House. Mirabelle spoke very little English, but dressed with French flair. Esmée and Daphne were fluent in both languages. Crispin told them to enhance their Frenchness; his family wouldn't know the difference between a middle-class Paris accent and a Marseilles working-class one. Daphne was quite sure they'd accepted Crispin's version of her background.

They had a fairy-tale wedding. Mirabelle couldn't believe the money Crispin spent on Daphne's wedding gown.

'A terrible waste,' she said, 'when you'll never wear it again. I could live on that for six months.'

'But Daphne won't need to,' Esmée had pointed out triumphantly. 'She's made her fortune by marrying Crispin Wyndham.'

Daphne let her mind linger over the honeymoon trip to Paris where she'd felt more at home than he did, and where she'd so enjoyed interpreting everything for him. He was a skilled and attentive lover who had eyes only for her. She'd had such hope for the future. It seemed life would be champagne all the way...

Now she pulled herself off the sofa, deciding to go out to cheer herself up. She'd wear her new powder-blue hat and coat, treat herself to lunch at Coopers, perhaps see if she could have a brace of pheasants delivered. None of the Wyndhams knew what good food was. They were content with their mutton and overcooked beef. She'd try and find a cook who could make French dishes. She'd go to that new bookshop too and buy some more books – they hadn't enough to fill the bookcase. But the house was lovely and she had a home of her own at last.

She sat down again with a little thump. It wasn't enough, and the resentment she felt for Crispin and Rosaleen for the way they'd treated her wouldn't go away.

124

When Daphne had been taken to Otterspool as a bride all those years ago, she'd found it more difficult than she'd expected to settle down. The Wyndhams were not friendly. Mostly, they kept themselves aloof, chatting together about things of which she knew nothing. Only her mother-in-law and her sister-in-law Frances made any effort to include her.

They seemed to spend their time doing things that Daphne could not. She knew nothing about sailing, and had never ridden a horse. Frances and Rosaleen had cars of their own, but Daphne hadn't learned to drive. Tennis was another problem. Frances suggested a coach, but Daphne didn't enjoy it. She wasn't much good at croquet either.

At that time, there were several maiden aunts, widows and grandparents, all with their own suites in the mansion. They played bridge and bezique on wet afternoons, and though Daphne was asked to join them, and Great-aunt Gertrude offered to teach her, she'd never played cards and was afraid of making a fool of herself.

The house had seemed very grand at first sight, but it was not all that comfortable to live in. It was a long time before Daphne could find her way round it. She and Crispin had a bedroom and a private sitting room where she spent most of her time while he was working in the office. She was expected to join the family at meals, and if there were guests she was expected to join in and help entertain them.

Rosaleen was almost her own age, a pretty girl. She'd expected to make a friend of her. In the early days, she'd sought her company.

'You've never played tennis before?' Rosaleen's eyebrows went up in condemnation. 'Or ridden a horse? Is there nothing you can do? Where have you been all your life?'

'In France.'

'Really? I'd probably die of boredom there.'

On another occasion, Rosaleen announced she was going shopping for clothes. 'Can I come with you?' Daphne asked. 'I love going round the big shops.'

'No, I prefer my own company,' Rosaleen said, and drove off in her own car. She never offered to take Daphne anywhere.

She knew Rosaleen was snobbish and when she hinted she considered Daphne's origins to be in the bottom end of society, Daphne at first assumed she saw members of the Diplomatic Service as being lower down the social scale than the Wyndhams. It wasn't long before she began to fear Rosaleen might suspect the truth.

Daphne got on better with Frances, who was John's wife and in the same position as herself. She heard Rosaleen bitching at Frances too, though Frances was related to the Wyndhams, and seemed to get on well with the rest of them.

Frances had more confidence than she had, and she didn't have to keep a tight hold on her tongue. Daphne couldn't relax and talk about her own family or her life before she was married. Crispin had warned her never to breathe a word to any of them about her pedigree. He said it wouldn't do to let it be known that he'd taken such a wife. It would let him down, and weaken her own position.

On Grand National Day, the first after Daphne and Crispin were married, the younger members of the family went to Aintree *en masse*. Daphne had never been racing before and found the long wait between races rather boring. The Wyndhams spent the time eyeing up the runners for the next race, talking to the trainers about form and putting their bets on at the tote.

Daphne was beginning to feel Rosaleen was baiting her. She was always asking questions about the Diplomatic Corps – questions which Daphne found hard to answer because she knew little about it. Now suddenly, she found herself pinned against the rail by Rosaleen, while Crispin and the others walked on ahead.

'What a disgusting liar you are,' she hissed at her, 'trying to pass yourself off as a lady when all the time you were a common barmaid.'

Daphne felt the strength ebb from her knees. All along, she'd been afraid the family might learn of this.

'Lived over the Lord Raglan pub, your whole family in the trade. I could see you were as common as muck. That was obvious from the start.'

'How...?' Daphne could get no more out.

'Foolish, as well as common if you thought you could keep that a secret. Henry told me, Henry Montague.' She smiled, a victory smile. It made Daphne quake. Rosaleen knew she had the upper hand now. 'Don't tell me you don't remember him? He says he often went with Crispin to the Lord Raglan.'

Daphne did remember him, and Giles Hurst and several others. They were Crispin's friends. She'd pointed out to Crispin that in the early days he'd rarely come to the pub alone.

'They won't tell Father,' he'd said. Crispin was always confident – overconfident, it seemed now. 'Why should they? They don't meet each other.'

Rosaleen was crowing with triumph. 'Dear Mama will be shocked. And as for Father–'

'Don't tell them,' Daphne pleaded. She was sweating though it was a chilly spring day. 'Please don't tell them.'

'Rest assured I will, unless...'

Daphne was filled with dread, she broke free and ran through the crowd as fast as she could. She didn't wait to hear what Rosaleen was demanding in return for her silence. She soon lost her, but she lost the rest of the party too and found that quite frightening. She heard the Grand National race being run over the loud speakers. She felt the fevered excitement in the crowd, but she was so gripped by panic she couldn't take any interest. She couldn't see anybody she knew. It was only when she thought of looking for Crispin's car in the car park and found it, that she was able to pull herself together.

The Wyndhams eventually returned to their cars, telling her how worried they'd been about her. Daphne held her tongue until she was able to get Crispin on his own.

'The little witch!' he swore when he'd heard her out. 'I'll half kill her if she spills the beans. Anyway, we are married, it's too late for them to carp about that. Don't worry, darling.'

128

Daphne did worry. She felt the family didn't accept her now. They'd probably send her to Coventry if they learned of this. Only later, did she ask, 'What did Rosaleen want for her silence?'

'Money. What else is she likely to want?'

'You've paid her?'

'No. It'll be all right.'

A few days later, Piers told her all Crispin's brothers had heard of her origins and the lies told about her family. For a long time, she expected to be summoned to Quentin's study, but the summons never came. It took Daphne a long time to recover from the shock of the partially leaked secret. She knew it was Rosaleen's way of showing the power she had, and knew she was taking pleasure in her embarrassment.

Rosaleen was making her life a misery. Daphne knew that if she was to be happy at Otterspool, she'd have to do something to improve their relationship.

On Rosaleen's nineteenth birthday there was to be a big party in the evening, but lunch that day was special too. The family were in good spirits. As she got up from the table, Daphne found herself with Rosaleen.

'Will you come to my sitting room for a minute?' she asked her. 'Crispin and I have a present for you.' Crispin had left Daphne to choose it. She'd deliberated for some time before deciding on a smart handbag of brown leather and gilt clasps.

While Rosaleen was unwrapping it, she said, 'Couldn't we try to be friends, Rosaleen? I'm sorry I wasn't truthful about my background, that I lied to you and your family.'

'I expect that was Crispin's idea.'

'Yes.'

'He was ashamed to tell us the truth, that we were having a common barmaid planted amongst us.'

Daphne winced. 'Even so,' she said, making a huge effort, 'I am your sister-in-law now. We're going to see a lot of each other.' She put out her hand. 'Can't we bury the hatchet?'

Her hand was ignored. She looked up to meet Rosaleen's contemptuous gaze. She was holding the handbag aloft. It was an expensive one. 'Your choice, I suppose?'

'Yes, I thought it the handsomest bag in Bunnies.'

'I suppose, to a barmaid, it would be. Not to my taste, I'm afraid.' Rosaleen stalked out, leaving the bag and the birthday card on her table.

Daphne collapsed on the couch and wept. She'd tried very hard to get on with Rosaleen although the girl had been nasty to her from the beginning.

She comforted herself with the thought that she had Crispin who loved her. Within six months of her marriage she found she was expecting her first baby. Esmée wrote and told her a child would make all the difference. The Wyndhams would accept her once she was the mother of their grandchild.

Having Adam had helped. The ladies of the family were besotted with him. When Clarissa was born two years later, Daphne decided that life had its compensations, especially as all the effort of looking after the children was taken off her shoulders.

Another thing she enjoyed was the feeling of status that being Mrs Wyndham gave her. She could go into shops to order goods to be delivered and her name and address always brought respect. And Crispin seemed to have little grasp on money. He never complained however much she spent. She would try to ignore Rosaleen's jibes.

She could feel herself itching for revenge, but she'd bide her time. If Rosaleen saw her as an enemy and wanted a fight she'd give her one. Daphne promised herself she'd make her suffer for this when she had the chance.

Chapter Seven

At tea time that day, Mr Wyndham asked Lorna how she was getting on.

'Quite well,' she told him. 'I've virtually finished in the west wing, but I need help to get the curtains down.' She explained about Hilda having too much work of her own to be able to help her.

'What about Daphne?' Rosaleen suggested. 'It wouldn't hurt her to tidy up after herself. She said she was coming again tomorrow, why don't you ask her?'

Lorna was quite sure Daphne would refuse to help take down curtains. It wasn't the sort of job she could see her doing. Jonathon came in in time to hear Rosaleen's suggestion.

'I'll give you a hand with them tomorrow morning,' he offered. That pleased her.

'It can wait until Sissie comes back,' Rosaleen snapped. 'It seems we can expect her at the end of the week.'

'Tomorrow,' he murmured, in an aside to Lorna. She warmed to him.

Jonathon had brought with him a thick sheaf of papers with details of houses for sale and rent. Lorna didn't feel the choice of house was any concern of hers and left them handing brochures backwards and forwards, and arguing about the merits of Aigburth as against moving across the river to the Wirral.

She finished her tea and let herself out of the house to walk across the grass to the edge of the river. Much of the garden was a wilderness of brambles and dense shrubbery, but on this part the grass had been kept cut. It had been a dark day and was already dusk. She'd hardly reached the riverbank when she heard Jonathon running after her. That pleased her too.

'I've left them to decide which houses they want to see,' he said. 'When they've made their minds up I'll drive them round instead of going to work.'

She smiled. 'Isn't it lovely here? You'll miss living near the river.'

'Very much, we all love it. There's the problem of the boats too; where we'll be able to moor them, whether we'll be able to find somewhere handy.'

'You enjoy sailing?'

'My favourite pastime. In the summer the family always does a lot.'

That made it all the more strange, Lorna thought, for Oliver to have drowned in a boating accident. She said, 'I understand your family earned your fortune from shipping.'

She saw him wince. 'So I'm told. We may have made a fortune once but we've lost it now. That modest sailing boat over there is mine, the *Water Gypsy*.'

'It looks very smart.' It had been recently repainted and didn't look modest to Lorna. She wondered if Pa would know how to sail it, if he'd ever had the opportunity to learn. She'd never heard him talk of seafaring with any great affection.

'Grandpa had it done up for me. It's mine now, but once it belonged to my father.'

'Did you have lessons on how to sail it?'

'Yes, all our family learn – at about ten or twelve years of age according to how keen we are.'

That pulled Lorna up. Even more strange that Oliver should drown in a boating accident.

Jonathon was smiling. 'I say, would you like a trip out in her?'

'Oh, yes, please, that would be lovely.' Lorna was delighted. She'd feel the waves below the boat and the wind in the sails; it would be a new experience.

His smile broadened to a grin. 'Sunday, if it's a fine day?'

He was eager and she liked him, but wasn't this

133

what her mother had warned her against? She'd let her enthusiasm run away with her in an unguarded moment. Her words came out in a little rush. 'I'm not here on Sundays. I go home.' She sounded brusque.

'Of course, I was forgetting.' Suddenly he was unsmiling and staring into the darkening clouds across the river.

Lorna could feel the blood coursing through her veins. She wasn't going to be dragged into an emotional relationship as her mother had been. History was not going to repeat itself. She did find Jonathan attractive but she was going to fight it. She had to find out what had happened to Oliver before she started anything like that.

'My mother likes to see me.' Her voice sounded strange. 'My father's away a good deal.'

'I'm afraid the weekend is the only time I get for sailing. Weekdays I have to work.'

'So do I,' she said quickly. She must not make friends with a Wyndham. She mustn't get involved on a personal level. 'What a pity.' She tried to sound light-hearted; she would have loved a boat trip.

'We can't keep you here in your time off.'

Lorna felt uncomfortable, but there was no sarcasm in his voice. He too was trying to keep things light.

'That yacht, *Spirit of the Wind*, what a lovely name.'

'It's Grandpa's.'

'Really!'

'I was taken out in her from a very early age.'

'It's old, isn't it?'

'Very. I think it belonged to his father before him, maybe even his grandfather, but like everything else here, it needs a lot spending on it. It's up for sale but no takers yet.'

Jonathon started to stroll upriver. Lorna fell into step beside him. 'We call this the river walk. I like to think of my forebears taking their daily constitutional along this very path.'

'The boats are all swinging round,' Lorna noticed.

'Yes, the tide's on the turn.'

'But why...?'

'We anchor them at the bow. When the tide's coming in the current pushes them back from their anchors so they face down to the river mouth. When it's going out it pulls them the other way so they swing and face upriver.'

'Oh! You certainly love ships.'

He pulled a face. 'I'd much prefer to go to sea than spend each day behind a desk.'

'If you'd been born a century or two earlier you probably would have done.'

He was smiling again and she sighed with relief. 'Yes, I'll certainly miss living near the river.'

Jonathon kept Lorna out on the riverbank until it was dark and very cold. When they returned to the house, he didn't want her to rush away. 'What have you been doing today?' he asked.

'Turning out rooms.' After a slight pause she added, 'Come upstairs and I'll show you.'

She led him through the labyrinth of bedrooms, dressing rooms and boudoirs, showing him how she'd laid everything out neatly. She

135

pushed lists she'd made into his hand. 'I'm afraid there's a lot of junk that needs to be thrown out too. I'll have to bring your grandfather or aunt up here to decide exactly what.'

'Stand over them, and press for decisions or you'll not get them.'

'So I've noticed.' Her smile came, lighting up her face.

'Aunt Maude will be back soon. She's better at making her mind up. We're a family of hoarders and hate to throw anything away.'

'All the more to put in the sale now.'

'Have you seen the attic? I don't think Grandpa's given any thought to what's up there.'

'I sleep in the attic.'

'Is that where Aunt Roz put you?' Her sea-green eyes sparkled up at him. She seemed so full of life.

'Next to Hilda. I've got Connie's room.'

He chuckled. 'I might have guessed. Apart from the eight attic bedrooms for staff, there–'

'Ten,' Lorna corrected. 'I've counted them. There's only three in use now and seven empty. That's my next job, sorting through what's been left in the staff bedrooms.'

He laughed. 'What I'm trying to say is that the rest of the attic is crammed with centuries of family possessions. I want to get a box to store the papers I'm coming across. Let's get some lamps and have a look. You'll be amazed.'

He lit two storm lanterns, which had been left outside the rooms in case the electric supply broke down, and they went up to the attic. Shadows swung creepily across the ceiling as they moved.

Lorna was shocked when she saw the vast array of stacked furniture and household goods. She could see a penny-farthing bicycle and an ancient wicker perambulator. Vast storerooms covered a good deal of the roof space of the building. She sighed when she realised all this would have to be sorted through before the auction took place.

'I can't believe... Some of it... That's a lovely chair.'

'I'm sure there's a lot of value up here.'

'I'll leave this until I've finished downstairs,' Lorna decided. 'It's a bigger job than I thought.'

Jonathon found a cabin trunk, a large black wooden box with a handpainted design in red and white round the name, 'J.J.P. Wyndham' and the date, '1832'.

'Isn't this a find? I'd like to keep it.'

'It must have belonged to your great-great-great-grandfather...'

'Who's to say how many greats? Just what I need for keeping the important things I come across.' The lid creaked on its hinges as he opened it up. It smelled pleasantly spicy inside. He sniffed. 'Made of cedar wood.' There were some very old clothes inside which he took out and used to start dusting the box down.

'No,' Lorna protested, catching at his arm. 'They might be as old as the trunk and worth something.'

'I didn't think... I'll leave all that to you. Give me a hand to carry this down to my bedroom.'

'I need a trunk too,' Lorna said. 'I haven't come across anything private or personal yet, but sooner or later I will.'

137

'Which d'you want?' He lifted his lamp high.

There were all manner of boxes stacked between the cupboards, chairs, mirrors and whatnots. She could see a pile of old leather suitcases against one wall and a Gladstone bag and a wicker basket, but she shook her head.

'This then. It's empty.' Jonathon chose another cabin trunk for her. 'Let's move it to your room.'

'Just to the door,' Lorna said. 'I haven't that much space inside.'

On the way downstairs with the trunk, he said, 'I'd like to take you to the office. I want you to talk me through the Cartwright business. Adam reckons he hasn't time. He's always rushing off to do something else he thinks is more urgent.'

'Of course. When?' she asked.

He liked her, he liked her willingness to help. It made him feel he'd eventually succeed.

'In a day or two.'

'I'll come whenever you like.'

They'd reached his bedroom door. Lorna sat down on the box. Jonathon sank down beside her on the other end. She was friendly; he mustn't take offence that she wanted to go home in her time off.

They'd set the lamps on the floor and light was shining up in her face, making her eyes look like green rock pools. He could see sympathy and understanding in them, which made him confide his big worry.

'I'm beginning to feel desperate about the way things are dragging on in the office. I'm fed up twiddling my fingers with nothing specific to do. I came home to do a real job, but now it seems

Uncle Crispin doesn't want to give it to me.'

'I'd like to see your office,' she said. 'I might soon be working there myself if your grandfather decides against writing the family history.'

'He won't.'

'Your Aunt Rosaleen might persuade him it's a waste of time.'

'Never that. She's more puffed up about family achievements than any of us. She thinks our family has the ability to run the world. She'll want our history written down so she can hand out copies to her friends and acquaintances and preen herself that she springs from excellent stock. If she has any objections, it'll be about paying your salary. If you were also working part time in the office she might be reconciled to that.'

Lorna laughed. 'I'd love to do the research for your family history, but it's not easy to understand the concerns of people who lived two hundred years ago. Those who lived more recently...' He saw she was watching him closely. 'They seem more like us. Your father had other brothers, didn't he?'

Jonathon knew he was being prompted, that she wanted to keep him talking.

'Yes, there was Uncle Piers – he was the next eldest and brought up to be a sort of understudy to my father. Groomed to take his place should the worst happen and Dad not be able to run things.'

'But it didn't work out like that.'

Jonathon said earnestly, 'Please don't ask Grandpa about Uncle Piers.'

He could almost feel Lorna's interest quicken. 'Why not?'

Dare he tell her?

'I'm sorry, am I asking embarrassing questions?'

He felt she was understanding more than she should from his words. 'His death upset Grandpa terribly.'

He could see doubt in her eyes. 'Not more upsetting than–'

'My father's? Perhaps...'

'Your Uncle Piers was killed in the trenches too?'

'No, but he was called up and had to go and fight. Crispin was called up too in his turn, but they both survived the war. Uncle Crispin went to Ireland to train others for the trenches but Piers spent most of the war in the front line. He survived Ypres and the toughest campaigns on the Somme.'

Lorna was hugging her knees. 'Pity your poor grandparents. They must have lived in daily dread.'

'Piers seemed to have a charmed life. When the Armistice was signed you never saw such rejoicing. Champagne was brought out, we were all ecstatic with relief. The family thought they'd got off lightly, only one son having to give his life for England.'

'But the war must have damaged your business?'

'Just about killed it off. I was a boy but I remember Grandpa being worried stiff.' The memories were painful for him. He understood

140

the nightmares Grandpa had lived through. 'Some of our ships were sunk by the enemy, some were requisitioned by the Government. Trade was at a standstill, apart from food and fuel. The shipping industry virtually ceased.'

'But when the war was over?'

'We had such high expectations. Grandpa thought the business could be revived and would soon be back to normal. We all thought the wealth of Edwardian times would return with peace, but no, those days were gone for ever.'

Her voice was insistent. 'So what did happen?'

Jonathon shuddered. 'Influenza swept round the world.' He stared straight ahead now, almost forgetting she was there. 'More died from flu than were killed in the war – friend and foe combined. By then everybody was run down and exhausted.

'Uncle Piers had been injured twice but not badly. He'd been patched up in hospital, he came home to convalesce and was then sent back to the front. He'd fought in the front line for over two and a half years. It had worn him down.'

'He caught the flu?' Lorna's voice was soft with concern.

'Yes, one of the first when it came to Liverpool. He was very ill. I remember the doctor coming in his trap twice a day. My grandmother devoted herself to Uncle Piers's needs. She'd set her mind on nursing him back to health. It was inconceivable to us that he should survive the war only to succumb to influenza in his own bed, but that's what happened. Grandma caught the infection from him and, a week later, she was dead too.'

'Oh! How dreadful for–'

'Yes, Grandpa was devastated. Well, we all were. To have known such triumph on Piers's return and then that. Perhaps we rejoiced too much. I wept for Grandpa as much as for Uncle Piers himself. I know it racked him. It was a double blow. To be honest, life for him hasn't been the same since. He's never really recovered.'

'And the business?'

'Grandpa was so upset at the time that I think he was unable to cope. We never regained our share of the market. Things picked up a bit, but now with this depression we're worse off than we ever were.'

Lorna asked softly, 'Was Piers married?'

That startled him. Had she guessed? He wasn't going to tell her the secrets of the dead. 'No.'

He could see she was keying herself up to ask something else. 'I'd find turning out his room a lot more interesting than all these guest rooms.'

Jonathon smiled. 'I thought it might be interesting too, that's why I told Grandpa I'd do it myself.'

Lorna stood up, so he did too. 'Piers's room was this one next door to mine. I'm not sure when I'll get round to it, though. There's always something more pressing I have to do.'

When she left him, he stood staring out of his bedroom window, wondering about her. There were moments when he felt drawn to her – she was very attractive – but there were others when she seemed more than a little nosy. And why would she be interested in Piers?

Lorna went slowly back to the attic floor and her own room, musing that she'd learned a great deal. Certainly a lot about Jonathon; he'd put himself out to spend time with her, to be friendly. But after all his disclosures about his father and his Uncle Piers, he hadn't mentioned his Uncle Oliver. It was almost as if he'd never existed.

She threw herself down on her bed and tried to think. Jonathon would have been about three years old when Oliver died. Would that be old enough for him to remember her mother when she'd been a nursery maid here?

Possibly not. But he'd surely remember Oliver's death. There would have had to be a post mortem, and the family would have been shocked and grief-stricken at such an unexpected death. Even a three-year-old could not fail to notice the effect of that on his family.

The next morning, Lorna was finishing her breakfast when Jonathon said, 'I'll give you a hand with those curtains before I go.'

He was still munching on a piece of toast as they went together to the west wing. 'I'm jolly glad you're here to help,' he said. 'You really get on with things, put us all to shame.'

'I could do Piers's room too, if you like.'

'No, no. I'll get round to it.' The curtains came down in record time in the four main rooms. Lorna and Jonathon were both coughing in the dust as they folded them up.

'I've got Grandpa to agree to seeing three of the houses I picked out yesterday. Aunt Roz isn't exactly enthusiastic but she's coming with us tomorrow so I'm hopeful we'll decide on one.'

Since Jonathon had talked about his relations and his feelings about them, Lorna was seeing him as an ally, though she'd told him nothing about herself. If she was to find out exactly what had happened to Oliver, it was better to keep her mouth shut for the moment. The family was secretive, even if Jonathon wasn't. She must be too. She reminded herself she must trust no one here. This family had driven her mother to attempt suicide.

When Jonathon had gone, Lorna went up to work in the guest rooms in the main part of the house. On the way, she had to pass his bedroom with the sea chest still standing outside his door. He'd said he intended to store the private possessions and personal papers of family members in it.

Lorna heard the lid thump down as she climbed the main stairs and from the corner of her eye, she saw the bedroom door next to it swing almost shut. She knew whoever had been looking in Jonathon's sea chest had gone into what had once been Piers's bedroom. She crept up the remaining stairs and along the passage.

She hesitated, but she was more than curious to see who it was. She pushed the door and it swung silently open to reveal Rosaleen rummaging through some papers inside the drawers of a tallboy. Lorna cleared her throat, which made Rosaleen spin round. Her cheeks were flushed.

'I'm starting to turn out this room,' she said. Lorna saw the movement in her cheek, and thought she was flustered at being caught.

She smiled. 'I think Jonathon wants to do it

himself,' she said. 'I've offered twice to do it for him, but he said no.'

The drawer of the tallboy was slammed shut. 'In that case, I'll leave it to him. I thought he might appreciate some help.' Rosaleen stalked off downstairs.

Lorna stood still, holding her breath until the woman's footsteps died away. Then she tiptoed over to the tallboy and opened the same drawer. It was full of letters; most had been removed from their envelopes. She picked one out. 'Dear Piers,' she read, before guilt shafted through her. It felt a bit like snooping. She dropped it back, rammed the drawer shut and went along the passage to turn out another guest room.

She told herself she was being silly. She'd be expected to read private correspondence and other private family papers before this job was finished. But she was convinced of one thing now: something important would be found in Piers's bedroom, but she couldn't see that letters addressed to him were likely to provide it.

The afternoon of the following day, when Lorna was going down for tea, she met Harold in his chauffeur's cap on the stairs, carrying up two heavy suitcases. 'Mrs Carey's home,' he told her.

In the hall Lorna saw another case, a hat box and a travelling coat. She heard a new voice as she opened the door of the white drawing room where the family had gathered for their tea.

'Come in, Lorna,' Mr Wyndham said. 'This is my young sister, Maude Carey. I've just been telling her what a help you are to us.'

145

Mrs Carey had a lined face that was parchment-coloured, and the same tall and stringy build as Quentin. She wore thick-lensed spectacles and looked even more frail.

She put out a hand to Lorna. 'Only two years younger than you, Quentin, and an equal prey to the rigours of old age.' She smoothed back her sparse white hair with fingers encrusted with flashing rings. 'I hope Rosaleen's given you a comfortable room?'

Lorna hesitated, then saw Rosaleen was eyeing her coldly. 'Yes, thank you.'

'Aunt Maude acts as our housekeeper,' Rosaleen said.

'Chatelaine of the house,' her father corrected.

'Well, I don't know about that. I try to help when I'm here.'

'What you mean, Aunt Maude,' Rosaleen said with some acidity, 'is that I do the work and you take the credit – when you're here.'

'Rosaleen, you know she's almost always here.'

'I do enjoy visiting my grandchildren,' Maude said. 'I didn't want to miss Thomas's birthday this year. It's his twenty-first.'

'Falls on the same day as Grandpa's,' Jonathon smiled at Lorna.

'Rather a pity, Quentin, I had to miss your birthday.'

'Did you have a nice time?' Rosaleen asked.

'Yes, Louise looked after me very well. She took me to a concert and to the theatre. You must see *Chu Chin Chow*, dear, if it comes to Liverpool. But they're all so busy, and the house is so small. I'm glad to be home.'

After that the talk turned to the new house they must choose. Out came the brochures again to show to Aunt Maude.

'We saw three very nice houses with Jonathon this morning, but Rosaleen didn't like them.' Quentin seemed to be losing patience. 'We've been out again this afternoon in the Daimler to see more.'

'Nothing suitable,' Rosaleen said. The number of discarded brochures on the floor was growing.

'Did you see anything you fancied, Jonathon?' Aunt Maude asked.

He was tucking into cherry cake. 'I liked that black and white one.'

'Oh no!' Rosaleen moaned.

'What d'you think, Maude? Do you fancy Gatacre?'

Lorna had finished her tea and decided to leave them to it. She needed to look round this house. There were so many rooms, some of which opened one into the other, that she'd got herself lost twice today already.

She'd seen little of the ground floor up to now and wandered round. She'd gone through an anteroom and found herself in another drawing room when she heard footsteps coming after her.

'I'm trying to get my bearings.' She was relieved to see it was Jonathon and not Rosaleen. 'Such a vast house. I could do with a guide. Can you show me round?'

'This is called the red drawing room, but I'm not the best one to be a guide. I ran wild all over the house as a boy but I don't know much about the furnishings.'

147

Lorna looked round. It was dark and oppressive, not as large as the white drawing room, but still large enough to hold a dance in. The windows were hung with crimson draperies, and family portraits in ornate gilt frames covered the deep red wallpaper. Over the fireplace, in pride of place, a large picture had been turned to face the wall.

'Why is that?' she asked.

Jonathon shook his head. He pulled a chair nearer to stand on and turn it back. It was a portrait of a young lady in an off-the-shoulder red satin gown. She had the family's fair colouring.

Lorna stared at it in surprise. 'It was on the tip of my tongue to ask if this was your Aunt Rosaleen, but...' She could see now the portrait had been painted in Victorian times. The white-blonde hair was styled in ornate ringlets, the lady wore a tiara of diamonds and rubies, and a matching necklace graced her long pale neck. She held a fan.

'Everybody remarks on the likeness. Spitting image of Aunt Roz. Well – when she was young. But she doesn't like to be told that.'

'Whyever not? She's utterly beautiful. Who was she?'

'Eudora May, a daughter of the house.'

Lorna was peering up at the signature in the corner. 'It was painted in eighteen fifty-two.'

'Eudora was the one black sheep in the family.'

'Oh! What did she do? Run off with a handsome young man? Marry against her parents' wishes?'

'No, she married a man they chose for her.'

'Well, then... What turned her into the black sheep?'

'She killed her husband.'

'What?'

'She found he'd taken a lover and flew into a mighty rage. She knifed him.'

'Gracious!'

'So you can see why Aunt Roz doesn't want to be thought like her.'

'Yes, but to turn her face to the wall? Did she do it?'

Jonathon shrugged. 'Who knows?'

Chapter Eight

Jonathon, too, thought it made no sense to turn Eudora's portrait to the wall. Smiling down at them at the age of twenty-two, Eudora made a delightful picture. He watched Lorna move on to study the portrait of a sea captain.

'Who is this gentleman?'

'I don't know. Wish I did.' He felt ignorant about so many things here. He didn't really feel at home. 'I don't know a lot about the portraits. The marine pictures are my favourites. I'll ask Grandpa to take us both round sometime and tell us what he knows.'

'Has a family tree ever been drawn up?'

Today, Lorna was wearing an Alice band to draw her light brown curls away from her face. He'd not noticed before the freckles on her nose or how her upswept eyelashes cast shadows on her cheek. He ought to make an ally of this girl.

149

She was trying to find her feet here just as he was after two years abroad, returning to find the place in turmoil.

'Not as far as I know. I haven't seen one.'

He led her through the blue sitting room, the Chinese sitting room, and the summer drawing room. There were family portraits in all of them. Some rooms opened one from the other; all were cold and unlived in.

'This is the music room,' he said, throwing open the door. 'And that's my grandmother's portrait over the fireplace.' Lorna studied it. 'Grandpa wanted her painted here at her beloved piano.' The grand piano was all closed down.

'To see her at this very piano...' Lorna sat down before it on the same stool. 'It makes her seem a living person.'

'I remember her well,' Jonathon said.

She lifted the lid and ran her fingers across yellowing keys.

'Can you play?'

'No.' Her smile dazzled him, her dimple came and went. 'Never had the chance to learn.' She got up.

'The family had to have a music room, though most of us aren't musical. Apart from Grandma, I don't think it was used much.'

He took her on to the gun room.

'Guns?' Lorna pulled a face.

'Two hundred years ago, they'd have needed them.'

'On their ships?'

'Yes, there were pirates about then. There's a couple of cannons out in the garden that came off one of the ships. Look at all these – flintlock pistols.'

'Rifles too.'

'Years ago, Otterspool would have been out in the country. There'd be game.'

'Some pretty dangerous-looking knives too.'

'Very ornate mountings on some of them. Grandpa loves them. I don't think he'll want them all to go in the sale.'

Jonathon led the way out to the garden room, which was largely of glass, and sank down on the window seat.

Lorna said, 'You should draw up a family tree. Then I'd have some idea who all these people were.'

'Grandpa is the person to do that. He knows more about them than the rest of us. But even so, I doubt if he could. He won't know exactly in what order our ancestors lived and died. Nearly two centuries provide a good many generations.'

'But you know the present generation and your father's. Why don't you start there and work backwards? Tell me about your father.'

Jonathon was silent for a moment. She was asking too blatantly for information. He wasn't sure he liked her burrowing into the family history. He had to remind himself that this was what Grandpa wanted her to do. He'd need her help to write a family history.

Her eyes were watching him again. 'It doesn't upset you to talk about your father?'

He smiled. 'Just collecting my memories. When Dad was killed in the trenches in nineteen sixteen I was nine years old. I couldn't believe I'd never

151

see him again.'

'What a loss that must have been.'

'I missed him so much I wanted to sleep in the bedroom he'd had as a boy. He'd moved to the west wing when he married. He was Grandpa's heir, you understand. I already have all his private papers and personal belongings and much of my mother's stuff too.'

'Where is your mother now?' Her disturbing eyes wouldn't leave him.

'America. I went out to see her. I've only just come back. Mum didn't want to stay here after Dad was killed.'

'Why not? It had been her home for some years, hadn't it?'

'Yes, since she was married.' He frowned. 'She didn't get on very well with Aunt Roz or my uncles.'

'Do you?'

Jonathon thought that more than pointed. Lorna was giving him the third degree. He said, 'I try to. Does it show?'

She seemed sympathetic. 'They don't draw you into the family circle.'

'They don't. I'm kept at arm's length and that's exactly how my mother felt – that they resented her presence, that she was another person the family had to support.'

'Your Aunt Roz thinks of Daphne in that way.'

'You're right, but she has Crispin to support her. When they were packing to move out, there were a lot of angry arguments. Roz and Daphne were always scrapping over who was going to have what.'

152

'I heard them,' Lorna said.

'My mother said all they ever thought about was money, and she wasn't prepared to fight for a share. She wasn't that interested in the Wyndham wealth. After the war, when Grandpa wanted to send me to boarding school, she left here. She lodged near me for a while but eventually went off to America and never returned. I spent my school holidays here so I didn't lose touch with the family, not entirely.'

'That was your mother's idea?'

'Yes. She married again, much to Aunt Roz's relief.' Jonathon had to smile. Lorna certainly knew how to extract the facts she wanted. 'I have two half sisters now, and her American husband will have to look after them as well as my mother. He isn't rich, just average professional American. He's a dentist.'

Lorna said thoughtfully, 'Your grandfather accepts you and wants you here.'

'Yes, but not the others, except perhaps Aunt Maude.'

'I'd have thought Adam would be like a brother to you.'

'No.'

'You shared the nursery here.'

'He was two years older and used to give me a hard time.' Jonathon dried up. She'd think he was a wimp to be bullied by Adam.

'Tell me about him.'

He'd rather talk about her, but no doubt she'd say she needed a bit of background to do what Grandpa wanted.

'I've never got on with Adam.' He couldn't

153

resist kicking out against him. 'When I grew older I couldn't bear the thought of going to the same school as him. I begged my mother to send me elsewhere.'

At thirteen he'd wanted to join the *Conway*, a training ship moored in the Mersey. His grandfather had been against that because he'd have been trained to be a Merchant Navy officer. But Grandpa had partly heeded his wishes.

'Where did you go?'

'Shrewsbury. I enjoyed it there but now it means I have no old school friends in Liverpool.'

'Then you went to America?'

'I spent another three years articled to a firm of accountants in Manchester, to give me what Grandpa sees as a useful background for the business.'

He'd far rather have been learning about navigation, but being a Wyndham meant giving up his personal wishes so he might take his rightful place in the family business later on.

'Once I was qualified, Grandpa agreed I should spend six months with my mother, who had settled with her new family in Newport, Rhode Island.'

'I imagine you had a good time there.'

He had. 'My mother's new husband owns a sea-going yacht and we all went sailing at the weekends. I loved that.'

Boats and ships had always been a passion with him, and once he'd shown he was a competent sailor he was allowed to take the *White Dove* out himself. He'd met other youngsters at the sailing club. He'd played tennis with them too and enjoyed having a lazy time on the beach in the sun.

'America seemed so free and easy.' So lacking in the formality and pomp he'd grown used to in the family. He dried up again. When the six months were up, he hadn't wanted to come home. Beside him, he saw Lorna shiver. There was a gale-force draught in the garden room. Some of the windowpanes were cracked, others were broken. It was growing dark now, and too cold to sit out here. She stood up. 'I'd better see if Hilda needs a hand in the kitchen.'

He watched her go and wasn't sorry. He didn't want to tell her about the girl he'd met there, and Lorna was a dab hand at shelling facts out of him.

Jonathon had written apologetic letters home to his grandfather asking for an extension of his holiday. He had a little money left to him by his father as well as a small income from the family trust, but not enough to pay his way in America, so to help out, he'd taken a job in a soda fountain serving ice creams and coffee.

He'd met Carla there, a dark-haired girl with a delicious tip-tilted nose, and become so enmeshed in love he couldn't bring himself to leave. She'd come home to Newport for her summer holiday and after three weeks had to return to her job in New York.

He'd been so certain of Carla that he'd followed her, and found himself an apartment and a job as photographer's assistant. He'd persuaded her to spend more and more time with him. She was a determined career journalist on the *New York*

Times and once he told her he was a chartered accountant she couldn't understand why he didn't get on with his career. He'd explained that his career was waiting for him back in Liverpool. He'd hoped at that stage to persuade Carla to return with him.

'Wow, a family business waiting for you?' she'd marvelled. 'But to have a real job here would be marvellous experience for you.'

'This is my holiday and I want to have fun doing other things. I'm not aiming to be the company accountant. A background in accounts is all I need, not day-to-day experience. I'll be working on the administrative side.'

Carla had thought that irresponsible. At her insistence he'd found himself a job in a bank and tried to make a go of it, but it hadn't worked out. He'd sensed her interest in him was waning.

Carla had said, 'All you limeys want is to laze about doing menial jobs.' By then he'd been developing a taste for Broadway and was taking her with him to the theatres. 'You're playing around.'

She'd ditched him for a man who was prepared to work and was as serious as she was about building a career. That had hurt. Jonathon had returned to his mother's house, but had not been able to settle back into their easy life. For him, the enjoyment had gone. He'd been made to feel he was drifting through life and needed more focus.

'Go home,' his mother had urged. 'You need a career you can get your teeth into, go home and take up your rightful place in the family. Work in

156

the business as your father did. You'll settle in Liverpool. It's where you have your roots.'

Jonathon had been persuaded, but he was beginning to think it had been a mistake. He got up, went slowly up to his bedroom and threw himself on his bed.

This was a mausoleum of a house. He'd forgotten just how cold and uncomfortable it was. Growing up in it had blinded him to its discomforts until he'd been to his mother's house in America. All these large draughty bedrooms, yet the family had to share a bathroom that was freezing cold, running with damp, and full of woodlice. And there was never enough hot water.

His aunt and grandfather, however, truly believed they were living in one of the finest houses in Liverpool. The thought of moving out genuinely distressed them. How could they be so blind? He, for one, would be glad to see the last of the place. He must do his best to make them choose something more comfortable.

Otterspool might have been OK when Grandpa was a lad, but these days? He was trying to live in a different age.

Daphne sat in front of her dressing-table mirror and gazed painfully at her reflection. During the twenty-six years of her marriage her beauty had faded and gone.

She'd tried every type of face cream from cold cream to vanishing cream but her skin had sagged and the lines had come. Nothing she did could prevent them growing steadily worse. She felt her husband's betrayal, and his family's lack of acceptance, had etched lines on her face.

Her figure, once so ripe and curvaceous, was shapeless and fat. She'd taken Mr Banting's advice on how to stay slim. She'd suffered pangs of hunger and lost the weight she'd aimed to, but the pounds had returned with a vengeance once she'd stopped starving herself.

Rosaleen, who was too thin, had told her with a self-satisfied smile that it was years of lazy living and greedy eating that had given her so many sagging rolls of fat. She'd lost her beauty and that was as hurtful as Rosaleen's continuing aggression.

Daphne had thought she could ignore her jibes, but her policy of turning a deaf ear had made Rosaleen try harder. She'd soon realised her power, and had become a master of the cutting phrase; she'd perfected the art of hurting and embarrassing her.

Daphne knew she couldn't compete; she hadn't the same verbal skill. It brought frustration and tension, deepening her frown lines and shortening her temper. Her nerves were worn down, and she was in a constant state of irritation.

Years ago, Rosaleen had tried to push her out of Otterspool in the way she'd pushed Frances out. With Adam already away at boarding school, Rosaleen had suggested it might be a good thing for Clarissa to go too. 'Then you could spend more time in France,' she'd said.

Daphne had understood she meant less time at Otterspool and strenuously opposed that.

'Clarissa should spend a few years at a French school then,' Rosaleen had suggested several times. 'Your French relatives would approve, wouldn't they? They'd want her to speak French like a native, and I'm sure they'd love to have more of your company.'

Daphne had responded by inviting her mother and grandmother to visit Otterspool. They came at least once a year and stayed for a month. She took the children for a return visit during the Christmas holidays.

She was determined not to be pushed out and tried to think of ways to turn the tables on her sister-in-law.

Daphne was impressed by the portrait of Eudora May hanging in the red drawing room. She'd seen Rosaleen's resemblance to her immediately. She had the same shaped face, the same proud and haughty look in her pale blue eyes, the same Scandinavian blonde hair. Daphne remarked on it when the family were assembled there before dinner one evening, expecting Rosaleen to be flattered. Instead she grimaced and turned away offended.

Daphne asked Oliver about it the following day when she found him on his own. Oliver was more studious and more interested in the family history than his brothers. He told her that Eudora May had stabbed her husband after he'd betrayed her.

'With another woman?' she asked.

'What else?'

'I thought perhaps money.'

Oliver laughed. 'No, another woman.'

'You Wyndhams have such fiery tempers.' She knew Rosaleen certainly had. She could blow up into a raging fury in seconds and it didn't take much to cause it.

Daphne stared up at Eudora's portrait. 'What happened to her?' she asked. 'Did she get away with it?'

'No, she was hanged – in eighteen fifty-nine.'

'How awful!' It was absolutely dreadful for a Wyndham. She tried to work out how old Eudora would have been.

'She was twenty-nine at the time.'

Rosaleen was not far from that age at that time and it gave Daphne an idea. She saw the bad feeling between them as a power struggle, with Rosaleen determined to vanquish her, but suddenly, after all the years of taking her kicks, she could see a way to even things out. Rosaleen had her weak spots: she was nerve-racked and full of hate, and had always had a troubled mind. Daphne could make her more jittery, wage a war of nerves; make her as mad as a March hare if she could.

The next time she found herself alone with Rosaleen in the red drawing room, she began to talk about Eudora, pointing out how much Rosaleen resembled her in looks, telling her she was a chip off the same block.

Quentin had told Daphne there were no ghosts walking in Otterspool because all the Wyndhams had had happy and fulfilled lives. Clearly he'd forgotten about Eudora. She told Rosaleen she'd seen her sitting in the red drawing room, working on an embroidery frame.

The following week when she went to the dining room for dinner and found only Rosaleen

160

there before her, she pretended to be shocked.

'I've just seen Eudora May.'

Rosaleen looked at her in stony silence, but Daphne knew she was strangely superstitious, believed in the occult, and had the sort of mind that was swayed by such suggestions.

'She was crossing the great hall, holding up the long skirts of her red satin dress.'

The colour was fading from Rosaleen's cheeks.

'I thought at first it was you, but you have no dress like that.'

'No.'

'And, anyway, she looked so old-fashioned and you were already here.'

When Quentin and Marina joined them, Daphne said, 'I'm sure I've just seen Eudora May's ghost crossing the great hall. Are you sure no one else has ever seen her?'

'Of course not,' they said in tones of brisk common sense. 'There are no ghosts in Otterspool.'

'But I thought Aunt Maude had seen–'

'That was a man,' Rosaleen said hurriedly.

When Aunt Maude came in for her dinner, she said that once she'd thought she'd seen a ghost in the hall.

'Just shadows,' Quentin said. 'It's often quite dark in there and the coloured glass in the windows–'

'There was a smell too,' Maude said. 'A strange smell.'

'I thought you said it was of soot?'

'Well, I wasn't sure. It was a bit like gunpowder.'

'Maude, you're letting your imagination run

away with you.'

Quentin didn't rebuke Daphne; she knew he wouldn't. He still treated her like a stranger, though she ate almost every meal with him.

She turned Eudora's portrait to the wall and when Rosaleen jumped with surprise to see it so, she denied touching it. It wasn't long before Daphne saw her looking warily over her shoulder. Rosaleen was growing more uneasy. The red drawing room was used less and less.

She was crossing the great hall with Rosaleen one sunny afternoon after they'd finished lunch. Daphne pounced suddenly on her arm, pulling her to a halt. 'There,' she said in a hoarse whisper. 'There, do you see her?'

The marble floor of the hall was a kaleidoscope of colours, greens and blues but mostly reds as the rays of the sun shone through the coloured glass windows.

'It's Eudora May. You saw her too, didn't you? You heard her satin dress swish as she walked?'

'Yes,' Rosaleen whispered, her eyes wide with fear. 'Yes, I saw her.'

Daphne felt a thrill of triumph. She'd got to Rosaleen at last.

All that week, Lorna had worked steadily and methodically through the labyrinth of rooms on the upstairs floor. Turning out guest rooms was not what she most wanted to do, but even so, she found the four-poster beds quite fascinating. Some were very grand, with canopies and drapes of embroidered silks; there were also candle snuffers in solid silver and warming pans in

162

hammered brass, which showed a way of life that had gone for ever. Though she craved to see the room that had once belonged to Oliver, Lorna knew she must not appear to be searching for anything in particular.

When she opened a door and found a well-worn rocking horse and an iron grate behind a large fireguard she knew she'd found the nursery. It was a series of small rooms opening one from the other, smaller than she'd imagined. It made her catch her breath to think of her mother working here.

Lorna felt totally involved now. She went round studying the framed religious texts on the nursery walls and looking at the shelves filled with children's books. Thrilling shivers were running down her spine. Mum would have carried children's meals from the kitchen to that table under the window. Possibly she'd have eaten here with them. She'd have made up the little beds in this night nursery, but here was another night nursery beyond. Mum must have slept in one of them. She would have made up these cots and pushed the prams, and probably have washed these tiny old-fashioned sailor suits. Had Jonathon sat on this child's chair? Had Oliver before him?

There were cupboards full of toys – dolls of all descriptions: some made from wax and stuffed with straw, others from china with real hair. She found building blocks and wooden carts that had been used by generations of Wyndham children. All this would have been familiar to her mother.

Lorna laid everything out with great care. The clockwork animals and trains would have amused

163

only more recent generations. Perhaps Oliver had played with these. Some had the winding key fixed in them, on others the keys were missing. Lorna came across a cardboard box of keys at the back of one cupboard and took time to see if she could find a key to fit each toy. She had keys left, though there were toys they wouldn't fit. One key was of better quality than the others. By the time she was almost ready to stop for lunch, she had automatons playing music and crocodiles shuffling up the table and snapping their jaws. Rosaleen came in.

She said crossly, 'I didn't want you to do the nursery. It would have been a labour of love for me. All these things,' she picked up a teddy bear and hugged it to her flat chest, 'they're part of my childhood.'

Lorna wasn't prepared to let Rosaleen get away with that. 'I do only what I'm asked.' She flipped her notebook to the front page to show the notes she'd made on her first morning.

'It was all agreed. Look, your father asked me to do the nurseries, d'you remember? You had first choice and said you wanted to turn out the china cupboards and sort through the butler's pantry.'

'I've finished those. I've even washed the china and got Sissie and Blossom to clean up the silver.'

Sissie Smith had come back to work that morning, a meek fourteen-year-old who could do nothing to please Hilda. She was still coughing.

'Who is Blossom?' Lorna asked.

Rosaleen sounded impatient. 'An old servant,

worked for us for years. Pensioned off now but still does a bit when we're busy.'

Lorna tried a different tack, and pushed the three keys she'd been unable to find homes for in front of her. 'Do you know what these are for?'

Rosaleen shook her head and picked out the most ornate one. 'This isn't for winding up a toy.'

Lorna rewound an automaton of tinplate animals playing musical instruments. 'Alexander's Ragtime Band' burst forth, while a monkey beat the drums, and a lion and a tiger raised saxophones to their lips. 'I think this is great,' she said.

Rosaleen pulled a face. 'It was Oliver's.'

Lorna's heart leaped. This was the first time she'd heard his name mentioned. 'Oliver? He was...?' She wanted desperately to hear more about him.

'My brother.'

Lorna held her breath.

Rosaleen stopped it playing. 'Probably bring quite a bit in the sale.'

'So could that teddy bear you're holding. Did that belong to Oliver too?'

'Edward Bear was mine. He's almost threadbare.'

'Yes, but I wouldn't throw him away.'

'I don't want to throw anything away.' She showed irritation again. 'These toys bring back such memories for me.'

'Memories, yes.' Lorna passionately wanted to hear them but didn't know how to encourage Rosaleen to keep on talking. 'You must have spent a wonderful childhood here.'

'Wonderful?' She looked sour and unhappy. 'I

think I had rather a bleak and solitary childhood. I missed a lot.'

'You had brothers, you were not alone.' Lorna hastened to add, 'Jonathon told me about his father and his Uncle Piers.'

'Yes, well, I've lost all my brothers apart from Crispin. That's another reason why my childhood wasn't happy.'

Lorna couldn't resist saying, 'But weren't you already grown up when the war started?'

Rosaleen dropped the teddy bear and stood up. 'The war ruined everything for us,' she said before rushing out.

Lorna sat back and tried to unwind. Had she groped too clumsily for information about Oliver? As far as she knew, his death had been the only family tragedy that had occurred before the war. And Rosaleen would have been twenty-four at that time, hardly a child.

She must have been very upset by it. Too upset, it seemed, to talk about it even now. Had something else clouded her childhood?

Daphne felt such satisfaction with her new home, that she often drifted from room to room, glorying in the good taste they reflected. Today, her eye came to rest on her portrait that Crispin had commissioned when she'd first become Mrs Wyndham and he'd been very much in love. She studied every brush stroke now. She'd been a slip of a girl of eighteen, with dark Mediterranean eyes and olive skin, the very opposite to the Wyndham family's washed-out northern colouring. Her hair had been long and silky and she'd worn it coiled on her head, but it was also curly, and little finger ringlets and curls always came to frame her face.

Her features were neat and even, her eyes wide and large. For as long as she could remember, her mother and grandmother had told her that her face was her fortune, and it had been.

She'd been a real beauty. Daphne admired the fulsome figure she'd had from her mid-teens, with a large bust, curvaceous hips and a narrow waist, which suited the very feminine Edwardian fashions of the day. When her picture had hung amongst the portraits of Crispin's relatives, she'd looked so much more vibrant, more lively than they.

Next to it on the wall, Crispin had insisted on hanging the French rococo mirror in a silver and Limoges enamel frame. He'd said he wanted it there, so she could see how much she'd changed. Daphne's satisfaction faded; she averted her eyes. She'd wanted Crispin to go on loving her after they were married. She'd tried her hardest to keep him at her side, but had failed to influence him ever after. She felt sick when she thought of how he'd ruined their marriage.

Daphne had known Ruth Detley since she'd first gone to live at Otterspool as a bride. Ruth had been a girl of fourteen then and her mother, who was a friend of Quentin's wife, Marina, brought her over to the tennis parties, boating parties and picnics they held. As she grew older, Ruth had been invited to the odd luncheon or dinner party too, as she was considered suitable company for the younger members of the family.

Rosaleen could be just as acidic to Ruth as she was to everybody else. Daphne thought she was jealous because Marina and her friend openly spoke of Ruth's 'flowering' in her late teens, and praised her poise and beauty. Certainly Ruth was attractive, with dark curly hair and an infectious laugh. She was outgoing, with a sense of fun, and was often the life and soul of the party.

On a weekend early in 1910, Marina had arranged a boating party to take advantage of the unexpectedly fine spring weather. They were all keen sailors. Quentin had a yacht and had given each of his sons a sailing boat of his own. They were to sail in a flotilla, taking family and friends upriver to have a picnic lunch in their holiday cottage near Fiddler's Ferry.

There had been an air of excitement about the preparations: the checking of tide times and barometers, and Marina had ordered a busy baking day in the kitchen.

Daphne was enjoying the trip. She and Frances had been told that the safest boat for the children would be Quentin's and they should travel on *Spirit of the Wind* too. They'd taken the nursemaid to keep an eye on the children, so they were able to relax. Ruth was in the party, and Daphne noticed Crispin was taking her on to his boat, but thought little of it, as Rosaleen and Aunt Maude were with him too.

Great-aunt Eliza Wyndham and Great-aunt Gertrude Slee helped Marina carry the baskets of food up to the little house and set it out on the table. 'A doll's house,' Marina had laughingly called it. It had only four bedrooms. Daphne

168

found it larger than her grandmother's house in Marseilles, which she'd thought a comfortable size.

Lunch was a jolly meal. There was beer for the men and sherry for the ladies. Afterwards, the family broke up into small groups and wandered off. Daphne didn't see Crispin go. The other members of the family never sought Daphne's company, nor seemed to welcome it if she attached herself to them.

She'd strolled along the shore following Oliver, the youngest of her brothers-in-law, and the children. He took an interest in his little nephews, and seemed to enjoy kicking a ball about with them. The nursemaid followed with Clarissa, and when they all stopped to dig sandcastles and hunt for shells and seaweed, Daphne sat down on a wall a little distance from them to watch. Growing tired of that, she sauntered back to the cottage where afternoon tea was being made.

It was mid-afternoon when the sun suddenly disappeared and it turned chilly, reminding them it was still only March. Great-aunt Gertrude shivered and reached for her shawl.

'Time we started back,' Marina decided, and started to repack the remains of the feast into the baskets. Daphne helped. It was only then that she noticed Crispin hadn't returned.

'Where's he gone?' Rosaleen demanded. 'Has anybody seen him?'

'Not since lunch.'

'We're all here, are we, apart from him?'

'What about Ruth?' her mother asked, now worried. Family members began calling their names. Daphne could hear them calling outside in the garden and in the lane.

'Rosaleen,' her mother said, 'please start carrying these baskets back to the boats.'

When Oliver got up to help her with the rugs and cushions, Daphne lifted two more of the baskets and followed them. The boats had been tied up to a long narrow jetty stretching out into the river. Rosaleen and Oliver went on board *Spirit of the Wind*. Daphne leaned over the side and put her baskets on the deck.

She went further along the jetty to Crispin's boat, meaning to see if he was there. She crossed the deck and opened the door to the cabin. In that blinding second she had the shock of her life. Crispin had been lying on one of the narrow bunks cradling Ruth Detley in his arms. Ruth leaped to her feet, straightening her clothes. Crispin stood up more slowly, a hangdog look on his face, knowing he'd been caught fair and square.

Daphne was speechless with shock. Crispin having an affair? With that plump lump Ruth Detley? But Ruth had 'flowered'. She was trying to work out how old Ruth was now. Twenty? She wasn't a child any more. Daphne found it hard to believe this was happening. She felt numb with hurt. She'd been betrayed. She turned and ran straight into Rosaleen's arms.

'Oh, so you've found out! I told him he had the luck of the devil keeping it from you this long.' She raised her voice to call back to her mother: 'It's all right, stop looking. Crispin and Ruth are here on his boat.'

170

Daphne felt gall rising in her throat. Keeping it from her? The rest of the family already knew? That was a very hurtful jab.

When she'd been pregnant with Clarissa and didn't feel like going out at night, Crispin had started going without her. Now he went out alone several nights in the week without asking her if she wanted to go with him. He told her he was going out with his friends for a drink, mentioned names like Henry Montague, Harry Yates and Giles Hurst.

What a fool she'd been to believe that. She knew better than anybody that Crispin could tell all sorts of fiction and make it sound like fact. He was still whispering that he loved her when all the time he had another woman!

Rosaleen was smiling at her, self-satisfied and smug. 'Getting a husband is one thing,' she purred. 'Keeping him, quite another.' Rosaleen knew how to score. She must have been waiting to say those words, knowing they'd cut to the quick.

Daphne could feel tears prickling her eyes. She wanted to escape but all the Wyndhams were coming down to their boats. She went on board *Spirit of the Wind*. This was changing everything for her. It was the end of an era. She'd really believed Crispin loved her and was a dutiful husband. He hadn't wanted to make love quite so often recently – she had noticed that, but put it down to the fact that they were both a little older and the freshness of marriage was wearing off. Now she stopped to think about it, he hadn't been quite so loving and attentive in other ways.

The return journey was cold. Marina called her

to join them in the day cabin but Daphne wanted to be alone. She couldn't face any questions about Crispin or Ruth Detley, couldn't talk about anything. She was frozen stiff when they got back to Otterspool and was shaking with fear too by then. What if Crispin should ask for a divorce? She didn't want to move out of her wealthy home. She had her children, the Wyndhams thought the world of them, they were their next generation. She was afraid that if she had to go, they would want to keep the children, that Crispin wouldn't allow her to take them with her.

Daphne tried to comfort herself with the thought that she was Crispin's wife, mother of his children and mistress of his household, even if it was only the west wing in his father's house. She wasn't prepared to give up that, even if he did have another woman. She'd had to fight hard to get this far. Where else could she go? Not back to Marseilles to live with her mother and grandmother – she didn't want that. She was determined to stay in Otterspool.

Shortly afterwards came great family anguish about Oliver's death. She knew Crispin and Rosaleen had been with him at the time and they said he'd had a fatal accident. Daphne was not that interested in the details; she was too wrapped up in her own worries.

Then her nursemaid confirmed what Oliver had said about having an affair with her, and told them she was pregnant.

'Just as if,' Rosaleen mocked. Daphne really didn't care, Frances would find another nursemaid to take her place.

The Wyndhams would not be concerned about Crispin's infidelity or the fact that his affair with Ruth Detley was turning out to be the first of a long line.

Daphne thought the Wyndham family was like a poisonous jellyfish with thousands of tentacles all ready to sting everyone it touched.

Chapter Nine

It was two o'clock that afternoon when Lorna got into Jonathon's car to go to the Liverpool office. He seemed tense and impatient on the journey. She knew he'd been out all morning with the rest of his family, looking at more houses.

'Didn't you see anything you liked?'

'We saw a beaut. Lovely garden, well away from anything else. Aunt Maude went overboard for it. I thought we'd cracked it.'

'But Rosaleen didn't like it?'

'No, she said it had no style. It wasn't formal or grand enough for her. I don't think we're looking for the same thing.'

Lorna could see he was fulminating.

'Aunt Roz found fault with every one we looked at. Grandpa suggested renting for a year to give us more time to find the right place. Roz wasn't happy with that. She carped all the time. "We should make sure we have a roof over our heads while we still have the money from the sale. You know how easily it disappears.'"

Lorna said, 'It would make it easier for your grandfather to decide what he needs to take with him if he bought straight away.'

'Gosh, how many times have we both pointed that out?' Jonathon sighed. 'Getting them to decide on anything is hard work. I left them arguing. It's a relief to get away for a few hours.'

The Wyndham office occupied the ground floor of an impressive building in Water Street, the prime business area of the city. Lorna had never been in a big office like this before. In retrospect, the Cartwright office seemed to have been very homely. Here, there were rows of desks in a big hall, each with a clerk bent busily over it.

Jonathon led her through. 'We've not renewed the lease on the Hamilton Square office. With the depression our business is tailing off and we have to cut costs.'

He took her to his Uncle Crispin's office but he wasn't in. 'I don't suppose Adam is either,' he said with an impatient toss of his head. 'They're more interested in their new house than looking after the business.'

Mr Buckler was in, but seemed none too pleased to be asked for the keys to the Cartwright files. He pulled his portly figure up from his chair with great reluctance to get them. His wing collar was smart and the handkerchief he drew out to wipe the perspiration from his forehead was snow white and freshly ironed.

'Why are the file cabinets kept locked?' Lorna asked Jonathon as she opened them up.

'Adam locks everything up before he goes

174

home. He doesn't like other people looking through his files, not even me.'

'Neither does Mr Buckler,' Lorna said, 'not even in working hours. How can anybody deal with the business if they can't get at the files?'

She pulled a chair up to his desk and started to explain what she'd done in the past. 'I wrote to every one of our clients telling them we'd sold to you and we were sure they'd be very well looked after.

'This one, Copelands, manufactures cotton cloth specially printed with designs for the West African market. They send out orders every fortnight. I booked space with Elder Dempsters for it, usually on the mail boat.'

It felt familiar territory to Lorna. She relaxed, knowing she could cope with anything here. She was pleased when a client's clerk she knew well called in with an order for shipping space and she was able to introduce him to Jonathon. Crispin returned just before closing time and seemed vexed to find her there.

Jonathon said, 'I couldn't pin Adam down to talk about the Cartwright account. I thought it would save him the trouble if I got Miss Mathews to fill me in.'

That seemed to displease Crispin further.

Jonathon went on, 'It would make sense to have her here in the office every day doing this, especially over the first months. We'd be more likely to keep the business.'

Lorna said, 'I'm enjoying sorting out the house contents for the sale.' She didn't want to give that up until she'd got to the bottom of what had really happened to Oliver Wyndham.

Lorna went home for her day off on Saturday afternoon. The little two up two down in Cleveland Street had always seemed small, but after getting used to the size of Otterspool House, it appeared to have shrunk again. The bathroom she shared with Hilda and Sissie was larger than the whole of their ground floor, though here everything was well cared for, highly polished and sparkling clean.

The atmosphere had always been cheery and welcoming, but even as a child Lorna had sensed that her mother had inner tensions. It was as though she held everything dear to her – her family and her little house – within protective arms. She lavished her energy on looking after them. Lorna felt surrounded by her love, but there was a prickliness about her.

Mum could flare up, with very little provocation, against anybody she thought might be attacking her little circle. Lorna thought her overprotective of her children, whom she hated to see leave home. She worried about them needlessly. Today, her mother looked drawn and anxious.

'How have you got on? How are the Wyndhams treating you? They don't suspect, do they, that you–'

'Hang on a minute, Mum.' Lorna kissed her cheek. 'Let me get my hat off.'

'I'll make a cup of tea and you can tell me all about it before Pam comes back. She's gone up Grange Road to buy some elastic.'

'How's she getting on at the secretarial college?'

'She loves it. She says they'll help her find a job if she passes the exams at the end of the course. I've heard from our Jim. He'll be home next week and Pa too.'

'Will I miss them?'

'Yes, they'll have gone back before next week-end.'

Lorna sat back in a familiar chair and tried to relax. She loved being home but it seemed nothing was quite the same now she'd learned of Mum's past. Even Mum wasn't the same. Her fingers were pulling nervously at her apron. 'Are they hard to please? Difficult?'

'Rosaleen is.'

'And her parents?'

'Mrs Wyndham's dead.'

'Oh! She was never rude or unkind to any of us, but working in the nursery... It was Mrs John or Mrs Crispin we had to answer to.'

Lorna told her mother the sad story Jonathon had told her, of how Piers had returned from the war only to catch flu.

'His mother nursed him and caught it too. They both died of it. I feel sorry for the old man.'

'Sorry for him? He was so proud; so full of himself, so powerful...'

'He's not powerful now. He seems melancholy, grief-stricken; everything's gone wrong in his life. He sort of leans on me, like Mrs Cartwright did, and he's kindly–'

'Kindly? You mustn't trust him, Lorna.'

'I'm just telling you how he seems.'

Her mother looked perplexed. 'But snooty, a proud leader of the family?'

177

'No, not snooty, and definitely not leading the family. The next generation is in charge now.'

'Mr Crispin and his wife?'

'Yes. Now, they're toffee-nosed and powerful. I saw him just for a few moments on my first night and again in the office. They've moved to a house of their own, you know?'

'Fancy that!'

'But Mrs Crispin comes round almost daily – to see what treasures are being brought to light by my sorting.'

'She would.' Her mother's face was twisting with dislike of her.

'Says it is her duty to come and help. But of course, she leaves all the hard work to me. She just mulls over all the things I've found to see if she can see anything of value to herself. She doesn't want to miss anything. I think they are all after as much money for themselves as they can get.'

'Just what I'd expect. They were mean-minded employers.'

'I don't think that, but not friendly like the Cartwrights. Apart from the old man they keep their distance from me.' Lorna deliberately avoided mentioning Jonathon.

That night, in the double bed she shared with Pam, they talked long after they'd put out their light.

'I like the typing lessons best. Shorthand isn't easy, but I'm determined to get up a decent speed. I want to get a good job like yours, and go to work in my best clothes. Almost all my friends from school have gone into domestic service.

178

They're scrubbing out other people's houses. I feel I've had a close shave and, but for you, that's what I'd be doing.'

'Families have to hang together,' Lorna said. 'Even the Wyndhams do that.'

She smiled into the darkness. The problem for her was that she wasn't sure which family she owed allegiance to. It could be both.

Back at work on Monday, Lorna turned out rooms as steadily and methodically as she could, but by mid-afternoon she felt she had to take a break and get a breath of fresh air. As yet, she'd not even looked at the buildings behind the house. She knew there must be stables because she'd seen Rosaleen in her riding habit, tapping the side of her jodhpurs with her whip, as she waited impatiently for her father to come down. As Quentin had walked with her towards the back door, her voice had floated back, 'I do hope Tom's managed to saddle up Beano.'

'I asked him to.'

'He forgot, Father, the other day.'

Lorna saw the stable block, a very handsome building with a clock tower over an arch that was large enough for a horse and carriage to sweep through. She went through to the stable yard, where the doors were mostly shut, indicating empty stalls. Only two seemed to be occupied. A dark head covered with a flat cap came to look out over one of them.

'Hello, Harold. I'm just looking round, thought I'd like to see the horses.'

Harold Jones said, 'Just finishing the mucking

out.' He was forking clean straw into the stall. 'This is Beano, Miss Rosaleen's horse.'

Rather gingerly, Lorna patted the nose of a handsome bay. She'd never had anything to do with horses and this one seemed huge.

'And that's Torkill. He's getting old like his master.'

'But Mr Wyndham still rides?'

'No. He knows he's past that, but he still likes a breath of fresh air. I put Torkill in the shafts of the trap. He drives that while Miss Rosaleen rides alongside.'

Harold showed her round the tack room, which smelled of leather. Highly polished bridles and saddles were hanging on the walls. The horse brasses were not so bright and the big display of rosettes was distinctly dusty.

'Did Rosaleen win all those?'

'Some of them. Miss Clarissa was keen on show jumping too at one time, and her brother.' He sighed. 'Those days are gone. I suppose the horses will all go soon.'

'Rosaleen wants her new house to have stables.'

'But will she get them?'

Lorna saw a bent old woman coming towards them carrying a large cabbage. 'It's not the horses we're worried about,' she said. 'Horses can be boarded out.'

'This is my mother,' Harold said. She was wearing wellingtons and a green tam pulled down hard to cover all her hair. 'Mam, this is Miss Mathews—'

'Lorna, please.'

'She's Mr Wyndham's new secretary. She's

180

helping to get the furniture and that ready for the auction.'

'I'm Blossom,' the old woman said. 'In the old days, the boss always had secretaries and valets and all that. We had twelve horses here at one time.'

'My dad looked after them,' Harold told her. 'That was his job.'

'Mr Wyndham used to keep a hunter and you should have seen the carriages they had.'

'The governess cart is still here if you want to see that,' Harold grinned at her.

'I meant the victoria and the barouche. Our Harold's the only outside help left. Used to be six gardeners here at one time, you know. Aye, things have come to a pretty pass nowadays.'

Blossom tucked a wisp of grey hair under her tam. 'I'm worried that none of us will have a roof over our heads for much longer. Lived here over these stables for the last fifty years, we have. Now we have to go.'

Harold said, 'I was brought up here and so was my dad, so none of us is looking forward to moving, and not knowing where...'

'I'm sorry, I didn't realise. Won't Mr Wyndham take you with him?'

'That depends, doesn't it?' The old lady was kicking at a weed coming through the cobble-stones.

'He doesn't know where he's going,' Harold explained, 'so nobody knows if there'll be space for us.'

'There's other reasons.' The old woman looked defiantly at her son. 'How do we know Mr

181

Wyndham will help us now?'

'Mam! Don't start that again. The boss won't hold it against us after all this time.'

Blossom took Lorna's arm and turned her away.

'Don't listen to her.' Harold was backing off. 'It's just tittle-tattle. Nothing in it.'

His mother's voice was confidential. 'There was awful trouble years ago. Our Harold... He was seventeen. You know how hot-blooded lads can be at that age. It was touch and go whether we were thrown out there and then.'

'Surely not!'

'But Tom's a good worker and he'd been here a long time. We made our Harold apologise.'

'What did he do?'

'You may well ask. I blame Rosaleen for it. She was leading him on. Such a flibbertigibbet she was then. Only fourteen and meeting the village boys in the woods. Hard to believe when you look at her now. She's gone real sour. It wasn't just our Harold, she went with others. He was the one caught with her, kissing her in the orchard. Not much more than kissing, though she'd got some of her clothes off. Not very nice and, of course, our Harold got the blame.

'Mrs Wyndham sent for us all to go up. She was shocked and the boss was furious. They didn't believe Rosaleen could do any wrong, and said the village boys were our Harold's friends. Packed her off to boarding school to get her out of the way after that. That's what they did.'

The facts were coming so fast Lorna could hardly take them all in. 'Mr Wyndham will help

182

you find another house, I'm sure.'

'He told me not to worry, that if there was no room in his new place, he'd find somewhere close for us,' Blossom said.

'There then.'

'I used to work in the house too, you know. Those were the good old days. Aye, it's right lonely now, nobody to talk to. Come up and have a cup of tea with me.'

'I'd love to, but I'm supposed to be working.' Lorna liked her ceaseless chatter. She'd learned a great deal about Rosaleen without asking one question. 'I should get back. Another time perhaps?'

The old woman sighed. 'Aye, another time.'

Lorna watched her go indoors before turning to leave. Across the yard, she could see Harold talking to a man who was polishing an old Daimler. She went over.

'It looks good, Dad. You've got a good shine on it.' Lorna was introduced to him. She'd heard him referred to as Tom in the house.

'Clean it is all I can do.' He had a toothless smile. 'Never learned to drive these things, or fix them when they go wrong. I leave all that to our Harold.'

'The trouble is, my mam and dad should have retired years ago,' Harold said. 'But living over the job like, they give a hand when needed. Dad helps me with the horses and the grass cutting, but Mam hardly does anything now and she misses it.'

Next to the Daimler was an almost new open Alfa Romeo sports car. Lorna admired the very latest design and immaculate red paint work.

'That's Miss Rosaleen's,' Harold explained. 'She drives herself. What I'd choose if I had the money.'

He paused when they reached the great arched entrance.

Lorna said, 'It's hard for you, losing your home. I feel for your mother.'

'Mam talks a lot about the old days,' he smiled. 'Still living in the past, really, but she's seventy-five, so there's some excuse.'

Lorna hurried back to the house, thinking over what he'd said. Talks a lot about the old days? Still living in the past? Blossom had worked in the house, she'd have known her mother. Lorna made up her mind to go back and talk to her soon. With a bit of luck, she'd learn a lot more about the family.

Now she'd put some distance between herself and Rosaleen by moving to her new house, Daphne wasn't keen on visiting Otterspool every few days, but, as Crispin pointed out, that girl Lorna was working through the guest rooms, turning up all manner of treasures. He pressed her to go, it wasn't often they were in agreement these days.

'Look out for anything of value,' he said. 'Mustn't let all those antiques be sold off. Impossible for us to collect things like this again. They don't often come on the market.'

She'd noticed he'd brought some guns back with him last time he'd been there, cased sets. One was a presentation pair of Colt model revolvers, hand-engraved, with gold and silver inlays at breech and muzzle.

Only last week, Daphne had been able to bring home a Roullet & Decamps musical automaton of a furry cat. It waltzed round its stand when wound up, and had green glass eyes. It was French, of course. Mirabelle had one similar and had told her it was worth a lot of money. Daphne felt she should go again today. She mustn't pass up the opportunity of getting more. She telephoned Otterspool House and was glad it wasn't Rosaleen who answered.

'There's so much needs doing, Aunt Maude, that I feel I have to come over and give Rosaleen a hand. Could you send the Daimler over to fetch me? Yes, thank you, any time Harold is free.'

Harold was at her door within twenty minutes – before she was ready. She made him wait.

Daphne had kept her keys. There was nobody about in the great hall when she arrived. She went straight upstairs to see if Lorna had turned up anything else of value, opening each door in turn to look round. She mulled over all the things that had been laid out where they could be seen, seeking treasure, and came across an attractive French brass spark guard. She admired anything French and decided she'd like it.

Sometimes Lorna left notes in neat handwriting, saying a piece of silver had been removed to the butler's pantry, or china to the still room. Daphne came across one.

'Two porcelain models of kestrels perched on flower-encrusted tree trunks, painted, marked Bow 1760.'

185

They sounded interesting. Daphne decided she'd take a look. She headed back downstairs with the spark guard, having seen nobody. There were many more pieces of china laid out in the still room. The kestrels were lovely; she must have those. She was looking for something to wrap them in when she heard Rosaleen's footsteps on the stone flags outside. She'd put the light on, so Rosaleen would know someone was here. She froze as the door swung back. Rosaleen's lip curled in contempt.

'Not again? What are you stealing now? We're losing half our things before the sale.'

Daphne felt her stomach muscles cringe; it was an effort to stay calm. 'You know your father told Crispin to take what he wanted. He'd rather these bits and pieces stayed in the family.'

'He didn't tell you to help yourself. Not you.'

There was no mistaking the malice in Rosaleen's pale blue eyes. Daphne found some newspaper and started wrapping up the kestrels. She was determined to have them.

'Leave those here. They're not yours to take.'

'Don't be silly, Rosaleen.'

There were several other pieces by Bow here but she couldn't look at them now, she had to get away. She'd learned to kick back at her sister-in-law.

'Your problem, Rosaleen, is that you have no life of your own. You interfere in things that don't concern you and which you don't understand.'

Daphne made a hasty exit and rushed round to the stable block only to find there was no sign of Harold or the car. Blossom told her he'd taken

Aunt Maude shopping. She had to creep quietly back into the house through the garden door, and telephone for a taxi to take her home. It was only when it was turning out of the main gates that she realised she'd forgotten the spark guard.

Daphne felt she'd been routed. She was seething. Rosaleen never missed a chance to jab her knife in, but it wasn't often she could get back at her.

Lorna went home again on the following Saturday and her mother sliced up cold pork for tea.

'We had the top end of the leg for dinner yesterday,' she said. 'Your dad and Jim have been home this week. We had a good time, didn't we, Pam? Took us to the pictures twice.'

To make up for the extravagance, Mum stewed shin beef for their Sunday dinner. Pamela went out after they'd washed up and Lorna told her mother what had happened during the week.

'Still nothing about Oliver, I'm afraid.'

Her mother frowned. 'It worries me to think of you there amongst that family.'

'I'm all right. They'll have forgotten about you, and, anyway, nobody could possibly know you're my mum. I told you Hilda was still there, didn't I? How did you get on with her?'

'Hilda's all right. Not a bad sort, but could be a bit sly. Fancy her still being there after all these years.'

'What d'you mean, sly?'

'Well, she's like them, another that looks after number one.'

187

'She's loyal to the family. Works hard.'

'Only if there's something in it for Hilda.'

'And Blossom Jones?'

'Is she still there too?' Her mother smiled. 'I liked her better. She never stopped talking. And her husband, Tom? I feel better about you being there now. D'you know, I'd like to send Blossom my regards.'

'No, Mum! I can't do that.'

'Come up to my bedroom. I've been going through my things.' She looked self-conscious. 'I found these. I thought I ought to show them to you.'

'What are they?'

'Newspaper cuttings.' Mum was biting her lip.

'"Tragic accident".' Lorna read the heading and her heart turned over. It was all there just as Mum had told it. The Coroner's verdict was accidental death. There was another cutting reporting Oliver's funeral and a blurred photograph of the family in full mourning. Mr Wyndham looked young and upright, Crispin a mere stripling. Both were staring straight ahead. The women were heavily veiled and could have been anybody.

'This is John, the war hero.' Mum's worn finger prodded at the faded newspaper. 'And this is Piers, who died of flu. In a way, the family got what it deserved.'

'Mum!' That brought home to Lorna just how much her mother disliked the Wyndhams.

'They did me down and if life itself made them suffer, then I'm glad. At the time I was so angry, I kept thinking up ways to get my revenge. I couldn't stop myself. I wanted to knife them, see them boiled in oil, but dream and fret was all I did. Fate took over and took revenge for me. They got what they deserved.'

Lorna swallowed hard and covered her mouth with her hand. Of course, Mum had suffered terribly; she hadn't been able to see her way forward; she'd even tried to end her own life.

'Oliver meant everything to me. I can still see him clearly in my mind's eye.' Lorna saw her mother's eyes go towards the wedding photograph of Sam's parents. She took it down from the mantel shelf.

'Your father... I mean Sam, hardly knew his parents. His father was killed in the Boer War and his mother died of tuberculosis.' Alice prised the frame open. From behind that photograph, she drew out another.

'This is Oliver.' She put a sepia photograph crazed with cracks in front of Lorna. It was easy to see how many times it had been handled.

'My father!' Lorna was enthralled. A young man smiled out at her. He had curly hair but though Lorna studied it for ages, she could see no other noticeable resemblance to herself.

'When you went back to Otterspool,' Lorna heard her own voice shake, 'back to see Daphne...'

'Rosaleen was there too.'

'You told them Oliver was my father?'

'Yes, I had to. I was scared stiff. I knew they'd tried to persuade him to change his mind about getting married, but he'd promised me nothing would do that. He said he'd made a will so whatever happened, you and I would be all right.'

189

'A will? Did you mention the will to them?'

'Yes. I was desperate for money. I owed for my room, and had nothing left to buy food.'

'And they gave you nothing?'

'Sent me off with a flea in my ear; made out I was trying to sponge on them, that Oliver had never made a will, that he had nothing much to leave anyway.'

'Had he?'

'He hadn't started working in the business. He spent a lot of time there in the school holidays but he wasn't paid.'

'Then how...?'

'He was given an allowance of two hundred pounds a year. He also said he had a share in a family trust that brought in a hundred or so more. By their standards I don't suppose it was much, by mine it would have meant wealth. My wage was twenty pounds a year and my keep.

'They said they didn't believe Oliver had had anything to do with me. They put it to me that the father was Ben, the under gardener, who'd run off with one of the housemaids although he was already married. They referred to him as "the local Casanova we were unfortunate enough to employ".'

Lorna sat back but continued to study the photograph.

'Mum, they're all very cagey about Oliver. They don't want to talk about him. The other day, Rosaleen said his name for the first time but afterwards, she shot off like a frightened hare. So I've found out nothing. But I will, sooner or later. I'll find out what happened to him.'

That seemed to satisfy her mother. 'What about the children? They were quite sweet really, the only Wyndhams who were. Perhaps they've grown up to be haughty and snobbish like the rest of the family?'

'Adam, yes. I'm not sure about Clarissa – I don't see much of her – but Jonathon, he's different. Friendly...'

'You be careful, Lorna. I wouldn't trust one of them. I don't want you ending up in trouble.'

Lorna was beginning to understand the true depth of the resentment her mother felt.

'Don't worry, Mum. I won't. I can look after myself. Anyway, forewarned is forearmed, isn't it?'

It ought to be, but Lorna found herself thinking about Jonathon when she went to bed. Pam was breathing deeply beside her, while Lorna relived the time he'd shown her round the red drawing room.

Chapter Ten

Jonathon no longer looked forward to Sundays. He usually took the *Water Gypsy* for a sail up the river, but it was raining heavily in the morning and he didn't feel like it – not by himself. If Lorna had been here, perhaps. He had to stop thinking about Lorna. She'd captivated him, was holding him in thrall, but like Carla, Lorna didn't always seem to welcome his attention. There were moments when she seemed open and friendly but others when he got the feeling she was definitely keeping him at arm's length. He was well over Carla now, but it would be more than hurtful if the same thing happened twice. It was making him hold back, half expecting another rebuff.

Jonathon had jobs to do but didn't feel like doing them. He started reading through some letters and documents he'd found in his parents' room, but they told him nothing new. He went for a walk in the rain.

On Sundays they had a larger than usual lunch, and Grandpa and Aunt Maude dozed in the afternoon. At supper time, Jonathon was down in the dining room early, not because he was hungry but because he was bored. The walls there were hung with marine pictures that never failed to interest him. He was studying them when the second gong went and his grandfather came in. Jonathon knew he thought the family portraits more decorative and artistic.

'I like our ship pictures too, of course. Did you know they're correct in every detail?'

'Yes.'

'Painted by men who loved the sea and understood ships.'

'They must have been good draughtsmen.'

'Painted for people who love ships too,' Quentin said. 'We ought to list all these pictures. I hardly know what we've got.'

'I'll help you. We could make a start after supper. You can tell me all about them.'

'Ought we to wait for the girl?'

192

Jonathon brightened up. 'Lorna will be back by then.'

Aunt Roz was late coming down and the meal proceeded slowly with all the usual formality. Jonathon drank coffee in the drawing room afterwards, expecting Lorna to join them at any moment. The trouble with a house of this size was that one couldn't hear people come and go.

Grandpa started telling him about the portrait over the mantelpiece. 'Let me get a notebook first,' Jonathon said, but the old man ambled off to his favourite chair.

Jonathon went to the kitchen and found Lorna tucking in to a plate of roast beef and pickles. Her brown curly hair was still damp from the walk up the drive. She looked very young.

'Hello,' he said, delighted to see her. 'I was coming to ask Hilda if you were back. Grandpa's going to take me round the family portraits. I wondered if you'd like to come too.'

'Yes, I'd love to.'

'He'll tell us what he knows about them and I'll make a list for the sale.'

'That's my job.'

He watched her butter another slice of bread. 'I didn't mean to interrupt your supper.'

'I've almost finished.'

Clearly she had not. Jonathon felt guilty. 'Really, you shouldn't be working until tomorrow.'

'This is hardly work. Wouldn't miss it for anything.' Lorna stood up, still eating. 'I'll need a pencil and paper.'

'I've got all that.'

'If, as well as a list of the pictures, I list your

ancestors and their dates, it will help us to put together a family tree later on.'

'That's what I thought. By the way, you've pushed him into deciding on a firm of auctioneers. He's got it all organised now.'

'The ones Mrs Cartwright used?'

'No, this firm is based in London. They have specialists who'll cream off the best of our stuff into their London auction rooms. They get the highest prices that way.'

'Good. I never thought of that.'

'The specialists are coming tomorrow, two in the morning to look at the pictures and the furniture, and two more in the afternoon for the silver and china.'

'Your grandpa will be finding this hard.'

Jonathon led the way to the drawing room. The old man had dozed off clutching his copy of the *Sunday Times*. Jonathon studied him, feeling a stirring of sympathy. His mouth was open, his skin wrinkled and his cheeks sunken. He looked none too well.

'Poor Grandpa,' he said. 'He finds it all exhausting. Really, he'd rather be left in peace.'

His voice caused his grandfather to give a little snort and pull himself up in his chair. His pale damp eyes looked at them vaguely, then he remembered why they were there. 'You're ready to list the paintings?'

'Yes.' Jonathon pointed to the portrait over the mantelpiece. 'Tell us about this man, Grandpa.'

'That's the man who founded the family fortune.'

Lorna stood on tiptoe to peer at it. It was of a

194

man in his early thirties with butter-blond hair and matching curly beard. His face was strong; his sea-green eyes seemed to be scanning the horizon.

'"Captain Lars Wyndham, seventeen fifty to eighteen twenty",' Jonathon read from the name plate beneath. Like most of the pictures in the house, the smoke of coal fires over the centuries had darkened it.

'We aren't starting in the right place.' His grandfather pulled himself to his feet and prepared to lead the way. They went round the great hall where the family portraits hung on chains from a high rail, large ones interspersed with smaller ones. He stopped in front of a blank oblong of paler panelling.

'Is there a picture missing from here?' Lorna asked.

'Yes, the portrait that used to hang there was of Captain William Wyndham and his wife, Viveca. She was the daughter of a Scandinavian sea captain and they had fourteen children. They founded the family.'

'So the family tree would start with them?' Lorna was scribbling in the notebook Jonathon had given her.

'Yes, Lars Wyndham, whose portrait you saw in the drawing room, was one of their sons. He built this house.'

'What happened to this picture?' Lorna wanted to know. 'It's sold already?'

'No, Crispin wanted it to hang in his new house. He had it professionally cleaned. It's come up wonderfully well. There's much more detail to be seen in it now.'

'Grandpa wants the family to keep as much stuff as possible,' Jonathon told Lorna.

'I wish we could keep it all together, but that isn't possible.' Quentin sounded sad.

'So that's why the Wyndhams are so fair,' Lorna said, 'the Scandinavian blood?'

'Yes. There were a lot of them in the eighteenth century. Mostly sea captains.' His grandfather mentioned the painters' names with pride and some had a familiar ring to Jonathon's ears.

Lorna said, 'Your family must have made a great fortune in their early days to have a collection of family portraits like this.'

Jonathon smiled. 'Shouldn't wonder if they didn't see themselves as aristocrats.'

The old man said, 'List each picture with the dates of the person portrayed and the name of the painter.'

Many were of men in the costumes of seafarers of the time, but some were in formal dress.

'William Wyndham Penn served on the town council,' Quentin told them. 'The only Wyndham to take an interest in that – must have been his Penn blood.'

The light was shining down on Lorna's hair, showing up gold highlights. 'Even if these were not family portraits,' she said, 'some are very attractive in their own right. Like this one.' They were looking at a picture of Mrs Drusilla Wyndham, a Victorian beauty. 'And this would enhance any room.'

They moved on to a family group picnicking on the banks of the Mersey. There were several more showing the house in the background, but there were so many generations, and not all could be dated. Jonathon couldn't envisage any sort of family tree.

There were more family pictures in the main drawing rooms and in the library. In the music room, his grandfather paused for a long time, looking up at the portrait on the chimney breast.

'My wife, Marina,' he said to Lorna, who was studying the picture too.

'She was beautiful.'

It made Jonathon look more closely. She had been beautiful in her youth. He could remember her clearly but by then she'd been middle-aged.

'I miss her,' his grandfather said. 'And I miss her music. She used to play Chopin for me. I shall hang this picture in my study in the new house.'

Jonathon could see how moved he was and ushered him to the summer drawing room. A growing number of oil paintings, watercolours, tapestry pictures and etchings were stacked against one wall. Lorna was bringing down pictures from the bedrooms, salons and boudoirs as she sorted through them. It was taking a long time to list them all.

She frowned. 'I find it hard to see your ancestors as living people who ate and slept.'

'And worked,' Jonathon said. 'They're remembered because of their work.'

'They worked hard,' his grandfather told them. 'They achieved a good deal.'

'Let's look at the marine pictures,' Jonathon urged when they'd sorted through all the others.

197

Quentin led them towards the dining rooms. 'These were the ships our family owned.'

The formal dining room was vast. As in the hall a multitude of oil paintings – mostly of ships under full sail – hung on chains from a rail.

'Are you going to sell these?' Jonathon didn't want to see them dispersed, but where would they be able to hang them in a small house?

'I'm afraid so, most of them, if buyers can be found. I know you're fond of them, Jonathon. You must choose one or two to keep.'

'Thank you, I'd like to.'

'This is Captain Lars's schooner, the *Flying Cloud*.' Quentin's silver-headed cane pointed it out. 'A very fast ship. Not his first – that was the brig *Viveca Mary*, thirty-six tons, over here.'

'Not very big then?' Lorna knew the ship Sam Mathews worked on was over six hundred tons.

'They were all small in those days.'

Lorna was studying the *Flying Cloud* carefully. 'Where did they trade?'

'Africa mainly,' Jonathon said.

'The west coast, the Guinea Coast,' Quentin told them, his face shining with pride.

Jonathon too studied the *Flying Cloud*. He'd read a good deal about vessels of that era. 'There are a lot of openings along the side. What could they be for? Would it be ventilation?'

'Yes. Don't forget they were sailing in tropical waters.'

Jonathon tensed. What he was looking at would provide added ventilation to the hold. He moved on round the room. The picture of the *Northern Light* showed it had the same openings, and the

198

Flying Fish, and the *Wave Crest* and the *Sylph*. The reason came back at him then, making him sweat.

'What cargo did they carry, Grandpa?' His voice seemed to squeak.

'Going out, it was trade goods.'

'You mean beads, hand mirrors, that sort of thing?'

'Yes, enamel goods and cotton cloth from Manchester. It was what the natives wanted. Even the missionaries needed to take goods of that sort. They bartered them for materials to build their churches. Our ships brought back gold. You've heard of Guinea gold? Ivory too, and palm oil – they called that liquid gold. Anything the coast produced that could be sold in Liverpool.'

Jonathon was afraid that wasn't the complete truth, and his growing shock and fear knocked the wind out of him.

'Some are by the finest marine painters of the time,' his grandfather went on. 'This is by Joseph Heard, and this is a Robert Salmon.'

Lorna was moving round the room, making notes of what she saw. 'I've never heard of those two, unlike the portrait painters.'

'Marine painters are specialists. They need a scientific eye; they're draughtsmen with an interest in ships' architecture. To them, it's not just art, making an agreeable picture.'

'And their pictures would be accurate in every detail?' Jonathon wanted that confirmed.

'Yes, they'd be painted from life, from the original vessel.' His grandfather sighed heavily. 'All long gone now. This is making me feel my own mortality.' He was heading for his study. 'Particularly since my allotted span is already over. Probably, I've spent more time on this earth than most of my forebears, but I've got less to show for it.'

When the study door closed on his grandfather, Jonathon stood with his hands in his pockets feeling sick.

The following morning, Lorna was surprised to find Rosaleen had come down to the dining room instead of having her breakfast in bed. Crispin and his family arrived ten minutes later and joined them at the table.

'Aren't they here yet?' Daphne wanted to know.

Crispin glared at his father. 'I thought you said early.'

'Nine o'clock is what they said to me.'

Lorna remembered then that the auctioneers were sending in their experts today to evaluate the furniture and domestic bric-a-brac.

'There's time for us to have a cup of coffee.' Clarissa yawned. Lorna admired her blue coat in the new loose and longer style.

'I'll have tea,' Daphne said. She looked peevish.

Lorna got to her feet. 'I'll tell Hilda.'

'Perhaps some more toast too,' Crispin called after her.

Hilda wasn't pleased. 'Why couldn't they have breakfast at home before coming?' she complained. 'Connie should be doing this.'

Lorna helped her assemble the cups and saucers. The toast was what Hilda had made for her own breakfast.

When Lorna took the tray to the breakfast room, old Mr Wyndham said to her: 'I want you to come round with us and take a note of what they say and the prices they suggest each piece should make.'

It seemed to her that the experts had come to advise him, but the rest of the family trooped behind him, hanging on to every word, and noting for themselves every price that was mentioned. Lorna thought they were afraid of missing out on something. They assessed the family portraits first and then the furniture.

Occasionally, Daphne or Adam would ask Quentin if they might have a piece of furniture rather than letting it go in the sale.

'I thought you'd already decided what you wanted for yourselves,' Quentin said irritably.

It seemed to Lorna that they were asking for items on which the experts put an unexpectedly high value. Crispin's family stayed to lunch, which threw Hilda into a worse mood. Afterwards, other experts arrived to evaluate the silver, plate and old china. Clarissa pushed herself forward so as not to miss a word of what was being said. When they came to a fine George III silver tea and coffee set on a salver, she asked her grandfather if she might have it. He agreed.

'I'll take it home with me,' she cooed. 'Thank you. I shall take good care of it.'

Rosaleen pulled a face, not wanting to lose it from the sale.

When, half an hour later, Clarissa asked if she might also have a vast collection of ornate silver cutlery in mahogany cases, Rosaleen's expression hardened. Later still they came to a toilet set of silver-backed brushes and cut-glass perfume bottles.

'I really love this, Grandpa,' Clarissa murmured, stroking the brushes.

'I'd rather like to have that myself,' Rosaleen put in, reluctant to see anything else pass to her niece.

'Please, Grandpa,' Clarissa wheedled. 'Please say I can have this too.'

'Well, provided you listen to your parents and put Dr Vincent McDonald out of your mind.'

'Thank you, thank you, Grandpa,' she replied easily. She reached up and kissed his cheek. 'I really love old silver.'

Lorna reckoned she'd been given more of value than the other members of the family. It seemed her grandfather doted on her and could deny her nothing.

Rosaleen looked grim as the day wore on.

The following Sunday evening when Lorna returned from her day off, she met Jonathon in the hall.

'I've been busy today,' he said. 'I've turned out my mother's rooms and rescued no end of oddments. She left cupboards full of stuff: watches that don't go, cigar cutters that must have belonged to Dad, old purses, that sort of thing. I've parcelled up everything worth having to send to her. There's a few photograph albums too.'

'I'd love to see them.' Lorna was keen. She was thinking of the one picture of Oliver that Mum had treasured for the last twenty years. 'It'll help me to see them as real people,' she said to explain her enthusiasm to Jonathon.

'Come up with me then.' Outside his room, he opened up the cabin trunk she'd helped him carry there.

'My father's watch,' he said, fondling a gold half-hunter. 'Everybody had pocket watches in his day. I think I might take it to a watch mender to see if it can be made to go. I might use it when I develop a paunch. Ah, here's the photograph albums.' He took out two leather-bound books and put them in Lorna's arms. 'We'd better go where there's a bit more light.'

'Down to the library?'

'Yes.' He led the way, carrying two more volumes, and slid them down on the handsome library table, while he fixed a lamp to shine down on the pages. Lorna couldn't take her eyes off him, his body seemed so lithe and graceful. She longed to touch him. Instead, she roughly pulled up a chair and opened one of the albums.

The strength drained from her knees when she saw the first photograph of three young Edwardian children with their nanny. She wondered if she'd come across a photograph of her mother. She hoped so.

The picture looked stiffly posed. The children were playing on the grass with the river in the background. One boy in a sailor suit had his arm round a spaniel, the other was engrossed with a toy train. The little girl was dressed in heavy frills and nursed a doll. All wore big uncomfortable-looking hats.

'You?'

'Yes, with Adam and Clarissa. I'm the one with the dog.'

'With your nanny.' Lorna studied the woman in uniform seated in a basket chair beside them. She was stout, with a pigeon chest. It was most definitely not her mother.

'Nanny Smithers. I was very fond of her.'

She turned a page, wondering how she could ask about her mother. Then a shiver ran down her spine. Here she was, young and pretty, laughing up at her with Clarissa, a baby in her arms.

'How many nannies did you have?' Lorna asked.

'That's Alice. She was our nursemaid.'

'If you had a nanny, what was the nursemaid for?' Her voice was unsteady.

'She tidied up the mess we made,' he grinned at her, 'washed our clothes and fetched up our meals. Alice used to play with us too and look after us at night. Here, take a look at this.'

He opened another album. The date, '3 July 1875', was embossed in gold leaf on the front.

'This is Grandmama on her wedding day.'

She was a beautiful young lady in a very ornate gown of lace and satin and corseted into an eighteen-inch waist, but it was the groom Lorna studied. Impossible to believe old Mr Wyndham had ever been such a handsome young man. She could see the family likeness in him here. He radiated youthful energy, delight at gaining such a bride and hope and high expectations for the future. It saddened Lorna that he'd become so disillusioned.

There was another photograph of a large group of exotically dressed guests taken in front of the house.

'Do you know who all these people are?'

He shook his head. 'I think this was my great-grandmother.'

'You should get your grandfather to put a name to all those he can.'

Lorna turned a page and the interleaved tissue paper and looked at a photograph of the tables laid for the wedding breakfast under the trees, with sun dappling the ornate silver and flowers. Another picture showing the five-tier wedding cake. What Lorna wanted to see were photographs of their children. She opened another of the albums and felt a little frisson of joy when at last she'd found what she was looking for.

Beside her, Jonathon said, 'They're mostly of family occasions, of course. Oh Lord! This is my christening.'

'Your parents... John and...?'

'Frances, my mother.'

They were standing side by side in a stiff and formally posed group picture.

'Would these be the clothes they went to church in?'

His father was wearing full morning dress; his mother was in high-necked satin and an enormous hat. Jonathon was in his mother's arms, wearing a robe of exquisite Honiton lace that reached almost to the floor. Lorna's finger went along the line of guests.

'I recognise your Uncle Crispin and Daphne.' Daphne looked proud of being part of so distinguished a family even though she must have been quite young then. Adam was not much more than a toddler and Clarissa was a babe in Daphne's arms.

'And Rosaleen, of course.' She was in her twenties at this time. 'Wasn't she pretty?'

'Quite the belle of the family,' Jonathon said drily.

Lorna took a deep breath. Her chance had come at last. 'Who is this?'

'My Uncle Piers.'

'And this?' She could guess, of course – the family likeness and she'd seen that other photograph.

'My Uncle Oliver.'

She dared to say, 'I've not heard you mention him before.'

Jonathon didn't answer immediately. To prompt him she asked, 'Was he killed in the war too?'

'No, he died in a boating accident before the war.'

'Oh, goodness! How awful, but a boating accident? You're all such keen sailors.'

He was biting his lip. She could see he didn't want to talk about it. She probed. 'What happened?'

At that moment, the lights flickered and went out.

'Oh, not again!' In total darkness Jonathon leaped to his feet. 'These power failures! There's nothing more infuriating.'

He struck a match and found some candles in elaborate sconces. He lit two. In the flickering light, he said, 'It happens so often we keep the candles handy all round the house. I'll have to go down to the power shed to see if I can get it on again. Harold isn't much good at this and the generator's worn out, like everything else here. You'll be all right?'

'Yes, of course. It's time I went to bed, anyway. Do you mind if I take these albums up to my room? I'd like to have a good look at them.'

Jonathon had gone. Candles and oil lamps were flickering in the hall and passages. Lorna went to the kitchen to get herself a small oil lamp, and then, making two journeys, she took all the albums up to her bedroom in the attic.

With a candle and an oil lamp alight, she opened one of the albums on her dressing table and pored over it. There were pictures of Oliver as a child. She had no difficulty picking him out from his brothers now. Oliver as a teenager sitting in a small boat, squinting up against the sun. That made her heart turn over. Was this the boat in which he'd drowned?

Lorna was captivated. She dipped into another album. More photographs of Oliver's parents and his siblings smiled out at her. Here was his family brought to life. It was hard to think of old Mr Wyndham as her grandfather, yet here was her family. The thought made her nerves twitch.

When the Wyndhams showed pride in their forebears, Lorna felt some of the shine fell on her. They were her forebears too, even if she was from the wrong side of the blanket.

Suddenly she heard shouts and people running about. A door slammed on the floor below. Lorna opened her door and peered down the black

207

staircase. Was that smoke she could smell? Fear shafted through her. Was the place on fire? She turned back for her candle and shot to the next room.

'Hilda? Are you there? Hilda?' She knew Hilda was in the habit of going to bed early. There was no answer and she found that unnerving. She went on to Sissie's door and banged on that.

'Yes?'

She threw open the door. Sissie's scared face peered over her sheet.

'I think there's a fire downstairs. Better get up. Is Hilda in bed?' She lit Sissie's candle from hers.

'Don't know.'

There was more noise down below. Lorna ran to throw open Hilda's door. Was she asleep? The room was in darkness and the draught blew out her candle. 'Hilda?' She had to return to her own room for the lamp. She went back holding it high. The bed was empty.

She heard Sissie's slippers slithering on the linoleum as she made for the steep stairs. There was a door on the floor below that led to their bathroom. Sissie snatched it open. Acrid smoke was billowing along the passage, making her cough. There seemed to be a lot of people milling round but Lorna's eyes were watering and through the smoke they seemed insubstantial shadows.

'It's all right.' That was Jonathon's voice.

Lorna groped her way towards the bedroom that years ago had belonged to Piers. The dustsheet had been pulled off the bed, together with pillows and a bolster and thrown on the

208

flames. Mr Wyndham was stamping on the last sparks while Jonathon was beating them out with Piers's cricket bat.

'I came back to phone for an electrician,' he panted. 'I can't do anything with that old generator. I decided I might as well go to bed.'

'Lucky you did. Whatever made you come to Piers's room, Rosaleen? What were you doing?' Her father was trying to force the window open. Jonathon had to help him. 'How could you be so careless?'

Rosaleen was choking with smoke and terror. 'I wasn't careless, I put the lamp down on the washstand.'

'Everything here is tinder dry. You know it would only take a spark for the whole house to go up.' Fear made her grandfather carp. 'We could all have been burned in our beds. Haven't I told you how dangerous it is to have all these naked flames about the house?'

'With the tiles, the washstand seemed the safest place.'

'But it wasn't.'

'The lamp slid off.'

'It couldn't slide off, Rosaleen. Don't be silly.'

'It did,' she wailed. 'I put a box of books on one end and after a few seconds everything slid off, including the lamp.'

Candles and lamps were held aloft to examine the washstand. It had a decided tilt. The feet on one side had gone through the floorboards, which were now badly charred. Hilda was sweeping up the broken glass and half-burned paper.

'The fire's burned a hole right through,' she

209

said. 'Just look at this.'

'Not the fire,' Rosaleen choked. 'I saw the hole before... Luckily there wasn't much oil left in the lamp. I noticed after I'd picked up that one. I was afraid it wouldn't last very long.'

'Surely it can't be...?' Jonathon took a penknife from his pocket and jabbed at the floorboards on the other side of the room. 'Butter soft!'

His grandfather took the knife from him and sliced a sliver off and crumbled it to flakes between his fingers.

'Dry rot!' He was aghast. 'It's spread here from the west wing.'

Lorna had noticed that some of the furniture left there had the same slightly skew-whiff look.

Jonathon had pulled part of a floorboard up and was examining little pools of sawdust beneath. 'The surveyor told us it would spread.'

'But this fast?'

'It's probably been going on for years unnoticed.'

The old man looked defeated. 'It's as well the place is going to be pulled down.'

The curtain behind the washstand was still smouldering. Jonathon yanked it from its rings. 'I must get this out of here.'

'And the carpet.' The carpet square was charred along one edge.

'No, don't take the carpet up,' his grandfather barked. 'The floors are dangerous; the carpet would prevent a person falling through. I don't think we should come in here. Have you finished sorting through this room, Jonathon?'

'I haven't started,' he said quietly. 'What were you doing here, Aunt Roz?'

'I thought I'd help you.'

'At this time of night? When there was no electricity?' Jonathon was on his hands and knees, peering at the detritus of the fire. 'A wooden box you said? Was that what you stood on the washstand? There are some bits of wood here. An orange box? What sort of books were in it?'

She shrugged. 'Just books.'

'Printed books? There's nothing left but burned paper, no charred covers.' He was stirring the contents of the bucket Hilda had filled with half-burned remains. 'Not private papers, diaries, that sort of thing?'

Rosaleen was almost in tears. There were black streaks on her face. 'How should I know? I didn't have time to look through them.'

'We'll never know now. Whatever it was has gone. You leave Piers's room to me, Roz. That's what we agreed.'

'Whatever's happened?' Maude Carey came fussing in, wearing a heavy sleeping net over her hair.

They were all trying to explain at once. Rosaleen dissolved in floods of tears.

'Come on, dear.' Aunt Maude put her lamp down so she could put an arm round her. 'You mustn't upset yourself. Not your fault. Come on, I'll see you into bed.'

'Sissie,' Hilda commanded, 'light the way for them, and make a hot drink.'

'Lucky you were in the next room, Jonathon,' his grandfather said. 'It could have been a lot worse.'

'At least the fire's out,' Lorna said, trying to

211

defuse the tension. 'You've got everything under control.'

Mr Wyndham was still being seized by bouts of coughing. 'You'd better be certain it's really out. We don't want it to flare up again once we all get to bed. Off you go, Hilda. It's getting late.'

'I'd better douse all these lamps and candles first.'

'I'm going down for a brandy.' The old man looked round. 'Would either of you like to join me? Bad for the nerves, a fire like that.'

'I'd better stay here,' Jonathon said grimly, 'just in case.'

'No thank you,' Lorna said. 'I'd rather go to bed.'

When he'd gone with his lamp she turned to Jonathon. 'Is Rosaleen expecting to find something of special interest in Piers's room?'

He gave her a strange look. She added, 'I saw her in here some days ago. She was looking through the drawers in that tallboy.'

'You know Aunt Roz, afraid she won't get her fair share of things,' he said easily. 'Making sure she keeps any valuables that turn up.'

Lorna smiled. 'I also heard her shut the lid of your cabin trunk as I was coming up the stairs.'

'Oh!' That made him straighten up. 'Give me a hand to lift it into my room now.'

As they stooped over it his hand brushed her wrist. Lorna felt a shiver of desire. She'd made up her mind to distrust everyone in this house, and she should. Jonathon wasn't telling her why he particularly wanted to turn out Piers's bedroom. There was something in there that all of them

212

wanted to get their hands on. Even so, there was something about Jonathon that drew her to him. She needed a friend here but she felt very wary about trusting him.

Chapter Eleven

Lorna was intensely curious about what the photograph albums could tell her. Each time she went to her room she dipped into them. She found pictures showing the family as they'd been around the time her mother had worked here. It made it easier to imagine what things had been like for her.

One evening she was taken completely by surprise to come across a photograph of Rosaleen as a bride. She hadn't known she'd ever been married and found it hard to believe. She'd even called her Miss Wyndham to her face and Rosaleen hadn't corrected her. So what had happened to the groom? Lorna studied his picture. Such a handsome man, with a waxed moustache with curly ends and dark hair brushed straight back from his forehead. In his morning suit, smiling down at Rosaleen, he seemed a husband any girl would be proud of.

On the spur of the moment, she picked up the album and knocked on Hilda's bedroom door. 'I've come across some old photograph albums,' she said, hoping Hilda would be interested and tell her more.

'Of the family?' She sounded cautious.

'I was wondering if you could help me – point out who all these people are. I need some idea – for when Mr Wyndham starts writing the family history.'

Hilda's big cotton cap was on the dressing table, her iron-grey hair was revealed to be straight and recently cut very short. She opened the album on her bed, stifling a yawn.

'Oh, it's Rosaleen's wedding. Wasn't she a lovely bride?'

'I didn't know she was ever married.'

'Oh yes, he was a Montague from Aigburth, and in business in a big way. Hotels, you know.'

'No, I come from the other side of the water.'

'Those are satin rosebuds round the hem of her gown, white and pink. She had real rosebuds to hold her veil on, and they matched exactly. Such a do, you wouldn't believe. Hundreds came to the reception. We had it here in the great hall and the garden.'

'What happened to him? The groom?'

'The war, you know.'

Hilda turned the page to look at a picture taken outside the church. 'I didn't see the actual wedding, of course. I was here preparing the wedding breakfast.'

'He died a hero, like her brother?'

'Yes, so I believe.'

'But why does she not count herself a widow? Call herself Mrs... What was it? Yes, Mrs Montague. Why does she act as though she's never been married?'

Hilda's dark eyes met hers warily.

214

'I don't think she counted the Montagues quite on a par with her own family. They'd made their money more recently and they weren't quite so rich. She wanted to revert to her own name. She's very proud of belonging to a family that can trace its line back through so many generations, almost like the aristocracy. They're all a bit strange, aren't they? Not like us ordinary folk.'

Lorna took the album back to her room, feeling there was more to it than that. She was disappointed Hilda hadn't told her more, and wondered if she'd been keeping a tight hold on her tongue.

The following day, after having lunch in the kitchen, Lorna was going back to work when she saw Aunt Maude heading towards the blue sitting room with her embroidery. It was a warm room because it got all the sun and Maude spent a good deal of her time there. Lorna decided to show her the photographs and shot upstairs to get them.

'Family photographs? Yes, I'd like to see them.' Aunt Maude was trying to thread a needle with red silk. 'Your eyes are better than mine, thread this for me, dear.'

She took off her thick spectacles and polished them. 'We've always been keen photographers. I expect you've found a lot?'

'Yes. Perhaps you can tell me who all these people are?'

Maude opened the first album, then got up and took them to a table in the window recess where the full sun fell on the page.

'Rosaleen's wedding?' She banged that album

shut and opened the other, flicking through the leaves quickly. That too was dismissed. She returned to her armchair. 'Those are professional photographs. Don't show them to Rosaleen, they'll only upset her. Pack them to go to the new house.'

'Perhaps Mr Wyndham–'

'Don't show them to him either. Just get them out of sight.'

Lorna knew she must have looked shocked. Aunt Maude added, 'Unhappy times for the family. No point in reminding us all of them now. Better forgotten.'

Lorna crept out. She'd learned one thing from Aunt Maude: the photographs held a story. She wished she'd taken them straight to Mr Wyndham, who might have told her, but now she couldn't. She hated having to pry into things that Aunt Maude thought were nothing to do with her. It wasn't something she normally did, but for her mother's sake she had to find out all she could before the chance was gone for ever.

The next afternoon, Lorna took two of the albums over to show Blossom Jones. Her son had said she lived in the past, that it was more real to her than the present. Lorna hoped to learn more. Harold was not about the stable yard but she found Tom grooming the horse Beano.

'Your wife told me to come over for a chat and a cup of tea when I had time,' she said. 'Would now be all right or will she be busy?'

He beamed at her. 'She's never too busy to chat. Nothing she likes better.'

He led Lorna to the back of the stables and up

216

a steep and narrow flight of stairs to the rooms above. His wife was making a stew, and the living room was filled with the scent of frying onions.

'You've come back. Nice to see you.' The stew pan was pulled to one side and forgotten. Lorna showed her the photograph albums and asked for help to put names to the family in much the same way as she had to Hilda.

'Old photographs? Oh, of Miss Rosaleen's wedding!'

They sat down at the table with the albums between them.

Lorna said, 'There doesn't seem to be any date on them – would you remember when she got married?'

'It was June, the roses were out. The summer before the war, nineteen thirteen it would be. The roses were lovely that year. She had them in her bouquet and her headdress.'

'Yes, she looks very happy.'

'Happy?' Blossom pulled a face. 'Well, if she was, it didn't last. He was a rotter.'

Lorna felt a glow of satisfaction. This was more like it. 'In what way?'

'It was her money he wanted, not her.'

'But he looks well-heeled, a real gentleman.'

'Not a gentleman! That's the last thing he was.' Her voice dropped. 'Even before the wedding, he had another woman and a son.'

That shocked Lorna. 'Then why marry Rosaleen?'

'Like I said, her family was rich, she had expectations.'

'But he looks quite a toff. Didn't his family

have hotels? He was one of the Montagues.'

'Yes, but he was a gambler too, couldn't stay away from the cards or the horses. His family thought a wife might settle him down, keep him away from temptation.'

'Poor Rosaleen! She found she couldn't?'

'Not a hope. Nothing could keep him away from the races. And she quite liked the night-life. Went out and about with him at first.'

Blossom's voice dropped another octave. 'She had a marriage settlement from her father. Hilda said it was ten thousand pounds and he went through it in next to no time.'

'No!' Lorna's curiosity was whetted. She huddled closer though there was nobody there to hear them.

'Our Wyndhams knew nothing about his gambling or the other woman. They encouraged Rosaleen – Crispin did specially. Henry Montague was one of his friends and they all thought him very suitable.'

'She'd feel used, let down. I don't wonder they didn't get on.'

'Didn't get on? They fought like tigers. You don't know her as well as I do.'

Blossom's wrinkled face lit up as she remembered more. 'She went to live in West Kirby with him. A fine new house she had. He persuaded her to use her money to buy it in their joint names. Later, Rosaleen discovered he'd taken out a big mortgage on it and used the money to pay off his gambling debts.

'Then she found he spent more time with his other woman. They said he preferred her to

Rosaleen. Her name was Betty; she used to be a parlourmaid in his father's house. He set her up in rooms and lived with her part of the time. I don't know whether it's true but they said Betty's father was in gaol, and Henry had supported her and her mother for years.'

Lorna knew that gossip would have been rife at the time. Rosaleen would have hated it.

'We heard all sorts of rumours about what he was up to, but he volunteered for the army, I'll say that for him.'

'Perhaps he was glad to get away by then.'

'Perhaps. Anyway, they made him a captain. He came here to the house once and had a terrible row with Mr Wyndham. Afterwards, Rosaleen came home looking awfully ill. In fact, she took to her bed for a time, and only began to look better after she heard he'd been killed.'

'But he died a hero in the war?'

'He was killed like a lot of others. I heard Rosaleen say she was glad to be rid of him so easily. That, for her, was much better than a divorce, and for him it was a fitting end. The Wyndhams celebrated.'

'So that's why she doesn't wear a wedding ring!'

'He was a fortune-hunter. For her it was an unhappy marriage. Rosaleen just wants to forget it ever happened. It cost the family a lot of cash. Harold says it made them much more money-conscious.'

Lorna was fascinated by what Blossom was telling her. She understood Rosaleen's preoccupation with money now. She'd returned to her own family and didn't want to miss out on a share of their wealth. Blossom went on to give it as her opinion that this experience had made Rosaleen and Crispin more grasping, that he thought Rosaleen's marriage settlement had been her share of the family money, and she shouldn't have more because she'd lost it. For the first time, Lorna felt sorry for Rosaleen. A marriage like that would change any woman, scar her for life. She could see Rosaleen wasn't happy now.

But what she couldn't get over was that Hilda hadn't even hinted at Rosaleen's misfortune. Hilda had said enough in the past for Lorna to know she had no love for Rosaleen. She'd expected her to open up, or at the very least make a passing reference to Rosaleen's unhappy marriage.

It surprised her to find Hilda showing such discretion. Perhaps it wasn't discretion, but loyalty to the family for whom she'd worked all her life? Hilda wasn't prepared to hand on gossip and rumour. If that was the case, Lorna would applaud it, but she couldn't help feeling Hilda might have her own reasons for saying nothing.

Lorna opened up the album of Jonathon's christening, hoping to get Blossom to talk about Oliver, who was pictured several times within. But the closing of one album had broken her concentration, and Blossom was looking at her clock.

'Is that the time? Tom and Harold will be in for their tea in five minutes and I've nothing started.'

'The stew?'

220

'For tomorrow's dinner. I didn't even make you a cup of tea.'

Lorna was aware she should be in the drawing room by now.

'We've had a lovely natter.' Blossom was putting her spectacles aside. 'I can't remember when I enjoyed myself so much. How about leaving that other book with me? I'd like to look through it after tea. Tom would too.'

'I'm sorry,' Lorna said, knowing she'd learn nothing that way. 'Mr Wyndham's instructions. I mustn't let things like this out of my possession. I'll bring it back another time, shall I?'

She knew that sounded as though she didn't trust her to take care of a few old photographs. Blossom's old face seemed to close up. Lorna was afraid she'd pointed out too clearly that it was her gossip she wanted. 'Photos bring the memories pouring back, don't they?' she said, trying to soften it as she took her leave.

Lorna had heard a great deal about Rosaleen's marriage and the effect it had had on the family, but she kicked herself for not starting with the other album. Finding out more about Oliver was more important to her. She had to run up to her attic bedroom to leave the albums before she went to the white drawing room. When she got there she found Rosaleen and her father had finished their tea.

'You do work hard,' Rosaleen said sarcastically. 'You'll need a fresh pot. Ring for Hilda.'

Lorna lifted the tea tray and headed towards the kitchen, glad there were no questions about what she'd been doing. On her return, she met

221

Jonathon in the hall. He held open the drawing-room door for her. Rosaleen and her father had already gone.

She poured tea for them both and watched him help himself to a buttered scone and piece of Swiss roll from the trolley.

'Place to ourselves.' He collapsed onto Rosaleen's favourite chair. 'I was thinking,' she could see him watching her, 'there's a film on at the Odeon that I'd like to see. *All Quiet on the Western Front.* Would you like to come with me?'

That took Lorna by surprise. She felt her heart turn over with pleasure. She wanted to say yes, she'd love to go with him, but...

She held back. This was not the way she intended to go. First, she needed to know whether she could trust him or not.

'That's very kind ... but I don't think I should.'

'Whyever not?' His bright blue eyes were staring at her.

'Your family wouldn't approve.' Even to her own ears she sounded prim and proper.

He was frowning. 'Not Aunt Roz, that's for sure, but does she matter?'

'I'm an employee here. I doubt your grandfather would like it.'

'Come on, you and I work hard.' He was persuasive. 'We deserve a break now and then.'

Lorna had felt a growing warmth in Jonathon's manner, but there were too many things she had to keep from him; too many things that would alter how he thought of her. She shook her head, unable to look at him now in case he saw how much she wanted to spend more time with him

222

and really get to know him. 'Better not.'

His voice had lost its warmth. 'What's the difference between going for a walk with me and going to the flicks with me?'

'You fell into step beside me,' she said, knowing he'd seen her leave and had run after her that first afternoon. She saw the pain in his eyes, and it pulled her up. It was as though she were saying she hadn't wanted his company.

'Right,' he said, leaping to his feet. 'I'd better go by myself then.'

She knew she'd hurt his feelings and was hurt herself. She wished things were different and she hadn't needed to choke him off, but she'd done the safest thing.

She had second thoughts about that over the following days. She could make herself do those things, but it was harder to stop thinking about him, fantasising about what she'd really like to do with him.

Lorna did her best to avoid him. She made a point of getting down to tea early and leaving the drawing room when she saw his car coming up the drive. At breakfast, she spoke to Quentin rather than to him. What she was doing in the house gave her plenty to talk about.

She brooded, always able to conjure up Jonathon's sun-tanned face and bright blue eyes in her mind's eye. She had read too many books and seen too many films not to know she was falling in love.

How marvellous it would be if she could respond to him as she wanted to, but she dared not. She was already hiding things from him; she

223

must hide this too.

Alice busied herself about the house, cleaning and cooking for Pamela and herself. But since Lorna had been working for the Wyndhams and coming home every Saturday, giving her news about them, they'd rarely been out of her thoughts.

She was pleased Lorna had come home again this afternoon, and saw right away that she was bursting with news. It raised her hopes, but when it all came out over their tea, it wasn't news about Oliver. Learning that Rosaleen had been married and it hadn't worked out left her a little flat. 'Serve her right,' she said.

'She had a very difficult time, Mum.'

'She gave me a difficult time too. You haven't found out anything about Oliver?'

Lorna was screwing up her face. 'Nothing. Where exactly was his bedroom? I haven't even found that out yet. Nobody mentions him.'

'It was the top room in the tower at the east end. There were three storeys just there.'

'Not near the other brothers?'

'Not near Piers. There were a lot of old aunts living with them at the time. Aunt Eliza Wyndham and Aunt Gertrude Slee. Mrs Wyndham's mother had the tower rooms for years – Oliver's grandmother, that is. When she found the stairs difficult to manage, they moved her down. It was only after she died that Oliver moved to her rooms.'

'I've cleared the tower rooms out already. I should have asked you sooner. I didn't realise.'

'You found nothing there?'

Lorna shook her head. 'Not even the usual collection of cricket bats and things a young man would have. I thought it was another spare room.'

'Somebody must have cleared out all his personal belongings.'

'Yes, I think that was done years ago, long before I went to sort things for the auction.'

Alice sighed. 'So when's this auction to be held?'

'They haven't decided yet. They're worried about having a large crowd in the house since they found the dry rot was spreading. Afraid someone might have an accident and go through one of the floors.'

'There's a stone floor in the big hall,' Alice remembered.

'Yes, marble. They can't decide whether to risk it and hold it there, or whether to have a marquee in the grounds. But that would mean everything had to be carried out to it.'

'In this weather? It would be very cold in a marquee.'

'They can't wait until spring. The house is sold with a completion date. I think they'll probably settle for the hall.'

'If they do, I'd love to go.' Alice had been toying with the idea for some time.

'Mum!'

'Who would recognise me now? I was a young girl then.'

'You're right. Rosaleen isn't the sort to remember what a nursemaid looked like. Nor Daphne.'

'There's Blossom and Hilda.'

'I doubt if they'll go. What could the staff

afford, even if they saw something they wanted?'

'Fancy Hilda still working there. What a dull life she's had.'

'I can guarantee you won't see her,' Lorna told her. 'The family won't want to be living there when the public invades their territory, that would never do for the Wyndhams. They'll move out before then and take Hilda with them. She'll have to stay home and cook dinner for when they return.'

Alice really wanted to see Otterspool House again. She'd never been able to accept Oliver's sudden death. Not knowing what had prevented him returning to her had brought a weight of grief and anguish she'd never been able to throw off.

She was apprehensive about going back to the house but determined not to let the public sale pass without doing so. She wouldn't get another chance.

Several days later, when she had finished sorting through the guest rooms, Lorna turned her attention to the seven empty bedrooms on the attic floor where once servants had slept. Most of them held two beds and one had three. It seemed that in days gone by, the staff would have had to share rooms. They were equipped with assorted patterns of cracked china jugs and basins as though they'd been expected to wash there. Lorna didn't expect to find anything of value here. The wardrobes were mass-produced and of plain deal. Their catches and handles were pock-marked with rust, as were the iron bedsteads.

Damp had distorted the small chests of drawers so they were almost impossible to open, but Lorna found nothing of use left in any of them. The pillows and eiderdowns were damp and mildewed, and in one room she found a mouse's nest in the straw palliasse that had once served as a mattress. She wrinkled her nose in distaste and fetched Rosaleen up.

'Oh, my goodness.' Rosaleen held a lace handkerchief to her nose. 'If we'd had a housekeeper these rooms need never have got into this state.'

'Shall I arrange for all this stuff to be burned?' Lorna asked.

'Well...'

She could see Rosaleen was reluctant to condemn anything as worthless.

'These straw palliasses anyway? Nobody sleeps on straw any more.'

'Good enough for servants.' Her eyes of blue ice were haughty, her voice hard. 'They might bring a few shillings in the sale.'

'Nobody will buy them in this state. Servants would refuse to sleep on them.'

'I expect these days they would. Servants don't know their place any more.' Lorna felt the implication was that she didn't know hers. She took Rosaleen to inspect the mouse nest. That clinched it.

'Yes, have the mattresses and pillows burned. They'll have to be taken outside. Get Harold to help you.'

'Right.'

'You could clear the attic next.' Rosaleen bustled along narrow passages to inspect it. 'The family have stored their surplus bits and pieces here in the roof space for generations.'

Lorna followed. She wasn't looking forward to this. The storage space covered a vast area stretching under the rafters. There were walls supporting the roof, breaking it up into compartments, all opening haphazardly one from another. There were no doors and in some places the walls had been completed and in others they had not.

'It's all such a jumble.' Rosaleen paused. 'There's so much crammed close together, it's impossible to see what's what.'

When they moved on, there was more of the same as far as Lorna could see. 'I must take care not to get lost. It could take me ages to find my way out.'

'There's more than one way down,' Rosaleen said. 'I say, just look at that.' It was a stuffed peacock in a big glass case, with all its tail feathers spread out. 'I remember that being downstairs. We had peacocks here when I was a child.'

Seeing the roof attics for a second time, they seemed to hold more than ever. Lorna remembered the penny-farthing bicycle, but there was also a Victorian bath chair and a sewing machine, which must have been one of the first ever made. Goodness knows what treasures she'd unearth when she started to move things round.

'This isn't going to be a room-by-room job.' She was appalled at the size of the task. Goods were piled up one on top of another.

'You'd better move all the furniture to one part first, and all the china to another and so on.'

'Perhaps, if I cleared out the spare staff bedrooms first, I could use them to divide things up.'

'Yes. The bedsteads can be taken out to the stables. Garden tools and such like will be sold from there.'

'I'll need help,' Lorna told her. 'Can I get Tom and Harold to lift the furniture about?'

'I suppose so. I don't want anything taken from here without me seeing it.'

'Of course not, Miss Wyndham,' she said.

Over the next few days, Lorna worked hard. Even with Tom and Harold with her, they kept losing their bearings and wasting time looking for a way out. Harold brought a piece of chalk so they could make white arrows on the walls. That helped.

Chapter Twelve

After lunch one Saturday, the telephone rang as Quentin was pouring himself a second cup of coffee. When Rosaleen returned from answering it she looked put out.

'That was Crispin. He wants to come to dinner tonight and bring all his family.'

Quentin sighed. Dinner time had been more peaceful since Crispin and his family had moved out. 'I thought we'd had the farewell dinner.'

'That's exactly what I said.'

'He must want something.' Maude looked up from her embroidery.

'What?'

'He wouldn't say.' Rosaleen helped herself to coffee. 'I mean, Daphne was here all yesterday morning – she might have mentioned it then instead of springing it on me like this. As if Hilda hasn't enough to do.'

'He could bring Connie back to help,' Jonathon pointed out.

'He did offer to do that. He's coming to ask you for something, I know.'

'He wants another of the pictures or more of the silver.'

Quentin didn't doubt they were right. He knew Crispin must be living beyond the income he was earning in the business. He and his family had always lived here and had every need fulfilled, but now he was having to meet his own expenses. He had extravagant tastes and a self-indulgent streak.

'That's why Daphne comes over all the time. She rushes upstairs to see if Lorna has discovered anything special,' Rosaleen said spitefully.

Quentin wished she wouldn't bicker with her sister-in-law. There was more than enough for them all.

'A very nice pair of silver candlesticks this morning,' he said. 'That fellow from the auctioneers said they were made by John Carter in 1769. I can't imagine why they were put up in the attic.'

'We could use those at Hedge End. Don't give them to him.'

Maude said, 'I'm glad Jonathon's found us a house we all agree on.'

'Well...' Rosaleen began. Quentin knew she had her reservations about it.

230

'It'll be comfortable,' Jonathon said hurriedly. 'Only eighteen years old. It dates from just before the war so it's sturdily built and with seven bedrooms and servants' quarters.'

'Six really; one is a slit of a boxroom.'

'There'll be plenty of room for us,' Maude insisted. 'I'm glad we've made the decision.'

Rosaleen's mouth twisted. She looked bitter. 'I'm glad you'll be buying it. At least I'll have a roof over my head in my old age.'

'You'd have that whatever we did, my dear,' said Quentin.

That evening, within five minutes of Crispin's arrival, Quentin knew Rosaleen was right about his motives. He used his keys and led his family into the drawing room unannounced. He poured sherry for Daphne and Clarissa as if it was his own home. Clarissa came to kiss him. She was a beautiful girl, the sort an old man could feast his eyes on, but she was dark like her mother instead of being blond like the Wyndhams.

At fifty, Crispin had a chin that seemed to be receding into his thickening neck, and hair that was silver on his temples but showed little because he was fair. He helped himself and Adam to a glass of whisky. 'So you've got yourself a house, Father?'

'I think we've found what we want at last.' Quentin couldn't help but notice that his son's paunch was expanding. 'It's very different from this, of course, but it has to be. Are you still pleased with your choice?' He knew he shouldn't have asked as soon as the words were out of his mouth.

'Ye-es, I see nothing I like better.'

'Nothing nearly so suited to our needs,' purred Daphne, whose eyes were going round the room as if assessing the furnishings. She was bulging out of a grey silk dress.

'It's a big place you've chosen,' Jonathon said. 'Do you really need all those large rooms?'

'We love them, we really do,' Adam said. 'The house is exactly right for us, isn't it, Mother?'

'You'll be leaving to marry some beautiful young lady shortly,' she answered.

'Have you got a young lady?' Aunt Maude wanted to know.

Quentin glanced at Clarissa; he wouldn't dare say anything like that about her. There'd been too many arguments about her unsuitable boyfriends already.

Crispin looked as though he had more important things to discuss. 'We've decided that perhaps we should buy our house.'

Quentin was shocked. Did he intend to take out a mortgage? He said as calmly as he could, 'Plenty of time to think about that. Didn't you take a five-year lease on the place only three months ago?'

'Yes, but it might be cheaper to negotiate a price to buy now,' Crispin replied. 'Everything's so damned expensive.'

'Wiser to leave it,' Quentin advised. 'Adam could be married within the next three years – Clarissa too – and it would be too big for the two of you.'

Crispin said haughtily, 'I should feel obliged to offer Adam a suite of rooms with us, if he did marry.'

'Are you thinking of it?' Rosaleen demanded of her nephew.

'No,' Adam said.

Crispin leaned forward in his chair and spoke earnestly. 'I mean, Father, when has a Wyndham ever had to buy his own house? Certainly not since seventeen seventy-three.'

The gong sounded outside in the hall, booming through the house. Rosaleen leaped to her feet, trying to put an end to the conversation. They all knew where it was leading.

'It's roast beef,' Maude announced. 'Sunday's lunch, but the best I could manage on the spur of the moment.'

'Very good it will be, I'm sure.' Quentin pulled himself to his feet.

Crispin and his family all remained seated.

'I was wondering, Father, when you planned to sort through the jewellery you keep in your safe?'

'Would you need any help to sort through it?' Daphne asked. 'It'll have to be done before you go.'

He thought that insufferable cheek on her part but bit back the retort that sprang to mind. 'None of it will go in the sale,' he said.

Clarissa smiled at him. 'In the picture you gave Daddy, Viveca Wyndham, William's wife, is positively weighed down with emeralds.'

'They're family heirlooms and small enough to take with me.'

'Drusilla, the Victorian beauty in the hall, wears a spectacular necklace,' Daphne said, 'but old-fashioned, not in modern taste at all.'

'Good as money in the bank,' Rosaleen said.

233

Quentin was afraid she might have heard him say that.

Crispin stroked his toothbrush moustache. 'Would you be prepared to give me one or two pieces to sell, so that I might buy my house? A roof over one's head is so much more important than keeping baubles like that.'

Rosaleen was stiffly erect at the door. 'Doesn't it occur to you that I might want to wear the family jewellery?'

'Let's have our dinner.' Quentin headed for the dining room. 'Hilda will be cross if we keep it waiting.'

He managed to move them to the table. The roast beef and Yorkshire pudding were superb, but it did not stop them bickering. Nothing would deflect their attention from the jewellery.

Crispin said, 'There are many pieces that no one would want to wear today, tiaras and such like.'

'You're acting like a vulture,' Rosaleen retorted, 'swooping on everything of value in this house to keep for yourself.'

'You don't understand, Rosaleen,' Crispin said angrily. 'I've had to find a lot of money to set us up in this new house and I've got nothing but my salary from the business.'

'And a share of any profit it might make at the end of the year.'

'If it makes a profit.'

'That's in your hands, isn't it?'

'Now Father's retired, I know it's up to me to look after the family, but you all expect me to provide a comfortable living, and these days it's much harder than it used to be.'

Rosaleen snarled, 'We can be sure you'll take the lion's share of anything you manage to make.'

It pained Quentin to see the envy pouring out of her. He knew she was afraid Crispin would get a larger share of the family money than she did.

'You know you'll get your hands on your share eventually,' Crispin retaliated.

'Goodness only knows when that will be.'

Quentin knew what they meant. They were beginning to sound impatient for his demise. 'I'm not planning on dying just yet,' he said. This made him feel dispirited. Rosaleen and Crispin had always fought like cat and dog. He'd hoped they would be on more amicable terms as they grew older, but they were getting worse.

'Don't let's spoil a good dinner by quarrelling,' he said. 'We'll look at the jewellery afterwards. I do think the pieces that aren't outdated ought to be worn by you ladies.'

'Of course they should,' Rosaleen agreed. 'Jewellery is meant to be worn, but you keep it locked away, Father, so we can't.'

Quentin didn't miss the nods of agreement from Daphne and Clarissa. They were all eager to have their share.

Clarissa smiled sweetly at him. 'Please, Grandpa, could I have the pink South Sea pearls that used to be Grandmama's?' Her fingers stroked her long elegant neck, which would show them off to advantage. 'In memory of her,' she wheedled. 'I'd think of her every time I wore them.'

'Your grandmama hardly ever did,' Quentin

told her sadly. 'She wore a five strand choker, like Queen Alexandra, most of the time.'

That disconcerted Clarissa. She wanted the South Sea pearls because they were alternated with diamonds and the necklace was valuable.

But Rosaleen was right, Quentin thought, he ought to give them Marina's personal bits and pieces. They hadn't seen the light of day since she'd died.

When they were finishing dinner, he told Connie to bring their coffee to his study. 'Come along,' he said, getting up from the table. 'We might as well open the safe now.'

How eager they all were then, and how keen to please him. He took his time pouring himself a glass of brandy and searching for the key. He opened the safe, aware of hungry eyes watching every move he made.

'I have some pearls that used to belong to Mother here, Maude. You should have her things.'

She lifted them out of their case and cradled them on her fingers. 'I remember her wearing these. Poor Mama. Where do I go these days to wear jewellery like this?'

'These diamonds were hers too, and these sapphire drops.' Quentin was aware of envious eyes appraising them.

'Keep them in your safe for me, Quentin. I can ask you for them should I want to wear them.'

He sighed and took out two large packets. He'd bundled all Marina's little boxes into them when she died and had never opened them since.

He shook out the leather cases on the table and opened them up. Only right that Rosaleen and

Clarissa should have these pieces now. He gave Clarissa the pink pearl and diamond necklace he'd bought for Marina on their twentieth wedding anniversary.

'Oh, Grandpa! Thank you, thank you, I do love this.'

She leaped up and kissed him, then wanted to try it on and demanded his attention to help her fasten it. He used to help Marina fasten it but his fingers could no longer cope with the little clasp. Daphne had to do it for her.

She stood smiling up at him, expecting some piece for herself. 'I love the ruby necklace Eudora May is wearing in her portrait,' she said. 'It hasn't dated one bit.'

He thought about it. Rosaleen wouldn't want the rubies; she'd developed an unfathomable fear of Eudora May.

Rosaleen laughed. 'There's a matching tiara, Daphne. When could you possibly wear that?'

Quentin saw his daughter-in-law flinch. 'Real family pieces, those,' he said gently. He hadn't planned to give away the antique pieces, and he was not fond of Daphne. He must not show it. 'But you're right. Rubies would suit your dark colouring. I have others here – a necklace and earrings.' He had to open several of the cases before he found them. 'A brooch and ring too.' He handed the lizard-skin case over. They'd come from Marina's side of the family; her parents had given them to her. He threw in another brooch made from a butterfly's wing. It was pretty and Marina had worn it a lot, but it was set in silver and worth little.

237

Jonathon's bright blue eyes were watching him too.

'Jonathon,' he said, 'your mother must have a keepsake.' He handed over the magnificent diamond and sapphire necklace Drusilla Wyndham had been wearing when her portrait was painted. 'Such jewels, satins and fancy hats the Victorian ladies wore to picnic with their children on the riverbank. Your mother loved this necklace.'

He smiled at Daphne. 'Frances didn't think it was old-fashioned. Once, John asked if she might borrow it when he took her to a ball.'

He'd been fond of Frances. 'She'd better have the earrings and bracelet that match. Mustn't break up the set.'

'Father!' The protest in Rosaleen's voice made him reckless. He picked out a ring and a brooch for Frances as well.

Another brooch glittered up at him. Diamonds set in platinum in the shape of a rose. 'A trifle for Lorna Mathews. I'll keep that for her.'

'That's much more than a trifle.' Crispin looked shocked.

'She's done so much to help. It's American, made by Tiffany. I don't know who this belonged to.'

'It's far too good for her.' Daphne looked close to tears.

Was it? Quentin turned it over in his fingers. Perhaps he should keep it until she'd finished the job, see how things went.

The rest he gave to Rosaleen. She was Marina's only daughter, after all. She opened up each little case with gasps of joy. He could see that Crispin was not pleased at this division of spoils.

'I was hoping you'd give me something I could sell to buy my house,' he said stiffly.

'Well, there's the rubies I've given Daphne and the pearls and diamonds I've handed over to Clarissa.'

'Absolutely not, Daddy,' Clarissa said. 'I've always admired this necklace.'

Quentin said, 'I don't want to part with pieces that have been in the family for a long time.' He meant to keep them for as long as he could.

'But is it fair?' Crispin protested.

'Of course it's fair,' his sister told him. 'Only the other week, Father gave you one of our most important portraits.'

'To hang over the mantelpiece of our new house,' Daphne agreed, 'to remind us that our ancestors earned a fortune and helped make the port of Liverpool what it is today. We're all very proud of it.'

Crispin said, 'I had to have the portrait cleaned and the frame regilded. It had grown quite shabby. It's a little too large for the room. Daphne complains that it dominates everything.'

'My eyes are drawn to it all the time,' she smiled.

'I don't mind that,' Crispin said. 'I'm more than proud of Captain William Wyndham and his wife, Viveca. After all, they founded our dynasty. There is no more fitting place for it.'

'Don't forget,' his father reminded him, 'you've promised not to sell it.'

With Tom and Harold, Lorna worked hard in the clammy airless attics for three whole weeks before she could see any semblance of order. It was gloomy even on the brightest of days because the few small skylights had never been cleaned, and electric light had never been installed up there.

Lorna took up the two storm lanterns from the garden room and Tom provided three more from the stables, but the attic was still full of shifting shadows. They disturbed whole armies of spiders, flies and beetles, and found generations of birds' nests, used, abandoned and returning to dust. Lorna took to borrowing Hilda's aprons and tying a scarf round her hair because there was so much dust flying about. It made Tom cough, and after a week it went on his chest and he retired to his bed.

It seemed that nobody had ever bothered to look in the attics before. All manner of things had been brought up here to be stored and then forgotten. In their first week the workers came across two fine rugs that had been carefully protected against dust, and the experts downstairs confirmed they were Aubusson. In the second, they found a pair of Meissen dogs. But there were trunks filled with clothes already worn till they were threadbare, uniforms for butlers, coachmen and maids, and boxes of invitation cards to hunt balls, and dinners to mark every occasion, all long since over.

With Harold's help, Lorna had moved the furniture to one end and had cleaned and polished it. She'd washed china and glass and spread out smaller items on the floors in the staff bedrooms. There were many articles the family just did not recognise and could think of no use for, and these were put all together in another room. She made lists of everything she could name and stuck numbers on those she couldn't.

This morning when she went up she found Harold already at work there.

'It's all junk at this end,' he said. 'Old animal skins, look. Heaven knows where these came from.'

'Some distant part of the Empire.' Lorna spread them out. 'Are they monkey skins?'

'This one looks like deer of some sort.'

Some had not been properly cured and were now decaying. Lorna was sorting these from others that remained in better condition when she unearthed a heavy bundle. Something had been tied up inside a skin. When she cut the string she came to what appeared to be an old piece of curtain and wrapped in that were several books.

As she took the good skins to the room where she was building up a collection of native spears, masks and drums, she wondered why anyone would go to the trouble of tying books up in that way, but she put them on one side, meaning to take them down to the library where the experts were already at work.

Harold was raising a haze of dust. 'Why keep old newspapers?' he grumbled. 'You'd think they could have thrown these out.'

'What are they?' Lorna asked. He was dragging several bundles of old newspapers, yellow and fragile with age, across to the growing pile of rubbish.

'Copies of the *Liverpool Chronicle* and the *Liverpool Mercury*. Gosh! This one's dated July eighteen thirty-five. That's nearly a hundred years old.'

Lorna brought a lamp closer and gently opened the paper out. 'Look, there's an advert here for the Wyndham business.' She began to read.

'Africa – to sail immediately for Sierra Leone. The remarkable fine fast-sailing barque *Neptune*. Now loading in Queen's Dock and will positively be dispatched as above. For freight or passage apply to master on board or Lars Wyndham and Sons, Head Office, Water Street, Liverpool.'

She found another dated 1845.

'*Liverpool Princess*, bound for Lagos – stands A1 at Lloyd's. Has the most part of her cargo engaged, now loading in the Salthouse Dock, east side. Burthen per register 110 tons. A very desirable conveyance for goods or passengers. Apply to Lars Wyndham and Sons.'

There were plenty more like it: 'The *Claris*, coppered and copper-fastened, bound for West Africa, will clear at the Customs House on the nineteenth inst.'

'Fascinating,' Lorna said. 'But we're wasting time.'

'Listen to this.' Harold peered closer. 'There's an account here of the *Great Britain* steaming into the Mersey for the first time.'

'When was that?'

'Eighteen forties. A leviathan of three thousand five hundred tons. Sightseers crowded both banks to see the vessel that Brunel designed and Prince Albert launched.'

'Harold, we'll never get finished at this rate.'

'I could spend hours on these.'

'We already have. Let's take some down to Mr Wyndham and I'll leave some outside Jonathon's room. They'll be fascinated too. We need to get on.'

'There's boxes and boxes of papers here.'

'Newspapers?'

'No.'

Lorna went to look. There were papers of all kinds: letters, account books, legal documents and diaries, none of which she had time more than to glance at. Handwritten in fading ink on darkening paper, and using spelling and language that was hardly recognisable, she was afraid they'd take years to decipher.

'Help me take these down too, Harold.' She had far more than it would take to fill her cabin trunk. 'The light's better downstairs, easier to read there.'

They made two journeys. Lorna left Mr Wyndham poring over a great bundle of old newspapers.

Harold said, 'Let's get a cup of tea from Hilda while we're down.'

They met Sissie on the way. 'Harold, I've been looking for you. Mrs Carey wants you to run her down to the church for eleven o'clock. There's a meeting or something she wants to go to.'

'Damn, there goes my tea. I'll have to have a

243

wash first. Tell her I'll be at the door in five minutes, Sissie.'

Lorna decided to skip the tea too. She went back to the gloom of the attic. The bundle of books that had been wrapped in the skin of a deer was where she'd left it. As she picked it up to take down to the library, she wondered if they had been deliberately hidden so that others wouldn't read them.

She took them nearer to her storm lantern to find out what they were. She could see no lettering on their spines. That made her cut the string that bound them to take a closer look. They were notebooks, some bound expensively in leather and some in cloth. She opened one and the name Oliver Wyndham leaped out at her, making her gasp.

At last! Wasn't this what she'd been looking for since she'd first set foot in Otterspool? She sat back on her haunches and started to read. His strong flowing script made her heart turn over. She thought she'd found his diary. Would she find out his true feelings about her mother? Discover his real intentions? She was convinced now that the books had been intentionally hidden to keep them private.

It didn't take her long to realise that Oliver had been writing his family history. It started with William Wyndham, who had founded the dynasty. She flipped through the pages: he'd put dates to all events, and ages to his ancestors.

Lorna got up to stretch her legs. It didn't make sense to her. Quentin Wyndham was talking of writing the family history when Oliver had already done it – already started it, anyway. Her first feeling was one of disappointment that this wasn't his diary, but it was still an important find. To have something in her father's own handwriting excited her. There was quite a lot of it – he'd almost filled this notebook. And even if the job wasn't finished, he'd made a good start on the hardest part.

Normally, she'd have taken such a find straight to Quentin, but because it was the first thing she'd come across that had been written by Oliver, she decided to say nothing for the moment to give herself time to look through it first.

The find filled her with elation, she was getting somewhere at last. She was bundling all the books together to take them to her own room, when she noticed another, more important-looking book. It was bound in brown leather with gold tooling, and fastened with a gilt clasp. She tried to open it and found she could not. It was locked, and that intrigued her. She was wondering whether she could force the clasp back when Harold returned, and she had to remove the books discreetly to her room, but for the rest of the day she was bubbling with anticipation.

After dinner that night, Mr Wyndham kept Lorna downstairs. He wanted to look over all she'd found and have her read out details from her notes. It was quite late when she went up to bed. She couldn't wait to get back to the family history Oliver had started to write but she was tired. She got into bed as quickly as she could and started to read.

Oliver wrote clearly and well. She was

245

immediately transported back to 1739 when William Wyndham, an apothecary with a practice in Liverpool, had married Viveca Svenson. She came from a Norwegian seafaring family and was said to have the typical colouring of that part of the world: beautiful ash-blonde hair, pale grey eyes and translucent fair skin. Her father, Lars Svenson, was the captain of a brig called the *Northern Light*.

Their first son, called Lars after his grandfather, was born in 1740, and he inherited his fair colouring. Growing up on the Liverpool waterfront he was fascinated with the ships and everything to do with the sea.

Young Lars looked forward to visits from his mother's family. He loved nothing better than listening to his grandfather and Uncle Tor talk about the sea and the distant ports they visited. He asked his grandfather if, when he was grown up, he could join his ship and be a mariner too.

'Of course you can, lad. I'll teach you all you need to know about navigation and seamanship.' He'd slapped him on the back and Lars knew he was pleased. 'He's a chip off the old block, Viv.'

But his father wanted him to become an apothecary like himself. 'To a young man, going to sea might seem a great adventure,' he told him, 'but when you're older, your happiness will come from a settled home with a wife and children. You'll need some way of supporting a family.'

When Lars was twelve, William apprenticed him to a fellow apothecary to learn the trade. Lars tried to accept his father's decision but he hankered all the time for the seafaring life. Many of the patients he saw were sailors and their ships in the Mersey continued to fascinate him...

Lorna could no longer see straight and could feel herself drifting off. She put the book down, determined that tomorrow she'd find time to read more of it.

Chapter Thirteen

The next night, Lorna went up to her room shortly after dinner and looked through the other journals she'd found in the bundle. There was one written by Lars Wyndham himself. This was not easy to read but she could decipher enough to understand that it had provided the facts on which Oliver had based his account.

She reached for another notebook and saw it was filled with Oliver's neat script. Glancing through, she was thrilled to find what she thought was a transcript of Lars Wyndham's journal and she could continue with the account of his life that she'd started yesterday. Lorna threw herself on her bed, propped the book on her pillow and settled down for a long read.

By the time Lars was fourteen, his grandfather had retired, and his Uncle Tor, who now captained the *Northern Light*, came to visit his mother. He brought her a parrot, an African grey he'd taught to say 'Hello pretty lady', and several other polite phrases to please her.

His uncle told Lars that he traded along the coast of West Africa. His ship would cast anchor where the huts of a village could be seen on shore. Canoes would immediately come out to trade, bringing palm oil in calabashes, elephants' tusks, coconuts, fresh fruit and provisions. Sometimes they brought parrots, which were much sought after because they fetched a high price in Liverpool.

In exchange, the natives wanted printed cotton and calico, muskets and ammunition, tobacco and pipes, gin, second-hand clothes and trinkets. Lars never stopped asking questions, and his enthusiasm for the sea received such a boost that he asked his father if he might change his career.

'That wouldn't be wise, my son. As an apothecary, you'll be better able to support a family. When you grow up, you'll find more satisfaction here, helping others. Your uncle talks only of the exciting things in his life, and they tempt you.'

'No, Papa, he's offered to take me as cabin boy. You know I've always wanted–'

'He tells you nothing of the dangers; of the storms, of the long lonely months away, and I fear there could be drunkenness and licentiousness aplenty on his ship.'

Lars argued half the night with his father, until they were both angry and his mother in tears. His parents were adamant: he could not go. When morning came, Lars ran away to join his uncle, but when he reached the Queen's Dock, he couldn't find the *Northern Light*.

The *Mary Trimmer*, a schooner of forty-two tons, was tied up in the dock, taking on cargo, and he asked a man leaning over the rail where he might find the *Northern Light*.

He spat a mouthful of tobacco juice into the water. 'She sailed on the morning tide.'

Lars was left gasping, knowing he'd missed his uncle. 'I was going to sail with her,' he said, 'as cabin boy.'

His anger had gone, leaving him cold with fright. Should he go back home and face his father? He'd left him a letter written at the height of his anger, and probably he'd have read it by now. He'd not be forgiven quickly for this.

'We're taking on crew,' the man told him, 'and still short of a cabin boy. Come aboard and speak to the mate, see if you'd suit here.'

To Lars the offer felt like a lifeline. 'Where are you bound?'

'The Guinea Coast.'

That settled it. He made up his mind to go if he could. Within half an hour he'd signed on as cabin boy and was being instructed in his duties. He was still shaking with fear when the *Mary Trimmer* cast off in time to catch the evening tide.

He discovered that she carried her weight in salt, together with all the items his uncle had mentioned and many more besides. She sailed for West Africa and travelled a thousand miles along the Guinea Coast before she began to trade. Lars expected them to load the calabashes of palm oil, gold and parrots he'd heard about. Instead they took on a quantity of beans, cassava, yams and fruit.

249

It took him some time to realise that what they really sought as cargo were human beings that could be sold as slaves. Lars had heard this trade condemned loudly by his father and by his father's friends, and was sickened when he found he was caught up in it. If anybody had jumped out of the frying pan into the fire, it was he.

Three months after she'd left Liverpool, the *Mary Trimmer* was sailing many miles up the Cross River through a country of mangrove swamps.

The voyage had not been without incident. There had been frequent fist fights amongst the crew as well as a knifing and, following an argument, one man had fallen to his death from the rigging. Lars heard it said that he'd been pushed off. He was scared stiff at finding himself on board such an evil ship and wished he'd listened to his father.

The *Mary Trimmer* had been anchored in the Cross River for a week, one of six European vessels. It was late afternoon of the seventh day and the heat of the day was dying. Lars was so tired he ached. He'd been working and on his feet since before dawn. He'd helped to receive and stow their cargo of slaves on board. Now the ship was getting ready to sail for the Caribbean.

He was on deck when he saw another ship coming up river. It looked familiar, and he couldn't take his eyes from it, hardly able to believe it was the *Northern Light*, but each second as it drew closer confirmed his hopes. He felt suddenly buoyant and filled with energy. When it was close by and he saw his Uncle Tor supervising the dropping of the anchor, all his fears had gone. He wanted to laugh with relief at his tremendous luck.

Lars made up his mind within moments to jump ship and join his uncle. He bundled together his few possessions, then let down a rope ladder that had just been stowed, climbed quickly down to the brown brackish water and slid silently into it.

He needed to swim only thirty yards before he was picked up by a canoe that had been selling coconuts to the crews of the anchored ships. From there, he was able to watch the *Mary Trimmer* weigh anchor and slip down river without him. For one English penny, he was paddled over to the *Northern Light* where he hailed his uncle from the waterline. Tor was more than surprised to see him but he welcomed Lars on board and listened to his story.

'I always knew the sea was in your blood,' he said, slapping him on the back in high good humour. 'I'll be glad to teach you all I know. I'll make a ship's captain out of you.'

To Lars, who had visited the ship several times while she was in dock in Liverpool, it was like coming home. He felt safe with his uncle, delighted he'd escaped from the evil of a slave ship.

After a meal, Tor said to him, 'Come on, we're going ashore tonight. You must listen and learn. A ship's captain needs to know a lot more than seamanship.'

'What are you going to do?'

'Have palaver with the chieftains. They control

everything here.'

Lars followed his uncle and was introduced to a tribal chief he met. They were taken to a barracoon filled with native men. Lars thought at first his uncle wanted to take on more crew.

'You're part-way to being a doctor,' Uncle Tor said. 'Help me pick out the healthy ones, the strongest ones.'

It was only when he saw the leg irons that Lars realised Uncle Tor was negotiating to buy slaves. It shocked him to the core. He'd thought his own family too high-principled for this.

He kept his head down and said nothing until they were alone and going back to the ship. Then, unable to hide his agitation, he said, 'At home, you never mentioned that you carry slaves.'

His uncle smiled. 'Your father would not approve.'

'He's very much against it.'

'So I keep my mouth shut. In England, some think it shouldn't be done. They get quite the wrong idea there, believing it to be cruel.'

'Isn't it?'

'It's like this, Lars: here in Africa, the different tribes have always waged war on each other. At one time, the tribal chiefs aimed to kill as many of their enemies as they could, but not any longer. Now they take as many unharmed prisoners as possible to trade with us, so you could say we save their lives.'

'All these European ships here... Are they all...?'

'Yes, that's why they come. You can see two Spanish barques here now and a Portuguese schooner. It isn't just the English. They would all carry on if we stopped. The trade brings prosperity to everyone.'

'But you're exchanging glass beads and little mirrors for human beings.' The thought sickened Lars anew.

'The chiefs choose what they want from our stock: salt, gin, cutlery and earthenware, pots and pans, tools that they can sell on. If they don't like what we bring they won't trade with us. Nobody gets rich more quickly than the chiefs, who capture their enemies and sell them to us.'

'There were women among them too, Uncle, and even children.'

'We don't carry women with babies at breast, nor those heavy with child. And isn't it better that they go to a life in another part of the world?'

'As slaves?'

'Nobody will be out to kill or capture them there. They'll be able to live in peace. Once good money has been paid for them they'll come to no harm. They'll be fed, clothed, housed and looked after. The Caribbean is a better place for them.'

'So slaving is not such a wicked thing?'

'That's something you'll have to decide for yourself, Lars, but you'll see we treat them kindly.'

'But those who travel on other ships?'

'We all treat them well. We've given over our trade goods in exchange for them – we don't want them to die, do we?'

Lars knew there was no way out for him now, he had to engage in slaving. He wondered if his father had guessed Tor's trade and that was why

253

he'd been so against him joining his ship. But he knew he'd be much better off on the *Northern Light* than the *Mary Trimmer*. He no longer feared for his life at the hands of the crew. Uncle Tor did not allow drunkenness on board.

The *Northern Light* could carry sixty-eight slaves. Those that had been bought remained in the barracoons on shore until the full load was assembled. The day before sailing, the ship's barber went ashore and shaved every head. On sailing day, they were all fed a substantial meal and then chained together in groups of ten and ferried out to the ship by canoe.

Lars heard his uncle give the order for them all to strip off as soon as they were alongside, women as well as men. This had happened to those boarding the *Mary Trimmer* too.

Lars turned on him. 'You can't say that's kind, Uncle.'

'It's not unkind. It's cooler for them and it keeps them free from vermin. We keep them naked throughout the voyage.'

Lars watched as the men were stowed in the hold, in spoon fashion, their heads in one another's laps. His Uncle Tor pointed out that the tallest were selected for the greatest breadth of the vessel, while the shorter ones and the youngsters were stowed in the fore part of the ship. Tubs were distributed so both sides had access. The women and children were crammed into the cabins.

'It's only until we're clear of the land,' Uncle Tor said. 'Once they can no longer swim ashore, then we only keep those in leg irons who cause trouble, and the children are allowed on deck during daylight. The adults have to take turns; we can't allow much mixing of the sexes.'

Lars found that the crew were all issued with guns.

'We're outnumbered three to one,' Uncle Tor explained. 'We don't want them to gang up on us. The guns are to deter them from that. We don't use them unless we have to. To hurt them is against our interests as well as theirs.'

Lars had to help at meal times. The slaves were fed twice a day, at ten in the morning and four in the afternoon. Grace was said before meals and the crew saw to it that each got a fair share. Refusal to eat was taken seriously.

The sick were separated as soon as possible and the whole of the forecastle used as a sickroom for them.

Buckets of sea water were hauled on deck so all could wash. It was the boatswain's duty to keep the ship clean and Lars's uncle was very particular about it. The tubs were emptied and scrubbed with chloride of lime, the upper deck washed and swabbed and the slave deck scraped and holystoned.

'You can always tell a slaver,' his Uncle Tor explained. 'The bulkheads and hatches are grated for ventilation and sometimes even the decks have additional gratings. When in light winds or calms, the gratings are taken off and some slaves are allowed to sleep on deck. We cover them with spare sails in the cool of the night.

'I aim to keep them as healthy and contented as possible. Every morning a dram of spirits is given

255

to each, and they are allowed to sing and play their tomtoms. Occasionally, I distribute pipes and tobacco. The barber shaves their chins once a week to keep them comfortable.'

The routine of the days at sea went on until they reached Havana. Before the slaves went ashore they were told to wash all over and each was given a new outfit of clothes to make them look smart. They were sold or exchanged for sugar, rum and tobacco. Then the *Northern Light* sailed up the coast of America to buy raw cotton for the Lancashire mills before returning to Liverpool.

Lars sailed with his uncle for several voyages and, as promised, was taught seamanship and navigation. He learned the perils that the West African coast had for ships: the sand bars that formed where the rivers met the sea; the treacherous movements of these sandbanks and the dangers of mists and mirages on a coast where there were no aids to navigation.

He learned a great deal about trade too. Rates were high because of these dangers and also because of the reputation of West Africa as being the white man's grave. He learned even more about slaving.

It was the early hours of the morning before Lorna closed the notebook and lay back, shocked yet enthralled. It seemed unbelievable, and yet it must be true.

Lars had found the trade repugnant, yet he'd engaged in it. Even if it was true that they'd treated the slaves with kindness during the voyage, it didn't excuse the fact that they sold them into a life of slavery. That stuck in Lorna's throat, horrified her, even though, two centuries ago, the world had been a cruel place.

She put her light out, but couldn't sleep. Her head was whirling with all she'd learned. She'd been so pleased to find Oliver's notebooks, believing herself to be near the end of her search, but what she'd found wasn't what she'd been looking for. It seemed incredible that the Wyndhams had earned their fortune in slaving! Especially as they'd spoken so often of the pride they had in their ancestors' achievements.

Rosaleen would be most put out if she knew. In an odd way, Lorna felt cheated herself.

The next day, Lorna found it hard to concentrate on her work in the attics. She tried, but her heart wasn't in it. Her mind kept returning to the notebooks. She'd put them out of sight in her wardrobe, having read only a fraction of what was there. At lunch time she allowed herself half an hour of reading. Harold was again helping in the attics so she had to work with him. When he knocked off for the day, she went back to the journals.

Tonight, after dinner, she settled down for another long read. She took a duster upstairs with her to use on the book covered with brown tooled leather and locked with a gilt clasp to keep its contents private. It didn't look as old as some of the others. The gilding on the leather was bright and shiny, and there was an attractive design on each corner that reminded her of something.

She sat back and tried to think. It was the key she'd found in the nursery toy cupboard that came to mind. Was this the same design as on that? Lorna shot downstairs to the nursery to get the key. She was right, it was the same design.

She was rushing back to her room when she saw Sissie dash up the attic stairs ahead of her almost in tears. Hilda was following her, mounting the stairs slowly and blocking her way.

'Sissie's worse than useless,' she said crossly. 'I asked her to sweep out the scullery.'

'I saw her doing it.'

'She never does anything properly. You could plant potatoes in the dust she left behind. Useless.'

Lorna could barely contain her impatience. 'You scare the living daylights out of her, Hilda. If you found less fault, if you were kind, you'd get more from her.'

'She'd try the patience of a saint.'

It was a relief when Hilda reached her own room and went in. At last, Lorna shot to her dressing table, picked up the leather-bound book and inserted the key. The lock turned easily, the hinge opened and she was able to inspect the contents.

On the frontispiece she read: 'The journal of Marina Wyndham.' Marina? Yes, Quentin's wife who had died so sadly after catching flu from her son Piers.

It was dated 1909–1910. Her heart leaped in anticipation. This covered the time when Oliver had died. Lorna turned to the end: there were a few blank pages. She flicked over those covered

258

in neat small script, reading a few lines here and a paragraph there, greedy with hope and excitement, expecting to find out more about Oliver's end. Her attention was gripped within seconds.

4 January 1910

How can I tell Quentin that the ancestors of whom he is so proud accumulated their fortune on the proceeds of slavery? If I told him Captain Lars Wyndham and the *Flying Cloud* carried trade goods to the West African coast to buy slaves, which he then transported to Havana, he wouldn't believe me. But I'm sure now that the Wyndham fortune was founded on slaving.

Oliver came to me in great distress when he discovered the truth. He'd long wanted to write his family history. I begged him to say nothing to anyone else, to leave the telling to me. I haven't slept properly since.

How can I possibly tell Quentin? He exudes pride as he shows visitors the pictures of the *Northern Light* and the *Wave Crest*. He thinks of his ancestors as adventurers, but honest and upright adventurers, who braved the dangers of the high seas to engage in legitimate trade.

8 January 1910

Oliver has worked on the family history all over the Christmas holidays, every minute that he hasn't been in the office with his father. I dread that Quentin will discover the family shame.

We thought it bad enough that the family engaged in slaving when it was legal to do so. But

Oliver has turned up far worse than that. The British Parliament abolished slavery in 1807. From then on it was against the law for British citizens and British ships to engage in it.

Lars Wyndham wanted to carry on the hateful trade. So did the Portuguese, Spanish and the French. The African chiefs didn't like the British attitude either, which would ruin their livelihood.

Captain Wyndham commissioned a new ship called the *Flying Cloud*. A clipper of 38 tons, she was 65 feet long, needed 22 men to sail her and could do an astonishing 10 knots. The passage from Cape Verde – that's on the bulge of West Africa – to Havana took forty days.

The *Flying Cloud* was designed and built in 1808 with the express intention of being able to out-sail the British naval ships that were beginning to blockade the slave ports of Dahomey and the Cross River, as they tried to put an end to the dreadful trade.

Oliver has discovered that the Wyndhams continued to engage in it for many more years, despite the risks. As late as 1836 new laws were being passed to curb the trade. Vessels flying the Spanish flag could be seized by the British if suspected of slaving.

If caught by the Royal Navy and found with slaves on board, the crew would be put ashore in some remote part of the jungle with no guns, food or water, where they would be the prey of wild animals and mosquitoes, and be unlikely to survive. Their ships would be destroyed and not sold on by their captors.

Fast sailing ships were much in demand to give

a better chance of escape. Many more were built, larger in size and capable of carrying more slaves.

That really shocked Lorna. The Wyndham ancestors had been rogues and criminals.

She was hooked on Marina's account and unable to close her journal. There were more details. Slavers made so much money from just one voyage that they sold the ship on and bought new, just in case the British naval ships had sighted it or had received information about it.

Lorna knew she would spend many more hours reading what was here. She also knew she'd been right about these books being intentionally hidden. Oliver and his mother hadn't wanted the rest of the family to know their own origins.

She asked herself if anyone else knew. Rosaleen did not, nor Quentin – they showed too much pride in their forebears – but what about Crispin? And if Quentin's wife didn't think he should know, and had kept it from him, Lorna wondered if she should tell him. She was being paid to read and sort all the family documents she came across; if she found something important she knew she mustn't keep it to herself.

She decided that when she'd gleaned all she could from these notebooks, the best thing for her to do was to hand them over to Jonathon and let him decide whether to tell his grandfather and the rest of his family or not.

Now she'd seen photographs of Oliver it was easier to believe her mother had been in love with him and he was her natural father. After the hours she'd spent poring over his handwriting, she could see him as a living, breathing person, upset when he found out his ancestors had been slavers.

She no longer felt in control of her emotions. They were raging through her, stirred up by reading in Oliver's own hand the account of how slavers operated. She couldn't help but compare Oliver with Jonathon; her mother must have been gripped by emotions like these.

Jonathon was rarely out of her thoughts. He'd been avoiding her since she'd refused to go to the cinema with him. She'd caused herself terrible heart-wrenching by doing that. When they came face to face at the breakfast table or at tea time, he hardly spoke to her. He kept his eyes averted.

Just to be near Jonathon sent cold shivers down her spine. She missed his companionship and the long talks they used to have. She began to wish she'd handled things differently, not choked him off. She'd made him as aloof as Adam and she could no longer reach him. But now she needed to speak to him on his own.

At tea time the next day, Rosaleen, her aunt and her father stayed on in the drawing room, talking about their new house. They were to take possession next week and were deciding which pieces of furniture they wanted there.

They did not plan to move in just yet because there was still a lot of work to do in preparation for the auction. Aunt Maude had ordered two pantechnicons, one to come next week to take some of their things and another to come when they finally moved.

It was a fine evening, but already dark. Lorna said to Jonathon, 'I fancy a breath of fresh air. You've been cooped up in your office all day, would you like a short walk?'

He stood up and said pleasantly enough, 'No, thanks. I've got something I want to do before dinner.'

'Right,' Lorna said, 'see you later.' She had no alternative then but to go. She walked quickly, cross with him but knowing she'd brought this on herself. He was retaliating by cold-shouldering her. She went as far as the river but the wind cut through her coat in an icy blast. As she returned the lights were on in the white drawing room and she could see Rosaleen with Aunt Maude, who was writing something on her knee. Lorna went straight upstairs and knocked on Jonathon's bedroom door.

'Come in,' he called. He was lying on his bed reading the *Liverpool Echo*. There were books, papers and clothing scattered on every surface.

'Oh!' He leaped to his feet and started tidying up. 'Aunt Maude said she'd bring me the list of furniture going in the vans, so I could add–'

Lorna cut across all that. 'I want to talk to you. I've discovered something important.'

'What?' His manner was cold, his eyes looked affronted that she'd dared to pin him down here.

She answered with equal brusqueness, 'Your ancestors made their fortune in slaving.' Her words seemed to scorch the atmosphere and hang between them. She thought from his face he didn't believe her. 'It's true,' she went on quickly. 'What made the port of Liverpool so prosperous in the time of your ancestor Lars Wyndham?'

He came closer and patted her arm as though to soothe her. 'I know,' he said quietly. 'It's all right, I know.'

'Since when?' She straightened up angrily. He hadn't told her and she didn't like that.

'The night we looked at the marine paintings.'

'But how?'

'I noticed ... Grandpa said they were true to life, accurate in every detail. It made me think.'

'What?'

'All our vessels from that era showed extra gratings. The only possible reason – to help ventilation in the hold. They couldn't allow the slaves to suffocate, could they?'

Lorna stared at him, trying to think back. 'Why didn't you say?'

'I was guessing, could only half remember... I had to make sure before I opened my mouth.'

'How can you make sure after all this time?'

'There are plenty more marine pictures in art galleries and there's books.'

'You read up on slaving?'

'Went to the museum too. I'm sure about it now.'

'You were clever to pick up on that,' Lorna told him. 'I looked at the same pictures and all I saw were tiny ships with billowing sails on rough seas.'

He smiled. 'Many seem to have been painted at the height of a storm.'

'And they're all so dark.'

'They need cleaning. I don't suppose they've ever been touched.'

264

'Your grandfather didn't see any more than I did.'

'His interest has always been in the business and the family. He hasn't read about slaving as I have. He's accepted what his father told him about his forebears.' Jonathon was eyeing her. 'How did you find out?'

'I found more notebooks. They'd been deliberately hidden.'

'We're not the first then, to uncover this secret?'

'No. They're in my room, come and see.'

He followed her up. She'd left the journals piled neatly on her dressing table. Everything else in her room was spick and span, not like his.

'Read this book first,' she said. 'Your Uncle Oliver started to write the family history, then in this one he transcribes Lars Wyndham's account of slaving. When you read this brown leather one you'll understand why I've told you instead of your grandfather.' He took the books and she heard him crash downstairs and his door slam.

A couple of hours later, Lorna was in the kitchen. She'd got into the habit of going down early to help when dinner was being dished up. Hilda's wrath descended on Sissie's head if she failed to keep up with her demands.

Lorna was chopping boiled cabbage on the stove when Jonathon came in. She felt all his old friendliness and was glad it had returned. He came close behind her and spoke softly over her shoulder.

'I've decided to tell the rest of the family. It doesn't make sense to keep secrets like this. After dinner, you bring our coffee to the drawing room.

265

I want you to stay.'

Lorna felt relief that he seemed to have put their rift behind him. She ate her dinner on the end of the kitchen table with Hilda and Sissie, and then did as he'd asked. As she slid the coffee tray down in the white drawing room, she saw the familiar pile of journals on the table.

'Black for you, Mr Wyndham?' she asked.

'Please.'

'I'll pour.' Rosaleen was pointedly rude. 'No need for you to stay.'

Jonathon said: 'I've asked Lorna to stay tonight.' She carried on handing cups of coffee round.

'Why?'

'Lorna's found these journals. Did you know, Grandpa, that Uncle Oliver started writing the family history?'

Quentin was busy lighting a cigar, and Lorna saw the match waver.

Aunt Maude said, 'Good gracious, did he?'

'Said he was going to,' Rosaleen scoffed. 'But he didn't get round to it.'

'He started,' Lorna told her.

Jonathon said, 'He discovered Lars Wyndham was the captain of a slaver. Slaving was the source of the family fortune.'

'Nonsense,' Rosaleen retorted hotly. 'How can that be?'

Aunt Maude crashed her coffee cup down. 'D'you know, I have sometimes wondered.'

Quentin's face had gone white, and his cigar was forgotten. 'The *Flying Cloud* was a slaver?' His eyes went to his favourite portrait over the fireplace.

266

'Uncle Oliver did his research and didn't want to carry on.' Jonathon was on his feet. 'Come and look at the picture of the *Flying Cloud* in the dining room.'

They trooped out behind him. He stopped in front of it, pointing.

'See these extra gratings in the hull? They're to let fresh air into the hold, so the slaves don't suffocate. All slavers had them. This journal was written by Lars himself. He gives all sorts of details about how he looked after the slaves on his ship.'

'Not easy to decipher,' Lorna said.

'I want you to read this one, Grandpa.' Jonathon opened the brown leather book and held it in front of him.

'Is this...? Yes, it's Marina's writing.'

'She didn't want you to know there'd been slavers in the family. She was afraid you'd be upset.'

'You must have it all wrong,' Rosaleen fumed. 'Father, you told me Captain Lars traded in gold and parrots. He wouldn't carry slaves, I know he wouldn't. There's never been any question.'

'He wanted it kept quiet, Aunt Roz. D'you know why?'

'Who would want to broadcast that?'

Jonathon looked at her. 'It was legal when he started...'

'Of course.' Rosaleen was shaking her head angrily. 'He wouldn't do anything illegal, would he?'

'It seems he did. The *Flying Cloud* wasn't built until 1808, a year after slaving was banned. Read

267

what it says in these journals. The Royal Navy blockaded the ports from which the slaves were being shipped. Lars needed a fast ship to outrun them. He and then his son kept on slaving until the eighteen forties.'

'Rubbish.' Rosaleen spat the word out. The nervous tic in her cheek was back.

'It's all here.' Jonathon patted the pile of journals.

Rosaleen pulled a face. 'I don't care what's there, it isn't true.'

Jonathon opened one of his own books. 'Listen to this.

'By 1800 Liverpool was handling ninety per cent of the world's slave trade. Many honest men, like William Roscoe and William Rathbone, fought hard to stop it, despite the prosperity it brought to the town. But the slavers carried on earning their fortunes in the dreadful trade right up to the first of May eighteen oh-seven, the date when British participation in the trade was outlawed.

'The point is that our family went on for many years after that date. Lars commissioned the *Flying Cloud* in 1808 with the deliberate intention of outsailing the naval ships who were trying to implement the ban on slavery.'

Jonathon slammed the book shut and pushed it on to his grandfather's knee. 'You'll have to read Oliver's account for yourself. Slaving went on almost to the middle of that century. They were breaking the law – why else would it be kept a secret?'

Lorna said, 'And the secret was kept for almost another hundred years.'

'Let me have one of those journals,' Maude said. 'Which would be best to start?'

'We were brought up to be proud of our ancestors.' Lorna saw Quentin Wyndham wipe away a tear. 'To think that Marina knew and didn't tell me.'

'She didn't want to hurt your feelings,' Jonathon said gently. 'She knew how proud you were of your roots.'

Rosaleen flared up. 'I still don't believe it. Some families are known to have been slavers but not the Wyndhams.' She turned on Lorna. 'No doubt you're pleased you've unearthed these beastly journals. You want to drag us down to the common level.'

Before she could answer, Jonathon laughed. 'No, Aunt Roz, we got ideas above our station. Our forebears were law-breakers and slavers. No wonder they kept it all quiet.'

Quentin looked bemused. 'Well, I'm not sorry. To know I came from a long line of criminals makes me feel better. If I'd come from a long line of honest and brave adventurers then I've failed to live up to them.'

'It's all ancient history now.' Aunt Maude was riffling through the pages of Oliver's journal. 'They looked after themselves, grabbed the best they could of everything.'

'Some of the present generation haven't changed,' Jonathon grinned, 'but they're not as good at it as their forebears.'

Chapter Fourteen

The family stayed in the white drawing room until it was quite late, arguing endlessly about the evidence that their forebears had been involved in the slave trade, and how they felt demeaned by it. Lorna sat a little apart, listening.

Aunt Maude was the first to decide it was bedtime. Lorna got up and said good night too. She hadn't reached the great hall when she found Jonathon had followed her out.

'Lorna, you did wonders, digging all that out. You really made them sit up.'

'But you worked it out for yourself, I'm still not sure how.'

'I didn't think I could convince the aunts.'

'I'm not sure you could have convinced me without the notebooks.'

'I read it up... I could show you.' Impulsively, he caught at her arm. 'Come with me to the art gallery in William Brown Street. I'll show you the marine paintings, then we'll go to the museum.' His eyes danced with enthusiasm.

Lorna didn't point out she was already convinced. She was ready to go anywhere with him. 'Are they different to what you have here? The ship pictures?'

'They explain it all. Saturday afternoon, yes?'

Lorna hesitated. 'Mum will be expecting me home.'

'Just for an hour or so,' he pleaded. 'You could go straight home afterwards.'

'I could drop her a postcard to say I'll be late. She'll keep tea waiting for me otherwise.'

'We can have tea in town, if you like. I know a place where they have very good cakes.'

'Not afternoon tea.' Lorna felt suddenly awkward. 'We have high tea at home. Sausages or kippers, something like that.'

'Will you come?' His gaze had great intensity. She'd thought their estrangement had cooled things down, that it would be impossible to get over that in an instant, but no.

'Yes, I'd like to. Thank you,' she smiled. 'A good thing, do you think? For the family to know the truth about slaving? To have it all out in the open?'

She could see from his face that he wasn't sure. 'It upset them but they ought to know what really happened. How silly their pride looks now. In a way it upset me. These are my forebears too. To think of them as slavers – well, it does make a difference.'

Lorna said nothing. She felt the same. My forebears too, she thought.

On Friday, the wind dropped and by nightfall, mist was gathering. On Saturday morning it was thickening and by midday, dense fog like yellowish grey cotton wool pressed against the windows, blotting out the view. Lorna had heard ships' foghorns blaring out across the Mersey all night. It was a ghostly sound from invisible ships.

Jonathon was late coming home for lunch. If

271

Hilda was instructed to have the meal on the table by one o'clock that was when the gong summoned the family to the table. Sissie had taken the bread-and-butter pudding to the dining room before she announced his arrival. Lorna filled a soup bowl for him from the pan kept simmering on the stove. She feared now that their outing would be cancelled. For once, she wasn't hungry and toyed with her lunch. She was finishing it when he came to the kitchen.

'It's a real peasouper out there today.' There was another ghostly blast from the river. 'Took me ages to get home, could hardly see my hand in front of my face.'

Lorna asked, 'It isn't safe to drive back into town?'

'The buses have stopped running. There's no other way you can get home.'

'There's trains,' Sissie said from across the table. 'Walk to the station, Lorna, then you'll be all right.'

'No,' Jonathon said. 'I don't want to be stuck here all day. We'll go as arranged.'

Lorna had already packed a small overnight bag. She was ready in moments and went out to his car. Sitting this close to him, watching his hands on the wheel, was quickening her pulse. They were in a world of their own. Impenetrable fog cut off everything else. It smelled of smoke and burned oil, a real industrial smell.

Lorna had never been to the Walker Art Gallery before. Their footsteps echoed eerily; few people were interested in art today. Every few minutes the foghorns blasted out from the river. She felt awkward and ill at ease. This wasn't what she was used to doing on a Saturday afternoon. She was unsure of him, did not know how to treat him, afraid this alliance was too fragile and would break down again.

Jonathon was earnestly pointing out the notes she should read, the points she should notice. Lorna couldn't concentrate; she was too conscious of him. She thought he must be able to see how much she liked him, how much she longed to be on better terms. It must stick out a mile. She hadn't half the guts her mother had had. She'd loved Oliver and held nothing back. Mum would have been all right if his family hadn't interfered. What had she done herself? Held back, been careful – been too careful and put him right off.

When they'd examined the marine pictures at length, he took her to the museum, which was close by. Lorna found lots to interest her there. They stayed until it was closing for the night. Out on the steps, Jonathon offered a cup of tea, but by then Lorna was tired. She thanked him with great formality and said she must go home.

'I'll run you to the station.'

'It'll be quicker to walk,' she smiled. Traffic was barely visible across the wide thoroughfares and seemed stationary for minutes at a time, the honking of motor horns blending with the louder noises from the river.

'You're right.' He tucked her arm through his and they stepped out quickly. Lorna could see the fog standing in beads on Jonathon's hair, tightening it into tiny curls at his hairline. At

273

Central Station he bought her a ticket and walked with her to the top of the stairs.

Lorna said, 'There's my train, waiting at the platform.' This was the terminus. She began to thank him again.

'You'll be all right now?'

'Yes, I can walk home from Hamilton Square, it isn't far.'

He kissed her cheek, a friendly kiss without passion. 'Take care,' he said. 'See you tomorrow night.'

Lorna ran down the steps to the train, feeling she had wings on her heels. Her cheek flamed where his lips had touched it.

When Lorna reached home a big fire was roaring in the grate and the table was set for five. The little living room was cosy and comfortable.

Her mother was quite excited. 'Not often I get all the family home together, but tonight you'll all be here. Our Jim docked this afternoon and Sam's taken him round to the Lighterman's Arms for a drink.'

'Lovely,' Lorna said. 'Haven't seen Jim for ages.' But the truth was that Jonathon was filling her mind. She could almost feel herself sparkle. 'What's for tea?'

'Boiled bacon.'

Pam was toasting herself in front of the fire. 'And I've made a cake and some scones.'

'Have you found out any more?' That was usually Mum's first question.

'Not about Oliver, but yes, something you'll be interested in.'

At that moment the menfolk of the family returned and Lorna said, 'I'll tell you later.'

After they'd eaten, they pulled their chairs to the fire and roasted chestnuts in the red-hot coals. There were only two armchairs because there wasn't space for more, but Mum had made cushion seats for the dining chairs, and when they were all home they used those. Pam liked to use a stool and tonight she rested her back against her father's knees while Lorna told them the story of how the Wyndham fortune had been made in slaving.

Alice was delighted and laughed aloud. 'That takes them all down more than one peg. They were so snobbish and thought highly of their ancestors and themselves. It's wonderful to think they've descended from criminals and villains. They looked down on me, thought I wasn't good enough to marry into the family.'

Lorna smiled. 'Rosaleen didn't believe it at first. Jonathon said Crispin was astounded when he heard. It hadn't occurred to them to doubt what they'd been told. It came as a blow to their pride.'

'What about the old man?' Alice asked.

'I saw him wipe away a tear and thought he was upset, but he said only because his wife had known and hadn't told him. And Oliver had known too and had stopped writing the family history.'

'Both were trying to shield him,' Sam Mathews said.

'He wasn't unhappy about it. He said, if he was descended from rogues he had less to live up to, and he'd always tried to be honest and fair, even if he'd let the house fall about the family's ears.'

Alice said, 'They were so proud of their roots, it must have hurt.'

Lorna was thoughtful. She decided to say nothing about Jonathon for the time being, afraid it would make Mum nervous. Instead she said, 'What were the four brothers like, Mum, when they were young?'

'Handsome, good-looking fellows, all of them, but a quarrelsome lot. Always bickering between themselves.'

'John, the eldest?' Lorna wanted to know what Jonathon's father had been like.

'The old man's favourite. As he was older than the others he used to keep them in order. Boss them a bit, but he was always polite to me, a real gentleman.'

'And Piers?'

'I didn't like him much. He could be rude and demanded a lot. He was very strange...'

'In what way?'

'Well...' Her mother was screwing her face up. 'He had a sort of... an unlawful tendency.'

'What?' Lorna demanded. 'He wasn't honest? He had a criminal record?'

'No, no, nothing like that...'

She could see her mother was embarrassed. 'What then?'

'It doesn't matter.' Alice was looking anxiously at Pam. 'Nothing. I'll make some cocoa. It's time we were all in bed.' She jerked to her feet and started rattling cups in the scullery. Pam went to help her.

276

Lorna was perplexed. Was there something else she didn't know about?

Half an hour later, when Pam had gone upstairs and closed her bedroom door, Lorna said, 'I don't understand what you were saying about Piers, Mum.'

'It was nothing.' Alice began collecting the cups together to wash them.

'It's no good you keeping secrets from me,' Lorna burst out. 'It's hard enough getting to the bottom of things at Otterspool. Come on, I want to know.'

'Well, they said he was a nancy boy.'

'What's that?'

'It means he wouldn't have looked twice at you or at Mum.' Jim was helping her out. 'He preferred men to women.'

Lorna asked, 'He wasn't married?'

'No.'

'If he didn't like women, if he didn't feel the normal attraction for them, why would he get married?' her brother asked.

Alice looked fluttery. 'Rosaleen was always asking girl friends home to meet him. I don't think she believed anyone as well bred as a Wyndham could be like that.'

'Did he have boyfriends?' Jim wanted to know.

'Yes, but they kept it very quiet.' Alice bit her lip.

'I've never heard of such a thing.' Lorna was amazed, and rather shocked.

'It's not a very nice thing to talk about,' Sam said.

'So you don't.'

'Nobody does,' Jim said. 'It's also against the law.'

'You mean he could be sent to prison for that?'

'Yes, men have before now.'

'Goodness!'

'He was close to his mother,' Alice said. 'Rosaleen and Crispin rather ganged up on him. They were inclined to do that if one of the family stepped out of line and wanted something the others didn't. They'd close ranks and try to talk him out of it. I think that's what happened when Oliver wanted to marry me.'

'This slavery business – bad news for the family, Lorna,' Sam chuckled. 'Bet they were sorry they'd paid you to find that out! I'm surprised you haven't been thrown out.'

'If it had been up to Rosaleen, I think I would have been,' she laughed.

Daphne had not been pleased to see Rosaleen on her doorstep one evening earlier that week, but when Crispin closed the front door behind his sister hours later, she sniggered.

'How the Wyndhams amassed their great fortune,' she mocked. 'They battened on poor Africans, carted them across the world and sold them into slavery. Are you still proud of your ancestors?'

'Shut up!' Crispin made for the stairs. It was time for bed. Daphne followed him up. She'd intended to have a bedroom to herself in this house. After all, Crispin often slept elsewhere. She never knew whether he'd return home or not.

'No,' he'd thundered, when he'd realised what she was doing. 'You're my wife and we'll share the same bed. What would the children think? And the servants?'

'I didn't think you'd care about that.' He'd never taken the trouble to hide from her that he'd had a succession of mistresses. And recently he'd given her to understand that he'd set up his present mistress in a place of her own. Daphne suspected this one was becoming a permanent fixture and he might even have had a child by her.

He let her know these things to hurt her, but it had been going on too long to cut her as it had. It was what she expected from him: he was a complete cad. His infidelities were a secret he kept from the rest of his family, though. He wouldn't want his father to know. Well, she'd married him for the status of being a Wyndham and she still had that.

'I don't see why I shouldn't have a room to myself. We don't need all these guest rooms. We rarely have guests...'

'Just your relatives,' he'd sneered.

That was another thing. All his close relatives lived under the same roof, but the family had resented her mother and grandmother coming for a visit.

There was only one dressing room to the main bedroom at Ravensdale House and Crispin had commandeered that. He came back to their bedroom wearing his silk pyjamas.

'Slavers,' she sniggered again as she undid her corsets and rubbed the rolls of fat that had been compressed all day. 'I can't get over them being slavers.'

'Hurry up,' he urged. 'Let's get the light out. I can't bear to look at you. You've got to stop gorging yourself. You're too fat.'

Daphne had heard this many times before. That too had lost its cutting edge. 'You're a bit of a barrel yourself.'

She giggled girlishly and then laughed outright. The news that the family had been slavers had delighted her. She'd seen how it had upset Rosaleen, who had said ten times that she didn't believe it. Even Crispin had been taken aback. But it seemed they'd have to accept it. There was irrefutable proof.

'It's that girl Lorna Mathews,' Rosaleen had complained. 'Father asked her to sort through our family papers and she's turning up things that would be better left undisturbed. I told him so.'

Daphne smiled. The family had made such a song and dance about their wonderful ancestors, but this brought them down a peg or two and she wouldn't be the only one crowing.

'How the mighty have fallen. Your forefathers were not the upright gentlemen you supposed. They were criminals and fortune-hunters and didn't care how they made their money. Slavers, ha ha.'

'Not slum trash like yours,' Crispin sneered, climbing into bed.

'You've always kept that fact hidden from your parents,' she taunted, 'but my relatives were always law-abiding citizens.'

The following day Daphne bought several books about the Liverpool slave trade. Her eyes had been opened; she hadn't realised slaving had been so widespread in the city. She left the books lying about where Crispin couldn't miss seeing them. He ignored them.

She displayed them on his bedside table so he'd see them when he went up to bed. Her reward was seeing him throw them across the room in a fit of temper.

'Did you know,' she said, trying to look wide-eyed and guileless, 'that some families dealt quite openly in the slave trade, and have streets in the city named after them? The Tarletons and the Earles?'

'Those families will have died out by now.'

'Or,' with all the innocence she could assume, 'those families stopped slaving when the trade became unlawful for British citizens. So they haven't quite so much to be ashamed of.'

He burst out, 'We have nothing to be ashamed of.'

'Crispin, being ashamed is not something you do. You could commit murder and feel proud of it.'

'I certainly could at this moment.' There was black rage on his face.

Daphne smiled; she heard him clatter downstairs and the front door slam. As she climbed into bed, she heard his car start up. Let him go, she'd had enough. Yes, she'd enjoyed that. It wasn't often she could give Crispin and Rosaleen as good as they gave her.

Her thoughts went back over the years, dwelling on the rare times when she'd had the upper hand. On Rosaleen's twenty-first birthday, there'd been big celebrations at Otterspool. At breakfast, Daphne had congratulated her on her coming of age.

'If you decide to get married, you'll have no need to ask for permission now,' she'd smiled. 'All you have to do is to find the right man.'

She sensed Rosaleen rather envied her own married state with two children, and that she was growing impatient about finding her life partner. The family thought it important for a daughter to marry well and ever since she was eighteen, her mother had been taking her about, and holding parties of every sort, from cocktails to tennis, so that she'd meet young men.

The problem was perfectly clear to Daphne. Rosaleen was seeking a partner from a social class at least as high as she rated her own family, and hopefully higher, so she could look up to him. He'd have to be wealthy, handsome, good-natured and amusing company. There weren't many men like that about.

Daphne lost no opportunity to point out the delights of marriage to her. Rosaleen would have a life and a home of her own, a partner to share everything, and eventually children. At the entertainments held at Otterspool for Rosaleen, Daphne looked over the young unattached men who were invited, and saw Rosaleen was not particularly interested in any of them, nor they in her.

She sympathised as the years went on. 'Such a

shame, getting older and still no sign.' Daphne talked of old maids and of being left on the shelf. 'Such a disappointment for a girl in your position.'

Rosaleen was twenty-seven in 1913 when she finally decided to marry Henry Montague. He was Crispin's friend and, because he used to accompany him to the Lord Raglan, he was no stranger to Daphne. It was he who had told Rosaleen she'd lived and worked in a pub.

Daphne had no reason to like him and could see no reason why Rosaleen should either. He was said to be rich – the Montagues were in hotels – but she knew Crispin had sometimes paid the bills he ran up at the Lord Raglan. She also knew that in addition to drinking a lot, he was passionate about horse racing, going from course to course during the season. Crispin had also told her that he gambled heavily.

Daphne thought his waxed moustache with curly ends made him look like a tailor's dummy, and she'd heard talk of wild parties and many women. Neither did she think he was madly in love with Rosaleen. After all, they could have married years ago.

Daphne was wary of him. In the past, he'd come to Otterspool only rarely when large numbers of guests were invited to a cocktail party or a dance, and she'd been careful to keep her distance. Now he and his family were coming when there were no other guests, and it was much more difficult to keep out of his way.

Daphne kept her mouth shut about his faults. She wanted Rosaleen to marry and move out of

Otterspool so that she'd be free of her corrosive company. The family said they were very pleased for Rosaleen. The wedding was a far more lavish occasion than her own. She told the bridal pair she hoped they'd be happy.

When she heard the first mention of Rosaleen's dissatisfaction with Henry, she wasn't surprised. She'd expected Henry to be a worse husband than Crispin. But things got so bad Rosaleen left him and came home to Otterspool and that was the last thing Daphne had wanted.

Rosaleen was upset, touchy and difficult to live with. Her parents tried to console her and gave her everything they could. Daphne thought her a spoiled only daughter and told her Henry's gambling habits had been well known to Crispin and she was surprised he hadn't warned her. She asked Crispin about Henry's drinking and his other women and, when Rosaleen had a go at her, Daphne recounted the details of her husband's sordid adventures. For once, fate had given her the ammunition she needed.

Rosaleen became depressed. Daphne had always thought she lived in a veiled world of her own, far from reality, a world she expected to mould to her every wish. She lived on her nerves, so it didn't surprise Daphne when she had a nervous breakdown. She thought Rosaleen deserved it.

Daphne thought the war years had been easier for her than for the rest of the family. Crispin was called up, but was given the rank of major and sent to Ireland to train others for the front. She enjoyed his absence and felt she would not be too worried if he met his end, but for him there was never much risk of that.

When John was killed, she tried to comfort Frances, but felt little grief herself. Frances, as the wife and then the widow of the family heir, was senior to Daphne in the Wyndham hierarchy. Although she was a distant cousin, Frances didn't have the fight needed to cope with Rosaleen, who was just as aggressive to her as she was to everybody else. Daphne wasn't pleased when Frances left voluntarily.

Daphne felt even less grief for Piers when he died. Her mother-in-law's death came as an almighty shock to them all, but Daphne didn't feel close to her, though she'd never been unkind. With Marina gone, Daphne began to see herself as mistress of Otterspool. Within days Rosaleen had elbowed her out, though she wasn't prepared to take on much in the way of household organisation. Aunt Maude took over much of the daily housekeeping while Rosaleen pretended she did it. She acted as hostess when they had visitors. To Daphne, she remained a thorn in the flesh.

By Sunday, the fog had cleared. Back at Otterspool that night, Jonathon came to the kitchen while Lorna was having her supper with Sissie and Hilda. He sat down at the table, drank tea and chatted. Hilda showed her disapproval, trying to move him out so that Sissie could wash up. Lorna went with him to the library. In that house there were plenty of places where they could get away from other people. The next day,

Lorna was just finishing her lunch in the kitchen when Harold brought a van driver in.

'He's come to collect some furniture and boxes,' he told them.

'Mr Adam's things,' Hilda said.

'Didn't they go on the pantechnicons in September?' Lorna wanted to know. 'To the new house?'

The van driver took a notebook from the pocket of his brown drill coat. 'These are to go to Queen's Drive.' He showed them the address.

Hilda was leading the way upstairs. 'You'd better come too, Harold. He'll need a hand to get the table downstairs.'

Lorna followed them. Within the coming days it would be her job to sort out the three rooms at the far end of the house. There was a bedroom with a huge four-poster, a sitting room looking out over the river and a smaller dining room.

She asked, 'Adam used these rooms?' Easy to see they'd had recent and heavy use. 'I thought all Crispin's family were in the west wing. In fact...' She remembered taking down curtains in what must have been Adam's bedroom there.

Hilda said stiffly. 'Yes, he moved here.'

'Why?' Lorna asked.

Harold sniggered. 'So he could entertain his own friends without annoying his mam and dad.'

'No thought for me,' Hilda complained. 'Or the extra trouble cleaning them would give. Often they'd want something cooked and we'd have to bring it all the way up here.'

'He held big parties?' Lorna wanted to know 'Played his gramophone?' She could see that here.

286

'Not big parties,' Harold said. 'I understand that most of the time, it was just one friend.'

'Oh,' said Lorna. 'He could entertain his girlfriend here without the family knowing.'

Hilda drew herself up. 'No, nothing like that, a friend from the office who liked opera. They played the records and followed the music from the score, that sort of thing.'

'He slept here? It's a five-minute walk to the nearest bathroom or lavatory.'

'It didn't bother him that I had to carry up hot water and empty his slops,' Hilda said.

'Look, he's stuck labels on the pieces he wants taken away.'

'He has loads of records,' Harold said. 'I helped pack them into these crates.' There were two, labelled 'Fragile', and marked with the Queen's Drive address. It seemed Adam wasn't planning to live with his parents.

'Is Adam not pleased with the house his parents have chosen?' Lorna asked.

'Yes,' Harold said. 'But toffs like him like more than one place to put their heads down, by the look of it.'

'Perhaps some of the records belong to his friend.'

'I can't stay gossiping here all day,' Hilda said sharply. 'I haven't the time.'

That moved Harold. 'We'd better start with the table.'

It occurred to Lorna as she followed Hilda back to the kitchen that she hadn't offered one item of gossip. It made her wonder just what she did know.

At tea time the next day, Lorna was in the drawing room with the family when Jonathon came home.

'Crispin said he'd come for a cup of tea this afternoon,' he told them. 'He wants to have a chat.'

'What about?' Rosaleen wanted to know.

Lorna poured herself a cup of tea and took it with a small slice of cake to her usual place near the window, a little apart from the others.

'The business,' Jonathon said. 'Mr Buckler's given him the half-yearly accounts.'

'I hope they aren't down again,' Quentin said.

'I'm afraid they are.' Jonathon was on his feet cutting a large slice of currant cake.

Lorna saw Crispin drive up and get out of a large powerful car. 'Here he is now,' she told them.

Jonathon came over to look and sat down beside her. 'He's not happy about the Cartwright business either.'

Lorna felt her stomach jolt. 'Why not?'

'He'll tell you.'

Rosaleen caught her eye. 'Crispin will need a fresh pot of tea,' she said.

Lorna got up and rang for Sissie. She wasn't going to fetch it today; she wanted to hear exactly what was said about the Cartwright business.

Crispin looked anything but pleased when he came in carrying a pile of ledgers and files. He slammed them down on an occasional table, rocking a vase of flowers.

'The Cartwright business isn't going to make

anything like the profit we were told it would,' he glowered at Lorna.

She put her cup and saucer down. 'I'm sure it will.'

'We were misled,' he insisted. 'The figures were inflated to make it seem worth the price asked for it. You paid too much for it, Father.'

Lorna knew that wasn't true. 'The price was fair. The figures I gave you were correct. The accounts were checked by our auditors.'

'Thring and Beddoes...' There was contempt in Crispin's voice. 'Buckler thinks they can't be trusted. Not a firm we'd heard of before. The Cartwright earnings are way behind schedule already.'

'Two of your clients have been lost.' Jonathon was frowning. 'They complained they weren't getting the attention from Adam that they received from you, Lorna.'

'Who've you lost?' she wanted to know. 'Really, I should be in your office all the time, a voice they know when they ring up.'

'I thought that was the idea,' Crispin retorted.

Lorna opened one of the ledgers he'd brought. It shocked her to find she couldn't understand the figures. 'You've changed the whole system of accounting!'

'This is the way we always work.' Crispin sounded indignant.

'It's just that I can't see...' She knew she was floundering. 'Does your method alter the way the totals work out?'

'It can't.' Crispin stroked his moustache. 'Either the business is earning what Mrs Cartwright said it would, or it isn't.'

Lorna took a deep breath and looked him in the eye. 'It's what I said the business was earning. You haven't been cheated. Mrs Cartwright would never allow me to mislead you.' She didn't like to hear Crispin accusing them of such a thing. But it worried her, and she felt responsible. 'I'd like to take these files and ledgers to my room. I need to look at your figures, see what exactly you've done.'

'Our accounts clerks are very reliable,' Crispin said haughtily. 'Mr Buckler guarantees their work, checks it over himself. And we'll need these books in the office tomorrow.'

'I'll look at them tonight. There'll be a mistake of some sort.'

'You're very sure of yourself.' His confident Wyndham eyes challenged hers.

Lorna could feel herself getting rattled. 'I should be. I ran this business myself for several years. Talked to the clients, booked cargo space, did the accounting and the writing of letters, everything. I know it backwards. If you'll excuse me, I'd better get started now.'

'I can take them with me in the morning,' Jonathon said. She rushed up to her room, feeling angry and confused, and spread out the ledgers for the last three months' trading on her bed. She was further shocked to find the figures nearly thirty per cent down on the previous year. She looked, but could see no reason for the fall. The cargo was being shipped by mail boat in regular small amounts – that didn't change much. True, two clients had taken their business elsewhere, but they'd never shipped large amounts, and Samsons, their biggest client, had put more business their way.

The figures had been divided up differently from the way she used to do it, so no direct comparison was possible. She found pencil and paper and did a rough calculation on losing the two small accounts and gaining more from Samsons and set them against the figure she'd expect them to earn. That should take them only around one per cent down. She studied the figures again, trying to see why they should differ so much, but had to give up. They made no sense to her.

She took the books downstairs to give to Jonathon. He'd been out for a walk and was taking his coat off.

'By my reckoning,' she said, 'the business is point nine per cent down on this time last year, not thirty per cent. Mr Crispin is wrong, but since he's changed everything round, I can't put my finger on where or why.'

They went together to the library and sat down side by side at the table. She talked him through her figures.

'I can't fault your arithmetic,' he said at last. 'But I only have your word for what the business made last year. Those figures are in the office.'

'I can remember, I know I'm not wrong.'

'Let's go and tell Grandpa. We need to get this sorted out.' He bundled up the ledgers and led the way to the drawing room.

Rosaleen was sipping sherry; Quentin was with her. He took a deep draught of his whisky when he'd heard them out.

'Crispin's gone, but you and he need to reconcile your figures. He's worried.'

'I'm worried too.' Rosaleen was indignant. 'If the balance at the bank is heavily down, what do your figures mean?'

'Crispin is running this in with our other business.' Jonathon frowned. 'There isn't a separate bank account.'

Quentin said firmly, 'Jonathon, take Lorna to the office in the morning and talk it through with Crispin and Buckler. You must straighten this out between you.'

Chapter Fifteen

The next morning, when Lorna travelled in to the office with Jonathon, the rain was dancing on the pavements and drumming on the canvas roof of his small two-seater.

'It's weather like this that makes me wish I'd decided on a saloon,' he said. 'I'm afraid this leaks a bit over your side.'

She felt they were more at ease with each other now, and that Jonathon had forgiven her for keeping him at arm's length. As they were drawing up outside the office, a motorcyclist passed them, wearing goggles, a tweed cap with a big peak and a yellow oilskin cape.

'That's Buckler,' Jonathon chuckled. 'I bet he's had a soaking this morning. He's always talking of getting a car – when he can afford it.'

Ten minutes later, Jonathon led her into the accountant's office. Mr Buckler was wearing a formal business suit, but Lorna noticed his trouser legs looked wet and he was trying to squeeze the creases back into them. Jonathon let the pile of ledgers he was carrying bang down on his desk. Lorna balanced hers on top.

She said, 'There's a problem here with the Cartwright account.'

Buckler surveyed them sourly. 'I've told Mr Crispin it's failing to perform.'

'We don't think so.' Jonathon's manner was positive. Lorna was glad of his support. She hadn't slept well; anxiety was crumbling her confidence. She knew she mustn't let Crispin see that.

'According to my reckoning,' she said, 'we are point nine per cent down on this time last year.' She placed her pencilled figures in front of him. He pushed them roughly aside.

'You can't compare with these. We've taken them into our own accounting system.'

'So I see, and it's hiding the true picture.' Lorna opened one of his ledgers and stabbed her finger on the figures. 'Orders are coming in and payments are being made promptly. I can't see the problem. Everything is performing exactly as we said it would.'

'According to our figures, it isn't.'

Lorna took a deep breath. 'By changing my way of accounting, it's hard to see what is happening. Wouldn't it be better to keep the figures separate until we're all satisfied that the former Cartwright

293

business is earning as it should? So much easier to check.'

Mr Buckler was steepling his fingers. 'The work to consolidate the account has already been done. It makes no sense to return to your outdated system.'

'But your figures don't tally with mine,' Lorna insisted. 'I've tried to make them but I can't.' The ledgers were passed backwards and forwards. 'There must be mistakes in your figures.'

'We need to look at the bank accounts,' Jonathon said. 'We can then pick out the amounts that have been earned by the Cartwright account.'

'You don't understand.' Mr Buckler was clearly losing patience. 'The figures have been amalgamated into Wyndhams' business. We can't separate them.'

'But if you can't do that,' Lorna asked, 'how can you say Cartwright business is down and we misled you as to the profitability?'

Mr Buckler was beginning to look uncomfortable.

Beside her, she felt Jonathon stir. 'She's right, Mr Buckler,' he said. 'My grandfather and I have decided it would be better if Miss Mathews came to the office every day and attended to this in future.'

'And what about Mr Crispin? He expects me to carry out his instructions.'

'He seemed very worried about it yesterday evening,' Jonathon said. 'But this morning, he isn't here. Or he hadn't come in when we started. I'll go and see if he's here now.'

Lorna could hardly believe it when he came

back and said, 'No.'

Once back in Jonathon's office, Lorna collapsed on his visitor's chair, deep in thought. His phone rang.

Jonathon lifted it, then covered the mouthpiece with his hand and said, 'A Cartwright client is being put through from Adam's office, because he isn't in yet either.'

'Let me take it.' The client wanted to book fifty bales of cotton cloth out to Lagos. There were two more orders before lunch time. Lorna dealt with them sitting at the end of Jonathon's desk. 'I'm distracting you here,' she said.

'You ought to have an office of your own.'

'A desk somewhere would do.'

'The desks are packed tight in the main hall because we've just closed our Birkenhead office. But neither Uncle Crispin nor Adam uses his office much. I get cross sometimes. All they seem to want is to draw their salaries.'

In the afternoon, Lorna took the bus back to Otterspool House because there was still a lot she needed to do there. At tea time, she went to the drawing room as usual, to find Jonathon there before her, talking earnestly.

He turned to her and said, 'I've been telling Grandpa and Aunt Maude about how ill at ease Mr Buckler seemed this morning. He insists the Cartwright account is not performing.'

'He didn't like us questioning his figures,' Lorna said. 'In fact he was quite embarrassed.'

'If he tells us the business is down,' Maude said, 'he must expect us to question his figures.'

Quentin helped himself to more tea. 'Starting

next week, Lorna, I'd like you to go in every morning. You're coming to the end of the job here. We need to keep that business and you're the best person to do it.'

'The customers all ask for her,' Jonathon smiled.

Lorna was deep in thought. 'Has Mr Buckler been with you long?'

'Ever since I can remember,' Jonathon said. 'You must have taken him on, Grandpa, in your time?'

Quentin had to think. 'He was a friend of your Uncle Piers. They went through the war together. We needed another accountant and he brought Buckler into the firm. He's been with us ever since.'

Lorna's mind was working overtime. What if he'd been Piers's partner, another with the unlawful tendency her mother had spoken of? Not that that would affect his honesty or lack of it, but it was against the law. She felt he wasn't honest. Why had he been in such a hurry to change the accounting system?

Jonathon said, 'Uncle Crispin accepts all Buckler tells him; he trusts him.'

'Perhaps he shouldn't,' Lorna frowned, and found they were all looking at her in surprise. 'Or am I being too suspicious?' She felt she had to justify that.

'It's only a few months since you bought Cartwrights. It's easy to see things haven't altered much. Why is he preparing you now for a down turn?'

Rosaleen looked up. 'Our profit has been going

steadily down for years, ever since you retired, Father. I think you and Jonathon should take another look at his figures.'

The following Saturday afternoon, Lorna was sitting on top of a bus going into town, on the first leg of her journey home. The bus had pulled in to a stop when she saw just in front of her a car turn into the drive of a large and rather smart detached house. She thought at first it was Jonathon's car, but she knew Adam had the same model. Both he and Mr Buckler got out. They were laughing together as they headed for the front door. Then Mr Buckler produced a key and let them both in.

She studied the house with interest, assuming at first it was the one Crispin had rented. But she'd heard that that was in grounds of two acres and was on the way to Speke Aerodrome so this couldn't be it.

When the bus stopped at traffic lights a few minutes later, she saw the name of the road was Queen's Drive and remembered that that was where Adam had had his belongings sent. It made her wonder if the house could be Mr Buckler's – it certainly hadn't been bought by Adam or she would have heard – but a big car had been parked in front of the garage and she'd seen him ride to work on a motorcycle on a very wet day.

She asked herself now if Buckler could be the friend with whom Adam shared his love of opera, and decided that when she next went to the office she'd look up Mr Buckler's address. Crispin kept all the personnel files in his room, but he was not often there and Jonathon now had keys to all the files.

The following week, on her first regular morning at the office, Lorna was working in Jonathon's room when he went out and left his keys on his desk. She was able to take a look at Buckler's file without anybody being any the wiser. His date of birth was given as 1889, which made him nearly forty-two. He'd qualified as a chartered accountant in 1915 and served in the Army Pay Corps until the end of the war, and his home address was given as Wervyn Street, Everton. Lorna knew little about suburban Liverpool but thought Queen's Drive a more up-market area.

She decided he must have moved house recently, but why did he come to work on a motorbike? Could it be that he didn't want to give the impression he was living beyond his income?

Jonathon was taking a careful look through Buckler's figures as Rosaleen had suggested. Every evening, between tea and dinner, Lorna helped him comb through the Wyndham accounts at the library table. He brought home the annual balance sheets of the Wyndham business for the previous five years, together with the ledgers that supported them. It took several sessions for Lorna to understand how they worked.

'They seem perfectly all right to me,' she said. 'But do I know enough about accounting?' Lorna felt full of doubt. 'Buckler called me a mere accounts clerk.'

Jonathon chuckled. 'He's trying to belittle you.

But I hold the same qualification that he does. I was articled to an accountancy firm when I left school.'

'Can you see anything wrong?'

'I couldn't at first,' Jonathon said. 'They seemed genuine enough; but I asked him for the bank statements for these years. I told him I needed them to check, and after a lot of time-wasting, he told me he'd destroyed them.'

'He doesn't want us to see them,' Lorna said, straightening up on her chair. 'They'd be filed away carefully, wouldn't they? Not like personal bank statements that can get lost or mislaid.'

'Exactly. For tax purposes, they have to be kept.'

'Can you ask the bank for copies?'

'Grandfather can. I've had a talk with him. He's a bit upset about this and he'll be going to the bank in the morning.'

It was only when they received the company bank statements and tried to reconcile the figures with those in the cash book that they found what they were looking for. After they'd been poring over them for a while, Lorna was frowning.

'D'you think the figures have been deliberately falsified?'

'The same thought occurred to me,' Jonathon said. 'But if they have, why haven't the auditors picked it up?' He pushed the company accounts he'd been looking at in front of Lorna.

'These figures are for nineteen twenty-eight. The auditors have signed and dated them as correct. Here look, Arnold C. Winter. The accounts for nineteen twenty-nine are signed as correct too.

'Something's very wrong here.' Jonathon had the open cash book in front of him. 'Look, May the tenth, according to this, Grimshaws paid a cheque to us for a hundred and forty pounds. But the bank statement shows a cheque being paid in of one thousand four hundred pounds on that date. It's quite obvious. What I don't understand is why the auditors didn't see it.'

Lorna felt quite fluttery. 'A mistake?'

'There's another instance here in June. Fifty-two pounds in the cashbook, but five hundred and twenty pounds on the bank statement.'

She was shocked. 'This runs into thousands of pounds.'

'Tomorrow,' Jonathon said, gathering the documents together, 'I'll call on Lowther and Winter, ask to speak to Mr Winter himself. This has to be fraud.'

Lorna shivered. 'This is scary.'

He shook his head. 'It's good news for you, isn't it? You were right about the Cartwright figures.'

'Maybe. And bad news for Crispin.'

'Let's keep this to ourselves for the time being.'

At lunch time the following day, Lorna was preparing to leave when Jonathon burst back into his office. His cheeks were scarlet.

'I was totally embarrassed,' he said, collapsing on a chair. 'Mr Winter told me they were no longer our auditors and hadn't been for the last six years. It seems Buckler wrote to him saying their services would not be required in future. He even dug the letter out of their files and showed it to me.'

300

'Mr Buckler signed it?'

'Yes, I've asked for a copy of it.' Jonathon was tight-lipped. 'Mr Winter said he was very surprised. His company had been auditing ours for decades and he thought we were on good terms. He spoke to Uncle Crispin on the telephone and he confirmed it. When I showed him his signature on our accounts, he said it was a forgery and that the reason was undoubtedly fraud. He advised me to go to the police.'

Lorna felt sick. 'I'm shocked. This means Crispin... Why would he want to? He owns a share of the business.'

'He's taking a lot more than his share, that's the point. I'm going home to talk to Grandpa before I do anything. The rest of the family are being done down. He thinks his father is too old to notice. And Aunts Maude and Roz have never had anything to do with business. Don't mention this to anybody here.'

'Course not, but it's time I went too. Can I have a lift?'

Lorna clung to the passenger seat as Jonathon raced the little car home. She was afraid they'd unearthed another Wyndham secret, one that would have an even greater effect on the family than finding their forebears had been slavers.

She said frowning, 'There's something else you should know. Buckler and Adam are ... well, great friends.'

'Are you saying Adam knows about this too?' Jonathon glanced at her. He looked shocked.

'Buckler's his partner, that's what I'm saying.'

'Partner? No...'

'Not business partner. They're both, you know, interested in men rather than women. Interested in each other.'

'Gee, what makes you say that?'

'I see and hear things. Can't avoid it sometimes.'

He glanced at her. 'What sort of things?'

She told him about seeing Buckler and Adam going into a house in Queen's Drive, though his address in the company records was quite different. 'He appears to own a large car too, yet we saw him ride his motorbike to work on a very wet morning.'

'He's careful about hiding things?'

'Yes, but Adam isn't. You know I cleared out his rooms?'

'I didn't know he had those rooms in the tower until you mentioned them.'

'Well, when I took out the paper lining from a drawer in his chest, I found some things which I think he'd hidden, but forgotten.'

'What things, Lorna?'

'There was a large envelope with some obscene drawings in, and a covering letter from Buckler. I can only describe it as a love letter.'

'Good Lord! You've kept them?'

'Yes, of course. They're in my room. I'll show them to you. There were other things too, poems. I wasn't sure what to make of them. I showed them to my brother Jim who said...'

'What?'

'He confirmed it was homosexual stuff, bawdy, not very nice. There's another thing. There's a notebook full of the poems addressed to Buckler that seems to have belonged to your Uncle Piers.

So it appears he was that way inclined too.'

'I didn't know!'

'You've been in America. And your family knows how to keep things quiet, doesn't it?'

'But I came back two weeks before you started. I've had longer–'

'You've been kept busy in the office. Take my word for it.'

'You unearth all our secrets.'

'Not all,' Lorna said, thinking of Oliver.

Quentin felt dispirited. He'd been going round the house looking into rooms that had been stripped bare. His family heritage was ready to be sold off. On top of that, he was very worried about what Jonathon might turn up in the accounts. At seventy, he'd felt ready to retire and had cut down on the time he spent at the office. He'd intended to keep control of the purse strings because he hadn't quite trusted Crispin to run the business properly, but within two more years he'd virtually given up. He'd given Crispin a freer hand as the years had gone on, but now he was regretting it.

Rosaleen had gone out and for once he'd lunched alone. Hilda hadn't made much effort – she'd given him the warmed-up leftovers from last night's dinner. He was drinking his coffee when Jonathon's head came round the door.

'Are you busy, Grandpa? Lorna and I would like a word.'

'You've found something? Come in, both of you.'

'Bad news, I'm afraid.'

'I should be used to bad news by now. What is it?'

Jonathon said, 'Following what Lorna found in the Cartwright account, we've been doing what you suggested—'

'I know that.' He was impatient.

'We've been looking closely at the Wyndham figures.'

'You sound as though you're addressing a public meeting. Get on with it, lad.'

'Company money has been taken. They've used more than one way of doing it.' He pointed out the Grimshaw cheque as an example.

Quentin's spirits sank. This was far worse than he'd imagined. 'Crispin should have picked this up. Whatever has he been doing?'

But Crispin had been so busy finding himself a fine house and making sure he got his full share of everything that he'd hardly had time to see what was going on in the office.

'We weren't sure at first whether these were mistakes or fraud,' Lorna said.

'Uncle Crispin must know about it.' Jonathon's eyes were misty with sympathy. 'Buckler couldn't do it without his knowledge. Large sums have disappeared over recent years. It's fraud. Has to be.'

Quentin couldn't get his breath. He felt he was being swamped in a wave of outrage. His own son! It wasn't just anger he felt, it was complete and utter shock.

'Crispin?' he choked. 'He's done this?' How many times had Crispin come here to his study complaining that business was being lost when all the time...? He'd never felt such helplessness, such a sense of futility.

Jonathon was pushing something else in front of him.

'What's this?'

'The copy of a bill for three hundred and twenty-five pounds. It was sent to Melkshams on the tenth of July. There's no record that it was ever paid, but no reminder was sent. And this is last year's receipt book.' Jonathon's finger was keeping it open. 'Nothing has been written on this stub, and there are several other blank ones.'

'Crispin is friendly with Peter Melksham. I've seen him in the office. I know we place regular cargoes for him – I see the paperwork – but no cheques come in from Melkshams though bills are sent. Nothing all last year. I think he must be making the cheques out to Uncle Crispin rather than to the firm, and he pays them directly into his personal account.'

Quentin felt the room spinning round. He held on to the arms of his chair. He'd felt disappointed with Crispin, angry with him too at times. What father didn't lose patience occasionally? But he couldn't forget the deep bond of affection that had been between them. Did Crispin not feel that affection for him?

It seemed he didn't, and the shock was taking his father to the edge of despair. He could feel tears welling, yet his grief was laced with love. He couldn't believe it – didn't want to believe it.

There was worse. Jonathon's voice went on, telling him that the accounts had not been audited for several years. As they were a private company they had no shareholders to satisfy, the accounts were for tax purposes and their own family use.

'Are you going to call in the police?' Jonathon asked.

Quentin had to think and his mind wouldn't move – old age was hell. 'Not yet. If Crispin is involved, then it's best handled within the family.'

'But how are you going to do that?'

He could hear doubt in his grandson's voice, knew he didn't think him capable of handling this. But he would. He couldn't have the name of Wyndham dragged through the courts.

'You go back to work this afternoon, and tell both Crispin and Adam that I'll come to the office tomorrow morning, that there's something I want to discuss. If they aren't in, ring Daphne and leave a message. If they ask what it's about, you've no idea. Absolutely no idea. Right, leave me now, I need to think. You work out what questions you want to ask. You too, Lorna.'

'Me?'

'Yes, I want you there. You spotted the problem. The rest of us trusted Crispin.'

Quentin got up and poked his fire into a blaze. He could feel anger rising like a tide inside him. He'd always put the good of the family first. Yet Crispin was stealing their income, cheating them. Cheating his aunt and his sister. Quentin wanted to think he was making genuine mistakes, but looking through the documents Jonathon had left with him, he knew that wasn't possible.

He didn't sleep well – his mind was working

306

overtime trying to find the best way to cope. By breakfast the next morning, his stomach was twisting and he had no appetite. He gave Jonathon and the girl an hour's start before getting into his Daimler to be driven to the office by Harold. His anger had gone cold; now he was nervous too. He needed to handle this carefully. He had to find out what had been going on since he'd retired. He'd never been as sure of Crispin as he had of John, but he hadn't expected him to be dishonest.

It wasn't easy to manage a business in which members of his family worked. He wanted to treat them generously, but the business had to thrive. Crispin didn't seem to realise he was bleeding it dry. It couldn't survive if he went on like this.

When the Daimler drew up outside, Quentin stood on the pavement for a moment, looking up at the window that had once been his office. The light was on; it looked as though Crispin was already there. He should never have allowed him such a free hand. Going up in the lift, it seemed so different, so strange. He'd been out to grass for the best part of a decade and was feeling every one of his eighty years.

Some of the older members of staff wanted to greet him, but he got himself to Jonathon's office as quickly as he could. 'Are you two ready? We'll hold the inquisition here.'

'Not Uncle Crispin's office?'

Quentin shook his head. 'I don't want him on home ground feeling comfortable. Let's have some tea first. Get three cups of tea for us, please, Lorna.'

He rearranged the chairs. 'We three will sit behind your desk and Crispin can sit well away from us on the other side, like this. You spell it out to him, Jonathon, tell him what you've discovered, and I'll take it from there.' He drank his tea in great gulps. 'Right, Lorna, ask him to come in now.'

Crispin looked rather disconcerted at the seating arrangements but he leaned back as far as the upright chair would allow, and crossed his legs in an exaggerated show of ease.

That stung Quentin to say, 'Miss Mathews has drawn my attention to the state of the company accounts. I'm quite alarmed.'

Jonathon put it to his uncle clearly that the figures shown were not the sums actually being earned. He called it an original concept of accounting and said the only reason for it was fraud.

'Nonsense.' Crispin was ready to laugh it off. 'I did warn you, Father, that we're losing profitability.'

'Yes, but when we bought the Cartwright account, you agreed with me that it would support the rest of our business.'

'Nothing to worry about yet,' Crispin said smoothly. 'Just teething troubles. We'll get it all sorted out. It's only four months since we took it over.'

He heard Lorna's sharp intake of breath. She said, 'But already by my reckoning one thousand eight hundred pounds have disappeared.'

Quentin pounced. 'And it's not just the

Cartwright account. Our own business is losing money too. Since I retired, we worked out that two hundred and... How many thousand did you say had disappeared, Jonathon? Perhaps Crispin you'd explain where it went.'

'I don't believe any such figure.'

'You say we're down, by how much would you say?'

'I don't exactly know, not without studying those figures you're talking about.'

'But it's your duty to study them as soon as they're drawn up. An enormous amount is missing.'

'Not missing, Father. We've failed to earn–'

Quentin felt his anger spark again. 'Missing, spirited away, money that was never put into our bank accounts. You've taken it, haven't you?'

'It's our own money, after all.'

'It's company money. It didn't belong to you. What d'you think we should do, Crispin?' he growled.

Crispin's forehead was shiny with perspiration. He crossed and uncrossed his legs, clearly rattled now.

He saw Lorna smile disarmingly at him. 'Yesterday, Jonathon and I had a chat with Mr Buckler. He could give us no clear explanation of where the money had gone either. He told us he was acting on your orders.'

Quentin saw the jolt that delivered. 'Is that so, Crispin? We need a yes or no to that, for a start.'

The silence lengthened. 'I suppose so.'

Quentin raised his voice. 'I want to know where the money has gone. What you spent it on. If you

309

don't give a satisfactory explanation, I shall call in the police this morning. I don't want Wyndham dirty linen washed in public, do you?'

Crispin's Adam's apple jerked as he swallowed. 'No.'

'Then tell me what you've done with it. That house you've moved to, I understood you to say you'd rented it? A five-year lease?'

'Yes.'

'Then where? Money doesn't just disappear.'

'Living expenses.'

That made him angry. 'Don't waste our time, Crispin. You lived with me. I provided all the food, paid for all services and for domestic help. Living expenses for you and your family have been negligible up to now.'

His son was surveying his shoes in silence.

'The telephone, Miss Mathews – get the operator to put you through to the police station.'

Crispin's face was ashen. 'No, wait a moment,' he said. 'Father, I have other responsibilities that you don't know about.'

'I thought we paid you a generous salary. It should be more than adequate for your needs.'

He was shaking his head.

'Tell us then.' Quentin leaned back. Crispin seemed to have regressed to a ten-year-old.

'I have another... Another home to support. I suppose you'd say a mistress – and a child.'

'Good God!' That took his breath away. This was worse than he'd imagined. A nightmare. 'Your child?'

Crispin drew in a long quivering breath. 'Yes, a girl of five.'

'Does Daphne know?'

'I think she guesses.'

'So you have two families. And you're supporting them like royalty?'

'Yes – no.'

Quentin shook his head in disbelief. 'There must be more to it than that, Crispin. Hundreds of thousands of pounds over the last eight years.'

'I told you, I've taken nothing like that amount. I've tried to be frugal–'

'Frugal, is it? Daphne demands money, I suppose?'

'She likes to dress well.'

'It has to be more than that.'

'No, Father.'

Quentin pushed a pad and pencil towards him. 'Write down how much you've taken from company funds and how often. Lorna, while we wait I'd like some more tea, please. Jonathon?'

'No thanks.'

'I'll have some,' Crispin said, licking his dry lips.

'Later, when I'm satisfied with what you write. I don't want you to be distracted.'

When the pad was returned to him, Quentin was shocked. 'You might as well own up,' he told him, pushing the pad back to him.

'No, Father, that's it. I keep telling you, the firm's losing profitability.'

Quentin shuddered. This was awful. He'd never suspected Crispin of double-crossing him. He took a deep breath. 'We've already come to the conclusion that's an out-and-out lie.'

'No. It's the truth.'

He was still trying to deceive. 'Who told you that?' Without waiting for an answer, Quentin pushed the pad in front of Jonathon. 'What d'you make of this?'

'If it's the truth, somebody else must have his hand in the till.'

Quentin pushed the pad to the other side, in front of Lorna. She nodded her agreement.

'I don't suppose,' Quentin said, 'that it has occurred to you that if you are seen to help yourself like this, others will see it as *carte blanche* to help themselves too?'

Crispin looked as if he'd been whipped.

'Adam, for instance?'

'He wouldn't!'

'We can soon find out. Ask him to come in, Miss Mathews. Tell him to bring a chair in with him.'

Lorna left the door ajar. Quentin heard Adam's querulous voice ask, 'What's going on?'

'A discussion,' she answered. 'Family matters.'

He looked distinctly uneasy when he saw his father.

'Well, Adam,' Quentin said, 'your father has just confessed to taking company money. I want to know if you've taken some too.' The colour had faded from Adam's cheeks. 'I want the truth. If I don't get it, I intend to ask the police to dig it out of you. Now, did you know your father was helping himself?'

Adam's answer was slow to come. 'Yes.'

Crispin looked shocked.

'Did he tell you?'

An even longer pause, then, 'No.'

'Who did then?'

'Buckler.' He swept his handsome yellow hair back from his forehead. He was sweating.

'And did he suggest you and he should take a little too?' Quentin waited. Then: 'Come on, the game's up.'

'How did you find out?' Adam's voice had faded to a whisper.

'I'm asking the questions. Give him the pad, Lorna. You've taken money from the company? Right, the next question is how much?'

'Well, I didn't keep–'

'Of course you didn't keep a record, but you must have some idea.' Adam blew his nose, mopped his forehead. 'When I needed it, I took a little.'

'To spend on what?'

'Trips to London, visits to the opera, records, things like that.'

'And you spent money on Mr Buckler?'

Adam flushed and glanced anxiously at his father.

'You've taken hundreds of thousands of pounds over the last eight years?'

'No, nothing like that.' He was as indignant as his father had been.

'That's the amount that's missing, Adam. It's gone somewhere.'

'I have a flutter sometimes,' he muttered. 'A little bet on the horses.'

'But not all this?'

'No, nothing like that.'

'Ask Mr Buckler to come in, Miss Mathews. Tell him to bring a chair.'

'I'll go.' Crispin's chair scraped back.

'Sit where you are!' Quentin thundered out with a confidence he hadn't felt for years. 'It's getting a little tight in here, but if you two shuffle up a bit there'll be room for one more.'

Buckler's plump face was a picture when he saw Adam and Crispin both trying not to look cowed.

'Sit down, Mr Buckler, do,' Quentin invited. 'We're discussing the company accounts, for which you, as company accountant, are responsible.'

Buckler's portly frame almost fell on the chair.

'We've ascertained that for the last six years they've not been audited. You told our auditors we no longer wanted their services and forged their signature so that I, and the rest of the family, would believe they had. That's a criminal offence as I'm sure you know, and could get you a prison sentence.'

Adam said in a strangled voice, 'I gave a few pounds to Clarissa from time to time.'

'So she knew too?'

'Father wasn't generous with her allowance. You know you weren't, Dad. She wants to run off with that doctor fellow. If she can get her hands on some cash she'll go.'

'Nonsense,' Crispin said. 'She wouldn't go against our wishes.'

'Mr Buckler,' Quentin was determined not to be side-tracked, 'there are hundreds of thousands of pounds missing and though Crispin and Adam have admitted taking a little of it, there's a huge sum still unaccounted for. So what have you

314

done with it? I assume you took some too?'

His small puffy eyes swung from Crispin to Adam. He was more than reluctant to answer. 'A little, yes.'

Quentin sighed. 'I'm getting impatient. This is dragging on. Where's that pad, Lorna? I want to know exactly how much.'

Buckler was shifting his weight restlessly.

'You admit you stole money. What did you spend it on?'

'Living expenses.'

'You're paid a salary, Mr Buckler, to cover those. Come on.'

'I bought a house,' he whispered. It was an admission wrung from him.

'That's more like it.'

Beside him Lorna groped across the desk for his personal file. 'That's where you live? Is it the address given here?'

'Er – no. I've moved recently.'

'To Queen's Drive?' Lorna smiled at Quentin. 'I couldn't help but notice some of Adam's possessions were going there too.'

'How much did you pay for it?' Quentin could feel himself bristling with rage. He'd been worried that he wouldn't have enough to house Maude and Rosaleen adequately and all the time this man was helping himself to their money. He'd thought of him as a loyal employee – Piers's friend, a family friend of long-standing.

'Three thousand, five hundred.'

'Good gracious! I imagine you got a very good house for that?'

'Yes,' Buckler gulped.

315

'Somewhat above the standard your salary as company accountant would stretch to?'

He didn't answer.

'What else have you treated yourself to, Mr Buckler?' Quentin had to strain his ears to hear his reply.

'A car.'

'But you come to work on a motorbike,' Lorna said.

'I have a car too.'

'What sort?'

'A Chevrolet.'

Quentin couldn't keep his voice low. 'No doubt of recent manufacture and more than your salary would stretch to?'

Buckler looked very hangdog now.

'And what else? There's still a good deal missing that you haven't accounted for.'

All three remained silent.

'You're investing some in your own name to enhance your pension?' Quentin guessed.

'No, no.'

'Then what?'

Buckler glanced guiltily round at Crispin and Adam as the silence dragged on.

'I'm waiting, Mr Buckler.'

'Hilda,' he muttered.

'What d'you mean, Hilda? I can't believe you even know her.' The silence dragged on. 'How do you know her?'

Adam cleared his throat. 'He visited my rooms once or twice.'

'In the tower? More than once or twice I suppose.'

'Yes,' Buckler conceded.

'We aren't talking about small tips for good service?' Again there was a heavy silence. 'But why give Hilda large sums of money? I never heard of anything so ridiculous. You might as well give handouts to all my employees.'

'Hilda demands it, sir.'

Chapter Sixteen

Hilda? Surely not! Lorna had thought the little office was getting stuffy but suddenly the atmosphere was chilled.

Beside her, Quentin Wyndham growled, 'What d'you mean, Hilda demands it?'

She could see raw fear on Buckler's fleshy face now. The heavy silence was broken at last by a whisper from Adam. 'Blackmail, Grandpa.'

Quentin looked stunned; took off his spectacles and polished them, put them back to scowl at his son, his grandson and Buckler. They were white-faced, silent and staring at their feet.

Lorna cleared her throat, feeling nervous. This would take for ever unless she took a hand. 'Hilda knows what goes on in your house, Mr Wyndham. She's been working for you for thirty-one years.'

The old man thundered out, 'What the hell has that got to do with it?'

She flinched but tried again. 'Hilda knows about Adam. That he's – different. Not...' She

317

could see Adam squirming.

'Not what?'

Quentin's face was blank. Lorna struggled on, 'Not interested in women. He prefers other men.'

His old eyes came up to meet hers, astounded. 'Good God!'

Crispin exploded, 'You stupid fools! I told you both to be careful, that nobody must know.'

Lorna was relieved to find Jonathon coming to her aid. 'Hilda told Lorna they played opera records there on the gramophone and that she took meals up to them. Presumably she understood what was going on.'

Crispin's face was scarlet. 'You should never have let Hilda anywhere near your rooms. Getting her to bring food up to you – what were you thinking of? That little ninny Sissie could have swept your rooms out once in a while. The whole point of them was that nobody would see what you were up to.'

Jonathon went on, 'Hilda knew Piers was a homosexual too, and that Buckler had been his partner first. Now he's with Adam.' He had to explain that again to Mr Wyndham.

'Under my roof!' he raged then. 'And with Buckler! Homosexual relationships are illegal, against the law. What a rotter you are, Buckler.'

What sounded like a gurgle came from Buckler's throat. He cleared it. 'How long has this been going on?' Jonathon asked. 'Was Adam a minor when you took up with him?'

Quentin sounded stunned. 'Is that right? You led him astray? In the eyes of the law that makes you, Buckler, guilty of–'

Lorna could see Adam shaking. Suddenly he sprang to life. 'No he didn't. You don't understand, any of you. I love him.'

'I can't stand any more of this.' Crispin was on his feet and extricated himself from the crush of chairs.

'Sit down,' thundered his father. 'I haven't finished with you yet. Whatever your excuses they aren't enough to placate me. What you've done to the family business is unforgivable. You've let the family down. You, Buckler, can consider yourself lucky if you don't go to prison. Not only falsifying accounts but carrying on an illegal relationship with my grandson.'

The old man was glowering. 'You are to make over your house and car as gifts to the company. I mean to have that much back. Go to Hammond and Lomax, the solicitors we retain. Ask Lomax to draw up the necessary documents for you. If you fail to sign them within three days I shall go to the police. You'll leave our employ immediately, without a reference or a pension.'

Buckler was loosening his collar. 'You can't cut me off without anything.'

'You'll still be able to work as an accountant, if you can find someone willing to take you on. I hope for your sake and theirs that you've learned your lesson. You agree to this?'

His eyes were pleading. 'A reference, please – I've worked here for twelve years. How will I get another job? It's not easy in this depression.'

'I'm not prepared to tell lies for you. If I told the truth, nobody would let you inside their doors. So do you agree to my terms or do I take

319

the matter to the police?'

Buckler looked grey and ready to drop. 'Yes, I agree,' he nodded.

'Go to your office and ring Mr Lomax for an immediate appointment. I want you to see him today.'

Buckler couldn't get out of the room quickly enough. The chair he'd been sitting on crashed to the ground.

'Adam?'

'Yes, Grandpa.' He looked terrified.

'Clear your desk, take your personal belongings from your office and go. I want you out of here within the hour and I don't want you to come back. You must find some other way to support yourself. You have a share in the family trust, but that's all you'll ever get from us.'

Adam got up and went without another word.

The silence lengthened. Lorna could see Quentin was thinking. At last he turned to his son and spoke with quiet deliberation.

'I blame you most, Crispin, because I put you in charge. I blame myself too, for trusting you. I knew you weren't working as hard as you should. You've let me, the firm and the family down. I didn't want you to leave my roof and I was disappointed that you didn't ask the rest of us to share your new home, but things being as they are, it's perhaps as well.'

'Father, I'm sorry. I never intended... I didn't realise the extent—'

'Crispin, I thought you were too intent on skimming the cream from the family effects at Otterspool to notice what was going on under your nose, but it's been going on for years, six at least and probably more. What I said to Adam applies to you as well. Out of here within the hour and don't come back. You had a sinecure, but not any longer. You'll have to support yourself too. I shall also be seeing Gregory Lomax. I intend to cut you and Adam out of my will. That's all I have to say. You can be on your way now.'

Lorna could sense Crispin's panic, but he too left without a word, leaving the atmosphere heavy with emotional angst. It surprised her to see the old man so strong. He'd steam-rollered the three of them.

'Lorna, you can take responsibility for the Cartwright business.'

'Thank you,' she said quietly. 'I'll soon have it running smoothly again. It's what I'm used to.'

His eyes fastened on hers. 'How did you find out? Adam a homosexual? I didn't know.'

Lorna could feel the heat running up her cheeks. 'I didn't know anything about ... that it existed. You told me to keep my eyes and ears open. For snippets about your family you could use when you came to write the family history.'

He nodded. 'I remember, but...?'

'That made me look closely at everything.'

'Hadn't Adam left by the time you came?'

'Yes, but I cleared out his rooms. He'd left things behind that puzzled me. My brother... Well, he explained things to me.'

'You've kept these things?'

'Yes, I'll show them to you.'

'You're very observant. You'd make a good detective.'

321

Lorna sighed. What had happened to her mother had made her more observant than she would otherwise have been, but she hadn't managed to find out anything about Oliver. Really, she wasn't observant enough.

Quentin was hesitating. 'You are sure?'

Lorna said, 'Adam admitted it, didn't he?'

'You're right, he did. That settles it then.'

The old man was pulling himself to his feet. 'Well, Jonathon, it seems you'll have to take charge here. Can you cope?'

Jonathon let his breath out slowly. 'I don't know. I'll try.'

'You haven't been with us long enough to find your feet. Perhaps if I came in for a few hours each week until we get things straight...? And you can always talk things over in the evenings. It'll take a bit of doing to get out of this mess. But, d'you know, I feel better already? And I shall enjoy having something to do.'

Quentin really did feel better, more alive. This had woken him up. He should have kept a closer watch on Crispin; he'd always known he wouldn't make the best of managers.

Beside him Jonathon said, 'What about Hilda? What are we going to do about her?'

Quentin groaned and dropped his head in his hands. He'd forgotten about Hilda! Was there no end to it? 'Blackmail! After all the years she's been with us, she stooped to blackmail. I thought she was one of the old school, that she gave good service. She'll have to go, of course. We'll deal with her in the same way.'

He didn't feel like facing Hilda. He hadn't the

322

energy to do more. Taking control like this, brow-beating those who'd been cheating him, was taking a lot out of him. He was getting too old to throw his weight about.

'In the meantime we shouldn't let her know we've dragged the story out of Adam,' Jonathon said.

Quentin wished his mind could still work quickly. 'If she did hear, what would she do?'

'Bolt,' Lorna suggested. 'Get away as fast as she could. She talks of retiring soon, as though she's making big plans, but she doesn't say what they are.'

'These plans – does she imply she'll have money?'

'No. She wouldn't, not if she's used blackmail to get it. Hilda's got a good grip on her tongue. But it isn't likely Adam or Crispin would tell her. She'll be no friend of theirs – they'd hate having to give her money.'

Jonathon said, 'All the same, we should get it over with today, before she wonders why no more money is being paid to her.'

'Will you need me for that?' Lorna asked. 'It's a bit embarrassing. I tried to make a friend of her.'

'It's embarrassing all round,' Quentin said. 'Right, I'll let you off but I'll need you, Jonathon. Got to have some support.'

'Shall I go back now then?' Lorna asked. 'It's what Hilda would expect and I've still plenty to do there.'

'Yes, but say nothing about what's gone on here this morning. Let's have more tea before you go.'

'Food is what we need,' Jonathon told him. 'It's

323

lunch time and I'm hungry. I'll send out for some sandwiches. Ham all right?'

'Yes. I don't want to leave until those three have left the building. I'll have a walk round and see how they're getting on.'

Lorna went to ask someone to organise the lunch.

'Grandpa, we need to give more thought to this. What about the company accounts? Who will take responsibility for them now?'

Quentin sat down hurriedly. He was no longer thinking on his feet. 'We'll get someone from outside. The staff here will have seen what's going on. They might try ... you know.'

'It'll take time to find the right person.'

'What d'you suggest?'

'That we advertise for a chief accountant today. But we could get Fred Nichols to fill in. He's only got six months before he retires.'

'Fred Nichols? I remember the name.'

'He's worked in accounts for years, but I think he'd be all right.'

A typist came in with the tea and sandwiches. When the door had closed behind her, Quentin said, 'We'll get him in here after we've eaten these.'

Daphne was having a good day. She looked round the little sitting room she'd fitted out for her own use and was pleased with what she'd done. The last of the curtains she'd ordered had been delivered and hung this morning. The design she'd chosen of cool green flowers on a white ground suited the room to perfection.

She'd chosen a pair of lamps for the hall, and they'd come too, and they complemented the décor. She'd found a cook who claimed to be able to cook in the French style and hired a new parlourmaid. For tonight, Daphne had ordered a special duck dinner. She'd finished fitting out Ravensdale and was delighted with the result. She was thrilled to have a home of her own at last.

She heard the front door slam so ferociously that the noise reverberated through the house. It surprised her because she hadn't heard the doorbell ring, which meant it must be Crispin. She rarely saw him at lunch time. She heard the door to his study slam too, and went to speak to him.

'How do you like your new curtains?' She crossed his room to pull the folds straight and feel again the richness of the green velvet. 'I'm pleased with them. I think they're really lovely, don't you?'

He growled 'To hell with the curtains.'

She turned to see him slumped at his desk, his face working with rage. She'd never seen him quite like this before and it made her shiver. 'What's happened?'

'We're finished. I always get blamed when something goes wrong.' His fury was building, his face scarlet and sweating. He jerked to his feet again. 'That girl–'

'What girl?'

'Lorna something or other.'

'Mathews. What's she done?'

'Raked through our accounts. Told Father we

weren't keeping the books properly – a terrible row this morning. He's thrown us out. Adam too. We're on our own from now on.'

'On our own? It's what you wanted, a place of our own. You like this house. I love it–'

'Don't be so bloody stupid. He's thrown us out of the firm. Cut us out of his will.'

Daphne could feel herself stiffening. 'You can't mean–'

'I do. No more money. Not from the family.'

'What will you do?'

'What can I do? I'll have to look for a job.'

She stared at him. Surely he couldn't be serious? Crispin didn't know what work was. 'What sort–'

His irritation boiled up. 'For God's sake! How do I know?'

'It's not your only source of income. Your mother left you–'

'Long since spent.' He looked tight-lipped, white with shock.

'And that trust fund.'

'That won't go far.'

Daphne suddenly felt unsteady. She sat down and gripped the arms of the chair. 'Have you had your lunch?'

He was frowning heavily and didn't answer.

'If you want something to eat, the cook could make you an omelette, or–'

'No,' he snapped.

She noticed then that he'd already poured himself a stiff whisky. She said, 'We've just moved in time. Lucky we've got this house.'

'Daphne! You don't know what you're talking

about. It takes money to run a place this size. Where am I going to get that?'

'Your father – he'll forgive you. He won't let us starve.'

'He's kicked me out.' He tossed back the last of his drink. 'I don't think he will this time.'

'I don't understand,' Daphne said. 'What did Lorna Mathews do to cause this?'

'Interfering little bitch. Why couldn't she keep her nose out of what doesn't concern her?'

The doorbell rang through the house. Before anybody could answer it, it jangled again, even more loudly. Crispin exclaimed with impatience and slammed out of his study in high dudgeon to answer it. Daphne followed and saw Adam on the step.

'You bloody fool,' Crispin swore. 'Why couldn't you be more careful? Come in.'

He took him back to his study. When Daphne tried to follow, he snarled at her from the doorway, 'This has nothing to do with you,' and shut the door in her face.

Daphne swore. She and Crispin had had mounting arguments with Adam. He hadn't slept regularly in his rooms in the west wing for some years, preferring to set himself up well away from the family at the far end of the house. Maude and Quentin knew about that, but didn't seem to think it unreasonable. But when they'd moved to Ravensdale he'd refused to come with them, and instead had moved in to live with that rogue Buckler.

That had caused a mammoth row. Adam had stormed out of the house and Crispin had blamed

327

her French ancestry for Adam's sexual deviation. Daphne knew she'd reacted like a fishwife.

'How do you explain Piers's problem then?' she'd screamed at him. 'Couldn't possibly believe such things could be in your family, could you?'

She'd thought by moving to Ravensdale and separating her own small brood from the rest of the family that she'd be free at last from the fighting and the intrigues. She'd been looking forward to having a more peaceful life. Perhaps this was just another storm in a tea cup that would blow over in a few days. Perhaps Quentin would relent – he usually did.

The new parlourmaid knocked on the door of Daphne's boudoir and announced that the lunch she'd ordered was ready. Daphne liked to have it here when she was alone. The trolley, set with silver and starched linen, was pushed in.

As soon as the door closed, she lifted the lid of the tureen. The soup smelled excellent and with the game pie to follow, there was more than enough for the two of them. She went in search of Crispin. If he ate now he wouldn't make a fuss in the middle of the afternoon by wanting something when the cook took her hour off.

She found him slumped over his desk, looking really down. Adam had gone. He followed her back to her sitting room without a word and accepted a bowl of soup. His arrogance had left him. He looked stunned. Daphne was beginning to think that their financial position must be really serious. She felt her first stab of fear.

'Something's happened? Something bad?'

'I keep telling you,' he said with growing irritation. 'That girl's caused havoc. Really, I blame Adam and Buckler. They should have been more careful with the Cartwright account.'

Daphne had never heard of the Cartwright account and it took time to get a clear picture of what had gone wrong.

'She'd been running it, knew what it should earn better than the rest of us. That fool Buckler tried to tell Father it wasn't making money.'

Daphne knew only too well that Crispin did little to earn the salary he was paid, but he'd never mentioned putting his hand in the till as well. This was news that made her shiver.

'I don't know how we'll manage. We should never have moved to this big house. It'll be too expensive to run. You should never have chosen it.'

'Don't blame me, you were keen on it too. You'll have to get another job.'

'How? There's a depression on. Nobody can get a job. Half the country is starving. Anyway, nobody else would pay as well as Father.'

'Not for what you do.' Daphne no longer cared if she showed contempt.

It was after three o'clock when Quentin climbed into the back of the old Daimler to go home. It had been a terrible morning. He couldn't yet accept what Crispin had done, and he still had Hilda to contend with. He had no option but to deal with her as he had the others.

He went straight up to his bedroom, collapsed on the double bed he'd once shared with Marina

329

and pulled the shiny blue eiderdown over him. He felt drained, absolutely exhausted. He slept heavily for over an hour, and, if not refreshed when he woke, at least he felt better.

He went down to the white drawing room to have his tea. The trolley was already there and Maude and Rosaleen were tucking in to walnut cake. They'd have to know about this. He went to sit near them on the sofa so he could keep his voice low.

'Fraud in the office! Crispin?' Rosaleen blew up in a fury. 'How underhand can he get?'

Quentin got up to make sure he'd closed the door. Hilda mustn't hear about this yet. It must come as a shock to her in the way it had to Buckler. He mustn't give her time to work out a story. But he was being paranoid – how could she hear anything over distances like these?

'Are you sure, Quentin?' Maude was looking at him over her glasses.

'Quite sure. Be glad you've kept well away from the office.'

Rosaleen raged on. 'The way Crispin went on about the business going down, we all believed him. No doubt Adam's in it too. We should have known they were up to something.'

'Buckler as well,' Quentin said, and explained briefly what they'd been doing. 'I've sacked the three of them. It seems Hilda's involved too.'

'But that's ridiculous!' Rosaleen's cup crashed back on its saucer. 'What can Hilda have to do with what goes on in the office?'

He explained how she'd used blackmail to get money from them.

330

'I'll sort Hilda out! We're not putting up with this.' Rosaleen was making for the door in high dudgeon.

'No, sit down.' Quentin raised his voice to a command.

Maude said quietly, 'Come here, drink your tea and calm down, Rosaleen.'

She sat down then.

'Maude, pour me a cup.' Quentin had always known she was better at controlling his daughter than he was, but she couldn't calm her.

'Father, they're riding roughshod over us. Lining their own pockets at our expense. We're the ones going short, having to move out of this house.'

'I'll deal with this. I'm just waiting for Jonathon to come. Ah, here he is now.'

'I want to be in on it,' Rosaleen demanded.

'No, you stay here. Leave it to us. We'll need cool heads to deal with Hilda.'

'Sit down, Rosaleen,' Maude said. 'You stay with me.'

Lorna came in with Jonathon and cut two slices of walnut cake.

'All's quiet in the office,' his grandson told him. 'I've left Fred Nichols to lock up for the night.'

'I want to get this over. Come to my study, Jonathon.'

Lorna was pouring tea, refilling his cup. 'Take these two cups with you,' she said.

'Lorna,' he said, 'before you have yours, will you go to the kitchen to tell Hilda I want to talk to her?'

It took Hilda longer to come than he'd

expected. Quentin felt poised on a knife edge. It had shaken him to see Rosaleen boil up in a rage.

A discreet knock on his door and Hilda's head came round. She'd put on a clean apron and her white cap was pulled down low on her brow. 'You wanted me, sir?'

'Yes, come in, Hilda.' He wouldn't ask her to sit; she rarely had in his presence. 'How long have you been working for us?'

'Thirty-one years, sir.' He'd noticed her eyes before, very dark, more black than brown, and they seemed to miss nothing.

'All those years, I've trusted you, Hilda, looked upon you kindly, even with some affection.' She understood something bad was coming now. Her back had straightened and her eyes were burning into him. 'But all that time you've been preying on me and my family.'

'No, sir!'

He outlined what had happened in the office this morning, what Adam had told him. 'Blackmail, Hilda, is an ugly crime. It would mean prison for you if you were convicted. You are to hand over to me the money you extracted from Adam.'

'I wouldn't blackmail anybody, sir.' Hilda looked offended at the very suggestion. The palms of her hands came together as though she were about to pray. 'Not Mr Adam. Anyway, what could I possibly blackmail him about? He'd have had to do something bad, wouldn't he? Something very wrong?'

Quentin couldn't cope with this. He wasn't used to the idea of having a homosexual in the

332

family. It would take a bit of getting used to.

Jonathon put it to her. 'Adam has a homosexual bent. He was paying you to keep quiet about it, wasn't he?'

'No! I didn't know that, sir! What a terrible shock! I can't believe... Of course you'd all want to keep that quiet. Wouldn't do to let something like that out. They could get into trouble for it, couldn't they?'

Quentin looked at Jonathon. Hilda was denying it! It surprised him to find she had more guts than Buckler.

Jonathon said, 'Both Adam and Buckler say you demanded payment for keeping quiet.'

She looked hurt at not being believed. 'I didn't know. How could I? I don't go to the office.'

'Mr Buckler has been in the habit of coming here over these last years.'

'Yes. I've taken meals up to Mr Adam's room, but they don't tell me anything. I'd never have guessed – such a nice young man, and a Wyndham. I wouldn't dare blackmail him about anything. I'd never do such a thing. No, sir, I haven't.'

Quentin was glad to find Jonathon taking over. 'Adam tells us he's handed over money to you. Large sums, on several occasions. We want it back. What d'you say to that?'

'He never did, sir. Never.'

Quentin shivered. She looked innocent. 'If you don't hand it back, Hilda, I shall go to the police with the whole story.'

'But then you'd have to tell them about Adam and Mr Buckler, and what they done was against

333

the law.'

Quentin almost swore. He had to keep calm. Hilda was more wily than he'd realised. 'It may not reflect well on Adam but you risk going to prison. I want that money back.'

'I haven't got any money, sir. You can see my bank books if you like. I haven't done anything wrong.'

Quentin was beginning to doubt that Adam had told the truth. 'Where d'you bank, Hilda?'

'The Post Office, sir. I'm saving up for my retirement. I have to.'

Jonathon stirred in his seat. 'You said bank books. That isn't the only bank account you have?'

'I have a bit in the Liverpool Savings Bank too. You can see them both. They're in my handbag in the kitchen. I've been out this afternoon to pay a bit more in.'

'Then yes,' Quentin said, 'we'd like to see them, please.' He knew there'd be nothing incriminating in them, or she wouldn't have offered. Hilda went to fetch them, looking very put out at being accused in this way.

Quentin sighed. 'I was sure we were getting the truth out of Adam.'

'We were. Why would they bring Hilda's name into it, if it wasn't true?'

'Keep your eye on her, Jonathon. We don't want her to do a bunk just yet.'

Moments later Quentin was inspecting her bank books. He was paying her fifty-five pounds a year and her keep. Hilda had paid three pounds into her account at the Liverpool Savings Bank this afternoon. The balance was seventy-four pounds and she'd accumulated that over the last twenty years. She had thirty-five pounds in the Post Office. That had been paid in in one sum, four years ago.

'I got that when my mother died,' she said with a proud tilt to her chin.

He was stumped. These weren't the sort of sums he was seeking.

'Will that be all, sir? I need to get the dinner in the oven. Should have been in ten minutes ago.'

'For the moment,' he said.

When the door closed behind her, he let the expletives rip. 'What have I done, Jonathon?'

Chapter Seventeen

Lorna felt a false friend as she sent Hilda to Mr Wyndham's study.

'What's he want?'

She had to pretend she didn't know. She'd been uneasy in Hilda's presence since she'd come back from the office on the bus. She returned to the white drawing room to have her tea. Rosaleen was boiling with fury.

'What's happening?' she demanded. 'Everybody with their hands in the till. And now Hilda – what's she been up to?'

Lorna didn't feel she should be discussing private family matters, though she knew Mr Wyndham must have told Rosaleen and Maude.

335

In any case, Rosaleen was so angry she was hardly taking anything in. Lorna made soothing responses while the woman spilled out hate against Hilda.

Lorna escaped to her bedroom as soon as she could and lay on her bed, trying to read. She had some of Oliver's notebooks and wanted to extract everything she could from them. For once she couldn't concentrate. She'd spent the afternoon in the attic trying to get on with the job there, but it hadn't been easy to keep her mind on that either.

Her head had been spinning after watching Mr Wyndham deal with Crispin, then Adam, then Buckler. She would never have believed he'd have the strength if she hadn't seen him do it. Not just physical strength either – it had taken mental and emotional strength to get the upper hand. He'd shown real vigour.

She was pleased to have been given a permanent job, delighted to be in charge of the Cartwright account again, and she knew she'd enjoy working in that office with Jonathon. Most of all, she was very pleased she'd diagnosed Mr Wyndham's business problem for him. Profitability had not been going down at the rate Crispin had led him to believe. Quentin had been loud in his praise of her before she'd left to catch the bus.

Lorna was tired and beginning to doze when she heard footsteps rushing upstairs. Hilda's bedroom door crashed back against the wall and she could hear drawers being opened and slammed shut again. It sounded as though she was in a furious hurry to pack. Quentin must have ordered her to leave right away.

She was making so much noise, Lorna knew she must be in a rage. Something banged against the party wall, something else was being pulled out from under the bed. Should she go and say goodbye? Not yet. She'd be better staying out of the way.

Then she heard more footsteps pelting up. She'd heard them so often on the lino-covered stairs to their attic that she realised she'd been mistaken earlier. *This* was Hilda!

Lorna heard her snarl, 'What are you doing?' Then the door slammed shut again. She sat up and swung her feet to the floor. There was somebody else in Hilda's room! Somebody else had gone there alone. She could hear angry voices, but the walls were thick in this old house and she couldn't catch their words. She recognised the other voice though: it was Rosaleen's. She must have come up to search Hilda's bedroom and Hilda had caught her in the act.

Lorna decided this was none of her business and she wasn't going to interfere. Rosaleen would have to talk her way out of it. But she found it impossible to read, impossible to do anything with that going on in the next room. She'd creep downstairs and get out of the way. She was half across her room when she heard Hilda choking and then a snatched and terrified scream. Lorna went instead to wrench Hilda's bedroom door open.

She was on the floor; Rosaleen was on top of her and had her by the throat. Lorna had no time to think. She hurled her weight against Rosaleen and knocked her away. It was only then she noticed the five-pound notes and one-pound notes all over the bed and the floor, and the home-made bag, with its drawstring neck wide open, showing bundles of banknotes still inside.

Rosaleen was panting. Her eyes seemed half out of their sockets. 'She's a thief.' She could hardly get the words out, she was in such a frenzy. 'Stolen our money. Look at all this, hidden in her drawer. We're short of money and she's taken all this.'

Lorna was helping Hilda to her feet. She was choking and coughing and weeping at the same time. Lorna could see the marks on her throat where Rosaleen's fingers had bitten in. She pushed Hilda towards the bed where she could sit down.

Rosaleen screamed: 'I'm going to fetch my father and send for the police. You'll not get away with this, Hilda.'

Within half an hour, Jonathon had found two ancient suitcases in the attic and Lorna was helping Hilda pack. Mr Wyndham had stopped Rosaleen phoning for the police. She was calmer now, having collected up the money and taken it downstairs.

'Where can I go?' Hilda's voice was hoarse. 'They can't put me out at this time of night.'

'It's only just six,' Lorna said. It had been dark for some time. 'Don't you have a friend who would take you in? A relative?'

'No,' her voice was agonised, 'nobody. This is

338

my home.'

Lorna had heard Mr Wyndham come up and deliver his verdict. 'You'll have to go, Hilda, after this. Blackmailing one of the family and then denying it. You almost convinced me you were innocent, that I was making a mistake. But now we've found the proceeds of your crime, you are guilty, there's no doubt about that. I want you out of here within the hour.'

'Can't I stay until morning?' Hilda looked shaken. 'I've nowhere to go.'

'Now, Hilda, please. Consider yourself lucky we haven't called the police. You could get a prison sentence for this.'

'What am I going to do?' Hilda implored. She looked terrified.

Despite what she'd done, Lorna felt sorry for her. Wasn't this what the family had done to her mother? And in her case for a nonexistent crime.

'I've seen a boarding house just down the road,' she told her, 'close to where I get off the bus. Would you like me to phone and see if they have a vacancy?'

Hilda groaned but nodded. Lorna ran downstairs to do it. Then she looked for Jonathon. He was in the library with his grandfather and great-aunt. Rosaleen was counting the money into piles on the table.

Lorna said, 'I've found Hilda a room in the boarding house down the road.'

'We don't care where she goes,' Rosaleen flared up angrily. 'She's to go from here and that's that.'

'She's a bit shaken,' Lorna reminded her. 'She

339

says you tried to throttle her.' Rosaleen had gone too far. 'She'll need help to get even that far tonight.'

Jonathon got to his feet. 'I'll run her down in my car.'

'There's no need for that,' Rosaleen snapped, 'mollycoddling her after what she's done.'

'I'm afraid there is. She'll never be able to carry two big suitcases and a box...'

'There, you see, she's already spent our money on luxuries for herself. Now she wants help to move them out of here.'

'It's not like that,' Lorna said. 'I've helped her pack. Considering that's all she's got to show for over thirty years' work, it's rather pathetic.'

There was a little silence. Then Quentin took five one-pound notes from the table. 'Give her these, Lorna, to help her on her way.'

'She doesn't deserve...' she heard Rosaleen rant as she headed back to the stairs. Jonathon came with her.

Hilda had put on her hat and coat and was sitting on her bed, still mopping her tears.

'They have a room for you at the boarding house,' Lorna told her.

'I'll run you down,' Jonathon said. 'Is this your luggage? Too much for my car, I'm afraid. I'd better ask Grandpa if I can use his Daimler.'

'You'll feel better when you've had a night's rest,' Lorna comforted. 'You'll be able to get on with your retirement plans. You wouldn't have worked on for much longer, would you?' She put the money into her hand. 'Mr Wyndham says this is to help you on your way.'

Hilda's black eyes, full of venom, swept from one to the other. 'It's the least you can do after the thirty-one years' service I've given. You wouldn't want to find me collapsed on your drive tomorrow morning, would you? The police might start asking questions.'

Lorna saw Jonathon's eyebrows rise before he bent to pick up her suitcases. 'Come with us,' he said to Lorna. 'I'm not sure where this boarding house is. There's plenty of room in the Daimler.'

She carried Hilda's cardboard box down, and left her sitting by the door, surrounded by her belongings. While Jonathon fetched the car, Lorna went to the kitchen. The Wyndhams would give no thought to dinner until they wanted to sit down and eat it.

Sissie was peeling sprouts at the sink. 'Where's Hilda?' Her face was working with anxiety. 'I've put the pork chops in the oven, but she'll go for me if she meant to grill them. She didn't say, and time's going on and–'

'Thank goodness. You've done the right thing.' Lorna told her what had happened.

Perhaps Sissie would cope better if she wasn't being heckled by Hilda all the time.

Lorna put Hilda to sit in solitary state on the back seat of the Daimler, then climbed in beside Jonathon. 'I can't believe you've never noticed this boarding house,' she said.

As he drove through the main gates, the large signboard was almost opposite. She heard him chuckle and guessed he'd known where it was. It pleased her that he wanted her company. They busied themselves moving Hilda's luggage inside the boarding house.

'She didn't even thank you,' he said as they walked back to the car. 'After all you did for her.'

'Didn't thank you either.'

'I did little enough. You stopped Aunt Roz–'

'I thought she was going to kill her. She was in such a fury.'

Instead of turning towards the stable block to garage the car, Jonathon parked some two hundred yards from the house, overlooking the river, and switched off the headlamps. Lorna could see two ships chugging up to Runcorn and the lights twinkling on the far bank.

He put out his hand to cover hers. 'You've got your wits about you, Lorna,' he said, 'seeing through what Crispin and Buckler were doing. We're all very grateful.'

'I know the Cartwright account, you see, and changing so soon the way I'd kept the books made it look as though there was something to hide.'

She could see him staring down at her. His voice was a soft murmur. 'Didn't you tell Crispin you expected to take the account over again? He should never have milked it. Underestimated you, didn't he? He thought you wouldn't find out.'

He put an arm round her shoulders and pulled her closer, kissing her fully on the lips. Lorna felt a thrill run down her spine and her arms went round him. He hugged her closer.

'You're good for us all, and specially good for me.'

342

The moon came out from behind a cloud and in that instant she could see tenderness, affection and perhaps love quite clearly on his face. Jonathon felt for her what she felt for him.

'I could take to you, Lorna,' he said softly. 'In fact, I think I already have.'

She hugged him tighter. He wasn't saying he loved her but that was what he meant; what she'd seen on his face. She'd felt his interest from the start and it had fanned the fire in her.

His chin was against hers. 'Do you think you could take to me?' he whispered.

Lorna's heart was pounding. 'You know I already have.' It was more than that, but how could she tell him now?

This was what she'd meant to avoid. This was what her mother had done – fallen in love with one of the family. Part of her wanted it desperately, was urging her on, but she couldn't talk about it to him. Not yet. She shouldn't let this go any further.

Lorna couldn't get to sleep that night. Her mind was racing with joy at one moment, only to be filled with dread the next.

There was a good deal about herself that Jonathon didn't know. She wasn't the person he believed her to be. Once he found out his ancestors were slavers, he'd said he viewed them differently. Would he see her in a different light when he found out who she was? Would he think she'd been spying on his family? Lorna knew now she was in love, but...

She was comforted because they were closer and on better terms. But would she still feel that when he knew she was another Wyndham relative?

The following week, Lorna unrolled a bundle of posters and felt a moment of panic when she saw they were advertising the auction. The date was given in black and white as 7 January 1931.

She'd been working at Otterspool House for more than ten weeks now and had found out almost nothing about Oliver. Once the sale was over, the house would be bulldozed down and the opportunity would be gone for ever. Already she was working here for only half the day and Christmas would mean time spent at home. She needed to get a move on. Time was running out, and so were her ideas on how to find out more.

This afternoon, she'd go and see Blossom again and take the photographs of Oliver. Blossom might tell her something new. It was mid-afternoon before Lorna could get away from Mr Wyndham. She shot upstairs to pick up two of the albums, made sure the one on top had several pictures of Oliver in it and hurried over to the stables. Harold was in the yard.

'Hello,' she said. 'Is your mother in?'

'She's not here. We've moved.'

Lorna's spirits sank. 'Where to?' She should never have left it so long before she came again. Things had blown up in the office and her time and energy had been spent there.

Harold was all smiles. 'We've got a nice little terraced cottage. Only five minutes' walk from the boss's new place. Once he'd signed for Hedge End, he told us to look for somewhere to rent nearby and he'd pay the rent. There's nowhere for us in his new house, you see. You must call on my mam. She'd love to show it to you.'

'It'll have to be some other time.' Lorna was biting her lip.

'Mam's right proud of it.'

Lorna took the albums back to her bedroom and tried to think of another way to unearth information about Oliver. She could take another look at the room which, according to her mother, had been his bedroom. She found her way to the tower, sat down on the single bed and looked round. She should have known this wasn't a guest room; they mostly had double beds, if not four-posters.

The wallpaper was faded and stained with damp, and the room looked drab with its curtains down and the bed stripped. She couldn't remember exactly what she'd taken away to add to the piles of china and bedding. She consulted the lists she'd made, but nothing seemed out of the ordinary.

She pulled out the drawers in the chest, but she'd emptied all of them and wiped them clean – nothing left here either. Her eyes came to rest on a small desk. A secret drawer perhaps? She pulled a chair up to it and hunted for one, but found nothing. She leaned back and tried to think.

After Oliver had died, Rosaleen and her brothers would have had plenty of time to take away anything they wanted from here. It would be normal, Lorna thought, for them to help themselves to his belongings: sports equipment, pens, books, anything like that would be a keepsake.

Rosaleen had shown no interest in this room. It had been left for her to turn out, therefore, she thought, nothing important belonging to Oliver would have been left here. It was Piers's room that had attracted Rosaleen's attention.

Lorna went back through the labyrinth of passages to that and looked inside. She could still smell the fire, though the window remained slightly open. Jonathon had turned the room out as she would have done. Everything was stripped bare. He'd never mentioned doing it, let alone that he'd found anything of special interest, yet Rosaleen had expected something to be found here.

Lorna was deliberately late going down to the white drawing room for afternoon tea. Mr Wyndham and Rosaleen had finished theirs, and Aunt Maude didn't seem to be at home. She waited until she saw Jonathon's car pull up in front of the house before fetching a fresh pot from the kitchen.

'Only biscuits?' he asked, helping himself to several. 'Bought biscuits?'

'Hilda's gone.'

'Grandpa said Connie was coming back.'

'She's here, but she doesn't bake.' As soon as he sat down she said, 'I see you've turned out Piers's room.'

'Some time ago.'

'Did you find anything of interest?'

He sighed. 'No.'

Lorna was disappointed. 'Rosaleen expected to

346

find something there.'

'Perhaps she did find it.'

'Not on the night of the fire. She was too frightened then to have hidden it from us. There were no papers or books?'

'Aunt Roz managed to burn them, if you remember.'

'Yes, it's just that ... if Piers had something to hide, he'd have hidden it well. He knew he was going off to fight. He'd have had plenty of time.'

'Why should he have something to hide? What makes you think that?'

Lorna looked up into his bright blue eyes She almost blurted everything out, about her mother, about the will she thought Oliver had made. It was on the tip of her tongue and the temptation was strong. Then Jonathon stood up to help himself to two more chocolate biscuits from the trolley, and the moment was gone.

'You've already unearthed Grandma's diary and discovered the family fortune was earned from slavery,' he said. 'What more can there be?'

Lorna shrugged. 'I've just got the feeling... Let's have another look. Come up with me when you've finished your tea.'

Upstairs, Jonathon helped her turn back the carpet to see if there was anything obvious in the floorboards. Apart from further evidence of dry rot there wasn't. 'Just four bare walls,' he said, 'and some furniture which isn't worth much.'

Lorna looked very carefully at the wardrobe, inside and out, stood on a chair to see if there was anything on top, and then at the tallboy and chests. When she'd finished, she was satisfied there was absolutely nothing to be found inside any of them. Yet the feeling remained: something was hidden here.

'Wishful thinking,' Jonathon told her.

Lorna was growing despondent. The weeks were flying by and she was no nearer finding out what had happened to Oliver than she'd been on the day she'd come. Every time she went home, her mother's hopeful eyes searched her face, and every time she had to disappoint her.

One afternoon, Lorna was in the library crating books to go to Hedge End with the family, when it occurred to her to consult the family Bible. An entry read: 'Oliver Cecil Pembury Wentworth Wyndham, born 10 January 1891.' A different hand in different ink had added: 'Died 10 March 1910. Drowned.'

The Bible also enabled her to work out Rosaleen's age. She was forty-four now, five years older than Oliver would have been. Lorna sighed. It didn't seem to get her any further.

The family were getting ready to move out. Rosaleen was packing up her own belongings. At intervals Lorna was summoned to her bedroom or private sitting room to remove what she didn't want to the rubbish dump Harold had made, and was told to burn it.

Lorna looked through the rubbish for documents, old diaries or notebooks, though she didn't expect to find anything that would help in her search; Rosaleen was too careful for that. Connie and Sissie swooped on her handbags, hats and coats with cries of delight.

'Don't let her see you wearing them,' Lorna warned. 'She told me to burn them.'

'What a waste! Nothing the matter with this hat. It's real posh.' Connie had snatched off her cap and was parading round the kitchen with it on. 'I'll wear it to church, she won't see me.'

Lorna thought it wouldn't have hurt Rosaleen to offer what she didn't want to them. Quentin turned out overcoats and old-fashioned shooting jackets and asked Lorna, who was helping him with his packing, to see if Tom or Harold could make use of them.

'I'm not going through my desk drawers,' he said. 'If the desk's too heavy the drawers can be slid out and carried separately, but there are these.' He waved his hand towards the cupboards in his study that were hidden behind the panelling. He opened the doors so Lorna could see the shelves piled high with documents and papers.

'I started writing a history of the house some time ago,' he sighed. 'I've got the original plans here and the bills showing what things cost.'

'That sounds interesting.'

'A labour of love, but I put it to one side – too busy at the moment – but I don't want anything to do with the house thrown out.'

'Course not.'

'I'll give you limited responsibility to throw out the rubbish. There must be lots of that, but if you're in doubt I'd like to see it first.'

Lorna nodded. 'I understand.' Her interest was quickening in the hope she might turn up something about Oliver.

'There are more cupboards upstairs,' he said,

'in my dressing room and in what was my wife's boudoir. I want her papers packed into boxes and taken to the new house. I'm concerned that we don't lose any.'

'I'll make sure you don't,' Lorna said, hugging herself gleefully. Just when she hadn't known what to do next, this opportunity had come up.

The move to Hedge End took place ten days before Christmas. The night before, Mr Wyndham said to Lorna, 'Has Maude made arrangements with you to come too?'

'No, I was rather expecting to stay on here for a few days until everything was packed up.'

He frowned. 'You can't do that, not stay by yourself. There'll be no heating or lighting. I'll have a word with her.'

It seemed he had a word with Rosaleen instead. She met Lorna at the bottom of the stairs an hour later and said rather grudgingly, 'Tell Connie to prepare a room for you at Hedge End. You can use it until we've got the sale over and done with.'

So Lorna packed her suitcase and rolled up her bedding, as did Sissie and Connie. The two servants were to travel to the new house in the front of the removal van and would take their things with them.

Lorna went to the office with Jonathon that morning as usual. He had moved into Crispin's office, which was rather grand, and now she had his old office to herself. At lunch time she had a sandwich with him.

'I'll come to Otterspool to fetch you at tea time,' he said.

350

'Make it early evening. By the time the bus gets me there and I get going, it doesn't give me long.'

When she let herself in, the old house looked forlorn with its furnishings almost stripped out. The windows were rattling in the wind. She kept hearing creaks in the old timbers and her footsteps were echoing eerily on bare boards and stone floors. It felt strange to think she was the only person in this huge old building. It had been one of those dull dark days and dusk came early. The electricity had been turned off, but Lorna was used to lighting the oil lamps now.

She still had more than enough to do here. Connie and Sissie had packed up what kitchen equipment they wanted and it had gone with them. Lorna was left to lay out and list the jelly moulds, the preserving jars and hot-water bottles that were surplus to requirements. There was a huge number of rusting fish kettles, cauldrons and griddles. She was more interested in sorting through papers and documents, but the mundane tasks all had to be done.

She worked on doggedly, but at six o'clock she was glad to hear Jonathon's voice calling her name. He breezed into the kitchen wearing a muffler and bringing a blast of icy air with him.

'Aren't you cold, Lorna?'

'A little. I've put on an extra cardigan.'

'The old place is a bit ghostly now,' he shivered. 'Not many girls would be prepared to work here after dark.'

'There aren't any ghosts. I asked your grandfather and he said none of his ancestors wanted to return to earth.'

He laughed, holding her coat out for her to slide her arms in. 'That's not what Aunt Roz says. She convinced Eudora May can't rest. She reckons she's seen her walking through the hall, wringing her hands and showing great remorse. Sitting in the red drawing room too.'

'Really?'

'I shouldn't be talking about ghosts, should I? Not when you'll be here by yourself tomorrow.'

'I'm like your grandfather, unlikely to see ghosts.' All the same, Lorna was glad to get into his two-seater and be driven away.

'In future I'll come for you on my way home from the office,' he said. 'That's long enough to stay by yourself.'

'I could take the bus.'

'No,' he said. 'You'd have that long walk down the drive in the dark. It's only for a short time, anyway.'

Lorna peered through the darkness with great curiosity as she saw Hedge End for the first time. The façade was of white stucco, long and low, with many windows beaming out light. She'd been told it was screened all round by tall trees and the drive wound through two acres of garden.

'It's a beautiful house! Rosaleen said it was small, but that's the last thing it is.'

'No view of the river,' Jonathon smiled. 'That spoils it for Grandpa.'

A wall of warmth met them at the door. The house had been newly decorated throughout; there was still a faint smell of new paint in the air. New carpet had been laid and the whole place looked clean and light and fresh.

'The kitchen's this way. You'd better get Connie to take you to your room.'

'What a lovely house.' Lorna had never been in one she liked more. 'And isn't it big?'

'Very big.' Connie's cap was almost sliding off her unruly red hair. 'But it's so easy to keep clean.'

'Only three bedrooms for staff,' Sissie told her from the sink where she was washing vegetables, 'and we've got a new cook starting on Monday.'

'That means you've been allotted a guest room. Come on, I'll show you.' Connie led her along straight corridors and landings that were well lit and warm. 'This is it.' She threw open a door. Lorna looked round, amazed. It was a very comfortable room with new chintz curtains and a thick carpet that covered the entire floor.

'Miss Rosaleen insisted on having a new bathroom put in next to her room, and then Mr Wyndham decided to have one too, so you'll be able to use this one. Isn't it lovely? Everything's so modern.'

By the time she'd unpacked her case, Lorna heard the dinner gong ringing through the house. She was heading towards the kitchen, expecting to help with the dishing up and then eat her dinner there. She met Jonathon coming up.

'I've come to take you to the dining room. Aunt Maude has overruled Aunt Roz, and you're to eat all your meals with us from now on.'

Lorna was glad she'd washed her face and combed her hair. When she reached the place set for her at the table, Mr Wyndham said, 'We all know you better now, Lorna. You've done valuable work for our family, both at Otterspool and in the office. We should all be grateful to you.'

Rosaleen managed to smile faintly in her direction.

Chapter Eighteen

Christmas was almost on her. Lorna was going home for the holiday, but still had a lot to do at Otterspool. She did not go to the office on Christmas Eve. Mr Wyndham told her to do as much as she could at the old house but to leave early.

As she passed through what had once been the main gates of Otterspool House, there were two posters screaming the date of the sale at her. When she came back, there'd be only twelve more days before the auction. After that her chance to get at the truth about Oliver's death would be gone for ever.

'Happy Christmas,' Pam sang out as she opened the door to her. There were colourful paper streamers crisscrossing the living-room ceiling, and the table was set for tea.

Her mother kissed her cheek. 'Now we're all home except Pa, who's somewhere in mid-Atlantic.' She had a fire roaring up the chimney to welcome her daughter.

'Have you found out any more?' It was the

question Mum always asked when Lorna came home. Her smile was hopeful.

'Not about Oliver.'

'I think of you as a sort of detective.'

'Not a clever one, I'm afraid. I'm running out of time. The house looks bare; what the family want to keep has gone to their new houses, and the cream of what was left has been moved down to London to await specialist sales.'

'There is going to be a sale at Otterspool?'

'Yes, that's all settled. It's to be held in the house. A temporary lintel has been put in over the original front door. That was thought to be cheaper than moving everything to a saleroom in town.'

'I can't believe there's any danger,' Alice said. 'The floors are marble in the main entrance, a lovely black and white pattern.'

'And in the great hall too. The furniture and other goods to be auctioned have all been brought down and stacked round the walls. The public won't be allowed anywhere else in the house except to the kitchens where the silver and china is being laid out.'

'I'd love to go,' her mother said.

Lorna looked at the large box that was taking up a good deal of space on the floor. 'What's this?'

'A present for all the family,' Jim told them. 'Pa and me clubbed together to get it.'

'What's in it?' Mum wanted to know.

'You'll have to wait until we've eaten. We want to do justice to that hotpot you've made.'

'We'll not have to wait until tomorrow?'

'No, this is the sort of present we open tonight.' Jim's eyes sparkled.

Lorna felt a tremor of excitement. 'It's all very festive.'

'I'm going to shut you ladies in the kitchen to wash up,' Jim said when the table had been cleared. 'And I'm going to set up our big present. No peeping now.'

Ten minutes later they crowded back into the front room to find him setting up a wireless.

Pam shrieked with joy. 'Will we be able to hear London?'

'I hope so,' Jim said smugly. 'I put up an aerial for it yesterday.'

'That's what you were doing up on the roof!' Mum laughed. 'You said there was a slate loose when I asked.'

Lorna looked round their enthralled faces, as dance music began to fill the room.

'There'll be special programmes over Christmas,' Jim said.

'It's as clear as crystal,' Mum said. 'It'll be such company for me when you're all out.'

'That's what I thought,' he smiled up at her. 'I suppose you've heard wireless before, Lorna?'

She nodded. 'Mrs Cartwright had one, and Mr Wyndham listens to the news and the weather forecast on his every evening.'

Lorna meant to enjoy the rest with her family, but she'd come across so many notebooks and papers in Marina Wyndham's boudoir that she'd brought some of them with her. She meant to skim through them during the holiday. She didn't expect to find anything very exciting – she'd read

356

through much that wasn't – but she had to make sure.

She had no time to do so until after they'd eaten the remains of the Christmas joint of roast pork on Boxing Day. It was a cold afternoon with rain sweeping along the street outside. They all decided to stay by their fire and listen to the wireless.

Lorna brought down the notebooks she'd pushed in her overnight bag, and cut the string that held them together. She found the careful housekeeping accounts that Marina had kept year after year, and her notebooks with drawings of the plants and flowers that grew in the grounds. She discovered Oliver's interest in how the tides corresponded with the phases of the moon and the notes he'd made on that and on ocean currents and prevailing winds. She'd even found old school books belonging to Rosaleen, who'd had a governess when she was young. In addition, the family were keen diarists, particularly Quentin's wife.

To start with, it had delighted Lorna to come across one of Marina's journals. She'd found the notebook Marina had kept in 1910, which had stopped abruptly the day before Oliver died. She had written nothing for many weeks after that. She had found many more. Marina had written in clear copperplate of dinner parties she gave, and bridge hands she'd won, and a great deal on the health of her mother.

Lorna had also learned how Rosaleen's marriage had affected her mother, and the heart-wrenching details of how she'd nursed Piers when he'd caught Spanish flu. That diary had ended abruptly before Piers's death. Lorna knew she'd been taken ill at that point and would write no more. She'd almost given up hope of finding any reference to Oliver's death, but she had to skim through long entries to make sure there were no references to it, because she was determined not to miss anything.

Lorna found the first notebook she opened was another of Marina's diaries. It was for the year 1915, long after Oliver had been killed, so she was expecting more about her social life. Marina used plain notebooks and wrote spasmodically when she felt the urge, rather than every day. Lorna read with only half her mind, listening to a play on the new wireless at the same time.

In January, Marina had written:

Aunt Eliza's end came at midnight with Quentin and me at her bedside. She was Quentin's great-aunt and had never married. She told me only yesterday that at eighty-nine she'd had enough of life and was too weary to go on. I shall miss her, but would not want her to suffer any longer. She looked so peaceful when we left her.

We went to bed afterwards but I could not sleep, though Quentin was off in an instant. Her death brought such painful memories of Oliver's end rushing back at me. I've fought almost daily ever since to keep such thoughts at a distance. I have to, it's my only way of staying sane.

He was at the threshold of his life, it promised so much, but he was idealistic and didn't understand that love and marriage might not always go together. He had more energy and exuberance than his older brothers, and was more intelligent too. He loved books and sailing and being taken by his father to the office. He was keen to learn all he could, about his forebears, and about managing the family business.

I was shocked to read his history of the Wyndhams and how their fortune was founded on slavery, but I found his sources in the library and know he was right. We couldn't show that to Quentin and even less to the world at large.

'Change it,' I told Oliver. 'The truth's been hidden for centuries. Change it. Nobody need know now.'

But he wouldn't. 'There have been too many lies and cover-ups already,' he said. 'Why add more?'

I feel so guilty about Oliver's death. No mother could grieve more for a son. I didn't want him to marry Alice, but better he did that than drown. As the men saw it, Oliver was letting the family down.

I was proud to take the name Wentworth Wyndham when I married. My relatives saw them as one of the great Liverpool families. I didn't realise then that it meant the name must be upheld at all costs; no slur must ever dim its shine, that the present generation mustn't let the family down.

Oliver would hear nothing against Alice and even made a will in her favour. A hand-written one without benefit of lawyers, but he executed it correctly as far as I can see, and had it properly witnessed. Crispin wanted to tear it up the day after he died. He said it was dangerous to keep. Oliver also wrote a letter to Alice that we never posted. I wanted to keep them. I can't bear to destroy any remaining remnant of Oliver's life. I hid them and wept. We've all kept so much hidden about dear Oliver.

I wonder about his child, though I know not whether it was a boy or a girl, whether it thrives or not. I feel haunted by it and want to see it. In bed, I fantasise sometimes about finding Alice, taking her child and bringing it up myself. I daren't talk about it to Quentin because he blames himself too. It's a terrible thing to lose one's youngest son, especially in circumstances like that.

Lorna felt fire shooting through her as she read it through a second time. At last!

'Mum, I've found something here about Oliver.'

'What?' The play on the wireless was about fox hunting. Bugles were sounding across the clatter of horses' hoofs. Mum was still following the hounds.

'Something about Oliver.' She watched her mother's dark eyes widen with surprise. 'Take it upstairs and read it in private.' She pushed the journal at her. 'Go on, read it. It confirms much of what you worried about.'

Lorna quickly looked through the other notebooks she had with her. No letter had been trapped between the pages. She moved to the armchair by the fire and heard one rider being tossed from his horse and receiving comfort from his girlfriend, following which he declared his love and the fox finally found refuge in his lair. She sat on, staring into the flames.

'I'm going to make a pot of tea,' Pam said, getting up. 'I'll take a cup up to Mum.'

Lorna looked at the clock. It was over an hour since she'd gone upstairs. 'Let me take it up,' she said.

She found Alice lying on her bed, her eyes heavy with emotion. She could see she'd been crying.

'Lorna, it's the best Christmas present you could have given me,' she said, mopping at her tears. 'Even better than the wireless.' Her smile was wan. 'But don't tell our Jim that.'

'We still don't know what caused his death.'

'I know he didn't mean to desert me.' Mum sipped her tea. 'That means so much. Something happened to stop him coming back.'

Lorna sat on the end of her bed. 'Marina wrote of hiding Oliver's letter…'

'And he did make a will! There've been times when I thought it was all in my head, that I must have imagined it.'

'I've had a quick look through what I brought, and there's nothing tucked between the pages, but I know there is more to find now. I'll go through everything with a fine-tooth comb when I get back. This has given me hope.'

'It's given me peace,' her mother said.

Lorna went back to Otterspool House feeling sure she'd be able to find the will and letter Marina had mentioned. She was equally sure his mother must have written more about Oliver, but if she were to find that, she'd have to read

361

through everything in her handwriting. She took a good deal of it back with her to Hedge End every evening, and read it in bed. She knew she had to as the deadline was so close.

There were so many documents, notebooks, papers of every description, both in Marina's boudoir and Mr Wyndham's study, that he came back to help. On his instructions, Harold carried great cartons down to the Daimler and more out to the garden to burn.

Lorna went home for New Year's Day and again for the following Sunday, after searching without success. Even her mother was giving up hope that she'd find anything more. They both knew time was running out. No longer was this just for her mother: Lorna hungered for information about her natural father and was desperate to get to the bottom of what had happened. Impossible to walk away from Otterspool House and accept that she'd never know the whole story.

She was trying to work out her next move. It seemed her only possible course would be to tell Quentin who she was. He'd know the full story and so would Maude and Rosaleen. She'd be raking up painful memories and was afraid they'd find it upsetting to talk to her about Oliver's death, but twenty years had passed and surely it wasn't too much to ask for Oliver's daughter?

Lorna had kept Marina's diary for 1915 open at the page where she'd written of her sad memories of Oliver's death. She now had proof that Oliver had told them of her mother's pregnancy. Quentin must have memories of his own and could no doubt tell her all she wanted to know. She hoped he'd be sympathetic and accept her for what she was, a Wyndham born on the wrong side of the blanket.

But even more urgent was the need to tell Jonathon. She saw that as more of a risk. She couldn't bear it if he decided he wanted no more to do with her. She'd made him tell her all about his life, searched out his secrets, but told him next to nothing about herself. She hadn't dared in case she was sent away from Otterspool House before she'd finished. She hadn't told any lies, just kept her mouth shut about certain facts. Until Jonathon knew the full story, she could never feel sure of him.

She hadn't quite finished clearing out Marina's boudoir and Quentin's bedroom, but if she found nothing more, then she'd have to tell the family.

Alice was feeling better, she was singing now as she went about her housework. She was enjoying cooking for herself and Pam and listening to the new wireless. That Oliver hadn't let her down made a huge difference. She was more curious than ever to know what had happened to stop him coming back to her and was determined to go to the auction. As the day drew closer she knew she was getting a bit jittery about it, and was pleased when Sam arrived home the day before.

'Will you come with me? I need somebody to hold my hand.'

He sat warming himself by the fire and said slowly, 'I've heard so much about the place, I'd like to see it, but... I know what it did to you.

Alice, are you sure you want to see it again?'

'Yes.' Alice told him about the entry in Marina Wyndham's diary. She'd copied it out before Lorna had taken it back. She got it out now to show him. 'It'll help me get things straight in my mind, though I'm better already. Soon the house will be gone for ever. This will be my only chance.'

'If that's how you feel about it, we'll go,' he said.

On the morning of the sale, Alice dressed carefully in a navy-blue outfit and a matching hat that was smarter than anything else she'd ever had. Sam wore a good alpaca overcoat and fur-lined leather gloves to hide his calloused hands. 'We look a pair of toffs,' he said as they set off.

'They'll be a moneyed lot going there, but we won't look too much out of place.'

'We can thank Lorna for these good clothes.'

'And Mr and Mrs Cartwright.'

'Well, he doesn't need this coat any more.'

'But I can't see why she threw out this lovely hat.'

When they got off the bus, Alice didn't recognise the surroundings. The road had been widened and there were streets of small houses and shops where once there'd been green fields. Only the eight-foot wall was familiar.

There were posters advertising the sale and large arrows pointing the way. Cars drove past them and there were quite a lot of other people walking up the drive. It saddened her to see how neglected everything looked. She held tightly on to Sam's arm as they turned the corner and the house came into view.

It took her breath away, it looked so beautiful, and it was just as she remembered it. The ivy growing up the walls of grey stone was now as red as rosy apples in the winter sun. As she mounted the steps to the front door, Alice could feel her heart pumping. There were weeds and grass growing in the cracks between the York stone slabs. Not that she'd ever used the front entrance in those far-off days.

An attendant at the door waved them through to the big hall. It smelled just as it always had – of age and damp, rather like a church. Alice had never seen such a crowd here before, nor the rows of chairs with cane seats. Sam sat down on one and pulled her down beside him. The auctioneer was already on his dais. His hammer slammed down.

'Sold for seventy-five pounds, at the back of the hall.'

Alice opened the catalogue Lorna had given her and found the previous lot had been a clock. She could see it now on the table, but didn't recognise it. She couldn't say she'd ever seen it before. It seemed an enormous sum for such a thing.

'Lot number fifteen.' Another clock was held aloft by a porter in a brown drill coat. 'Dating from about eighteen hundred.'

Alice thought it rather ugly but the bidding went even higher. She knew there was nothing here she and Sam could afford even if they wanted it. She relaxed and looked round slowly. Nothing much else had changed. The great fireplace went up to the roof and the black beams were lost in the shadows. The winding staircase was still beautiful.

As Lorna had said, the great hall was shabby and cold. It had always been cold in winter, even when the fire was roaring up the great chimney. The family had shut themselves away in their suites of rooms and the nursery had been cosy.

An elderly woman was standing near the grate, gazing round the hall. To Alice, her face was familiar but for a moment she couldn't place her. There had been so many relatives either living here or visiting regularly in those earlier days.

Was she Mr Wyndham's sister? Yes, that was it. She didn't appear to have changed all that much. Still upright, with a lively face. Her gaze was coming closer, Alice felt the blood rush to her cheeks. What if she recognised her? They hadn't given a thought to other Wyndham relatives. Alice moved slightly, to put more of Sam's bulk between them. The forthright gaze passed over her and was now back on the auctioneer. Alice was able to breathe more easily. Silly to worry. She'd looked very different when she was seventeen.

Sam nudged her. 'There's our Lorna.'

She was at the door, looking round, although she'd said she might be working in the office today. She looked radiant. She had seen them and was coming over, her face lit up with smiles, a young man following in her wake. Alice's heart began to drum again.

'Hello, Mum.' She bent to kiss her cheek. 'You

366

found the place all right? Pa, you're home again! I hope you won't be going back before the weekend?'

'Afraid I will, love.'

'Lovely to see you anyway.' She kissed him too, then turned. 'This is Jonathon Wyndham.' She smiled round at him. 'My parents.'

That made Alice go weak at the knees. She wouldn't have known Jonathon – he'd been a toddler of three when she'd last seen him. He'd grown into a tall and handsome young man with the fair Wyndham colouring.

'Very pleased to meet you, Mrs Mathews.' He shook hands with them both and called Sam 'sir'. He was smiling. Alice steeled herself to meet his gaze. She remembered his deep blue eyes, but there wasn't a glimmer of recognition in them, thank goodness.

His expression was open and friendly. 'I don't know how we'd have managed without Lorna,' he told them. 'She's been a wonderful help to my family in arranging all this.'

He excused himself and went. Lorna sat down next to her. Alice gripped her hand; her own felt cold.

'That's old Mr Wyndham.' Lorna pointed out an old man sitting right in front of the auctioneer.

Alice studied his back. He'd had a full head of hair in the old days but now it was white and wispy and she could see his pink scalp shining through.

'I wouldn't have recognised either of them,' she whispered.

'I told you, everything changes in twenty years.

People are changed by what life throws at them too.'

Alice couldn't take her eyes away from Mr Wyndham. She'd thought him a powerful man. Now his shoulders were bent and he looked frail, but he was still head of the family. He was peering myopically at a notebook in which he was making notes. Everybody was deferring to him.

Lorna whispered: 'I must go to him. He'll want me to keep a record of what things make. He'll want to compare it later to the auctioneers' list. Bye, Mum. So long, Pa.'

Alice watched her slide into the seat next to the old man. He'd been so strict, so much in control of everything. She recognised his side view when he turned to greet Lorna, but he was withered with age. Alice gave herself up to thinking of the family as they'd been all those years ago, when Oliver had been like Jonathon. She'd come to lay her ghosts.

She saw Rosaleen then, standing by the door. She'd been a pretty girl once; now she looked a gaunt and stringy old maid. She was elegantly dressed in the latest style and her hair, which was fading in colour, showed it had received recent attention from a high-class hairdresser, but she looked unhappy and unfulfilled. Having money hadn't bought what she wanted in life.

Alice's attention was caught by Jonathon, who'd come back and was looking round the hall. The auctioneer's hammer came down on another lot and in the moment's lull he made his way over to where Lorna was sitting. She was talking to

368

Mr Wyndham and Jonathon touched her shoulder to get her attention and his hand stayed there. A gesture like that must mean... Alice felt suddenly cold.

'D'you see that, Sam?'

Lorna had turned so Alice could see her face in profile; she was smiling up at Jonathon, who was bending over to talk to her. His face was betraying an intimacy that made her shiver.

Sam whispered, 'They seem to have hit it off.'

'It's what I was afraid would happen.' Alice knew she was talking too loud, and was glad when the bidding opened on a collection of vases.

'He seems a nice lad.'

She gripped Sam's hand. 'He's one of *them*. The same thing could happen to her as happened to me.'

He was shaking his head. 'They're different people, Alice. Lorna's older than you were.'

'So's he. Older than Oliver was.' She was grasping at any comfort.

'They're both more worldly-wise too.'

'But she knows how dangerous it could be. I warned her.'

'She said, "Forewarned is forearmed."'

'But it doesn't seem to have made any difference. She's given no hint, has she? She's keeping it quiet.'

'If there's anything to hint about.'

'I'm sure there is.'

'Lorna's afraid it'll worry you, that's why she's keeping it quiet.'

'I am worried.'

'Ask her next time she comes home. She'll tell

you. Who's that who's just come in?'

Alice felt apprehensive. 'Talking to Rosaleen?' It had to be Daphne. 'Mrs Crispin.'

'The woman you worked for? The one who treated you so badly?'

'Yes.'

Once she'd been attractive too; now she was very much overweight. Daphne had found fault with almost everything she and Nanny had done and they'd both feared and dreaded her visits to the nursery. When Alice had pleaded for help for herself and Oliver's baby, she'd refused point-blank, been rude and sent her away penniless.

Alice had held a grudge against both her and Rosaleen ever since, but the years had not treated either of them well. They'd always seemed parsimonious if not mean with the staff. She guessed they were here to make sure they got their share of the money being generated by this sale.

She didn't know why Daphne should have such lines of discontent on her face, but it made Alice think that perhaps she herself had been just as well off with Sam. He'd been unfailingly kind and generous with what little he had. She squeezed his hand.

'Are you ready to go?' he whispered.

Alice was.

When the last lot went under the hammer, Quentin felt exhausted. He was stiff with sitting still for so long and it took effort to get to his feet. He wanted to get outside to his car and distance himself from all this, but the auctioneers stopped him, wanting to talk.

'A good sale, sir. Good prices, attracted a large crowd. We'll let you have the paperwork in a day or two, but we could phone you tonight with the amount it's made.'

'Yes, thank you.'

The crowd had surged to the entrance by that time and he hadn't the strength to push his way through. He was glad when Lorna took his arm; he needed more than his stick to lean on. Harold leaped up to help him down the front steps, which made him feel a decrepit centenarian, but it was such a relief to sink on to the back seat of the old Daimler.

'Are you coming home with me?' he asked.

'I'd better wait for Jonathon,' Lorna said. 'I've already accepted a lift from him. We can probably add up the figures faster than the auctioneers, and we won't be far behind you.'

'Good,' he said, though he didn't care that much. From what he'd heard, he was sure the sale had made more than he'd been expecting, which ought to please him. Yes, it did please him, but parting with the trappings of the house had reduced him to an emotional wreck. He wiped a tear from his cheek, glad of the privacy of his car now gliding on its stately way. It had been a wrench he hadn't expected to feel so deeply.

He thought of the hammered brass canopy over the hearth in the hall – who could possibly use such a huge thing these days? But somebody had paid good money for it. And the stained-glass windows too. The buyer was prepared to take them out of their frames and set them up elsewhere. Should he perhaps have built another house for the family and taken them with him? It had never occurred to him to do that, and it would take more energy than he had these days. He'd taken on a house that had been designed to suit another family, not the Wyndhams. To Captain Lars, such a thing would have been unthinkable.

The Daimler was pulling up in front of Hedge End. The lights from the entrance were beaming a welcome. By the time Quentin had got himself out on the gravel Harold had rung the bell and Sissie had opened the door for him. The warmth surrounded him in the hall. Otterspool had never been able to do that. This was a more honest house, not at all grand, built for a middle-class family without pretensions, but there were fewer draughts and more comfort than Otterspool had ever had.

The telephone rang as he reached the door of his study. Hedge End had more of these new-fangled things – too many for him. He ignored it. His study was smaller than the old one. Cosier, Lorna had called it. It had a gas fire he could light himself, but that was not as comforting as the real thing.

He wanted his tea, but there was no bell to pull here to get attention. Already it was late for tea, and luncheon had been a mere picnic on the library table that had already been sold to someone else. He sank down on his chair and wished somebody would answer the telephone. Then he heard the front door slam and Rosaleen's quick steps across the hall. The phone was silenced – peace at last. His eyes closed. He needed a rest more than anything.

Seconds later, his study door slammed back. 'Father, Crispin's distraught. Clarissa's run away.' Rosaleen's cheeks were crimson.

'Run away?' He didn't feel he could cope with anything more today. 'She's old enough to look after herself, isn't she?'

'Crispin's on his way over to see you.'

'What for?' That made him sit up again. 'I thought I'd made it clear... What does he expect me to do? She's his daughter.'

'Clarissa's left a letter for you. He's bringing it over.'

Quentin sighed. 'Let's have our tea, Rosaleen. I'm much in need of it.'

Crispin and Daphne arrived five minutes after the tea trolley came in. Daphne was mopping her eyes with a lace handkerchief. 'Where has Clarissa gone? Taking off when we turn our backs. She's taken all her clothes.'

'I'm afraid she's eloped with that awful fellow. She's going to get herself into trouble.' Crispin was beside himself. 'She'll cause a scandal, ruin her name.'

Daphne was angry. 'Her cousin Edmund wants to marry her. He asked Crispin for her hand. She'd have been much better doing things properly with him.'

Quentin helped himself to another piece of fruit cake. 'I can't see there's anything I can do about it.'

'She's letting the family down, besmirching our name.'

'She's not the only one to do that,' he sighed.

'We all have. It's hard to say who's done the most harm.'

'Open her letter, Father. I want to know what she says.'

Quentin ripped open the envelope. 'Where's my glasses?' Daphne pushed them into his hand.

Dear Grandpa, *he read.*

Today is my wedding day. I chose it because I knew you'd all be at the auction and Father would not come and cause trouble. It's to be in the register office at two o'clock. I would have preferred the church with my family round me and all the trimmings, but Father has shown Vincent the door and Mother doesn't want me to marry at all.

After the wedding, we are going up to Scotland for a few days, where I am to meet my new in-laws. They are arranging a service of blessing in their church, so you see, our marriage will be legal, and done with as much ceremony as my family's attitude allows.

Vincent has accepted a new job in West Africa and we'll be away for eighteen months. By then, when we come home on leave, everything will have calmed down. We'll be travelling out on the mail boat that leaves from Liverpool on the 26th of this month. I'm on cloud nine.

I hope, Grandpa, you will understand that I love him. At twenty-three, I'm old enough to make up my own mind about who I marry. Edmund Wyndham Yates will not do. I can't put up with Father forcing him down my throat, and at the same time, talking Vincent down. I wish it didn't have to be like this. Forgive me and wish us well.

Love from Clarissa.

'Father, what does she say?'

'She was married at two o'clock today.'

'What? Didn't she know it was the auction?' Daphne was angry.

'How could she have forgotten that?' Crispin demanded.

'She didn't forget it,' Quentin said slowly.

'She went behind our backs.'

'We didn't see the letter until we got home an hour ago,' Daphne fretted. 'She knew we wouldn't be able to be at her wedding. It should have been a family occasion.'

'I'm sorry I missed it,' Quentin said. 'She chose today because she knew you'd be tied up elsewhere.'

'If I'd known,' Aunt Maude said, 'I'd have gone to the register office and skipped the rest of the auction.'

'So would I.' Daphne was mopping her eyes. 'I feel cheated.'

Quentin handed the letter to Crispin. 'It sounds as though she was expecting you to make a real fuss.'

'Clarissa's letting the family down,' Crispin declared. 'I'd have stopped it if I could. Marrying a chap like that, she'll rue the day. I told her, but she wouldn't listen.'

'She's had the best all her life.' Daphne was in floods of tears now. 'After all we've done for her.'

Quentin sighed. 'Let's look on the bright side.

At least she is married, so there'll be no scandal. All we can do now is to wish her well and hope she'll be happy.'

'With him?'

'I've never met him. He's her choice.'

'Of course you have, Father. She brought him to dinner once at Otterspool. This is your fault, you made it possible for her to do it.'

'Nothing to do with me.'

Rosaleen turned on him. 'Of course it is. You gave her all that jewellery and the silver. She'll have sold it by now to pay for this. She may be back before long for another hand-out.'

'We aren't all like you, Rosaleen,' Daphne said as she made for the door.

Chapter Nineteen

The weeks were passing. Daphne knew Crispin was running up an overdraft at the bank. During the first week or two, he'd given her a little money for housekeeping, but that had dried up long since. He'd given a week's notice to the new cook and parlourmaid and they'd already gone.

Since her wedding day, Daphne had not had to worry about money. Everything she'd wanted, she'd been able to buy. She'd always known it was family money she spent. That Crispin didn't have to earn it, made her allowance feel all the more secure. Only now that his father had cut him off did she realise what a fallacy that was.

She knew she'd grown soft, become used to comfortable living and had lost the ability she'd once had to pay her own way. What was worse, she was afraid Crispin had never had that ability. Unlike his father, he had no talent for making money.

When he began looking for another job, Crispin had had offers, but he'd been too fussy about what he would accept. A business acquaintance of long standing had offered him the position of accounts manager in his firm. He'd turned it down without giving it much thought as being too lowly a position for him. A few weeks later he'd been forced to accept a job as a ledger clerk. He'd lasted only three days in that. In a second job in the shipping business, this time with Wyndhams' competitors, he'd lasted one week.

Without money, Daphne didn't know how to keep the household going. Already, she'd run up bills with the grocer, butcher and coal merchant. She knew Crispin had even more owing to their wine merchant. She was seeing him with fresh eyes. In recent years, the only things she'd valued about him were his wealth and status.

Daphne was also worried because Crispin was spending more time with his mistress than he was with her. It used to be one or two nights a week but since his father had dismissed him from the firm he was staying away much more. She hadn't seen him for the last week.

He'd even admitted to her that he had an illegitimate daughter, though he didn't speak about the girl to the rest of his family. She'd known Ruth Detley was the first of many mistresses, and guessed he'd set up his current one in a house of her own and that was where he stayed when he didn't come home at night. Exactly where that was she didn't know. Tonight he'd gone without telling her anything and she had no idea when he'd be back.

It seemed the last straw for Clarissa to have gone off and got married without saying a word. She couldn't have chosen a worse time. Daphne felt as though she'd been abandoned. Having neither of her children at home made her feel vulnerable, as though her reason for being with the Wyndhams had suddenly been taken from her. It heightened her feeling of impending disaster.

She wandered round her empty house, comforting herself with the thought that she was Crispin's legal wife; mother of his legitimate children and mistress of his official place of residence. He may no longer love her, but she'd been an exemplary wife. Until now, she'd felt her position was secure.

But Crispin and Adam were in trouble, Clarissa had gone, and their home was only rented and costing more than they could afford. What was she to do now? She felt sick when she thought about it. She was frightened of what the future might hold.

For the first time, Daphne regretted marrying Crispin. He hadn't been honest; he hadn't treated her or his parents as well as he should have done. He'd cheated her by chasing after other women. He'd cheated his father too, by not looking after the family business. Daphne was afraid she'd paid too high a price to be his wife. She'd lost her looks in the years she'd given him, and was going to end up with very little unless she took matters into her own hands. She had had more than enough of Crispin and could no longer rely on him to look after her interests.

She looked up, and through the drawing-room window, saw him drive up to the front door. It was as though thinking about him had made him materialise. He got out of his car, came up the front steps and then she heard his key turn in the lock.

She waited for him to enter the room, but he went straight on upstairs. He was ignoring her and that made her lose her temper. She ran up after him and found he'd opened a suitcase on the bed and was throwing his clothes into it.

She snapped, 'What are you doing?'

'What does it look as though I'm doing? I'm packing my things. I'm moving out.'

Daphne felt the strength ebb from her knees. She had to hold on to the bedstead. 'Why?'

'I should have thought that was obvious.'

She tightened her grip. He preferred his mistress to her?

'No,' she said.

'I can't afford to live in a house like this.'

'But what about me?'

'You chose it. You wanted it.'

'We chose it together. You wanted it too.'

'Not any more. My circumstances have changed.'

'You've signed a five-year lease on this house. You're legally liable to pay the rent for that

379

period.' She knew his only way out would be to find another tenant to take over the lease. 'I don't suppose you care–'

'That'll be your problem now.'

'No.' Daphne had already taken legal advice on this. She'd been to see the solicitor who was retained for the business. 'Fortunately, the lease is in your name. With your usual high-handedness, you didn't even want mine on it as joint tenant. It's entirely your problem.'

He snapped the case shut and pulled up another. 'We'll see about that.'

She knew he was the sort who would renege on the rent when he had no more money. 'Where are you going?'

He ignored her and went on pulling clothes from his wardrobe. Why had she ever thought him handsome? He was fat and his eyes were tiny slits under puffy lids. Anger shafted through her.

'Answer me, you slob. You've bought a house for your lady friend, haven't you? You're going to live with her?'

'Yes, but it's not much of a place. You wouldn't like it.'

'What am I going to do?'

'You wouldn't deign to live there.'

'Not with a whore like her...'

The slap across her cheek made her stagger backwards. If she hadn't been holding on to the bed rail she would have fallen. She said through clenched teeth, 'Go to your mistress and your bastard. I certainly don't want you here.'

'You've been making that clear.'

This was a further blow to her pride. 'I hate you.'

'Mutual, I assure you.' He slipped the locks shut on the second case and looked round the room. 'I'll be back for my pictures and the rest of my things.'

Daphne was furious. As she listened to the sound of his car pulling away she knew she'd see precious little of him in future. From now on, she'd have to look after herself.

She strode through the elegant rooms of Ravensdale House, boiling over with resentment, knowing she couldn't continue to live here. She despised Crispin. He was useless, incapable of doing anything. It was only the family power of the Wentworth Wyndhams that had kept him afloat this long. He indulged himself, followed every whim without giving any thought to earning a living, to loyalty or responsibility. He was a decadent fool.

Daphne was frightened. She knew now that moving to a house of their own was the worst thing she and Crispin could have done. For years she'd wanted it, longed for it, but if they'd stayed at Otterspool she'd at least have been left with a roof over her head. Quentin wouldn't have thrown her out.

She decided she must see him. She was going to tell him what Crispin was doing to her. He'd be sympathetic; he'd understand how impossible this was for her. Without giving herself time to think, she telephoned for a taxi and half an hour later, feeling uneasy and not a little queasy, she was ringing the front doorbell at Hedge End.

As it happened, Aunt Maude was just crossing the hall and let her in. 'Hello, Daphne. Come in. You're just in time for tea.'

She followed her to the sitting room where Quentin had hung the portrait of Marina in pride of place. The room was much more comfortable than the white drawing room at Otterspool. Rosaleen, thin to the point of emaciation, was already pouring tea. She looked up and pulled a face that was anything but welcoming.

Quentin seemed to struggle as he got to his feet to greet her. 'Daphne! Hello, come and sit down.'

She said nervously, 'I expect you're wondering what brings me here.' She knew by the way three sets of pale Wyndham eyes were sizing her up that they expected it to be trouble.

'There's something... I have to tell you. You ought to know. Crispin is leaving me.' She was unable to keep the bitterness out of her voice.

'Divorce?' Rosaleen looked shocked. 'Crispin wouldn't do such a thing!'

Daphne let her anger bubble out. 'He wouldn't, you're quite right. He wouldn't be bothered. It would be too much trouble. Besides, he hasn't the money to pay for such frills. He's moving in with his current ladylove and bastard child. He's abandoned me.'

Even Aunt Maude gasped. Rosaleen's face showed horror.

'Are you sure?' Quentin asked.

'Oh yes. He's going to leave me in the big house he chose, with all the bills to pay.'

Quentin sighed heavily.

Daphne turned on him. 'You've put him out of

382

the business. I know you have your reasons, but what about me? I've never done you any harm.'

She watched him purse his lips in thought as she rushed on.

'Crispin can't support himself. He sees it as a logical step to stop supporting me, an economy.' Daphne could feel tears prickling her eyes. 'It's damned humiliating after twenty-six years of marriage that he can walk out on me; that he prefers someone else. He doesn't give a thought to my position. What am I to do?' She took out her handkerchief and blew her nose.

'I'm sorry,' Quentin said, his face furrowed with concern. 'I should have given more thought...'

Aunt Maude pushed a cup of tea into Daphne's hand. 'You must let us help you.'

Daphne knew none of the Wyndhams really liked her, but they wouldn't approve of this sort of thing in the family. As Quentin understood it, women should be looked after. He'd never deal harshly with them. He was a gentleman.

'Perhaps... I could make you an allowance,' he said.

'Surely, Father, that's not necessary!' Daphne didn't miss the spiteful look Rosaleen shot in her direction. 'You must talk to Crispin, point out that he–'

'A small allowance,' Quentin said, 'but enough for you to live modestly.'

Relief came, blessed relief. Daphne felt it flooding through her. She wouldn't have to look for work.

'Thank you, that would be such a help, such a weight off my mind. It would be so difficult to find a job at my time of life.'

'You mustn't think of that, my dear. If Crispin doesn't see it as his responsibility to look after you, then I certainly shall.'

'I can't thank you enough.' Daphne dried her eyes. 'I'm very grateful. The only other thing I could think of was throwing myself on my mother, but she's growing old and needs–'

'No, no. Leave it to me. You have a bank account of your own?'

'No, Crispin felt... He saw to everything, settled my bills, gave me a little allowance for clothes.'

'We'd better open an account for you now. I'll see to it.'

She would have liked to ask how much of an allowance he meant to give her, but didn't dare. She must not upset him.

'I feel I can breathe again. I'm very grateful, thank you again.'

Daphne took her leave, knowing that, after all, she wasn't going to starve. Harold had been summoned to drive her home. Relaxing on the back seat of the Daimler and feeling somewhat mollified, she decided to go to the pictures by way of celebration.

She rapped on the glass partition and asked him to take her into town. She hadn't been out for ages and it was doing her no good to mope by herself at home. There was a new talkie showing, *The Blue Angel*, with the sensational new star Marlene Dietrich. It would do her good to see that.

It was late when she returned home that night but she felt much more cheerful. Now Quentin

384

had promised her an allowance, she would be happy to sever all connection with Crispin. But of course, she had her regrets.

She loved living in this very beautiful house. It was the first home she'd had of her own and she'd been here such a short time. But it was a mirage, it couldn't last, and she'd been very frightened she'd be left with nothing.

She could walk out now, and get another house for herself, but it wouldn't be like this. Daphne drifted from the elegant drawing room to the dining room, admiring their beautiful plaster ceilings. Here she was surrounded by Crispin's belongings, things he valued, things he'd said he would come back for. What remained of their wealth was tied up in this antique furniture they'd brought from Otterspool. Of course, she could take a few pieces with her to furnish her new house, but this lovely table would be too big – most of the furniture here would be.

She could, of course, sell off a few pieces and bank the money in her own name. Why leave it all for Crispin? She decided it would be wise to do so, and the sooner she started, the safer she'd feel.

There was a long silence in the Hedge End drawing room when Daphne left. Quentin watched Maude lay aside her embroidery and begin putting the cups back on the tea trolley. She picked up the cake. 'Bought slab cake – it wasn't very nice. We haven't done as well for cake since you sacked Hilda.'

'Hilda had to go,' he said. 'Oh dear, I do despair

385

of Crispin.'

Rosaleen's face was screwing up with fury. 'You don't have to give Daphne money. She's not your problem,' she screamed.

'I feel I should.'

'How much will you give her?'

He daren't mention a figure – Rosaleen was against him giving her anything. 'I haven't decided yet.'

'You're a fool, Father,' she flared up. 'What's the point of saying we're hard up if you're going to throw money at the wall like this? An allowance! It'll go on for years. You can guarantee she'll live to a ripe old age now.'

'Rosaleen dear, you mustn't upset yourself...' Maude tried to comfort her, but she leaped to her feet and rushed from the room.

'Oh dear! She isn't herself.' Quentin pulled himself to his feet to go after her, but he could no longer get up stairs quickly. He heard her bedroom door slam before he reached the landing. He tapped on it. 'Rosaleen?' There was no answer, he hadn't expected one. He went in to find his daughter had thrown herself across her bed like a frustrated child. He sat beside her and put an arm across her heaving shoulders.

'Leaving Otterspool is hard for us all, Roz, but we'll get used to living here. This is a comfortable house – in many ways, it's better.'

'It's not just that,' Rosaleen wept. 'It's Daphne. She always has a sob story, and you always fall for it. Giving her money!'

'I can't just ignore what's going on.'

'Of course you can. Serve her right. But it's

386

Jonathon too and Lorna Mathews – they cause nothing but trouble for us all.'

'No, Rosaleen. Lorna helped–'

'That's what you think. That's what she makes you think but she's nothing but trouble. They frighten me.'

'There's nothing to be afraid of, dear.'

'But there is. Crispin too – he scares me more than anybody. And Hilda. They're all after our money. Crispin would do anything–'

'No, Rosaleen. Hilda's already gone and we'll probably hear little from Crispin in future.'

'I hate him, hate them all. Nobody cares about me.'

'I care about you,' Quentin said. 'I care very much. You're my only daughter, and I love you.'

Rosaleen seemed to pour out such hate, envy and fear. Why should she feel frightened? Why so jealous?

She was quieter. Her shoulders had stopped heaving. 'I hate...'

'I'll cover you with your eiderdown,' he said. 'You have a little rest, then come down before dinner and have a glass of sherry with us.' He tiptoed out and went back to the sitting room.

'How is she?' Maude asked.

Quentin shook his head. 'Impossible to reason with her when she's in a mood like this. When she comes down for her dinner, I'll suggest she sees the doctor. Her nerves are shot to pieces. She's wearing us both out.'

Quentin's mind was already on something else. 'I've been thinking about Clarissa. It's the twenty-sixth tomorrow. She'll be catching the

387

mail boat to West Africa. We could go down to see her off. If we don't, we won't see her for another eighteen months.'

'Would she want to see us?'

'I think we should. Her quarrel wasn't with us. I'll go alone if you don't want to come.'

'I'll come, Quentin. I wouldn't like her to think she's cut herself off from the whole family. We'll go and say goodbye to her.'

'Always been fond of Clarissa.'

'What time does her boat sail?'

'We'll have to ring Elder Dempsters to find out. You do that, Maude. I don't hear well on the telephone these days.'

'I'll do it now,' she said, getting up. It took only a few minutes.

'They say the ship will be tied up at Princes Dock from midday until five to take on passengers. Then it will pull into the river to wait for the high tide to cross the bar. Visitors are allowed on board.'

'Then we'll have an early lunch and go as soon as we've finished,' Quentin said. 'What about Daphne? Should we ask her if she wants to come with us?'

Maude studied him for a moment. 'No, you're too soft-hearted. Clarissa's run away from her parents. Daphne read her letter, she knows she'll be leaving on that boat. There's nothing to stop her going down to make her peace if she wants to. Better if we let her do things her way.'

The next morning, Quentin bought a large bunch of carnations for Clarissa. 'I feel sorry that she had to get married in such a furtive way. I'd have liked to make a fuss of her.'

It was a dark winter's day and there was a cutting wind off the river.

The ship was painted white all over except for its yellow funnel. 'Looks very summery,' Maude said.

'She'll be sailing in tropical waters.'

As they went on board they were caught up in the busy hustle and bustle of sailing day. Maude was at the purser's desk asking for the newlyweds' cabin number, when Quentin nudged her arm. 'Here she is.'

Clarissa was coming down the main staircase on the arm of her groom. She looked radiant.

'Grandpa!' she squealed with delight when she saw him.

'Couldn't let you go without saying goodbye.' He gave her a hug. 'You look as though marriage suits you.'

'Oh, it does, it does.'

'Grandpa bought some flowers for you.' Maude had carried them. 'He thought you should have some token of our affection.'

'Lovely.' Clarissa buried her face in them. 'They smell heavenly.'

'Good afternoon.' Dr Vincent McDonald was at his most formal. 'I fear I should apologise for stealing Clarissa from her family and whisking her off to the other side of the world.'

'Not to us, though I'm sorry we won't see so much of her from now on.'

'Vincent's been worried sick.' Clarissa beamed at Quentin. 'But the arguing had gone on long enough. I didn't want him to sail for Nigeria

389

without me. It was the only way.'

'It bothers me that you're going to the West Coast,' Quentin said. 'Not a healthy place, and our ancestors ... well, you know what they did there.'

'Vincent won't be dragged into anything like that,' she laughed. 'He's a medical missionary.'

'I'll take good care of her,' the doctor said.

'Grandpa, you're not cross with me?'

'Your mother and father are. You should make peace with them.'

'We tried, Grandpa, truly we did. We stayed at the Adelphi last night. I telephoned Ravensdale three times to ask them to forgive me and come and have dinner with us, but there was no reply. I tried twice after dinner too. Have they gone away?'

'Your mother's there. She came out to Hedge End to have tea with us yesterday,' Maude said. 'I'm surprised you didn't get her.' Maude didn't know whether to tell her that her parents had parted, but decided not to. It was not her place to do that. 'I'll tell her we've seen you and that you tried to contact her.'

'Come and see our cabin.' Clarissa was excited. It was light and spacious.

Afterwards they had afternoon tea in the lounge. The call for all visitors to go ashore came all too soon.

'I'm glad we came,' Quentin said as they made their way down the gangplank. 'He seems a pleasant enough fellow.'

'I'm glad she had the guts to defy Crispin. She was bubbling with happiness the whole time.'

'I think she's done the right thing,' Quentin said. 'Dr McDonald couldn't take his eyes from her.'

It was the following Friday, and Daphne got up late and, after a substantial brunch, went into town, taking a few pieces of silver in a bag. She'd never had to put herself in this position before and was afraid it was going to be a humbling experience. She could feel her heart thudding as she pretended to study the luxury goods displayed in the window of one of the smartest shops in Liverpool.

An elegant George III tea and coffee service sparkled under the light, set as it was against a background of black velvet. She was looking for a discreet notice offering to buy fine silver and jewellery but couldn't see one. She told herself that didn't mean that they wouldn't. The door swung open as a customer came out. Daphne peered in, wondering if the sales staff would recognise her. She'd been inside several times as a customer to buy jewellery.

Seeing that the shop was now empty, she hoisted the bag on to her hip, took a deep breath and marched inside. She could feel herself blushing with embarrassment as she told the man behind the counter why she'd come – she kept her voice so low that she had to repeat herself. His manner was very formal.

'We might be willing to purchase from you,' he said. She jumped when the doorbell pinged and more customers came in, and was relieved to be led off to a small back office where the manager came to speak to her.

She had to give her name. She'd been hoping that wouldn't be necessary, but the public auction had acquainted everybody in the trade that the Wyndhams had silver to sell. She laid out the snuff boxes and candlesticks she'd brought, and her head swam as she watched the buyer scrutinising the hallmarks through an eye glass.

'London, eighteen forty,' he murmured. Then, 'Chester nineteen twelve.'

Daphne's mouth was dry. She took from her handbag the butterfly brooch that Quentin had given her, and was surprised at the high price offered for that. As each price was suggested, she accepted it without comment, wanting only to bring this toe-curling meeting to an end. After she'd rushed from the shop, she wondered if she might have got a little more if she'd pressed for it.

Outside on the pavement again, she could feel the beads of perspiration across her forehead drying in the cold air. She felt better now it was done and she had a little money in her handbag. She needed to buy some food to take home – her larder was empty – but before she did that she'd reward herself with a cup of coffee and a cake to blot out that awful experience. She set off towards the Kardomah Café.

She was boiling with resentment. She deserved better than this from Crispin. He'd treated her despicably. She was striding along without looking where she was going when she almost bumped into a girl in a blue two-piece. It made her stumble and drop her empty bag. The girl bent to pick it up for her.

'I'm sorry.' She was smiling at her.

It was only then that Daphne recognised her. 'Hello, Lorna. I've not seen you for a while.'

'I'm just going to catch the bus up to Otters-pool. I'm working in the office every morning now.'

'Working in our office?' Daphne realised as soon as she'd said it that she should no longer refer to it as 'our office'.

'Yes, I'm working on the Cartwright account again.'

It embarrassed Daphne to realise Lorna must know what had happened to Crispin. The girl was directly responsible for her present difficulties. Would she also know he'd left her?

She was about to make her escape when a passing gentleman raised his trilby to Lorna. 'Good afternoon, Miss Mathews.'

'Does he work in our office too?' Daphne asked.

'No, for the auctioneers who managed the sale.'

'No, you're wrong.' It helped that she could correct Miss Know-All who had ruined them financially. 'I've never seen him before.'

'The sale for Cartwright's, I mean, not your sale.' The girl was still smiling. 'Mr Wyndham used a London firm. Bamfords are based here in Liverpool, in this building here.' Daphne felt she'd been taken down another peg.

Lorna was pointing to a row of windows at first-floor level. 'That's their office up there.'

Daphne read the sign: 'H.W. Bamford and Sons. Dealers in Fine Antique Furniture'.

'They're one of the foremost Liverpool firms.'

The idea came to Daphne like a flash of light, and was so simple she couldn't understand why she hadn't thought of it before. Instead of trying to sell small pieces a few at a time, she could walk into Bamfords and ask them to come out to Ravensdale, and sell everything on her behalf.

'Do they buy as well as sell?'

'Oh yes.'

Daphne tried to think. Would she be able to do it without Crispin finding out? He'd said he was leaving her for good, but he'd come back to collect the rest of his things. If she could sell everything in Ravensdale that would bring money, get Bamfords to move it all away, then she'd pack up her personal belongings and move out before Crispin discovered what she was doing. Then she'd have something to show for the years she'd spent as his wife. She'd have more than just Quentin's allowance.

She waited until Lorna Mathews had disappeared in the direction of the bus stop and then went through the glass doors and climbed the staircase to Bamfords' office.

As always, the name Wyndham brought her deference. She was shown to a private room, and asked if they would come out to Ravensdale to assess the furniture, pictures, silver and old china she had there.

'We'll be very pleased to.' The antiques dealer was opening a ledger. 'Mr Crispin Wyndham, Ravensdale House? Your husband, I presume?' He held his pen against the entry, turned it round so that she might read it.

'Yes...' Daphne was shocked. She could feel the strength draining from her knees.

'He came in a few days ago and arranged for us to call. In fact, I've been trying to telephone you this morning to arrange a convenient time. I couldn't get an answer.'

Daphne's telephone hadn't rung this morning, but she could see that the phone number he'd written down wasn't hers. There was an address too, in Aigburth, which must be where Crispin and his lady friend were living, where he intended to stay. Her head was swimming. Crispin had already taken steps to sell off all the antiques. He intended to handle the arrangements. This must mean that all the money raised would be paid over to him.

It looked as though he planned to cut her out altogether. Well, perhaps he intended to give her something, but she'd be dependent on his goodwill, and in her experience, he didn't have a lot of that. Crispin was greedy. He'd certainly made these arrangements without mentioning them to her. She didn't trust him.

The man was looking at her through his thick glasses. 'Perhaps, we could arrange a time now?' he said.

Daphne swallowed hard. What could she do to make sure she got her share? Surely after a marriage lasting the best part of thirty years she was entitled to something? She couldn't think straight.

'Yes, of course.' She tried to smile, not let him see that this altered her plans completely.

'Our Mr Singleton will call to assess the pieces

395

you have. I was going to suggest next Wednesday morning.'

Today was Friday. Her mouth was dry. 'There's quite a lot.'

'Yes, your husband listed some of the pieces for us.' He took a typed document of several pages from the folder in front of him, turned it round and slid it in front of Daphne. The first item on it was a Regency sewing cabinet.

Daphne felt rage and indignation boiling up inside her. That wasn't Crispin's to sell. It had been a wedding present from Mirabelle, her grandmother. Her family wanted to give her things she could show to the Wyndhams with pride. Daphne had chosen it herself. She ran her eye down the list. Her portrait was on it too. When that was being painted he'd made out it was a gift to her.

His address was on the document. He'd kept that a close secret! She memorised it: number 31, Arbuthnot Road, Aigburth, Liverpool.

'It seems likely that we'll have to arrange for specialists–'

Daphne said forcefully, 'Wednesday isn't convenient, I'm sorry.' She had to stop this but she couldn't think how. She had to delay it, give herself time to think.

'Thursday morning, then?' he suggested.

'I'm so sorry...'

'Would Friday suit you, madam?'

'What about the following week?'

'Er – we're heavily booked that week. Sales for probate. But we could manage Monday.'

Daphne had to agree.

'Monday the ninth then, at nine o'clock?'

She found herself out in the street, feeling fluttery. It had come as an almighty shock, but she'd kept her head and arranged things to give herself more time. She didn't want to see an assessor from Bamfords on her doorstep ready to sell everything off on Crispin's behalf. She must decide now what to do.

Daphne had managed to pick up a taxi before it occurred to her that Crispin might well ring Bamfords to make his own arrangements. Then he'd find out that she had taken over. She collapsed in the corner of the seat, a trembling nervous wreck.

Chapter Twenty

With her job at Otterspool almost at an end, Lorna was feeling the pressure. She was seeing much more of Jonathon now she was spending her mornings in the office. She shared a sandwich lunch with him almost every day. He'd taken her to the cinema, and for short walks. He kissed her many times and was making it obvious that he loved her.

Lorna enjoyed his company, wanted even more of it, but it was tearing her in two. She was trying to hold him at arm's length, slow him down. There were too many things he didn't know about her that he should before their relationship went any further. This was tightening the pressure on her. These last few nights, she'd wished the family good night, saying she was tired as soon as dinner was over.

'Aren't you feeling well?' Jonathon had asked tonight.

'Yes, just tired.'

She'd gone to her room and got herself ready for bed, and was skimming through another of Marina's diaries, when she found herself reading an entry beginning, 'Today is the anniversary of Oliver's death.' Could this be what she had been looking for? She went on.

At breakfast, none of us spoke of it but it was there between us, a heavy burden to bear. Rosaleen was tearful when the men went to the office, she's by no means over the nervous breakdown it gave her. Quentin says I should talk about Oliver to her, but she leaps to her feet and rushes from the room if I try.

'It's over and done with,' she screams. 'Nothing will bring him back. For God's sake let's forget about it.'

Rosaleen worries me deeply. Not only have I lost my son but my daughter is much altered by his death. I fear it's blighted her life. Probably blighted all our lives. John looked very stern and sober at breakfast so I know it is on his mind too. I would have liked to keep Oliver's writings as mementoes – it would have been a comfort to have them now – but John insisted on putting them away.

I fear he thinks some of them might be incriminating if they fell into the wrong hands. He said he thought they'd bring back bad memories for me, and Rosaleen couldn't stand any more.

Lorna sat up and pummelled her pillows. She could feel the blood coursing through her veins. She'd been right: the Wyndhams had done their best to put Oliver's death right out of their minds and possibly hide the true facts. Marina had hidden her diary and the family history Oliver had written, and now she was saying John had put away other things belonging to his brother. Perhaps included were the letter and the will his mother had spoken of.

But where had he put them? Not in the attic, which might have seemed the safest place. Lorna had been through everything there very carefully. Not in the library, where a few hardback journals might have been hard to find amongst so many others.

She decided she'd have another careful look round tomorrow, though the house had been cleared and everything sold. She realised the odds were against her, and really, she had no alternative but to tell the family who she was. There was no other way she could find out more.

She was dreading having to do that. She felt Quentin liked and trusted her, and in retrospect it seemed underhand to come into his house and burrow through the family's personal papers for her own ends. Rosaleen would see it as spying.

It was raining when Lorna got off the bus the next afternoon, and she was cold and wet by the time she'd hurried up the drive and let herself in to Otterspool House through the kitchen door. It seemed only marginally warmer inside.

She went straight up to Marina's boudoir, telling herself if there was anything important still to be found this was the most likely place, but the room was bare. She went to the bedroom close by that Quentin had shared with her. There wasn't anything to do here either. It was only mid-afternoon but already the daylight was fading. Lorna ran down to the kitchen to light one of the oil lamps she'd left there, then went to have the last look round she'd promised herself.

Jonathon had said he'd found nothing of interest in the room he and his father had used. But his father had been killed in 1916, and Piers could have removed anything after John's death and hidden it in his own room to keep it safe, though Jonathon had said he'd found nothing in Piers's room either.

She'd believed him. Could the will and the letter still be there? Jonathon's bedroom was cold and empty. There was nothing but bare floorboards and bare walls. Piers's room next door was the same, apart from the fire damage and the dry rot. Lorna surveyed it from the threshold. The carpet had gone from here now. There was nothing.

She had to tell Jonathon who she was. It made no sense to keep this to herself any longer. She was afraid his feelings would be hurt if the first he heard of it was with the rest of his family. If she told him first, it might seem that she cared about what he thought. She wanted to explain why she'd refused his early invitations to go boating and to the cinema.

Tonight she'd tell Jonathon on the way to Hedge End, and she'd tell the rest of the family over dinner. There seemed no other way to find out what had happened to Oliver. She wouldn't have many more nights under their roof, so the sooner she did it, the better.

'Lorna? Are you ready? Where are you?' It gave her palpitations to hear Jonathon calling her. It reminded her the time was on her. She mustn't lose her nerve.

'Coming.' She picked up her lamp and ran downstairs. His small torch seemed a pinprick of light in the great hall. He switched it off, put it in his pocket and took her storm lamp from her. Then one arm went round her shoulders and he pulled her close to kiss her.

'Jonathon...' She was on the point of telling him at that moment.

'Did you have a last look round? I don't know how you can bear to be in this freezing black place now. I could hear the deathwatch beetle in that panelling by the window. Let's get out of here.'

'I've left my bag in the kitchen. Have to pick that up first.' He came with her, holding on to her arm.

As they set off for Hedge End in his small car he seemed lighthearted, chatting about a Cartwright client who had ordered more shipping space that afternoon.

Lorna felt apprehensive. They'd talked a good deal about the work they shared in the office. He'd told her how much he valued what she'd done. He'd kissed her as nobody had before, and made her feel a riot of emotions. She loved him, but her own secret was a heavy weight between them, and there were still times when she could feel him holding back, as though he didn't quite know where he stood with her. Even now, she wasn't sure whether telling him would help or whether it would blow their relationship sky high.

He was staring out on to the road. The lights were flickering past. Lorna felt half paralysed. She had to tell him now while they were alone. It was hard to start.

'Jonathon,' she choked out at last, 'I've been misleading you, not telling you...'

'What?'

'The time has come when I have to...'

She could see him smiling. 'What are you trying to say?'

'I think I'm related to you.'

He took his eyes off the road to shoot a startled glance at her. 'Related? Honest?'

'Yes.'

'Well, guess what? When I first saw you, I thought you were another of the distant Wyndham tribe.'

'Not so distant,' she said.

'What d'you mean?'

'All these things I've dug out about your family – Oliver having an affair – well, I'm Oliver's daughter.'

She heard his gasp. He pulled the car hastily into a side road and stopped.

'Oliver's daughter? But why didn't you say so? Why hide it?' He was staring straight ahead. She couldn't see his face, couldn't even guess what he was thinking. 'I'm stunned. Knocked out, but I can't see...'

She told him then how she'd first heard of Oliver Wyndham and how distressed her mother had been.

'If I'd told your grandfather on the day I first came here, do you think he'd have believed me? Would he have given me free rein to look through all his personal papers?'

He shook his head. 'Maybe not. Aunt Roz would have had a fit.'

'And for my mother's sake I wanted to find out all I could. You wouldn't believe how upset she was. It was my chance to help her. She didn't want me to come at all. To Mum, it was like sending me into a lion's den. She was afraid I'd be torn apart and thrown out as she was.'

He turned to her then and she breathed a sigh of relief. 'Alice didn't have much to thank us for.'

'No.'

'But you've found out what she wanted to know, from all these journals and diaries?'

'Not all. What did happen to Oliver? Why did he drown? He could swim.'

Jonathon was shaking his head again, biting his lip.

'That's why I have to confess now. You were only three at the time but the rest of your family will know. It'll be burned into their minds as badly as it is in Mum's. I came here for her sake and because I wanted the job, but now I need to know too. Oliver was my natural father, and I have a right.'

403

She saw him smile in the semi-darkness. 'You've been like a terrier shaking out facts. I thought you were downright nosy. You asked a lot of questions about my parents.'

'I had to, if I was to find out anything.'

'Lorna, you found out a lot about the family that we didn't know ourselves. We're grateful to you.'

'I felt like a spy.'

'You should have told me. Why didn't you?'

'I was afraid you'd tell the others and Rosaleen would throw me out.'

'I'd have kept my mouth shut. I felt there was something... I knew something was keeping us apart.'

She shook her head. 'Couldn't, I just couldn't.'

'You should have trusted me.'

They stayed parked in the side road for a long time. It was a bitterly cold night but Jonathon was holding her close and Lorna shared his warmth.

'I love you,' he told her. 'You've fascinated me from the day I first set eyes on you, yet I hardly know anything about you. You've got Wyndham blood in your veins but you've had a very different upbringing from the rest of us.'

'You must come and meet my other family.'

'I did meet your mother at the auction. So that was Alice. I didn't recognise her.'

'You were only three when you last saw her. She remembers you. She warned me not to get involved with anybody at Otterspool. She's scared some disaster will overtake me too.'

'I guarantee it won't. Everything's different

these days.'

He'd never kissed her with such passion before. It felt as though the barriers that had been between them were now down.

'We've missed our tea,' he said when at last he switched on the engine to drive on. 'In fact, it's almost dinner time.'

That made her nervous again. 'How do I tell them, Jonathon?'

He laughed. 'The same way you told me. I'm delighted to have you as a cousin.'

'But what about your grandfather? He's going to be shocked.'

'He's fond of you too.'

'I hope he is. I hope he's going to forgive me.'

The house felt blissfully warm as they went in. Jonathon sniffed. 'Roast beef for dinner, I think.'

'With apple pie. Connie's surpassed herself.' Aunt Maude was crossing the hall. 'You're late tonight. The first gong sounded five minutes ago.'

Lorna felt nervous as she hurriedly rinsed her face and changed her dress. She stayed in her room until the last moment, not wanting to face the family. As she saw it, she had a confession to make. When she took her place at the table, Jonathon gave her a supportive smile. Connie brought in the soup tureen and set it in front of Aunt Maude, who started to ladle it on to plates.

Now, she told herself, while Connie isn't here. Tell them now. As usual, they all waited until Quentin said grace. Then Lorna watched them take up their spoons. Now, she urged herself.

Mr Wyndham met her gaze and asked: 'Have you anything more to do at Otterspool?'

'No. I won't need to go back again.'

'Good. You've done very well for us, Lorna. I'll probably take a last look round tomorrow.'

'Take Harold in with you, Quentin,' Aunt Maude advised. 'I'm afraid you'll fall through a floor somewhere.'

'It's very unsafe upstairs without the carpets.' This wasn't what Lorna wanted to talk about just now, but there were other things she had to sort out. 'From now on, I'm to spend all my time in the office, yes?'

'Yes,' Mr Wyndham said. 'That was what we agreed, wasn't it?'

'And I'm to live at home?'

Jonathon caught her eye across the table. 'I don't want you to move out. I won't see nearly as much of you. There's no hurry, is there?'

'No, but it's just as easy to get to the office from my home as it is from here.'

'Lorna's right,' Quentin decided. 'There's no further point in her living in. She wants to spend more time with her own family, Jonathon.'

That made her shudder. She had to tell him!

'Perhaps at the weekend,' he said.

Lorna couldn't listen as they went on talking about the minutiae of the day. She could feel her throat growing tight with tension as she spooned up ham and lentil soup.

'There's something I must tell you,' she managed at last. Jonathon smiled at her encouragingly. Three other pairs of expectant eyes came up to meet hers.

'My mother's name was Alice Carpenter.' It came out like an announcement. She could see

406

the name meant nothing to them. 'You employed her once... She worked at Otterspool...'

'Who?' Rosaleen demanded. 'Who worked at Otterspool?'

Jonathon tried to help. 'Alice, our old nurse-maid.'

'I think I remember her,' Maude said. 'A small dark girl.'

'Alice?' Rosaleen's face took on a look of thunder. 'Her? Your mother?'

'Yes.'

There was stunned silence while they took that in.

Then Lorna went on breathlessly, 'Mr Wyndham, I found some entries in your wife's diaries that show she understood that Oliver and my mother–'

'You crafty bitch.' Rosaleen's spoon crashed back on her plate. There was another stunned silence.

'Rosaleen!' her father protested.

'Let me explain.' Lorna was determined not to get angry.

'You'd better!'

'I knew nothing of this,' she turned again to Quentin, 'when you offered me a job here. My mother was very much against my coming. I made her tell me why and was very shocked. She told me my natural father was Oliver Wyndham.'

'That's a lie.' Rosaleen was furious.

'Hush,' her father said.

Lorna felt stricken; her voice was little more than a whisper. 'My mother's husband adopted me. I never for one moment believed him to be other than my true father. He was always kind and loving. We were poor but I had a happy–'

'She's come here to demand money. She's another who wants to call herself a Wyndham, pull herself up on our shirt-tails.'

'No,' Lorna said firmly. 'I came to find out what had happened to Oliver.'

'You're just stirring up trouble. It was we who suffered.' Rosaleen's fury lashed at her. 'I lost my brother.'

Quentin said, 'I lost my son. So terribly sudden.'

'It made me quite ill.' Rosaleen sounded savage.

Lorna went on with quiet dignity, 'My mother … apart from what she read in the newspapers, was told nothing about his death. He left her in lodgings, telling her he was going back home to collect some clothes, get some money and return to take her to Gretna–'

'That's all lies, a figment of her imagination.'

'No, she's had twenty terrible years, knowing he was dead, but not knowing what happened to him. It would settle her mind, allow her to put all this behind her, if she knew the truth.'

Maude sighed. 'We were all very upset. A terrible time for the family.'

Lorna took a deep breath. 'My mother was left without money, without a home and no one to turn to, and she was expecting me.' She looked Rosaleen in the eye. 'She came back and pleaded with you to help her, but you refused. You'll understand she was more than upset when I tell you she tried to commit suicide.'

They were staring at her, horrified now.

'But she didn't, did she?' Rosaleen said spitefully.

'No, obviously not. I'm here. A sailor fished her out of the Mersey just in time.' Lorna was fighting back the tears. 'Won't you please tell me why Oliver drowned?'

'The *Topsy* was run down by a larger vessel,' Quentin said. 'There was a thick fog on the river. They didn't see her.'

'But I thought they stopped river traffic if there was dense fog?'

Rosaleen let out a little scream, leaped up from her chair and rushed from the room. There was another moment's shocked silence.

'She took it very badly,' her father said gravely. 'Her nerves... She had a breakdown. Was in hospital for almost a year.'

Lorna couldn't suppress a sob. 'I'm sorry. You'll have to excuse me too. I can't eat now.'

She got up with as much dignity as she could muster and went up to the bedroom she'd been allotted. She flung herself across her bed and wept into her pillow. She didn't know how long it was before she got up to get herself a handkerchief. She lay back on the bed feeling a nervous wreck. The house was quiet apart from an occasional clatter of plates from the kitchen below. Eventually she got up, rinsed her face again, combed her hair, and tried to pull herself together. She was hungry and needed to go down to the kitchen to get herself something to eat. She heard the tap but didn't at first realise it was on her door.

'Lorna, can I come in?' It was Jonathon's voice.

'Yes.' A glance in her dressing-table mirror confirmed her worst fears. Her eyes looked red and puffy.

'Are you all right?' His anxious face came round the door. 'Ah, Lorna, you're upset.' She saw he'd brought a tray with him. He slid it on the dressing table and put his arms round her in a comforting hug.

'Nervous reaction,' she gulped. 'Are they furious with me?'

'Not Grandpa or Aunt Maude. You explained it well – about your mother.'

'Yes...'

He pulled her down to sit beside him on her bed. 'You should have told me sooner.'

'Yes.' She should have done, before she'd worked herself up into this state.

'I've brought you a beef sandwich and a slice of apple pie. You've got to eat something.' He brought the tray closer.

'Thank you, coffee too.' She bit into the sandwich.

'We've read Grandma's diary entries again, the ones you copied.'

'Just to prove it wasn't a figment of my mother's imagination?'

'We talked it over. Aunt Maude said Oliver was always writing, and he was a keen diarist. She thinks he may have left more, and when pressed, Aunt Roz said she thought her brothers had hidden some of Oliver's papers.'

'She doesn't know where?'

'Does it matter now? You've found enough to

410

provide proof. The family accepts it. You've got the truth out in the open.'

'It matters to my mother.'

'The will?'

'I doubt she expects to inherit anything after all this time, but the letter Oliver wrote to her, that would make all the difference. I've searched everywhere and I found what your grandmother hid, but nothing else. I worried that you'd found it.'

'You did ask me, and the answer's still no.'

'Rosaleen was expecting to find something in Piers's room, I'm sure.'

'But she didn't, and I went through everything that was taken out with a fine-tooth comb.'

'They're hidden somewhere, I'm sure. If only...'

'Shall we go back and have a last look round? Well, when you've finished your coffee?'

'I did that myself this afternoon. Everywhere's stripped bare, but...' Lorna felt restless. She wanted to be doing something, however hopeless it seemed. 'Why not?'

'It wouldn't hurt to look now before the place is pulled down.'

'In the room you were sleeping in too, Jonathon. Your father might have hidden something.'

'I doubt we'll find anything there. Hang on, though, there's an electric fire fitted in the fire-place. I could take it out if I took some tools, look behind that.'

'Would anybody hide papers behind a fire?'

'I don't know how much heat goes out of the back.' He chuckled. 'Come to think of it, not a lot

411

came out of the front. If the papers were put into a tin first, that should keep them safe. It's a long shot, but so's everything else now.'

As they were going downstairs, she asked, 'Is Rosaleen over the shock?'

'Not really. Grandpa went to her room to talk to her. He's worried. He says the nervous break-down she had after Oliver died wasn't the last, and it doesn't take much to push her over the brink. What with the auction, and moving here, and Otterspool having to be demolished, she's a bit on edge. He doesn't think she can stand much more.'

Otterspool House felt even more icy than it had this afternoon. It echoed to their footsteps, and Lorna was glad to have Jonathon to cling to. They'd brought two large torches, which filled the place with moving shadows.

'A bit creepy now, isn't it? Strange to think this was home last month.'

The stairs creaked as they went up. Jonathon lifted the light high when he reached the threshold of the room he'd used.

'Doesn't it look awful now it's bare? You hold both torches while I take this electric fire out.' He'd brought a large screwdriver and a hammer to do the job.

'How old is that fire?' Lorna asked. 'It doesn't look as though it's been here since nineteen ten.'

'Dad was living in the west wing by then. It might have been put in when I was nine and wanted to sleep here.'

412

'That means it's an unlikely hiding place.'

Jonathon was easing it out. Soot, dust and twigs had fallen down the chimney behind it. He used his hammer to make sure there was nothing more solid amongst the rubbish.

'Shine the light up the chimney,' he said. 'Sometimes there's a ledge.' He was feeling upwards with his hammer and dislodging soot. 'No, nothing here.'

'You've got soot on your face.' Lorna couldn't help but smile.

'Not only on my face, look at my hands. Pull my hanky out of my pocket, will you?'

Lorna put her hand in his trouser pocket. It seemed an intimate thing to do. She could feel his warmth and the hardness of his hip. Pulling out his handkerchief, she wiped the smudge from his cheek. That was intimate too. She wouldn't have risked that before today.

He picked up the torch. 'We aren't going to find anything here. Let's have a look next door.'

'Don't forget the dry rot's bad in here,' she said.

In Piers's room, the floorboards and window frame had been scorched and blackened by the fire. So had the wallpaper, and some of it was hanging loose. Jonathon prodded at the floorboards with the long screwdriver. They were crumbling. 'Don't come into the middle of the room,' he said. 'It isn't safe.'

The small iron grate was similar to the one in the room next door, but no electric fire had been fitted into it.

Jonathon said, 'Better have a look up this chimney. They don't go straight up in a house as

413

old as this and they're all interconnected. There may be a ledge, but if I can't reach it nobody else would have been able to either.'

The room looked desolate. Lorna felt half mesmerised by the shadows flickering round the walls. 'It's hopeless. There's literally nowhere else.'

The wallpaper had fallen away on one wall, and her gaze came to rest on some dark stains in the uneven plaster. She'd seen nothing quite like this anywhere else in the house. Keeping close to the wall she went nearer and aimed the hammer she was holding at the centre of the stain. The plaster cracked, and dust and bits flew back at her face, making her shut her eyes.

'Lorna! Lorna, there's something there.' There was no mistaking the excitement in Jonathon's voice. 'You clever girl.' He snatched the hammer from her hand and was tapping gently all round. 'There's something plastered on to the wall.'

Lorna's spirits were soaring though she couldn't see for the dust in her eyes. 'Is it? Is it?'

'I think so. Why else would it be here? Whatever it is there's fungus growing through it. Ugh.'

'It smells of mould and decay.' Lorna finished wiping her eyes and held her hanky against her nose.

'Stinks horribly and feels damp. I've got it now.' Jonathon tore a large envelope off the wall. 'It's quite heavy.'

Lorna shone the torch on it. 'No writing on the outside.' Part of the thick manila envelope had rotted, and more paper could be seen inside.

'There are two notebooks as well.'

She whooped with delight. 'This must be it. What I've been looking for all these weeks.' She threw her arms round Jonathon and felt his tighten round her in a hug of triumph. 'At last!'

She laughed as kisses rained down on her face. He held her close for a long moment, then he was laughing too. 'You've stained your coat.'

'So have you.'

'We're both going to smell terrible, cuddling close to this thing. Let's see if I can get rid of this fungus.' He scraped some off with his screwdriver.

The floor creaked ominously beneath their feet. 'Let's get out of here before we go through it,' Lorna said. 'Oh, I'm so happy.'

'You don't know what's in it yet.'

'Somebody wanted it hidden, so it must be important. There's nothing else there?'

Jonathon was prodding round, knocking more plaster off the wall. 'No. Come on.' He took her hand and towed her back to the landing.

'Do you think it was Piers who hid it?'

'Must have been – this was his room. It couldn't have been Rosaleen. She knew about it but didn't know where to look. It's got to be what you've been searching for.'

On the journey back to Hedge End, Lorna directed the torch on to the envelope on her knee.

'There's a diary in here.'

'Another of Grandmama's?'

'No. Oh gosh, it's Oliver's! Marvellous, my luck's turned.'

'Can you see any date on it?'

'Oh, nineteen oh-nine, and yes, it goes on to March nineteen ten. Perhaps now we'll find out what really happened.'

Chapter Twenty-One

Jonathon led the way, hurrying along to his grandfather's study. The air was fragrant with cigar smoke. They found the old man stretched out on his chair behind his newspaper.

'Grandpa, we've found it.' Jonathon's eyes were dancing and his cheeks rosy.

'What I've been searching for all along,' Lorna said. 'More papers belonging to Oliver.'

'And his diary.'

They'd woken him from a doze. Quentin pulled himself upright in the chair, blinking at them. 'What's that?'

In the bright light, Lorna could see the envelope had almost rotted away. She emptied the contents out on a table. Some of the papers inside were stained and rotted too.

'Oliver's diary.' She reached for it and thumbed through to the last pages that had writing on them.

'Read it aloud,' Jonathon said. 'We're all dying to know what's in it.' Lorna started reading, her voice shaky.

'March the ninth, nineteen ten. None of the family wants me to marry Alice.' She shivered with anticipation. 'I have asked my parents for permission and though they haven't refused outright they certainly haven't granted it.

'My father thinks me young and foolish. All my family treat me as though I should still inhabit the nursery. Perhaps they're right. I've certainly done a very foolish thing.

'"Get married?" I saw even Mama's eyebrows go up in shock.

'"At your age?" Father's eyes rolled heavenwards as though asking for divine help to make me see sense.

'Now my brothers and sister know, the whole family is united against me. Rosaleen says they have to protect me. At nineteen, I can't convince them that I'm serious about marriage, but I know I have to.

'"Who's the lucky lady?" Crispin always has a sneer in his voice. Because he's older, he thinks he's superior. I knew it wouldn't help to tell them it was Alice. They'd never see that she could inspire such passion, such need.

'"Not the nursemaid? For God's sake, Oliver! Grow up." I know growing up will only make me love her more.

'"You can't!" Rosaleen was aghast and echoing Mama's words. "The nursemaid? You can't possibly. We must keep you out of her clutches."

'They're trying to tell me Alice is a scheming money-grabber, out to feather her own nest. I can't convince them that money is the last thing she thinks of. It is always their first thought, though they have so much already. It doesn't make sense.

417

'They tell me our business is not as profitable as it used to be. I hear that all the time. The truth is they don't want others given a claim to be kept by it. I feel absolutely desperate. I've got to do something, but I can't think what. I half expected this but I have to get round it somehow.

'Today, Daphne paid Alice off and sent her away in disgrace. It's because I've asked for permission to marry her. I haven't told anybody she's with child. I can't make up my mind whether it would make my family more sympathetic or totally condemning. I'm afraid it wouldn't bring about the permission I so much need. At the same time, I'm so terribly ashamed of myself. I should have had more self-control and more thought for Alice's wellbeing. I can only plead love and my need to convince her of it.

'I could arrange the wedding and lie about my age – say I'm already twenty-one. But my family is so much in the forefront of Liverpool society, everybody has heard of the Wentworth Wynd-hams. The registrar might wonder why there is so little fuss being made of my wedding when at the nuptials of John and Crispin there were great celebrations that are still being talked about. It might not take him long to find me out, and I really have to marry Alice.'

Lorna paused and wiped her eyes. This would be balm to Mum. Oliver's thoughts when he went back to Otterspool were exactly what she needed to know.

'At dinner tonight, I confessed to the family why

418

I have to do it. That I was about to add to the next generation of Wyndhams. Mama was totally shocked at my behaviour, Father condemning.

'"She's just the nursemaid," Crispin said. "You don't have to worry that you've got her pregnant. Father, she must be paid off. Twenty pounds should do it; she won't expect a lot."

'"Perhaps another ten, if she promises to keep her mouth shut," Mama suggested. "We don't want you talked about, do we?"

'Rosaleen looked at me spitefully. "Pay her off, though it's an awful waste of money. Have you no common sense?"

'I told them then that I'd never pay Alice off. That I meant to live with her and our child, come what may. That I was going to pack my things and go. That I could give up the family more easily than I could give up Alice.

'"She'll not make you happy for long," my mother pleaded almost in tears. "You'll be poor, not know where the next penny is coming from. Let us pay her off and you can go away to college and get on with your life. You can't give up your plans for her. It would ruin everything for you. Think of the future."

'I do think of the future, that's the trouble. I think of how Alice will fare. Besides, I want to be with her. The thought of parting is unbearable.

'Crispin sneered. "You'll forget her in a year. You can't expect help from the family if you turn your back on us. It'll be the end for you."

'"Think carefully before you do anything," Father said, looking very stern. "Take your time. This will affect your whole future."

'I've come up here to my room but I'm so angry, with myself as well as with them, I can't think of anything but of Alice waiting for me to return to her, and I'm sure she'll be worried stiff.

'March the tenth, nineteen ten.

'It is now two in the morning and I can't sleep. I've written a note to Alice and I've made up my mind, finally and for ever.

'I choose Alice. Father has threatened to stop my allowance and I've already spent the last payment I received from the trust fund. It will be July before there is more from that source. I would very much like us to start as man and wife, and I know that's what Alice wants.

'It will be very wrong of me to accept their offer to pay Alice off when I have every intention of doing the opposite, but it's the only way. I have to get money from somewhere. I think I might even argue the amount up to fifty pounds. I'll have a try.

'We'll go to Gretna Green first and if we're lucky there'll be enough to start us off in rooms of our own while I look for a job. I can always sell my boat if things get hard.

'If my family don't want to know Alice, then I'll manage without them. I don't care.'

Lorna looked up to find Jonathon's blue eyes on her. They were shining with tenderness. 'I can understand his anguish.' His voice shook a little. 'Uncle Oliver was in love.'

Lorna nodded. Her mother would be in no doubt about that.

Quentin's head felt on fire. He was shocked. Piers had told him Oliver had tried to go back on his promise; take his money and go to his lover. But to hear it planned in Oliver's own words... The nursemaid must have turned his mind. It hurt that Oliver could more easily give up his family than her, but there was no mistaking his agony as he'd made his decision.

It was like hearing a voice from the grave. He picked up the journal and flicked through the pages. It was definitely Oliver's writing; there could be no doubting this was genuine. He couldn't drag his eyes from the girl. His granddaughter? Yes, he had to believe that now. He'd never seen her all excited like this before.

'I've hoped and prayed that something like this would turn up,' Lorna's sea-green eyes were glistening, 'to throw more light...'

He had to admit he'd taken a fancy to Lorna when he'd first met her. It had never occurred to him she might be Oliver's daughter. He'd given no thought to the possibility that Oliver might have one. Even now it was hard to believe, but she was tall and slim, the Wyndham build. She had eyes of sea green, just as Lars's eyes had been described. She wasn't as fair, though. There must be plenty of English ancestry in her too.

Rosaleen had been hysterical when she'd heard the story, accusing Lorna of spying on them. That's exactly what she had been doing, but they had a lot to thank her for.

She'd seen through Crispin and Adam, nosed out what they were doing to the business, and found hidden lives behind what they were showing to him. Now he'd sorted that out, the business would earn enough to keep the family.

She'd also turned up those other diaries and papers proving the Wyndham fortune had been earned from slaving. That had come as an almighty shock to him too. Quentin looked at the decomposing envelope and shuddered. He didn't want to find out it contained more heart-rending facts.

Jonathon and Lorna were reading silently now. Quentin turned over a familiar envelope that had already been opened. It was stationery of the sort Marina had always ordered for Otterspool. They used it still. Rosaleen had had more printed with their new address.

This was in Oliver's handwriting too and it sent cold shivers down Quentin's spine. He took the note out slowly, bracing himself for more.

10 March 1910

My darling Alice,

It is two in the morning and I cannot sleep for thinking about you. I know you'll be worried that I'm not back with you by now. There is no need to be. I've packed most of my possessions as well as a suitcase of clothes to bring with me.

My father has arranged that Piers will go to the bank when it opens this morning, draw out some money and bring it to you. He'll want you to sign for it and promise to go away and never return. Do whatever he asks without fuss, but tell him nothing, absolutely nothing. We must have that money. I'm writing this so you'll know what's happening and be ready to deal with Piers.

Father insists I go to the office with him this morning. He believes he can stop me seeing you, but I intend to give him the slip. I'll have to come back here to pick up my things but I hope to be with you by midday. I'll get Tom to deliver this to you on his way home from taking us to the office.

I've drawn up a will and I'll get Hilda and Blossom to sign it before breakfast when I know I shall catch them on their own. I've left everything I own to you, though it is little enough.

My family are very much against what I intend to do and though it makes me sad, my mind is made up. We'll leave for Gretna Green as soon as we can and get married. All will be well, you'll see. This is the last night we will have to spend apart.

All my love always,
Oliver.

Quentin was fighting to control his emotions, but this was bringing them flooding back. He handed the letter to Lorna, who read it silently, and when she looked up at him her eyes were shimmering with unshed tears.

'What happened to stop him going back to her?' Her voice was anguished. 'I still don't know... She never received his letter or his will. And certainly nothing resulting from it.'

Quentin could see Lorna felt bitter about that. 'You were there.' Her eyes fastened on him and seemed to accuse. 'What exactly did happen to Oliver?'

Guilt was tightening his throat. 'I blame myself.

I should have involved myself more.'

'Weren't you involved?'

'I took Oliver to the office with me that day, but I went to a meeting and gave no more thought to him. I didn't miss him until lunch time. Things were happening there that needed my attention. Important things.'

'Not as important as Oliver losing his life?' Lorna stabbed at him.

It made him shake his head, numbed him with pain. Hadn't he gone through this a thousand times?

'The money he spoke of?' she asked. 'Did you do anything about it?'

'Yes, the night before we'd sat down as a family and talked about Oliver's trouble. He'd asked me for fifty pounds to pay the girl off. I agreed, on condition he promised never to see her again. It seems from this letter he had no intention of keeping that promise.' He'd expected Oliver to stand by his word.

'Was Oliver happy with that arrangement?'

'He said she might have difficulty cashing the cheque. Fifty pounds was a large amount for someone like her. I made it out for cash, not wanting to put her name on it. I was afraid that would be proof we'd paid a largish sum to her, and might come to light later. I wanted to keep the matter as private as possible.'

'What did you do?'

'I suggested Piers go to the bank and cash the cheque, take the money to her and get her to sign a receipt. I didn't want Oliver to see her again. Piers agreed to do this.'

'It was cashed? The money was drawn out of your account?'

'Yes.'

The colour had faded from Lorna's cheeks. 'It seems Piers was somewhat devious.'

'Not just Piers, it's a family trait,' Jonathon said gravely. 'Why Piers? My father was the eldest, why not him?'

'I don't know... Yes, I do. Your maternal grandmother died just a few days before. She lived in Gloucester. They say troubles never come one at a time.'

He watched as Lorna turned back the pages of Oliver's journal. 'Yes, there's something about that in here.' She was reading again.

'March the sixth, nineteen ten.

'Poor Frances is distraught. She's just heard her mother was thrown from her horse last Tuesday and has been in a coma ever since. Hunting was her passion. Frances went down by train today to see her.

'March the seventh, nineteen ten.

'Frances telephoned to give us the bad news that her mother had passed away without ever regaining consciousness. She was a widow, so it seems Frances will have to pack up her belongings and put her house up for sale. John came back from the office immediately and started to pack. Father said that Mama must ask Frances if she wanted help to sort things out, and go down too for the funeral.'

Quentin felt the painful memories rushing back. 'It was such a long time ago, a different world. Everything was serene until Frances's mother died. That was the first of our troubles. We were all upset and worrying about Frances and how she'd cope.

'When Oliver came to my study, bringing his mother with him, saying he wanted to talk to us both, I thought at first he wanted to go with her for the funeral.'

'You were shocked?' asked Lorna.

'Yes, I was proud of what he'd achieved at school. We thought of him as the brains of the family. And then when he asked for permission to marry the nursemaid and not take up his place at Oxford, well... Where was the sense in throwing away all he'd striven for? Brains he might have, but where was his common sense?'

Quentin stopped. He could see Oliver's young face before him now, earnest and shining with sincerity. He'd thought him honest and clear-headed. Anger had made him bark at him, 'What a waste, to throw away your big opportunity.'

'But he didn't want a career outside the business?' Lorna asked. 'He wanted to join his older brothers and work there?'

'Yes, that was always the plan, but I thought he was more intelligent. I expected more from him. We'd talked about him training to be an accountant or a solicitor, so he'd have some expertise. Or at least, that he should join another company for a time to widen his experience. I was disappointed in him and so was his mother. We felt he was letting us down.'

Quentin sighed. 'My brother, Sebastian, did much the same thing thirty years earlier. My mother had a French maid who saw to her personal needs. She was packed off back to France with a little money and no more was heard of her. Though I often heard my mother complain she was never able to find anybody as good at pressing her clothes or titivating up a tired hat.'

'But you still haven't told us how Oliver died.'

Quentin reflected that Lorna had Oliver's earnest sincerity and, like him, she never gave up. Why hadn't he noticed the resemblance before? To think of her being Oliver's child wrung his heart.

'I thought he'd come to his senses. I had no premonition of disaster. I got on with my work and left all that to Piers.'

'But you knew at lunch time that Oliver had gone?' Lorna prompted.

'Yes. Rosaleen telephoned. I was in a meeting but I went out to talk to her. She sounded frantic...'

'What did she say?'

'She and Piers and Crispin had found Oliver had no intention of keeping his promise, that he was hellbent on seeing the nursemaid, and they were going to take him to the cottage for a day or two to try to make him see reason.'

'How did Rosaleen find out?' Lorna demanded fiercely.

'I don't know... They might have seen Oliver's journal. He'd written down what he intended to do, hadn't he?'

427

'Aunt Roz read it?' Jonathon was flicking over the pages. 'I know we have, but it's one thing to read private papers when the writer has been dead for twenty years and quite another if he was there with them.'

'It isn't likely he'd tell her,' Lorna said. 'He'd want to give the whole family the slip.'

'We should be asking Aunt Roz these questions,' Jonathon said. 'She was with him at the time.'

Quentin couldn't suppress a grunt. 'She took it hard. It'll upset her again if you question her about it now.'

'Grandpa, you're trying to tell us about things Aunt Roz did twenty years ago. I think Lorna's entitled to hear it direct from her, even if it does upset her.'

Quentin couldn't stop his gaze going to the girl, couldn't help but feel sympathy for her. 'Rosaleen was ill. She had a nervous breakdown after Oliver drowned.'

'My mother tried to commit suicide,' Lorna said softly. 'She suffered too. Will Rosaleen still be up?'

'Probably. She doesn't sleep well, doesn't go to bed early.'

'I'm going to get her.' Jonathon was on his feet.

'Be gentle with her,' Quentin pleaded.

'My mother needs to know what really happened.' Lorna was trying to explain. 'She never quite got over it. And since I believe Oliver to be my natural father, I really want to know too.'

When Jonathon went, Quentin poured himself some brandy. Lorna declined but he kept the bottle handy. Rosaleen might need some.

'I'm trying to understand how you must feel,' he told her. 'We should have taken more care of you and your mother.' He was growing anxious; Jonathon was taking a long time. How would Rosaleen take this?

They came at last, Jonathon leading her in. She was wearing a pink satin dressing gown, and her manner was nervous and hostile. 'What d'you want?'

'We think you can help us get at the truth.' Lorna pulled up a chair for her. 'Jonathon and I have found more papers belonging to Oliver, as well as his diary for the days before he died, but it doesn't tell us—'

'No!' Rosaleen leaped to her feet and attacked the musty papers. 'No, you mustn't read them.' She grabbed a document and tore it to shreds.

'Leave them alone, Rosaleen,' Quentin said, but she was taking no notice of him.

Jonathon had to pull her physically away from the table. She was fighting him off like a wild thing but he got her back to the chair. He stood behind her, his arms on her shoulders.

'We just want to know how Oliver died,' Lorna said gently when she had quietened down.

'Why ask me?' Her hostility had changed to raw aggression.

'You were there with him, weren't you?'

'No, leave me alone. It's all over and done with long ago.' She let out a piercing scream. 'Don't resurrect that now.'

'We just want to talk it over quietly between ourselves,' Jonathon said gently.

'No, it wasn't my fault.'

'My dear,' Quentin said, 'of course it wasn't.' He was afraid he should never have allowed this. They weren't going to get anything from her anyway.

'I can't stand your everlasting questions.' Rosaleen screamed again and threw herself back at the table, sweeping all the papers to the floor.

Lorna too had realised the futility of it and was trying to soothe her. 'All right, you go back to bed.'

But it was too late. Rosaleen was beyond being soothed and they could do nothing with her.

'I'd better find Maude,' Quentin said with a heavy heart. 'She'll know how to handle this.'

Lorna and Jonathon found it hard to persuade Rosaleen back to her room. She struggled and fought them off. It was Maude who got her into bed.

'I think we'd better ask the doctor to come out,' Quentin said. 'He'll give her a sedative. She'll never sleep otherwise.'

'Yes, do that,' Maude said. 'Leave us, she needs quiet. I'll sit with her for a while.'

Lorna looked contrite. 'You were right, I shouldn't have pressed her. I'm sorry.'

Quentin felt exhausted. He'd had as much as he could put up with today. He no longer had Jonathon's energy, and he feared for his daughter. He should never have let them question her. They didn't realise how fragile her nerves were. He could have told them more about Oliver, it was just that he needed time to think these days.

Chapter Twenty-Two

Quentin felt shaken. He hated to see Rosaleen like this, and she was getting worse. On the way downstairs, he asked Lorna to phone for the doctor to come out to her. He hovered in the front hall while she did it, needing confirmation that he'd come that night. Lorna was putting the phone down when the front doorbell rang. Quentin almost swore with exasperation, he couldn't cope with visitors now.

'Crispin!' he said irritably. 'What brings you here?'

'I wonder if we could have a private word, Father? I need to apologise – for so many things.' There was a conciliatory smile on his plump face.

That made Quentin think. It seemed Crispin wanted to be forgiven. Possibly he was hoping to be reinstated in the business. He had almost barked out that he wasn't going to relent when he realised it would be easier to get information from him in his present mood than it would be from Rosaleen. And it would spare her any further upset. Crispin had had a few weeks to try standing on his own feet and was no doubt finding it hard.

'We'll have the private word later, Crispin, if you don't mind? At the moment, we're in the middle of something else. Come in. Perhaps first you could help us with this.'

'What is it?' Crispin looked more than willing to help. He'd come round offering an olive branch.

'Lorna would like you to explain something to her.'

'Oh!'

Quentin knew Lorna would not be in Crispin's good books. He blamed her for exposing what he and Buckler were up to. The old man poured himself a glass of brandy and offered it round. Only Crispin accepted. Lorna was picking up the papers Rosaleen had scattered over the carpet. Jonathon told him what they were, and where they'd been found.

'It seems Lorna is Oliver's daughter,' he said.

'What?' Crispin laughed nervously. 'Whatever gave her that idea?'

Jonathon ignored that and started to question him. 'You were on Oliver's boat the day he died, weren't you?'

Crispin was reluctant to admit it. 'Yes,' he said at last.

'But you came to the office with me that day,' Quentin said. 'You were at that meeting.'

'I was, yes.'

'When did you leave?'

'We went through all this at the time,' Crispin said in a burst of irritation. 'We had to protect Oliver. We had to stop him going back to that nursemaid, keep him out of her clutches. We believed he'd thank us for it when he came to his senses.'

'Hang on,' Jonathon said. 'Let's start at the beginning. You discovered Oliver didn't intend to

432

keep his promise, that he planned to go away with Alice. How did you find out?'

'For heaven's sake, what does it matter now?' Crispin's manner was more truculent.

'It matters to me,' Lorna told him with a touch of Wyndham sharpness. 'I want to know.'

Crispin looked at her and shrugged. 'It was Piers who found out, Hilda told him.' That made Quentin shiver.

Then they heard a scuffle and Rosaleen's voice in the hall. A second later she threw open the door and raged in with Maude at her heels.

'I heard you come,' she spat at Crispin. 'You're trying to put all the blame on me. You always do.'

'No, Rosaleen, come on back to bed,' Maude said. 'It'll only upset you more.'

'I'm staying,' she screamed. 'I want to know what you're saying about me.'

'All right,' Quentin said gently. 'Come and sit down then. We haven't said anything about you, but stay if you wish.' He poured some brandy for her. 'It's better if we talk to Crispin about this. Then we won't upset you.'

'He'll tell lies, he always does.'

Quentin turned to his son. 'You said Hilda told Piers. How did she come to be involved in this?'

'She heard us arguing with Oliver and knew the score. Rumour was rife. Every servant was either for or against Alice. You must have known it was being talked about all over the house.'

Quentin shook his head. Marina had looked after household matters; his mind had been on the business. He knew the servants listened, of course, but he'd never worried much about what they heard. He'd thought he'd done what was needed: taken Oliver with him to the office that morning to keep him away from the girl while Piers handed the money over to her.

'But how did Hilda–' Jonathon asked.

Rosaleen flared up. 'She was a real busybody, poked her nose into everything.'

Crispin's mouth pursed. 'Oliver was stupid enough to ask Hilda and Blossom to witness a will he'd drawn up. He took it down to the kitchen early that morning.'

'Surely Oliver would have more sense than to explain it was his will they were witnessing.' Quentin felt exasperated. 'They wouldn't know what it was.'

'Hilda didn't need things explained to her,' Crispin replied. 'She'd find some way to get a peep under any paper he put on top. She always wanted to know what was going on, and this threatened to be a scandal we'd want to hush up. She could have guessed Oliver didn't intend to pay Alice off, that he was planning to go away with her. She and Blossom watched him go over to the stables with a letter. Hilda took morning tea up to Piers's room herself that day to tell him.'

'Why would she do that?'

'To take Alice down a peg. Hilda was jealous of her. If Oliver married Alice, she'd have gone up in the world. You must have known what Hilda was like.'

He hadn't. 'I'm learning. And Hilda expected favours in return?'

Crispin pulled a face.

'So it was Piers who told you?'

434

'Yes, told Rosaleen too.'

'Don't bring me into this.' Her flailing hand caught her brandy glass and knocked it to the carpet. It didn't break.

He watched Maude leap up to ring for a maid to mop up the mess but there were no bell pulls in Hedge End. 'A cloth...' she said distractedly. 'It'll mark the new carpet – I'll get a cloth.' Quentin silently picked up the glass and refilled it.

'After Hilda told you about the letter, what did you do?' Lorna asked Crispin, her voice cold.

'I got up early and took a walk over to the stables. I found Tom grooming the horse before putting him between the shafts. I asked him for the letter, told him Oliver had changed his mind, that I'd be seeing Alice myself that morning and would deliver it.'

'You opened and read it? That's how you learned of Oliver's intentions?'

'Why not? We needed to know.' Quentin watched Crispin shrug again and felt he hadn't known his children. He'd thought them all upright and honest. 'Then?'

'We changed our plans to suit. You took me in to a meeting, but I slipped out so I could keep an eye on Oliver. I followed him when he left the office to come home to pick up his bags.'

Quentin tried to remember. 'I sent Tom back with the carriage to take Piers to the bank. I suppose he did go?'

'Yes, you know he did.'

'But the money was never handed over to the nursemaid?'

435

'No.'

'Nor was the letter given to her,' Lorna added bitterly, 'though it was addressed to her. None of you went near her. You and Piers decided to keep them apart.'

'It was what Father wanted,' Crispin insisted, 'what we all wanted, what was best for him. Even Mother couldn't talk sense into him.'

Quentin shivered. Marina had said nothing about that to him.

'I suppose you all jumped on Oliver when he came home?' Lorna asked.

'Yes, and it was all Piers and I could do to keep him in his room. At lunch time, Rosaleen had a good idea. She slipped a couple of Aunt Gertrude's sleeping pills into some soup and brought it up for him. That gave us a few hours' peace to think about what we should do. Otterspool was too close to Alice. If he got away, he could walk to her boarding house in twenty minutes.'

Lorna shook her head. 'What did you do?'

'We had a holiday cottage at that time, upriver, near Fiddler's Ferry. We decided to take him there in his own boat.'

'It was a foggy day, wasn't it?' Lorna remembered her mother saying how bad the weather had been, how surprised she'd been that anyone had gone out in a boat.

'It was a still day and the morning mist was thickening by afternoon.'

'And you still went? In a sailing boat?'

'It had an auxiliary engine, so we didn't think it mattered. But the fog became a real peasouper towards evening.'

'There's quite a bit of river traffic going up to Warrington,' Jonathon said. 'Didn't you see that as a risk?'

Crispin shook his head. 'There was much less twenty years ago. But we were run down by a coastal tramp, a larger vessel. It knocked a hole in *Topsy*'s hull and we couldn't stay afloat.'

Quentin felt the brandy coming back up his throat. 'All four of you were in on it? You too, Rosaleen?'

'Yes.'

'So you might all have drowned?'

'We managed to swim ashore.'

'But not Oliver?' Jonathon asked. 'Surely he'd have been stronger than Rosaleen?'

Crispin said, 'You're a good swimmer, aren't you, Roz?'

'Wasn't he?'

'Ye-es.' Quentin could see Crispin was feeling pressurised. He was casting anxious glances at him now.

Lorna said slowly, 'I don't understand how you meant to keep Oliver at the cottage.'

'Piers and I would have come back in Oliver's boat, stranding him there until we went back.'

'In a cottage?' Jonathon asked. 'Was there no road he could use?'

Another anxious look from Crispin. 'Yes, but it was quite isolated at that time.'

'Fiddler's Ferry is not that far from Warrington. Couldn't he have caught a bus or train back to Liverpool?'

Quentin could see his son beginning to sweat. 'He'd have to walk first, but yes, I suppose so. We

437

always went by boat.'

Jonathon said, 'Aunt Roz was planning to stay with him?'

'Yes, to look after him.'

'You mean, to make sure he didn't leave?'

'We didn't want him to leave.'

'Rosaleen wouldn't have had the strength to stop him,' Lorna said. 'If he'd wanted to leave, he could have done. Did you tie him up?'

Quentin saw Crispin's Adam's apple jolt as he swallowed hard. The clock ticked fussily.

'You'd have to,' Lorna went on. 'Had you already done that? You had, that's why Oliver drowned, wasn't it?'

Crispin's face was scarlet. 'Of course not,' he blustered. 'We wouldn't have done such a thing.'

Quentin jerked to his feet. He remembered what had been said at the inquest. It was etched on his mind. 'You said Oliver was thrown when the ship hit you, that he must have bumped his head,' he reminded him. 'That's what you told the Coroner.'

'Yes, that was it.'

'You didn't think of helping him?' Lorna asked.

'We didn't realise he needed help at the time, didn't know he'd been injured.'

'And it was every man for himself in the panic?' Jonathon wanted to know.

Rosaleen was holding her hands against her face. '*Topsy* turned over, the hull was crushed. I was thrown out and hardly knew what was happening. Oh God! It was all so long ago, why rake it up now? It's very upsetting.'

'Nearly finished now,' Lorna said. 'Was Oliver's

body washed up by the tide?'

Crispin's face was stiff with hostility. 'No, Piers and I recovered the damaged boat the next day. His body was still in the cabin.'

'And there were bruises on his head?'

Another long-drawn-out silence. Then Quentin said, 'Minor bruising in several places but not much on his head. His right wrist was most marked.' He felt sick.

It was Jonathon who said, 'He was tied by his right wrist to something in the cabin. And you didn't think to free him?'

'It wasn't that simple,' Crispin flared. 'We didn't get the chance. It happened too quickly. Besides—'

Rosaleen started to weep. 'He's going to deny it, but it was Crispin's fault. He forced more sleeping pills down Oliver so he wouldn't fight us off and turn the boat round.'

He turned on his sister. 'You silly fool, we agreed to keep quiet about that.'

He was upsetting Rosaleen. Her face was scarlet and wet with tears. 'He's going to tell you it was all my fault, that it would never have happened if I hadn't brought the handcuffs.'

'What handcuffs?' Quentin felt his mouth go dry with shock. 'A toy?'

'No,' Crispin said, 'real ones. We found a cabin trunk full of very old ones – leg irons, neck irons, that sort of thing, up in the attic. We used to play with them.'

'Handcuffs that could have been used to restrain slaves?' Jonathon asked.

'How could I keep him safe without?' Rosaleen

wailed. 'He was much stronger than I was. I had to lock one cuff to him and one to the handle of a locker.'

Quentin felt the hairs on the back of his neck crawl with horror. 'But why didn't one of you release him? You must have known he wouldn't stand a chance.'

'We thought Piers would have done it.' Crispin moistened his lips. 'We went through purgatory, all of us, when we realised what had happened.'

The colour had drained from Rosaleen's face. It was grey. 'We were afraid the wreck of the *Topsy* would be found with him in it,' she whispered. 'It would look like murder. But we didn't intend it, I swear. That's why Piers and Crispin didn't come home that night – they had to find the wreck before somebody else did.'

'To take the handcuffs off Oliver?' Quentin asked.

'Yes.' Rosaleen slumped back on her chair looking lifeless now, almost in a torpor.

Quentin found it hard to believe he'd lived through all this and understood so little of what his children had done. His mind had been on other things, but even so...

'Come back to bed, Rosaleen.' Maude tried to lift her from the chair. Jonathon went to help. She shuffled quietly back to her room between them.

'Rosaleen feels guilty,' Quentin realised. It made him shudder.

'Of course she does,' Crispin said irritably. 'Why else would she have these nervous breakdowns?'

Lorna looked stunned too. 'She feels it was her

440

fault Oliver drowned. How awful to have that on her conscience.'

'It was her fault,' Crispin said, 'very definitely her fault. She insisted on the handcuffs.'

What hurt Quentin most was that his children had deliberately kept these awful facts from him. With hindsight, he was sure Marina had known too. She'd have wanted to shield him.

It was getting late. Connie and Sissie had already gone to bed when the doctor rang the doorbell. Lorna answered the summons and took him upstairs. She knocked softly on Rosaleen's bedroom door and Aunt Maude opened it. In the room's semi-darkness Lorna could hear Rosaleen's voice rambling on. She ran back down to Quentin's study.

'Well, Father,' Crispin was saying, 'I came to have a private word with you.'

Lorna found Crispin staring at her. 'What about some coffee?' She knew he wanted to get her out of the way.

Jonathon got up too. 'I'll help you make it.'

'Malted milk for me, please,' Quentin said. 'I'll just give Rosaleen time to settle before I go to bed.'

'Had I better make some for her and Aunt Maude too?'

'Yes, if you would.'

As Lorna went to follow Jonathon to the kitchen, she heard Crispin say, 'Father, I've given you the help you asked for, but can we talk about something else now?'

It took Lorna and Jonathon some time to find

441

their way round the cupboards and the new utensils. By the time they had the drinks prepared, the doctor was coming down alone. Jonathon saw him out, before taking a tray upstairs.

Lorna was taking her tray to Quentin's study when Crispin came rushing out. 'Aren't you staying for your coffee?' she asked. He pushed past her without a word and the front door slammed behind him.

Quentin still looked shocked. 'He wanted his job back. Expected to get it, I think. Expected a reward for telling us. Ah, there you are, Jonathon. He couldn't believe you were doing his job.'

Lorna found a clean folder in which to store Oliver's papers. 'I'd like to take my mother's letter to her,' she said. 'You agree she should have it?'

'Of course.'

'What I don't understand,' Lorna went on, 'is why they didn't get rid of all this, burn it straight away? It's incriminating.'

Quentin's bleary eyes looked at her over the rim of his cup. 'Time mellows everything. A hundred years from now, when everybody mentioned is long gone, future generations of the family will think it romantic. It's Wyndham history. It's sacrosanct, mustn't be destroyed.'

Lorna shivered. 'At least I know what really happened. It was an accident. Though an accident that needn't have happened.'

'They twisted the facts to clear themselves of blame,' Jonathon said, 'tried to cast a very different slant on the truth.'

'A sad tale of wrong decisions,' Quentin said slowly, 'motivated by selfishness. They botched what they tried to do and then showed total cowardice by leaving Oliver to drown.'

'Our ancestors were slavers,' Jonathon sighed. 'Can't expect us all to turn out saints.'

Quentin said sadly, 'I do wish we'd let Oliver do what he so much wanted.'

It was very late that night when Lorna went up to her bedroom. They had talked over every aspect of Oliver's sad end and the part Rosaleen and Crispin had played in it. The details had sickened her but now, several hours later, she'd pushed all that behind her.

She propped her mother's letter up on her dressing table satisfied she had all the answers at last. In addition, she'd made a clean breast to the family about what she'd been doing and who she was. That was off her conscience and they hadn't thrown her out. But what was making her really sizzle inside was thinking about Jonathon and their future.

She wrote a postcard to her mother, filling it with tiny squashed writing to get it all in. 'I'll be home for good on Saturday. Jonathon has offered to help me bring my bags. Can we ask him to stay for tea?'

She thought for a moment. As Jonathon had driven her to the office this morning, she'd hardly been able to drag her gaze away from him. She'd never felt like this about anybody before. Why had she thought him less handsome than Adam? He looked upright and honest.

443

Yet she was doing exactly what Mum had warned her against. Lorna hoped she wasn't going to worry herself sick about this. She ought to drop some sort of a hint before they came face to face. She wrote: 'I'm sure you'll like him.'

She sucked her pencil for several more minutes, then added: 'I'll be able to tell you all you want to know this time. The Wyndhams know who I am and we know exactly what happened to O.'

She didn't want to say it was good news because she'd found it shocking and sad. She ended the card, 'Can't wait to tell you.'

When she got into bed, her head was whirling and sleep was a long time coming.

When Daphne had come out of Bamfords' office after learning that Crispin had arranged to sell off all their antiques, she'd rushed home in a panic and started packing. She collected up silver photograph frames, powder bowls, dressing sets, most of which had been given to her as gifts. She stopped to weep with rage that he could do this without saying a word to her.

She'd given herself ten days to make her plans and carry them out, but now she was afraid that was too long. Crispin would find out what she'd done if he rang Bamfords, and he was hardly likely to wait a week before doing that.

It gave her a terrible afternoon and evening. If she didn't get this right she could be virtually penniless for the rest of her life.

When she went to bed, she tossed and turned, unable to get to sleep. At midnight, she got up to look in the telephone directory. She urgently needed to find another firm she could ask to sell everything on her behalf. She could find only small firms offering house clearance, and they would never get the worth from the antiques here. She went back to bed feeling cold and defeated, but the next morning she woke up at the usual time, feeling calmer and knowing exactly what she must do.

She'd hire a removal firm to load everything up and take it away before Bamfords came on Monday the ninth. She wouldn't leave anything for Crispin to sell. Her first idea was to send it out to Marseilles where it would be impossible for him to get his hands on it. During the last years of her grandmother's life, her mother had moved in to look after her, and was now living alone in the house, but it would not be big enough to store all this furniture.

Daphne had gathered enough information about exports and imports from the Wyndhams to realise it might take her some time to book space on a ship and to get any licences, if needed. Anyway, she didn't want to live in France, she'd rather stay here.

That morning, she went out to try and make arrangements with a removal firm. She wanted to make it as difficult as possible for Crispin to trace her, so did not consider the firm he'd booked to move them from Otterspool. Instead, she chose a smallish firm based in another suburb some distance away.

The owner thought she'd need two vans to move all her things, but he was booked up until Thursday of next week. She told him how urgent it was, and almost went to try elsewhere. But she was afraid she'd not find anybody who could move her things any sooner, and she felt too panic-stricken to go on trying. She might waste time.

It was arranged that the packing of china and glassware would start on Thursday of next week. The first van would come on Friday morning, with the second on Saturday morning. The house would be cleared by Saturday afternoon. She knew her belongings would have to go into store for the time being, and he helped her book space for them.

That afternoon she toured the offices of local estate agents, seeking a house to rent. She didn't want a grand house like Ravensdale – it would have to be much smaller – but she wanted it in a good area.

She'd been through all this quite recently and knew exactly what she must do. The first thing was to decide exactly where she wanted to live. It needed to be at some distance from Hedge End, and also some distance from Aigburth, where it seemed Crispin was now living. She thought of Southport and of West Kirby on the Wirral.

She came home with a clutch of papers giving details of the properties available, and flung herself down on the new sofa to rest. She could see her fingers shaking against the papers and felt a nervous wreck. It was as though Crispin was just one step behind her and closing fast.

There were two small houses in West Kirby that sounded suitable. She lifted the telephone and arranged to see them both on Monday. If she could decide quickly, if she could get away before Crispin realised what she was doing, she'd take him by surprise instead of the other way round.

Either of the two houses she saw would have suited her purpose. She didn't expect to like them, she was going a long way down market. She decided on the one with the cheaper rent. It was up on the hill and had a pleasant view. It was a little larger than the house in Marseilles, with two good-sized bedrooms plus a smaller one, quite a comfortable sitting room with a small dining room and kitchen. It would have to do, but it was a doll's house compared with Ravensdale. She paid a month's rent in advance as requested and collected the keys. She felt better now she had her escape route organised, and if all went according to plan, she'd do it with a day to spare.

She returned to Ravensdale and walked through the rooms, marking the pieces she wanted to go direct to her new home. She was pleased to have found somewhere so quickly. It meant she could have what she needed delivered directly there.

Daphne felt fraught through the days of waiting, expecting Crispin to come round at any moment. When the removal firm delivered some packing cases she began to pack in earnest. On the Thursday, two men worked with her, packing all day.

Friday turned out to be a very cold morning, but she was up early and ready when the removal van backed in to the drive. Everything she'd need in her new house was clearly marked and separated from the things going into store. Daphne found it a gruelling day but by that evening, she'd moved in to her new home, she had her bed made up and most of her furniture in position. The house felt bitterly cold – it hadn't been lived in for some time – and she hadn't the energy to light more than one fire. Though she had many more boxes to unpack, her home was taking shape. She felt elated. This time she hoped to beat Crispin at his own game.

After tomorrow, when Ravensdale was cleared, and the remaining antiques were beyond Crispin's reach, she'd be able to finish unpacking here at leisure. When she'd had time to recover from this rush, she'd find a suitable firm to help her, and sell off everything she didn't want. That would provide her with some capital, and perhaps then she'd be able to afford a somewhat better house. She filled two hot-water bottles and, aching with fatigue, she went to bed.

Chapter Twenty-Three

Daphne was up before her alarm went off the next morning. She'd slept only fitfully, woken very early, and felt too driven with anxiety to lie in bed. She had to get up and get started. It was Saturday, and if all went well, by this afternoon she'd not have to worry any more about standing up to a furious Crispin.

The house felt icy but she had no time to light a fire. She made herself tea and toast and ran out to catch an early train.

It was a cold dark day with heavy cloud. On the station platform she heard someone say that snow was forecast. She hoped it wouldn't come before what was left of the contents of Ravensdale were packed up and moved into store.

When Daphne opened the front door of Ravensdale, she found a letter on the mat. It was from Quentin, telling her to go to the Liverpool Savings Bank and see the manager.

'I've arranged to pay in a monthly sum to cover your basic living expenses,' he wrote, 'the first of which will be waiting for you. You will need to provide a specimen of your signature before the account can be validated.'

Quentin had been generous. Daphne was pleased, and decided to call at Hedge End before going back to West Kirby to thank him for his generosity and to say goodbye to him and Aunt Maude.

She had a headache. It felt like a tight band round her head and she knew she wouldn't be able to relax until Ravensdale was cleared and she could get safely away. It helped to see the removal van backing up to the front door so that work could begin.

Daphne was taking down the new curtains when she noticed the first snowflakes falling. The removal men joked about being snowed in here for days, which made her panic so she hardly knew what to do next. But the snow shower wasn't enough to build up on the ground, and work didn't stop.

By mid-afternoon, it was beginning to snow in

earnest, but by then Ravensdale House had been stripped of everything, including its carpets. Daphne watched the last loaded van pull out of the drive, feeling exhausted but relieved that the snow had held off and all had gone according to plan.

The rooms were echoing and empty; there was little left but some golf clubs Crispin had bought but never used. She'd thrown a mound of his clothes over a spare tea chest, in which he could pack them.

Looking at the swirling snow, she wondered if she should go straight home, but decided to risk a trip to Hedge End. She had to stay on good terms with Quentin to ensure he continued to pay her the allowance.

She had two small bags of oddments she wanted to take to her new home, but she wouldn't take them with her. She must give the Wyndhams no clues as to what she was doing. Crispin was going to be furious when he found out, and none of them must know her new address. She must make it impossible for him to find her.

She rang for a taxi and, when it arrived, locked up Ravensdale, leaving her two bags just inside the front hall. When it drew into the drive at Hedge End, snow was still falling heavily and building up on the ground.

Aunt Maude, buttoned up in a heavy coat with a thick scarf over her hat, had almost reached home.

'I walked down to the shops to get some chocolate biscuits and a Victoria sandwich,' she said. 'Doesn't everywhere look pretty? I didn't expect so much snow, a very heavy fall. It'll spoil the garden.'

'It'll pick up when spring comes.'

'Do come in. You're just in time for tea.' Maude shook the snow off her coat before taking Daphne to the sitting room. Quentin was already there; she'd known it was a good time to visit. Sissie was right behind them, pushing in the tea trolley.

'We'll have some of these biscuits now, Sissie,' Maude said, giving her the shopping bag. 'And we'll need another cup and saucer.'

She was looking at the trolley. 'No we won't. Lorna's gone home and Jonathon won't be in for tea today. Didn't I tell you?'

Daphne accepted a cup of tea and waited until Aunt Maude sat down beside her on the sofa.

'Quentin,' she said, 'I came to thank you for making me such a generous allowance. You're very kind. And I want to say goodbye.'

'You're leaving Ravensdale?'

'Crispin expects me to. He's arranging to sell off most of the furniture.'

She could see Quentin didn't like that. 'He promised to keep those pieces in the family.'

'Where will you go?' Maude asked.

'To Marseilles to stay with my mother for the time being,' Daphne said, having to tell a white lie. 'I'm off tomorrow.'

'Much the best thing – to return to your mother. She'll be a source of comfort to you.' Aunt Maude patted her arm.

Daphne sighed and said sadly, 'I feel as though I've been hammered. I need a rest and peace to

451

get over this turmoil. It's a horrible end to twenty-seven years of marriage.'

'We're all very sorry,' Maude said.

'And very disappointed with Crispin,' Quentin frowned.

Daphne dabbed her eyes with her lace handkerchief. 'Then I hope to find a modest home for myself and live quietly.'

'Here d'you mean, or in Marseilles?'

'I haven't decided. I need to think about that.'

'You're being very sensible.'

'As befits a woman of my age. I shall try to make a life for myself. You wouldn't think it unreasonable if I took the furniture I'd need to furnish a small place? I've lived with those pieces all my married life. They seem like my own.'

'Of course, my dear. You must take what you want. I'm sure Crispin would expect you to do that.'

With her own business settled more satisfactorily than she'd dared hope, Daphne bit into a chocolate biscuit. It was only then she thought to ask after Rosaleen.

It was Aunt Maude's turn to sigh. 'She's not very well, I'm afraid. Resting in bed. Her nerves... Well, you know Rosaleen's always lived on her nerves. She said she'd try to come down for tea but it doesn't look as though she will.'

'We're worried about her,' Quentin said.

Daphne reflected that she was getting her just deserts. She'd made Daphne's life a misery for years.

'Rosaleen takes all our troubles to heart. Moving here has been an upheaval for her, poor girl. She needs stability, always has.'

'Needs it more than the rest of us,' Aunt Maude said. 'I must take a cup of tea up to her.'

Daphne knew this would be her last chance to even up the score. 'Let me do that.' She stood up to pour it. 'I must say goodbye to her before I go. Shall I take her a piece of cake too?'

'No, she isn't eating,' her father said.

'Yes, Daphne.' Aunt Maude turned to her. 'Cut a small slice of Victoria sandwich, try her with it. It would help if she ate something.'

'She's very edgy,' Quentin said. 'Try to soothe her.'

Daphne climbed the stairs gingerly so as not to slop the tea. It sounded as though her sister-in-law was in a worse state than she was herself. She knocked on Rosaleen's bedroom door and went in. The room was in semi-darkness with the curtains drawn.

Rosaleen was lying on the bed. 'Who's that?' She jerked to a sitting position and leaned over to grab something from her bedside table.

'It's only me, it's Daphne. I've brought you a cup of tea.'

She busied herself putting it within Rosaleen's reach and pulling up a chair. It was only when she slid the cake plate across her counterpane that she saw the knife in her hand. Daphne gasped with shock.

Rosaleen looked at her vacantly. 'I thought you'd gone, that you and Crispin had a house of your own.'

Daphne was struggling to get her breath. 'Yes, we have Ravensdale. You've been over to see it

453

several times.'

'Ye-es, I remember you showing me round. Quite a big house. Father thought Crispin should have asked us to move in with you.' Rosaleen was glowering at her, turning the knife over and over in her hand, making the light glint on its savage blade. 'But you didn't want us there.'

Daphne hadn't realised Rosaleen was this nerve-racked. 'Crispin wanted us to be on our own. Try some of this cake. Aunt Maude thinks you need to eat more.'

'I don't want it.'

Daphne said with assumed calm, 'Don't do that, Rosaleen.' She went to take the knife. 'You're making me nervous.'

Rosaleen jerked back; the cake plate slid to the floor but didn't break. 'Don't touch me.' Her hand now gripped the knife like a dagger with the blade pointing at Daphne's heart. Hurriedly, Daphne pushed her chair back.

She recognised the knife. Lars Wyndham was holding it in his portrait. Quentin had called it a hunting knife. It had a silver handle, a curved blade and a sharp point. It used to be kept in the gun room at Otterspool. In this house Quentin had a glass case in the hall where he displayed one or two of his favourite muskets and knives.

'It wasn't me that did it.' There was pent-up fury in Rosaleen's voice.

'Did what?' Daphne eased her chair back further still. Rosaleen needed a doctor. She was hovering on the brink of another nervous breakdown. She looked as though she could kill if she didn't get something to calm her down.

454

She'd been bad last time but not like this.

'Oliver was fastened to the locker that day,' Rosaleen's troubled eyes met hers, 'with his own handcuffs. Crispin did it, but now he says it was me – that it was all my fault.'

'Your fault that Oliver drowned?' Daphne's mouth felt as dry as sand. The official family explanation had been that it was an accident. Now it seemed that wasn't the exact truth. Rosaleen looked guilty. It had been playing on her mind. At the time, Daphne hadn't thought much about it, hadn't much cared one way or the other. It had happened just after she'd found that Crispin was in love with Ruth Detley.

It came to her in that split second how she could take revenge on both Crispin and Rosaleen at the same time. For years she'd suffered humiliation at their hands. Daphne's only method of revenge had been to manipulate Rosaleen's thoughts, twist her mind, until she felt fear and suffered too.

Daphne hated Rosaleen almost as much as Rosaleen hated her, and as for Crispin... Hate was too mild a word for what she felt for him. She loathed him. She'd been disillusioned by his need for other women – jealous of them too, if she was to be honest. He'd been insufferably rude to her for years, treated her with contempt, and she was frightened of his violence.

His wealth had prevented her leaving him – that and the children. Now his wealth had gone but he had another woman to go to, a life to enjoy. He'd planned to leave her high and dry with nothing. That was a raw hurt. She'd taken all his antiques – that was some revenge but she ached for more. Quentin had asked her to soothe Rosaleen, but it would suit her better to do the opposite.

'You could get your own back on him,' she told her. 'He's always done you down, done us all down.'

Rosaleen was jabbing the point of the knife at her eiderdown, cutting little slits in it. A feather wafted out and slowly came to settle on Daphne's arm.

'Father should never have brought that girl here. She's exposed all our secrets, things best kept hidden,' Rosaleen fretted.

'Lorna Mathews, you mean?'

'I hate her.'

Daphne realised that Lorna must have insisted on hearing all the details of Oliver's death, just as she'd revealed every other family secret.

'I hate her. She's brought nothing but trouble on me since she came.'

'No,' Daphne said as gently as she could. If she was to get Rosaleen to do what she planned, she must deflect this hate from Lorna to Crispin.

'Lorna Mathews has done you a lot of good. She pointed out to your father how Crispin was stealing money from the business. He said it was his own, but he was taking money that belonged to you and your father.'

'So she did.' Rosaleen looked confused. 'What's the matter with me?'

'It's Crispin you should blame, not her.'

Daphne took a deep breath. This was an un-expected chance to aggravate Rosaleen's state of mind, make her worse, drive her over the edge of reason. Set her on a course that would lead her to attack Crispin on her behalf. Perhaps hack at him with that knife? How richly he deserved that. She just might do it. After all, Rosaleen had attacked Hilda when she found her stealing family money.

'Your father's very pleased with Lorna,' she said in a conversational tone. 'Because of her, in future, the business will provide enough money to keep the family.'

'Crispin was taking it for you and his own brood.'

'No, I saw precious little of it and neither did Clarissa.' Daphne felt indignant. 'He was taking the family wealth to spend on loose women and giving the family a bad name. He has no morals and doesn't care what hurt he inflicts on us.'

'Oh, Crispin! He never takes the blame for anything.' Rosaleen's eyes gleamed with hate. 'He blames others when things go wrong.'

'He tried to say it was Adam and Buckler who were defrauding the business.'

'He blamed me for Oliver's death. Oliver was my favourite brother. I wouldn't have hurt him.'

'That's Crispin's way,' Daphne said softly. 'Why should he have all the money and all the fun? You should stand up for yourself, try to get your own back. It's what he deserves. You'd be doing it for the family.'

Rosaleen didn't seem to be taking notice. She was staring straight ahead. Her fingernails were bitten down to the quick.

'Crispin cheats us in many ways,' Daphne went on. 'He persuaded you to marry Henry Montague, didn't he? He said you'd be missing so much in life if you didn't.'

'Henry was his friend.' There was malice in Rosaleen's pale eyes now.

'Not really his friend, more his accomplice. Crispin knew what he was like. He told me Henry had been sponging on him for years. He deliberately handed the problem on to you.'

'Everybody said he married me for my money.'

'Well, he did. Crispin never cared what he did to the rest of his family.' All Daphne's loathing of her husband spilled out, but Rosaleen's need for revenge frightened even her.

'Do you know what I'd like to do to him? I'd like to kill him.'

Daphne took a deep breath. How easy it was to get Rosaleen to do her bidding. 'You do that.' She knew she was the one with the power now.

'I will.'

'He's let me down as much as he has you.'

Rosaleen was ripping her eiderdown with the knife now, pulling handfuls of feathers out, tossing them into the air.

Daphne stood up and brushed them off her dress. 'I came up to say goodbye. I'm going back to Marseilles for a while.'

That same Saturday morning, Lorna woke up still crackling with energy and delighted to be going to the office with Jonathon.

Yesterday, winter had tightened its grip. This morning was overcast, with a cutting wind and a yellowish tinge to the black clouds. Snow was forecast.

It did snow a little during the morning, but just

a few flurries that melted away. At lunch time, Jonathon took her to a café round the corner where they had soup and ham sandwiches. Lorna was more concerned now with how he would see her family and whether they'd take to him. It had been a tight fit to get her big suitcase and overnight bag into his little car.

'Would it be better to cross the river on the luggage boat, or drive up to the bridge at Runcorn?'

Lorna laughed. 'Easier to take the underground and leave the car at the station this end. We'll be at Hamilton Square in three minutes. Usually I walk from there, but with this case, it might be better to take a bus.'

Once Lorna and Jonathon were the other side of the Mersey, the day seemed darker still and it started to snow. The dusting of pristine white made the streets and pavements look dirty. She could see Jonathon looking round with interest.

'I've seen the docks from the river many times, and been to New Brighton and Rock Ferry but never here.'

The house in which she'd been brought up seemed tiny. She rattled the letter box and her mother opened the door, pulling them inside quickly. The only light was from the fire roaring up the chimney.

Lorna introduced him. 'You met my mum at the auction, but you didn't know then she was your old nursemaid.'

'Alice?' He seized her hand. 'Fancy seeing you again after all this time.'

'You can't remember me.'

'Not what you looked like, but I remember that you played with me and put me to bed. I was fond of you.'

'And this is Pam, my sister, and... Pa, you're home!' He was coming down the stairs. 'That's marvellous.'

'Only Jim is missing.'

'Isn't this cosy?' Jonathon warmed his hands at the fire. They pulled chairs closer and sat down and talked of Jim and of the wintry weather. Lorna knew her mother would be on tenterhooks until she heard what they had learned about Oliver.

'Make a cup of tea, Pam,' Lorna said, and started to tell her.

Jonathon helped her out, describing their holiday cottage and Oliver's boat. 'Both have gone now,' he said. 'The cottage was sold quite recently.'

To recount the story of Oliver's drowning brought a lump to Lorna's throat again. She could see the effect it was having on her mother; her eyes were glistening with tears.

When there was no more she could tell her, she said, 'We found the letter Oliver wrote to you.'

Jonathon apologised. 'It's being delivered twenty years late, I'm afraid, and it was opened, by Aunt Roz and her brothers.'

'Go up to your bedroom, Mum, and read it in private.' Lorna pushed her towards the stairs. 'Pam and I will get tea on the table.'

'It's liver and bacon,' Pam said. 'I'll start cooking. Spuds and sprouts with it in your honour,' she told Jonathon.

'Gosh, I'm causing a lot of trouble.'

'Mum doesn't want you to be hungry.' It was only when Lorna went out to the yard to collect some potatoes from the covered bucket there that she realised snow had been falling heavily for some time.

'It's sticking on the road.' Sam Mathews came out to refill the coal scuttle. It was getting dark. He made up the fire and drew the curtains.

Later, when they were finishing their meal, Jonathon said, 'I think the family let you down, Alice. Don't you feel bitter?'

'I did feel sorry for myself, but Sam looked after me. I was worried about Lorna. I didn't want her to go to Otterspool...'

'She's been afraid the same thing would happen to her,' Sam said.

'I guarantee it won't, Alice,' Jonathon said. 'I'll make sure no harm comes to her. I know the family let Lorna down too, ignored her, let her be brought up in poverty. Oliver wouldn't have wanted that.'

'I didn't know what I was missing,' Lorna smiled.

'Bringing up three kids hasn't been easy,' Sam told Jonathon, 'but things are better now they're grown up and two of them are earning.'

'Won't be long before I am too,' Pam said.

'And Lorna's generous with her pay.'

Jonathon's bright blue eyes met hers. 'I didn't think of it like that.'

'Don't think I've had a deprived childhood,' Lorna said seriously. 'I haven't.'

'We've always been short of money,' Pa said.

461

'Always scraping round for more.'

'You gave me a happy childhood,' Lorna insisted. 'I was well cared for, surrounded with affection. This little house always seemed a place of comfort, still does. Don't smile, Pa – I don't mean material comfort. It feels safe and secure, a place where nothing bad could happen to any of us.'

'We look after each other,' Alice smiled.

'So you see, Jonathon, I did very well here. There's no need to be sorry for me. I didn't lose out, not measured in care and love.'

'You make me feel proud,' Sam said, 'when you say things like that. I suppose it must have been a social embarrassment to have a Wyndham being born out of wedlock.'

Daphne went down the Hedge End stairs, feeling victorious. She was amazed at how easy she'd found it to manipulate Rosaleen. How much easier her life would have been if only she'd been able to keep influencing Crispin in that way.

She paused on the landing to look out at the snow, but today she hadn't thought carefully enough beforehand about what she was doing. She'd forgotten to give Rosaleen his new address. She'd never find him. Should she go back?

No, Rosaleen was never likely to kill Crispin. She was like a hamster on a wheel; she did only what she was used to doing. It looked as though she was going to need hospital treatment again. Serve her right.

Daphne put her head round the sitting-room door to ask Quentin if she might ring for a taxi to take her home. 'Harold will be in the greenhouse, Daphne. Why don't you get him to run you there?'

'Thank you,' she smiled. 'That's kind of you.'

'Send Connie out to tell him.'

Daphne had planned to pick up her bags at Ravensdale and go straight down to Liverpool Central to catch the West Kirby train. She couldn't let Harold take her there in case he mentioned it to Quentin. He could drop her at Ravensdale and she'd phone for a taxi from there.

Quentin looked uneasy. 'How did you find Rosaleen?'

'Agitated, I'm afraid. Not at all her usual self.'

'The doctor said he'd come again tomorrow.' Aunt Maude was frowning. 'We did wonder whether we should ask him to come today instead, but she seemed better this morning.'

Daphne sat making conversation until she saw the Daimler pull in front of the house. Then she kissed Aunt Maude and Quentin goodbye, and thanked him again for his generosity. She didn't want him to have second thoughts about paying the allowance he'd promised her.

She went outside, swinging her handbag, feeling as carefree as a child let out of school. It was all over now. She was more than pleased to have seen the last of the Wyndham family. She had to pull herself up and go carefully down the front steps, which were covered with more snow than when she'd arrived. It was still swirling down.

The staid old Daimler was gliding along at walking pace, Harold being very careful. The

463

snow was building up on the roads and on the trees, making the place look like a Christmas card. The sky was black; it looked as though there was plenty more to come.

As Harold nosed the car into Ravensdale's short drive, Daphne saw how beautiful a covering of snow made it look and was full of regret at having to leave before she'd had time to enjoy living here. She was going to miss this lovely house, but she'd managed to turn the tables on Crispin and get Quentin to give her an allowance. That brought both satisfaction and elation. She was winning.

While she waited for Harold to open the car door for her, she realised the house looked empty now she'd taken down all the new curtains. Perhaps the snow would distract him, and he wouldn't notice. But even if he did, he'd be unlikely to see Crispin and mention it before tomorrow.

'Thank you, Harold,' Daphne said hurriedly, 'and goodbye. You'll not see much of me in future.'

She was humming a little tune as she went carefully up the steps to the front door and let herself in. She'd put the telephone on the hall windowsill when the table it had stood on had been carried out to the removal van. Before lifting it, she looked through the window. Harold had got back into the Daimler. He was beginning to reverse back round the side of the house in order to drive out. Daphne was searching in her handbag for the taxi rank number when she heard the screech of brakes.

Startled, she jerked her head up to see why.

Crispin's car had come up the drive, blocking the Daimler's path. She leaped back from the window, wanting to hide, and was so fluttery, she tripped over the two bags she'd packed and left ready. She was in a cold sweat and could feel goose pimples coming up on her arms. Crispin was going to find she'd stripped the house bare.

Harold was out in the snow and walking over to speak to Crispin. Whatever they were talking about was taking a long time. Daphne could hardly breathe. She saw Crispin's car reverse to give Harold room to turn, then he pulled forward in front of the door.

Daphne could feel her heart pounding with dread. If he came inside, he'd find the house empty. He'd be furious with her, completely livid. She pulled her coat closer and went out to him.

'What have you come here for?' She attacked while she could.

'To pick up some of my things.'

'I wish you'd stay away. Leave me alone.'

'What's Harold doing here?' Crispin looked angry already. 'Have you been over to see Father? What have you been telling him?'

'The truth – that you've left me for your fancy woman.'

'You can tell him what you like. Father's washed his hands of me. You couldn't make things worse than they are.'

Harold hadn't reached the end of the drive when a scarlet Alfa Romeo sports car shot through the gates on screaming tyres. The snow was pushed aside in a dirty mound as the driver brought it to a frantic stop. Harold was now

465

blocked in again.

'Good God!' Crispin swore. 'What's Rosaleen come here for?'

Daphne could hardly believe Rosaleen had left home wearing a pink satin dressing gown over her nightdress. Not on a day like today! She'd got straight up from her bed! Sick with horror, Daphne watched her jump out of her car and come running up the tyre tracks towards them, still brandishing the knife. She was wearing pink satin slippers!

Daphne let out a screech of terror, knowing instantly what Rosaleen meant to do. Panic-stricken, she tried to run to the safety of the front door, but the steps were slippery, and she almost lost her balance. But she reached the door and turned round, ready to rush in and slam Rosaleen out if she came near.

'What's the matter with you?' Crispin sounded cross. The snow was falling more lightly now. Against it, his face looked grey and grim.

Daphne was in time to see Rosaleen use the momentum of her run to swing her arm and jab the knife at Crispin's neck. She saw the blood spurt out immediately but Rosaleen continued to lunge at him with the knife. Her first stab had taken him by surprise but now his arms were flailing, trying to keep her at a distance.

Daphne heard him croak, 'You crazy – fool...' He fell back against his car.

'I hate you. I've always hated you.' Rosaleen was flicking the knife at his face now. Daphne could hardly breathe. She could see the slashes oozing blood, and she was stiff with horror. She'd never meant to cause this.

Crispin pushed himself off the car to grab at his sister's arm. He was trying to take the knife from her, but the blood was pumping out of the wound at the side of his neck. He could no longer stand alone and was leaning over, supporting his weight against her, covering her with blood and twisting at the knife in her hand. He was too heavy for Rosaleen. His weight pushed her off balance and they fell together to the snow-covered ground.

Rosaleen let out a horrific scream. Daphne saw her fall on the knife, and under their combined weight it went deep into her chest. Harold came running up, his face frenzied. 'Oh my God, did you see that?'

Daphne was appalled. It had all happened so quickly. She staggered into the house to phone the police, but the phone was swinging away from her and everything was going black.

'Are you all right?' She was vaguely aware of Harold standing over her, of him shuddering as he spoke to the telephone operator. He left her to lie where she'd fallen, left the front door open as he rushed outside again. Daphne couldn't move. She felt convulsed with terror. Had she caused this?

She could hear Harold shouting for someone to help him, but she could not; he sounded desperate. Eventually she heard other voices, other vehicles. Daphne pulled herself painfully to her feet, her side hurt where she'd fallen. There was an ambulance just inside the gates. She couldn't see either Crispin or Rosaleen because several policemen were blocking her view.

She felt her way to the kitchen. It was the only place where she could sit down. She hadn't thought it worthwhile to remove the scrubbed kitchen table and hard chairs. She filled a tumbler at the sink and tried to drink, but she could feel the scalding vomit coming into her mouth. She bent over the sink and turned the taps full on.

Quentin folded his newspaper and yawned. He'd read every word in it today. He heard a door bang upstairs and footsteps running overhead.

Maude was busy stitching at her embroidery frame. She looked up, frowning. 'We hear so much more in this house.'

'Sound carries here.'

The footsteps hurtled downstairs and the front door banged. Quentin felt uneasy. 'That couldn't be Rosaleen?'

'Doesn't sound like her. She never gets out of bed. Wouldn't even come down to tea.'

He struggled out of his chair and was going to the window when the sitting-room door flew open and an agitated Sissie almost shouted: 'Miss Rosaleen's gone out in her dressing gown. I couldn't stop her. She pushed me out of the way.'

'In this weather!' Maude was shocked. 'She'll catch her death of cold.'

Quentin was at the window in time to see her backing her sports car out of the garage. The tyres slithered as she spun it round too quickly, then she cut across the bend in the drive leaving

468

black tracks and crushed crocuses in the virgin snow covering a flowerbed.

'Oh goodness!' It frightened him to see her driving so erratically.

'It's not safe for her to go out,' Maude said beside him. 'Not safe for anyone in this weather.'

Quentin asked, 'Did she say where she was going?'

'No.' Sissie was behind him, wringing her hands. 'What can we do?'

'Collect up the tea things,' Maude said briskly, 'and take the trolley back to the kitchen.'

Quentin was more than worried. When the door closed, shutting off the tinkle of crockery, he said, 'Where can she be going? In such a hurry too.'

'Back to Otterspool? It's played on her mind, having to leave.'

He mopped his forehead with his handkerchief. 'Why now?'

'Or to Ravensdale?'

'No, she's just spoken to Daphne. She sat with her for quite a while. Why would she go after her like that?'

Maude was shaking her head. 'In her nightdress and dressing gown too.'

'A pity Jonathon isn't here. He could have gone after her, made sure she came to no harm.'

'It has to happen on the one afternoon he isn't. Perhaps there was something else she wanted to say to Daphne.'

'She could have lifted the phone.'

'She might just come back on her own.'

'I'll send Harold to look for her when he comes

469

back,' Quentin decided.

'He's only just gone.'

'Ravensdale isn't far, but even he won't be there yet. I might try phoning in a few minutes.' Quentin felt very much on edge. 'There's nothing else we can do, is there?'

Over the last few years, Rosaleen had been losing contact with the few friends she'd had.

'I'll ring Grace Edgerton,' Maude said. He stood listening beside the phone while she did it. 'She says she hasn't seen her since before Christmas.'

'Try Laura Sandforth,' he suggested. Maude reported a few moments later that Laura said she'd invited Rosaleen to her birthday party last week, that she'd telephoned to say she'd come but hadn't turned up. There was no answer when Maude tried to ring Ravensdale.

She sighed. 'Rosaleen's a terrible responsibility when she's like this.' She put her embroidery away. 'I'll go up to her room and see if she's left any clue.'

Quentin went to his study and poured himself a brandy. He had to do something to calm his nerves. He was heaving with impatience but waited as long as he could, before ringing the Ravensdale number again. This time the receiver was picked up and a voice he didn't recognise repeated the number. He asked for Daphne. When she came to speak to him, he could hear tears in her voice. Such a change in her! She'd seemed perfectly normal when she'd left a short time ago. Now, she was hardly coherent and kept stopping as though to consult someone else.

'What's going on, Daphne? Is Rosaleen there?'

'I'll come straight over,' she said. 'Harold's here, he'll bring me back.'

'What about Rosaleen?'

But he heard the phone click back before he'd got the question out. That did nothing to soothe him. He poured himself another brandy and insisted Maude have one too. He was afraid something must have happened to his daughter.

Chapter Twenty-Four

It was only when Alice went to the kitchen to wash up that she noticed how deep the snow had become. 'It's over eight inches on the windowsill. How will you get home in this, Jonathon?'

He peered through the curtains in the living room. 'Will I be able to get across the river?'

'Yes, it's an underground line, the trains won't stop,' Lorna assured him. 'But you'll have to drive through the city and out to Hedge End, which worries me. Will your little car be able to get through?'

'It'll be dangerous,' Alice said. 'Traffic will be sliding all over the place. You'd better stay the night. You can have Jim's room.'

'That's very kind, but–'

'Do stay,' Lorna urged. 'That would be the safest. I want you to. It's Sunday tomorrow; you could spend most of the day here with me.'

He smiled. 'That sounds all right, but I'll have

to phone home. They'll worry if I don't. Where's the nearest phone box?'

'Near the station,' Pam said, 'or there's one near Charing Cross.'

'The station,' Lorna decided. 'I'll come with you.'

'I can't drag you out in this. I could walk back there.'

'You might get lost. I'm coming with you.'

Alice decided Jonathon couldn't possibly go out wearing his own shoes. She fitted him out in Jim's wellingtons and heavy coat.

'Put your galoshes on,' she said to Lorna, 'and wrap up warm.' She wrapped a scarf round each of them.

Outside it was dark, the streetlamps reduced to a dim glow by the thickly swirling snow. Already it was impossible to see the edge of the pavements, the road was filled with level snow. Tracks made by the last vehicle to pass were almost obliterated.

Lorna clung to Jonathon's arm as they both slithered along. More than once he held her upright. The snow was like a blanket; everywhere seemed unusually silent. Most people were staying home by their fires. Near the station there were more footprints and tyre marks in the snow but the two telephone kiosks were empty.

'Come in too,' Jonathon invited, holding the door open for her. 'It'll be warmer inside.' Lorna squeezed in while he took his gloves off and blew on his fingers. 'Not a lot warmer. Let's hope the snow hasn't brought the wires down.'

It hadn't. Lorna could hear the number ringing. Aunt Maude lifted the receiver almost immediately. 'Who?' she asked. 'Who?'

'It's Jonathon. Are you all right? You sound a bit–'

'Yes, Daphne should be here any minute now. She'll be able to tell us... Such snow... I hate to think of anybody caught out in it.'

'That's why I'm ringing,' he said, sliding his free arm round Lorna's waist. 'Lorna's mother has invited me to spend the night with them. It'll be safer than driving home.'

'Good, much the best plan.'

'I'll be home sometime tomorrow. Don't expect me early.'

'All right, dear.'

'Are you sure you're OK? You sound a bit ... you know – at sixes and sevens.'

'We're worried about Rosaleen... Oh, here's Harold bringing Daphne now. Goodbye.'

'Has something happened, Aunt Maude?' he asked, but she'd already put the phone down.

'What's the matter?' Lorna wanted to know.

'They're worried about Aunt Roz. Nothing new about that.'

Lorna felt his other arm slide round her too. 'We can't get any closer,' she said before his mouth came down on hers.

'Lorna,' he lifted his face three inches from hers, 'your nose is cold.'

She smiled. 'I'm cold all over.'

'I do love you. You're great.'

Lorna felt full of love for him. Jonathon was at his most earnest.

'I don't like the idea of seeing you only in the office. I want more of your company, not less.'

She nodded. 'That's how I feel.'

'We could get married,' he whispered. 'Then I wouldn't have to part from you ever. How d'you feel about that?'

'Get married? I'd love to,' she laughed. Sparks of excitement were shooting through her.

'We will then. We'll consider ourselves engaged. I do love you, Lorna – have done almost from the first day you turned up at Otterspool.' He hugged her. 'But you didn't like me much.'

She shook her head. 'I did, but I wouldn't let myself love you. Didn't dare.'

'With what happened to your mother, I can understand that.'

'I was scared the same thing could happen to me. I couldn't trust you.'

'I give you my word, you can be quite certain of me.' He smiled at her. 'I'm so happy, everything's coming right for me now.'

'And for me.'

'Let's get back to that fire. It's too cold to stay here.'

When they left the shelter of the phone box, Lorna hardly noticed the wet snow blowing in her face. The walk home through the snow, clinging on to Jonathon, felt truly wonderful. They were laughing as Pam let them in.

'You look like two snowmen,' she said. 'Shut the door quickly.'

Lorna and Jonathon peeled off their outdoor clothes on the doormat. Sam Mathews got up. 'I'll give these a shake at the back door and hang them in the kitchen. Come to the fire. You must be frozen.'

Lorna took Jonathon's hand and drew him to the fire with her. 'Actually, I feel warm. Tingling all over. Jonathon has just asked me... Well, we're going to be married.'

After the first stunned moment, Pam squealed with delight and Lorna was being hugged by each of her family in turn. 'Such good news. We hope you'll both be very happy.'

'As happy as your mother and I have been.' Pa landed a smacking kiss on Lorna's forehead. 'We ought to have a drink on this,' he said. 'I'll nip down to the pub and get a bottle of sherry.'

'No, Pa, it's terrible outside – freezing cold and very slippery.' Lorna held on to him. 'Let's have tea instead.'

'Are you sure? This is a big occasion. We ought to celebrate.'

'We're very happy and we're here with you. That's more than enough.'

'I'll put the kettle on,' Pam said. Sam built the fire up even higher, and they pulled their chairs closer.

'I want you to know I'm delighted.' Alice could see Lorna was sparkling with pleasure. 'When I saw you together at the auction, I rather sensed that something was in the wind.' She patted Jonathon's knee. 'You're doing what Oliver wanted to do.'

'You and he paved the way for us,' Lorna said.

'I do hope it will be all right – with your family, Jonathon.'

'Mum, don't forget my pedigree. I'm half Wyndham anyway.'

'I'll make sure no harm comes to Lorna. But

she can look after herself – she knows how to sort my family out.'

'Mum's afraid it'll be you who's harmed,' Lorna pointed out. 'It was Oliver who–'

'Things are different now. We don't all live together and we're a much smaller family. I think we live more normal lives. No harm will come to any of us.'

Alice looked thoughtful. 'Now I know exactly what happened to Oliver, I can put the past out of my mind. I've been silly, when all the time I've been very contented with the family I have.'

'Quite right,' Jonathon said. 'I don't know whether you'd have been happy with us at Otterspool. Some of my family would have made it harder for you than they did for Aunt Daphne.'

'I wouldn't have been comfortable amongst them, I see that now. They were too grand for me. I'd always have been better off with Sam.'

'Pa is one of the best,' Lorna smiled at him.

'The future looks rosy for all of us,' Pam said, handing round cups of tea. 'Even for me, though I don't think I'll ever do as well as Lorna.'

'Course you will,' Lorna said. 'Give yourself time, you're doing fine. Well on track.'

'I got full marks in the typing test we had on Friday, the only one in the class to do so.'

'There you are then. That's something to be proud of.'

Pam turned to Jonathon. 'It was Lorna's idea I should learn shorthand and typing. She's paying for me.'

'Lorna's that sort,' her mother said fondly. 'She'll do anything for us.'

'It's a Mathews family trait, isn't it, Pa?' Lorna said. 'We look after each other.'

Lorna was late waking up the next morning. Beside her Pam was still sleeping, her dark hair spread across her pillow. The house was quiet, she made herself lie still a little longer, though she felt more like singing and jumping for joy.

The bedroom curtains were closed, she could hear a soft patter against the window. The light coming in was whiter than usual. If it stopped snowing, she'd take Jonathon to the park after breakfast. It would be a winter wonderland today. There'd be snow and icicles hanging on the branches of the trees, and perhaps the lake would be frozen over. Pa said he'd seen it solid with people skating on it, but she never had.

When she got up and opened the curtains, Lorna found it was gentle rain not snow that she'd heard on the glass. Outside, much of the snow had disappeared. The family sat for a long time round the breakfast table and afterwards finding the rain had stopped, Lorna took Jonathon out for a walk.

By then little avalanches were sliding off roofs, the roads were wet and shiny and the snow that remained on the pavements had turned to dirty slush. The lake was black, the grass looked tired and the cold was still intense.

'Not a very nice day,' Lorna shivered.

'For a Sunday it's excellent.' Jonathon held firmly on to her arm. 'I always miss you on Sundays when you come home.'

After Alice's Sunday dinner of roast pork and

apple pie, Jonathon said, 'Come home with me. We'll tell the family we're engaged. I'll run you back here this evening.'

'Only right you should,' Alice told Lorna, but they sat on round the table, talking with great zest about all that had happened, so it was mid-afternoon before they stood up to clear away.

Lorna and Jonathon set off for Hamilton Square station to catch the underground. 'I'd better phone to say I'm bringing you over for dinner,' he said, when he saw the phone boxes.

'Don't give any hints as to why,' Lorna said. 'Better if we do it face to face – more exciting.'

They both squeezed into the phone box again. Lorna heard it ringing for a long time. It was Sissie who eventually picked up the receiver to say a nervous, 'Hello?'

'Jonathon here. Ask Aunt Maude to come and have a word with me, would you?'

Lorna could hear Sissie's soft snuffles and squeaks, then, 'Who's there?'

'Sissie, it's Jonathon,' he said more slowly. 'I want to speak to Mrs Carey.'

There was more shuffling. 'She's ... she's gone to her room to lie down.'

'Really? I didn't think she ever did.'

'Yes.'

'Grandpa then.'

There was silence. 'Are you still there, Sissie? Mr Wyndham, get him to come to the phone.'

'I can't,' she gasped. 'He's busy, there's people with him.'

'Oh! Then tell him I rang and I'll be home for dinner, and I'm bringing Lorna with me.'

478

Another silence. 'Have you got that, Sissie?'

'Yeah... Mr Jonathon, something–' At that moment the pennies ran out and they were cut off.

Jonathon and Lorna clung together giggling. 'Poor Sissie,' he said. 'I didn't know she was scared of the phone.'

'Scared of most things. She needs jollying along.'

It was dark by the time they reached Liverpool and walked to the car. Jonathon didn't start the engine immediately but took Lorna into his arms and kissed her.

'We've not had much time for this up to now,' she smiled.

Some time later, when he started to drive, Jonathon looked very serious. 'Now I've had time to think about what I'm offering you...'

She teased. 'You've not changed your mind?'

His hand left the wheel to pat hers. 'Of course not.'

'It's what I want, Jonathon.'

'But is it? There's Rosaleen, you see. She's a big responsibility for Grandpa and getting more than Aunt Maude can manage. I don't feel I can move away. I know it's a lot to ask, but would you be willing to live at Hedge End too?'

'I haven't had time to think. Would your grandfather want that?'

'I'm sure he will and Aunt Maude will. They're old, Lorna; they've always had a big family round them. They'll need us there.'

'Rosaleen won't like it.'

'She'll need us too. We'll sound them out and

479

see what they think.'

When he parked outside the front door, Lorna said. 'There aren't many lights on in the house.' Other times when they'd come back after dark, the house lights had blazed out a welcome.

Jonathon opened the front door with his key and Lorna went down the hall. The house was silent and still. Usually at this time in the evening, the air would be filled with the scents of dinner cooking, and Sissie would be bustling between the kitchen and the dining room.

'Has the dinner gong sounded, d'you think?' Jonathon asked. Driving back they'd been afraid they'd spent too long in the car and would be late.

'The dining table isn't set yet,' Lorna whispered as they passed the door. 'Something's happened.'

Jonathon looked in the sitting room – it was empty – then went on to his grandfather's study.

'This is where you all are,' he said. 'Hello, Aunt Daphne.' She looked up, her eyes red and swollen. 'What's the matter?'

Lorna felt the sombre atmosphere immediately. There was a grim twist to Quentin's mouth. His eyes were glittering with unshed tears. She could see Aunt Maude had been weeping too.

'It's Rosaleen...' Quentin told them. 'A terrible... She's dead, and Crispin too.'

Jonathon heard Lorna's shocked gasp. He too was appalled. 'An accident?'

'No, Rosaleen went berserk and attacked Crispin with a knife,' Aunt Maude told them.

'We think he was trying to take the knife from her but she'd mortally wounded him,' Quentin

480

faltered. 'Harold thinks Crispin had turned the knife round, that he passed out and collapsed against her. They both fell and their weight must have driven it into her. I really can't get over what happened.'

Lorna felt awash with horror. It took her a few moments to take in the dreadful facts. Jonathon asked questions, his face like parchment.

'Crispin dead. Such a shock.' Daphne was shivering. 'I can't believe it.'

'Pour her more brandy,' Quentin said to Jonathon.

'She was too much for us,' Maude sobbed. 'Too great a responsibility.'

'You all need a meal,' Lorna told him. 'It's dinner time.'

'I told Sissie to hold it up,' Quentin said. 'We felt we couldn't eat.'

'You'll feel better if you do,' Jonathon said firmly. 'We all will.'

Lorna got to her feet. 'I'll go and see how it's getting on.'

In the kitchen, she found Sissie sitting with her elbows on the table and her head in her hands. 'Isn't it awful?' she said. 'What Miss Rosaleen's done?'

'Don't think about her,' Lorna advised. 'We're ready for dinner now.' The fire in the range had died back and there was no sign of anything being cooked. 'What are we having?'

'Pheasant.'

A brace of pheasants were set in a baking dish with bacon laid over the breasts. They were still raw.

481

'Why didn't you start to cook them?'

'I've never done pheasants. Mrs Carey said she'd see to them. When I asked again, Mr Wyndham said they couldn't eat anything. Poor Miss Rosaleen...' her teeth were chattering, 'and Mr Crispin.'

Lorna put an arm across Sissie's shaking shoulders. 'They want to eat now,' she said. 'Where's Connie?'

'It's her day off.'

'No time to cook these now – we'll have something else. Are there any eggs?'

'Yes.' Sissie fetched a tray of two dozen from the larder.

'Set the table for five. I'm going to make scrambled eggs on toast for us. What about you? Shall I do enough for you too?'

'Comfort food,' she told the family when they were all sitting at the table.

'It'll be in all the papers tomorrow,' Maude fretted. 'Anything about our family always is, splashed on the front page.'

'I was there.' Daphne was still shivering. 'I saw it all. Such a terrible shock. No warning, but Crispin was so much stronger, I thought he'd have been able to hold her off.'

'Daphne, it seems she caught the main artery in his neck with her first blow.' Quentin was a little better now. 'Fortunately, Harold had driven Daphne over and was still there. He was able to tell the police what had happened and identify both.' His voice shook. 'They came here, though, with Daphne. Awful.'

'They asked if we'd had the doctor to her.' Aunt

482

Maude dabbed at her eyes again.

'He's been here a lot recently. She had pills to calm her,' Jonathon reminded her.

'I thought she was taking them,' Maude said. 'I gave them to her morning and night.'

'The police found she'd been throwing them under her bed,' Quentin said quietly.

'I handed them to her with a glass of water. I thought she was swallowing them – if only I'd made sure.'

'I should have done more,' Jonathon said.

'You mustn't blame yourselves,' Lorna said firmly. 'Rosaleen should have been in a nursing home, not here. Nobody should have expected you to cope with her.'

Quentin managed a half-smile in her direction. 'I'm glad you're here to help us cope now. I thought you'd left us, that you were going to live with your own family.'

'Yes, well...' She looked at Jonathon, thinking this was hardly the moment to announce their good news.

Aunt Maude intercepted the look. 'You and Jonathon? I did just wonder...'

'I brought Lorna back with me to– We're engaged. We're going to be married.'

'I told you, didn't I, Quentin?' Maude smiled at him.

'Well, yes...'

'I only asked her last night,' Jonathon protested.

'I sensed love was in the air.'

'Was it that obvious?'

'Not to me,' Lorna said.

'Maude's the born romantic,' Quentin smiled for the first time.

'Congratulations, Lorna,' Daphne sighed. 'You've done very well for yourself.'

'It's Jonathon who's done well for himself,' Quentin corrected. 'We hope you'll be happy, Lorna.'

'I know I will.'

'Not the best moment to announce it,' Jonathon said ruefully.

'It is,' his grandfather told him. 'Not all that's happened tonight is bad. It gives us something happier to think about.'

When they'd finished eating their simple supper, Lorna asked if they'd prefer a cup of malted milk instead of coffee and suggested an early night. They agreed.

'I must go home.' Daphne was still dithering.

'If I could borrow Grandpa's Daimler I could drop you off when I take Lorna into town,' Jonathon suggested.

'Don't go home tonight, Daphne,' Maude said, 'not to an empty house, not after what's happened. We can give you a bed here for the night.'

It took Daphne a moment or two to make up her mind. 'Perhaps I should stay. I'm absolutely shattered and there's no reason for me to go now.'

'You stay too, Lorna,' Quentin added. 'We'll need you here over the next week or so. There'll be a lot to see to.'

'I'm dreading the funerals,' Maude frowned.

Quentin looked at his sister. 'Maude isn't up to the housekeeping at the moment and your room

484

is still here. I'm sure Jonathon would like you to stay.'

'Yes.' He met her gaze and half smiled. 'You know I would.'

'My family will be expecting me back tonight,' Lorna frowned, 'and we haven't a phone. They'll be worried if I don't go.'

It was Quentin who came up with the answer. 'Jonathon could phone a telegram through. Your mother would get it almost as soon as you could get there. What d'you say?'

Lorna smiled. 'It'll give them a bit of a shock to get a telegram but yes, I'll stay.'

'Thank you,' Quentin said.

Daphne borrowed a nightdress from Maude and almost fell into the bed Lorna and Sissie made up for her. She was glad to stay the night. The journey to West Kirby would have been too far tonight.

She slept heavily for a few hours but at three o'clock she was wide awake again. She felt she was over the shock and had her wits about her again. She told herself she needn't have driven herself so hard after all. Now Crispin had been killed, all the antiques would be hers, and if she'd stayed in Ravensdale, Quentin would probably have paid the rent for her. She would have been better off if she'd done nothing at all.

Quentin had been kind. She'd offer to return the portrait of William Wyndham to him and anything else he might ask for, and she must remember to ring up Bamfords first thing on Monday morning and cancel their visit. In a

485

month or two, when things had died down, she'd get them to sell the rest of the stuff.

She was not sorry Crispin was dead. He'd deserved what he'd got. Not sorry about Rosaleen either – she suffered at her hands for decades. Daphne knew she'd have to go to the funerals and play the mourning wife, not to mention the sorrowing sister-in-law.

Also, she might have to think of some tale to tell Quentin to explain why the house had been emptied. But no, that wouldn't be a problem now. If he asked, she could say Crispin had emptied the house. He was not here to contradict her. And she'd say she was postponing her visit to Marseilles until after the funerals. She'd go when all this was over. She'd need a rest by then; it would do her good.

She could come back to her house in West Kirby and speak of it as a place she'd just found, but even that didn't matter now. She'd wanted to cut herself off from all the Wyndhams, in case Crispin should find out from his family where she was living, and come to make trouble. Now she was safe from that too.

With her mind made up, she was able to settle down to sleep again.

Daphne had to return to Hedge End after Crispin had been laid to rest. It was a sad occasion and Daphne wasn't looking forward to coming back tomorrow to go through it all again for Rosaleen. When the other guests were leaving, she looked round for Quentin to ask if Harold could run her to the station.

'Yes,' he said, 'but don't leave for a moment. I want to talk to you about something.'

Jonathon offered her another glass of sherry. Daphne sat down on the couch to drink it, while Quentin and Maude saw their remaining guests out.

'I'd better help Connie clear up,' Lorna said. 'She'll have a lot to do.'

'I'll give you a hand.' Jonathon followed her out.

'Lorna's a nice girl. Jonathon could do a lot worse,' Quentin said when they'd gone.

'She's very pleasant,' Maude agreed.

Daphne thought Lorna was going to have an easier time of it than she'd done. 'What did you want to talk to me about?'

'It's rather a delicate subject.'

Maude took over. 'Quentin has been worrying. About Crispin having another daughter.'

'A child we know nothing about,' Quentin said.

Daphne pursed her lips, her voice was harsh. 'And a mistress.'

'I'm afraid the child will grow up in poverty. She'll be in the same position as Lorna, wondering about her father.'

Daphne waited, wondering if the old fool wanted to pay them an allowance too.

'We don't know where to find them.'

She knew her guess had been right. Well, that whore wasn't going to get any help from her. She'd rather she starved in the gutter. Daphne didn't want to think of that mother and child living comfortably on an allowance from the Wyndhams.

'I was wondering if you have her name and address.'

'No,' she denied. 'Crispin didn't talk to me about them.' Why should she make things easy for a woman like that? Daphne took out a lace handkerchief and mopped at her eyes. 'I didn't ask. I really didn't want to know.'

'Of course not, I do understand.' Quentin patted her hand. 'I've talked to our solicitor. He says Crispin hasn't made any provision for them. The will I suggested he make when he married you still stands.'

'Yes.' Daphne knew; she'd been pleased about that. Not that Crispin had much to leave her now, but at least there'd be no quibble about the antique furniture.

'He suggested I advertise, but without knowing her name... It's difficult.'

'She might get in touch with you,' Maude told him briskly.

Daphne reflected that any sensible woman would. 'If she's really in need, she probably will,' she assured him. 'Sorry I can't help.'

Over the sad days that followed, Lorna was very busy. She and Jonathon had to go to the office to keep the work up to date. He'd taken over the management so recently he didn't feel he could allow any let-up. In addition, there were the funeral arrangements to see to as well as taking over some of the housekeeping chores from Aunt Maude.

'I'm glad I've a lot to do,' Jonathon said. 'It takes my mind off what's happened. When I feel really low, I think about us getting married. That buoys me up.'

Quentin was grieving. 'All my five children dead before I am. No parent imagines such a thing will happen, not even in their worst nightmares.'

'Don't forget you sent Crispin packing,' Maude reminded him. 'And he was doing his best to come back into the family fold.'

'I was on the point of forgiving him.'

'He'd have done the same thing over again given half a chance, you know he would.'

'Poor Rosaleen.'

'Perhaps... One shouldn't speak ill of the dead, but I do worry about the part she played in Oliver's death.'

Quentin sighed. 'That was a long time ago. All the same, it's like going through a dark tunnel.'

'There is light at the end,' Maude said. 'You have a grandson you can trust who looks as though he's going to follow in your shoes.'

A month later, when they were all beginning to feel the worst was behind them, Lorna and Jonathon returned to Hedge End one afternoon as Sissie was pushing the tea trolley up the hall. Jonathon helped her manoeuvre it beside the chintz sofa where Maude usually sat.

Quentin looked up. 'Have you two made up your minds yet about when you want to get married?'

'We put our plans on hold,' Jonathon said.

'I know you did, and I thank you for that. Do you want to talk about them now?'

'We decided it all depended...' Lorna smiled

489

from Quentin to Maude. 'I mean, on whether you'll let us live here with you.'

'My dear child,' Quentin was struggling to his feet to kiss her, 'if you're willing to live with two old codgers like us, we'd be delighted. I don't mind admitting that I had some misgivings. I thought you'd be looking for a house of your own.'

'No, Grandpa. I think we'd all be better off if we lived here.'

'Lorna? I thought all wives longed for a house of their own. You don't mind?'

'I think I could settle down very happily here at Hedge End. This is a beautiful house.'

'I couldn't afford anything as grand as this,' Jonathon beamed at his grandfather. 'And if we have somewhere to live, it means we can get married straight away. Say this spring? What about it, Lorna – do you fancy being an Easter bride?'

'Yes, oh gosh, yes, that's wonderful.' She could hardly believe it would happen so soon.

'Moving in to live here–' Quentin said –'as far as I'm concerned there could be no better arrangement. We know you'll fit in very well.'

'I'm quite thrilled.' Maude got up to kiss Lorna too. 'We must open some champagne later.'

'In the meantime,' Quentin said, 'how about some tea?'

Lorna poured it while Maude cut the chocolate Swiss roll into slices. 'Bought in, I'm afraid. Can you bake cakes, Lorna?'

'It's a long time since I tried. My little sister's good at it, I'll get her to show me.'

'That would be marvellous.'

'Hang on, Aunt Maude,' Jonathon said, 'I need Lorna's help in the office. We need to get the business on a firm footing. That's more important than cake.'

'The engagement ring...' Quentin began.

'We haven't had time to think of that,' Jonathon protested. 'We've been so busy.'

'What I was going to say ... there's no sense in buying another. I've still got quite a collection in my safe. That's if you don't mind wearing a Wyndham family ring, Lorna?'

'No – I mean I'd be proud to.'

'I'd like to think of you wearing one of our heirlooms.'

'I thought you'd handed out the jewellery to the ladies of the family,' Jonathon said.

'Not all of it. I kept some to sell later, if I needed to. But I'd rather it was worn. I'll open the safe now and you can choose.'

Lorna felt overwhelmed as she looked at the collection of rings Quentin was spreading out on the coffee table in front of her. 'What d'you fancy? There's this ruby with a diamond each side.'

'That was Eudora's ring,' Maude said. 'Old-fashioned. The stones aren't cut in the way they do them today.'

'Or there's this sapphire in a circle of diamonds?'

'What a display. Better than most jeweller's shops.'

Jonathon came over. 'That sapphire belonged to Drusilla.'

'Not that or Eudora's ruby,' Lorna decided. 'I'd

491

like diamonds.'

'A solitaire? Or would you prefer three stones?' Jonathon slid a ring on her finger. 'Or what about a whole cluster?'

'No,' Maude said, 'that's more a dress ring.'

'I love this.' Lorna moved her hand so that the three large diamonds caught the light. 'But it must be worth a fortune. Are you sure?'

'I'm quite sure. As it happens I bought that ring myself. Your grandmother wore it, Jonathon. I couldn't bring myself to part with it before, but now, for a new Wyndham bride, I quite like the idea.'

'It's lovely,' Lorna breathed.

'Does it fit?'

'A bit large,' Jonathon said.

'I'll have it made one size smaller,' Quentin slid it from her finger, 'and it needs a clean and a polish first.'

'Thank you,' Lorna said. 'You're very generous.'

'I'm not. Jonathon will have his share of all this one day. There's something else I've been meaning to give you for some time – a brooch.' He opened a little leather box and put it in her hand. 'In return for – well, you know...'

'I brought trouble on you. I'm afraid I opened up Pandora's box.'

'You did,' Maude said, 'but the way the family was carrying on we were heading for disaster, and Quentin was blaming himself.'

He nodded. 'I told you I was quite relieved to learn our ancestors weren't honest, clever businessmen. Family folklore was setting standards that were too high. I felt guilty that I couldn't provide for the present generation as they had. You helped me save our family business. You gave me back my self-respect.'

'Lorna's brought the family into the twentieth century,' Jonathon said proudly, 'and brought all our skeletons out of the cupboards.'

A smile lit up Lorna's face. 'The brooch is absolutely beautiful.' It was platinum, set with diamonds in the shape of a rose. 'I've never seen anything so lovely. I don't know how to thank you.'

'You've earned it and you'll be joining the family now.'

'Always has been part of the family,' Jonathon reminded him.

The publishers hope that this book has given you enjoyable reading. Large Print Books are especially designed to be as easy to see and hold as possible. If you wish a complete list of our books please ask at your local library or write directly to:

Magna Large Print Books
Magna House, Long Preston,
Skipton, North Yorkshire.
BD23 4ND

This Large Print Book for the partially sighted, who cannot read normal print, is published under the auspices of

THE ULVERSCROFT FOUNDATION